PENGUIN BOOKS

The Flicker Men

Ted Kosmatka is the author of *Prophet of Bones* and *The Games*, a finalist for the Locus Award for Best First Novel. His shorter fiction has been nominated for both the Nebula Award and the Theodore Sturgeon Memorial Award, and he won the 2010 Asimov Readers' Choice Award. He works in the video game industry, and is a full-time writer at Valve, publisher of mega-hits such as *Half-Life* and *Portal*.

The Flicker Men

TED KOSMATKA

PENGUIN BOOKS

PENGUIN BOOKS

UK | USA | Canada | Ireland | Australia
India | New Zealand | South Africa

Penguin Books is part of the Penguin Random House group of companies
whose addresses can be found at global.penguinrandomhouse.com.

First published in the United States of America by Henry Holt and Company, LLC 2015
First published in Great Britain by Michael Joseph 2015
Published in Penguin Books 2016
001

Set in 12.5/14.75 pt Garamond MT Std
Typeset by Jouve (UK), Milton Keynes
Printed in Great Britain by Clays Ltd, St Ives plc

A CIP catalogue record for this book is available from the British Library

ISBN: 978–1–405–91065–1

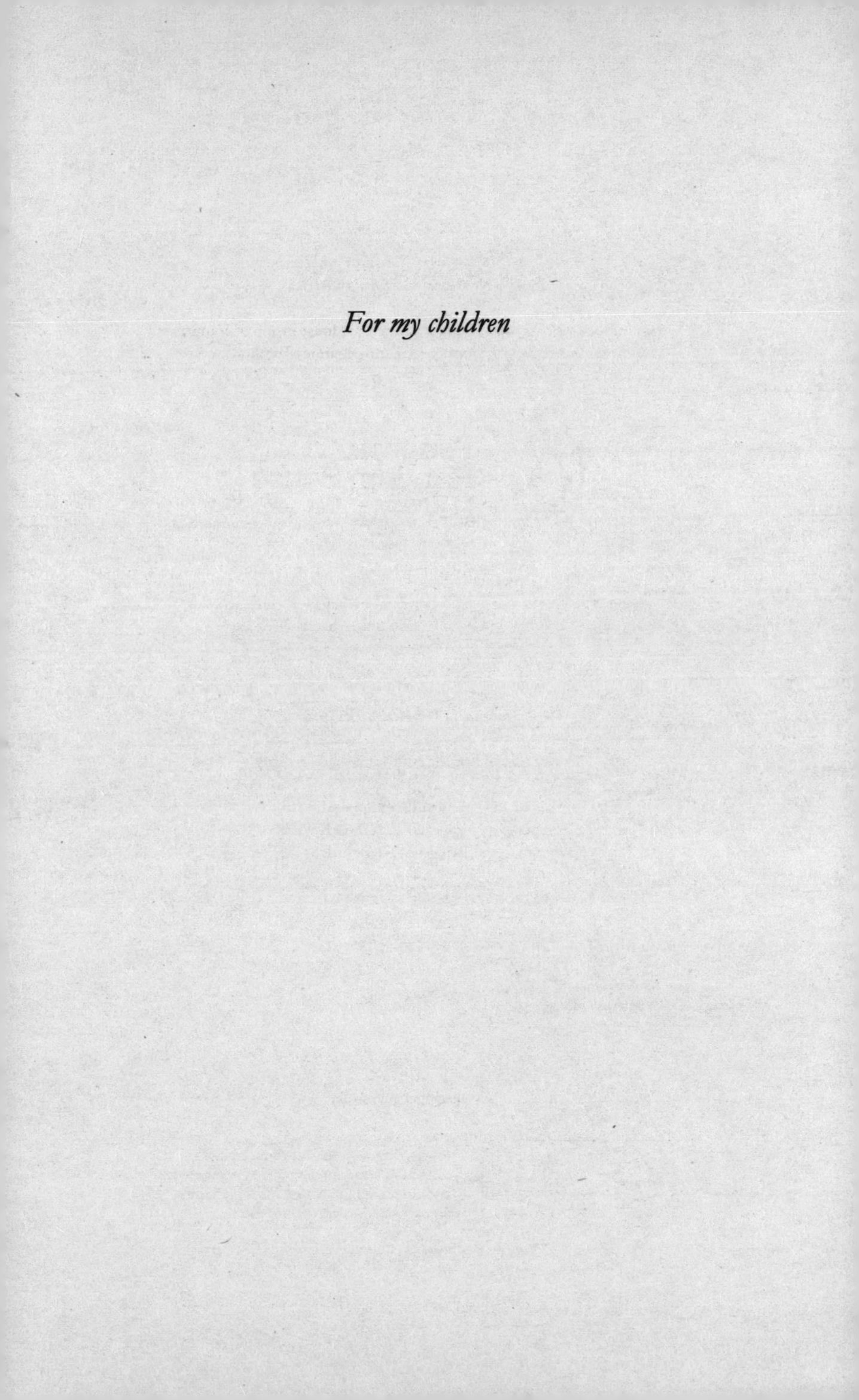

For my children

PART I

It is impossible that God should ever
deceive me, since in all fraud and deceit
is to be found a certain imperfection.

– Descartes

I sat in the rain with a gun.

A wave climbed the pebbly beach, washing over my foot, filling my pants with grit and sand. All along the shore, dark slabs of rock jutted from the surf, sharp as broken teeth. I shivered as I came back to myself and for the first time realized my suit jacket was missing. Also my left shoe, brown leather, size twelve. I looked for the shoe, scanning the rocky shoreline, but saw only sand and frothy, sliding water.

I took another pull from the bottle and tried to loosen my tie. Since I had a gun in one hand and a bottle in the other – and since I was unwilling to surrender either to the waves – loosening my tie was difficult. I used the gun hand, working the knot with a finger looped through the trigger guard, cold steel brushing my throat. I felt the muzzle under my chin – fingers numb and awkward, curling past the trigger.

It would be so easy.

I wondered if people had died this way – drunk, armed, loosening their ties. I imagined it was common among certain occupations.

Then the tie opened, and I hadn't shot myself. I took a drink from the bottle as a reward.

Another wave rumbled in. If I stayed here long enough, the tide would roll over me, drown me, and pull me out to sea. This place was nothing like the dunes of Indiana, where Lake Michigan caresses the shoreline. Here in Gloucester, the water hates the land.

As a child, I'd come to this beach and wondered where all the boulders came from. Huge, dark stones like pieces of shipwreck. Did the tides carry them in? Now I knew better. The boulders, of course, were here all along – buried in soft soils. They are left-behind things. They are what remains when the ocean subtracts everything else.

Thirty yards up the beach, near the road, there is a monument – a list of names. Fishermen. Gloucestermen. The ones who did not come back.

This is Gloucester, a place with a history of losing itself to the ocean.

The wind gusted.

I told myself I'd brought the gun for protection, but sitting here in the dark sand, I no longer believed it. I was beyond fooling myself.

It was my father's gun, a .357. It had not been fired for seventeen years, five months, four days. The math came quickly. Even drunk, the math came quickly. Always my most resilient talent.

My sister, Marie, had called it a good thing, this new place that was also an old place.

A new start, she'd said over the phone. *Away from what happened in Indianapolis. You can do your work again. You can continue your research.*

Yeah, I'd said. A lie she seemed to believe.

You're not going to call me, are you?

Of course I'll call. A lie she didn't.

There was a pause.

I mean it, Eric, call me. If anything goes wrong.

Farther up the beach, a white-winged tern leaped into the air and hung stationary against the wind, frozen like a snapshot, before it wheeled and lifted into the sky and was gonc.

I turned my face away from the ocean and took another burning swig. I drank until I couldn't remember which hand held the gun and which the bottle. I drank until they were the same.

I

During the second week, we unpacked the microscopes. Satvik used a crowbar while I used a claw hammer. The crates were heavy, wooden, hermetically sealed – shipped in from some now-defunct research laboratory in Pennsylvania.

The sun beat down on the lab's loading dock, and it was nearly as hot today as it was cold the week before. Perspiration dripped from my forehead.

I swung my arm, and the claw hammer bit into the pale wood. I swung again. It was satisfying work.

Satvik smiled, straight white teeth in a straight dark face. 'Your head is leaking.'

'Melting,' I countered.

'In India,' he said, 'this is sweater weather.'

Satvik slid the crowbar into the gash I made, and pressed. I'd known him for three days, and already I was his friend. Together we committed violence on the crates until they yielded.

The industry was consolidating, and the Pennsylvania lab was just the latest victim. Their equipment came cheap, bought in bulk, shipped in by the pallet load. Here at Hansen, it was like a holiday for scientists. We opened our boxes. We ogled our new toys. We wondered, vaguely, how we had come to deserve this.

For some, like Satvik, the answer was complicated and rooted in achievement. Hansen was more than just another Massachusetts think tank after all, and Satvik had beaten out a dozen other scientists to work here. He'd given presentations and written up projects that important people liked. He'd impressed someone.

For me it was simpler.

For me this was a second chance given by a friend. A last chance.

We cracked open the final wooden crate, and Satvik peered inside. He peeled out layer after layer of foam packing material, making a pile on the floor. It was a big crate, but inside we found only a small assortment of Nalgene volumetric flasks, maybe three pounds weight. It was somebody's idea of a joke – somebody at the now-defunct lab making a statement of opinion about their now-defunct job.

'The frog is in the well,' Satvik said, one of his many opaque expressions.

'It certainly is,' I said.

I had cause to come East again. I had cause not to. Both had everything, and nothing, to do with the gun.

The sign is the first thing a person sees when driving up on the property: HANSEN RESEARCH, in bold blue letters, tastefully offset from the road and surrounded by an array of carefully assembled shrubbery. A hundred feet beyond the sign are the gates, decorative and black, left open during business hours. From this entrance, you can't see the building at all, which in the real estate sector surrounding Boston speaks not just of money but *money*. Everything out here is expensive, elbow room most of all.

The lab complex is tucked into a stony hillside about an hour upcoast of the city. It is a private, quiet place, shaded by trees. The main office building is beautiful – two stories of reflective aluminum spread over the approximate dimensions of a football field. What isn't aluminum is matte black steel. It looks like art, or like what art might look like if translated into an architectural structure built to house the world's best scientific minds. A small, brick-paved turnaround curves up to the main entrance, but the front parking lot is merely ornamental – a rudimentary asphalt pad for visitors and the uninitiated. The driveway continues around the building, where the real parking, the parking for the researchers, is in the back. Several smaller adjunct buildings stand at the far end of the lot. These are the out-labs, buildings north and south. The tech facilities and lab spaces. Beyond there, standing off by itself like a big gray battleship, is W building, the old warehouse unit.

That first morning, I parked my rental car in front of the main office and walked inside.

'May I help you?'

'They're expecting me,' I told the receptionist.

'Your name?'

'Eric Argus.'

The receptionist smiled. 'Please take a seat.'

I sank into a leather cushion. There were three chairs and a nice, complicated painting, done in reds and blues. The painting could have doubled as a technical schematic of some kind, all lines and angles, suggestive of some hidden order. The exact sort of thing an engineer might pick if charged with the task of decorating a lobby.

Two minutes later, a familiar face rounded the corner, and I stood.

'Jesus,' he said. 'It's been too long.' Jeremy shook my hand and pulled me into a quick back-clap. 'How the hell are you?'

'I've been worse,' I said. Which was the truth.

He hadn't changed much in the intervening years. Not quite as skinny. His unruly blond hair now tamed into a business cut. But still that same easy way about him. That same easy smile.

'And you?' I asked.

'This place is keeping me busy, I'll say that. More than a hundred and fifty researchers now and growing all the time.'

He walked me back to his office. We sat. And then came the offer, like this was just business – like we were just two men in suits. But I could see it in his eyes, that sad way he looked at me, my old friend.

He slid a folded sheet of paper across the broad desk. I unfolded it. Forced myself to make sense of the numbers.

'It's too generous,' I said, sliding the paper back to him.

'We're getting you cheap at that price.'

'No,' I said. 'You're not.'

'Your work at QSR more than justifies it. We can set you up with high-scale integration, parallel cores, whatever you like.' He opened his desk drawer and pulled out a gray file folder. He placed the folded sheet of paper inside. 'You can pick up where you left off.'

'I think there's been a misunderstanding.'

'Just let us know what you need. Considering your patents and your past work – '

I cut him off. 'I can't do that anymore.'

'Can't?'

'Won't.'

That stopped him. He leaned back in his leather chair. 'I'd heard that rumor,' he said finally. He appraised me from across his desk. 'I'd hoped it wasn't true.'

I shook my head.

'Why?'

'I'm just done with it.'

'Then you're right,' he said. 'I don't understand.'

'If you feel I came here under false pretenses – ' I began climbing to my feet.

'No, no.' He held up his hand. 'The offer is still good. That's a solid offer. Sit down.'

I sank back into the chair.

'We can carry you for four months,' he said. 'We hire the researcher, not the research. Probationary employees get four months to produce. That's our system here.'

'What would I be doing?'

'We pride ourselves on our independence; so you can choose whatever research you like, so long as it has scientific merit.'

'Whatever I like?'

'Yes.'

'Who decides merit?'

'Peer review, ultimately, in the publications, assuming your work gets that far. But before that, you have to get past our review board here. Probationary hiring is at the recruiting manager's discretion, but after four months, it's not up to me anymore. I have bosses, too; so you have to have something to show for it. Something publishable or on its way. Do you understand?'

I nodded. Four months.

'This can be a new start for you,' he said, and I knew that he'd already talked to Marie. I wondered when she'd called him.

I mean it, Eric, call me. If anything goes wrong.

'You did some great work at QSR,' he said. 'I followed your publications; hell, we all did. But considering the circumstances under which you left . . .'

I nodded again. The inevitable moment.

He was silent, looking at me. 'I'm going out on a limb for you,' he said. 'But you've got to promise me.'

That was the closest he'd come to mentioning it. The thing people were so careful about.

I looked away. His office suited him, I decided. Not too large, but bright and comfortable. The window over his shoulder looked out on the front parking pad, where I saw my rental parked. A Notre Dame engineering diploma graced one wall. Only his desk was pretentious – a teak monstrosity large enough to land aircraft on – but I knew it was inherited. His father's old desk. I'd seen it once when we were still in college nearly a decade ago. A lifetime ago. Back when we still thought we'd be nothing like our fathers.

'Can you promise me?' he said.

I knew what he was asking. I met his eyes.

Silence.

And he was quiet for a long time after that, looking at me, waiting for me to say something. Weighing our friendship against the odds this would come back to bite him.

'All right,' he said finally. He closed the folder. 'Welcome to Hansen Research. You start tomorrow.'

2

There are days I don't drink at all. Here is how those days start: I pull the gun from its holster and set it on the desk in my motel room. The gun is heavy and black. It says RUGER along the side in small, raised letters. It tastes like pennies and ashes. I look into the mirror across from the bed and tell myself, *If you drink today, you're going to kill yourself.* I look into my own blue-gray eyes and see that I mean it.

Those are the days I don't drink.

There is a rhythm to working in a research laboratory. Through the glass doors by 7:30, nodding to the other early arrivals; then you sit in your office until 8:00, pondering this fundamental truth: even shit coffee – even mud-thick, brackish, walkin'-out-the-pot shit coffee – is better than no coffee at all.

I like to be the one who makes the first pot in the morning. Swing open the cabinet doors in the coffee room, pop the tin cylinder, and take a deep breath, letting the smell of grounds fill my lungs. It is better than drinking the coffee, that smell.

There are days when I feel everything is an imposition – eating, speaking, walking out of the motel room in the morning. Everything is effort. I exist mostly in my head. It comes and goes, this crushing need, and I work hard not to let it show, because the truth is that it's not how you feel that matters. It's how you act. It's your behavior. As long as your intelligence is intact, you can make cognitive evaluations of what is appropriate. You can force the day-to-day.

And I want to keep this job; so I do force it. I want to get along. I want to be productive again. I want to make Marie proud of me.

Working at a research lab isn't like a normal job. There are peculiar rhythms, strange hours – special allowances are made for the creatives.

Two Chinese guys are the ringleaders of lunchtime basketball. They pulled me into a game my first week. 'You look like you can play' was what they said.

One is tall, one is short. The tall one was raised in Ohio and has no accent. He is called Point Machine. The short one has no real idea of the rules of basketball and for this reason is the best defensive player. His fouls leave marks, and that becomes the meta game – the game within the game – to see how much abuse I can take without calling it. This is the real reason I play. I drive to the hoop and get hacked down. I drive again. The smack of skin on skin. Welts take the shape of handprints.

One player, a Norwegian named Ostlund, is six foot eight. I marvel at the sheer size of him. He can't run or jump or move at all, really, but his big body clogs up the lane, huge arms swatting down any jump shot made within his personal zone of asphalt real estate. We play four-on-four, or five-on-five, depending on who is free for lunch. At thirty-one, I'm a few years younger than most of them, a few inches taller – except for Ostlund, who is a head taller than everyone. Trash is talked in an assortment of accents.

'My grandmama shoots better than you.'

'Was that a shot or a pass? I couldn't tell.'

'Ostlund, don't hit your head on the rim.'

Some researchers go to restaurants on lunch hour. Others play computer games in their offices. Still others work through lunch – forget to eat for days. Satvik is one of those. I play basketball because it feels like punishment.

The atmosphere in the lab is relaxed; you can take naps if you want. There is no outside pressure to work. It is a strictly Darwinian system – you compete for your right to be there. The only pressure is the pressure you put on yourself, because everyone knows that the evaluations come every four months, and you've got to have something to show. The turnover rate for probationary researchers hovers around 25 percent. Friendships with new hires can be fleeting.

Satvik works in circuits. He told me about it during my second week when I found him sitting at the SEM. 'It is microscopic work,' he explained.

I watched him toggle the focus, and the image on the screen shifted. I'd used an SEM in grad school, but this one was newer, better. As close to magic as I'd ever seen.

A scanning electron microscope is a window. Put a sample in the chamber, pump to vacuum, and it's like looking at another world. What had been a flat, smooth sample surface now takes on another character, becomes topographically complex.

Using the SEM is like looking at satellite photography – you're up in space, looking down at this elaborate landscape, looking down at the Earth, and then you turn the little black dial and zoom toward the surface. Zooming in is like falling. Like you've been dropped from orbit, and the ground is rushing up to meet you, but you're falling faster than you ever could in real life, faster than terminal velocity, falling impossibly fast, impossibly far, and the landscape keeps getting bigger, and you think you're going to hit, but you never do, because everything keeps getting closer and sharper, and you never hit the ground – like that old riddle where the frog jumps half the distance of a log, then half again, and again, and again, without ever reaching the other side. That's an electron microscope. Falling forever down into the picture. And you never do hit bottom.

I zoomed in to 14,000x once, like God's eyes focusing. Looking for that ultimate, indivisible truth. I learned this: there is no bottom to see.

Satvik and I both had offices on the second floor of the main building, a few doors down from each other.

Satvik was short and thin, somewhere in his forties. His skin was a deep, rich brown. He had an almost boyish face, but the first hints of gray salted his mustache. His narrow features were balanced in such a way that he could have been alleged the heir to any number of nations: Mexico or Libya or Greece or Sicily – until he opened his mouth. When he opened his mouth and spoke, all those possible identities vanished, and he was suddenly Indian, solidly Indian, completely, like a magic trick, and you could not imagine him being anything else.

The first time I met Satvik, he clamped both hands over mine, shook, then said, 'Ah, a new face in the halls.

How are you doing, my friend? Welcome to research.' And that's how the word was used – *research* – like it was a location. A destination that could be arrived at. We were standing in the main hall outside the library. He smiled so wide it was impossible not to like him.

It was Satvik who explained that you never wore gloves when working with liquid nitrogen. 'You must be sure of it,' he said. 'Because the gloves will get you burned.'

I watched him work. He filled the SEM's reservoir – icy smoke spilling out over the lip, cascading down the cylinder to drip on the tile floor.

Liquid nitrogen doesn't have the same surface tension as water; spill a few drops across your hand, and they'll bounce off harmlessly and run down your skin without truly wetting you – like little balls of mercury. The drops will evaporate in moments, sizzling, steaming, gone. But if you're wearing gloves when you fill the reservoir of the SEM, the nitrogen could spill down inside the glove and be trapped against your skin. 'And if that happens,' Satvik said while he poured, 'it will hurt you bad.'

Satvik was the first to ask my area of research.

'I'm not sure,' I told him.

'How can you not be sure? You are here, so it must be something.'

'I'm still working on it.'

He stared at me, taking this in, and I saw his eyes change – his understanding of me shifting, like the first time I heard him speak. And just like that, I'd become something different to him.

'Ah,' he said. 'I know who you are now; they talked about you. You are the one from Stanford.'

'That was eight years ago.'

'You wrote that famous paper on decoherence. You are the one who had the breakdown.'

Satvik was blunt, apparently.

'I wouldn't call it a breakdown.'

He nodded, perhaps accepting this; perhaps not. 'So you still are working in quantum theory?'

'I'm done with it.'

His brow creased. 'Done? But you did important work.'

I shook my head. 'After a while, quantum mechanics starts to affect your worldview.'

'What does this mean?'

'The more research I did, the less I believed.'

'In quantum mechanics?'

'No,' I said. 'In the world.'

3

There are days I don't drink at all. On those days, I pick up my father's .357 and look in the mirror. I convince myself what it will cost me, today, if I take the first sip. It will cost me what it cost him.

But there are also days I *do* drink. Those are the days I wake up sick. I walk into the bathroom and puke into the toilet, needing a drink so bad my hands are shaking. The bile comes up – a heaving, muscular convulsion as I pour myself into the porcelain basin. My stomach empties in long spasms while my skull throbs, and my legs tremble, and the need grows into a ravening monster.

When I can stand, I look in the bathroom mirror and splash water on my face. I say nothing to myself. There is nothing I would believe.

It is vodka on these mornings. Vodka because vodka has no smell.

I pour it into an old coffee thermos.

A sip to calm the shakes. A few sips to get me moving.

It is a balancing act. Not too much, or it could be noticed. Not too little, or the shakes remain. Like a chemical reaction, I seek equilibrium. Enough to get by, to get level, as I walk through the front entrance of the lab.

I take the stairs up to my office. If Satvik knows, he says nothing.

*

Satvik studied circuits. He bred them, in little ones and zeroes, in a Mather's Field-gated Array. The array's internal logic was malleable, and he allowed selective pressure to direct chip design. Like evolution in a box. The most efficient circuits were identified by automated program and worked as a template for subsequent iteration. Genetic algorithms manipulated the best codes for the task. 'Nothing is ideal,' he said. 'There's lots of modeling.'

I didn't have the slightest idea how it all worked.

Satvik was a genius who had been a farmer in India until he came to America at the age of twenty. He earned an electrical engineering degree from MIT. He'd chosen electrical engineering because he liked the math. After that, Harvard and patents and job offers. All described to me in his matter-of-fact tone, like of course it had happened that way, anybody could do it. 'There is no smart,' he said. 'There is only trying hard.'

And he seemed to believe it.

Myself, I wasn't so sure.

Other researchers would come by to see the field-gated arrays set up around his workstation like some self-organizing digital art. The word *elegant* came up again and again – highest praise from those for whom mathematics was a first language. He stood crouching over his work, concentrating for hours. And that was part of it. His ability to focus. To just sit there and do the work.

'I am a simple farmer,' he liked to say when someone complimented his research. 'I like to challenge the dirt.'

Satvik had endless expressions. When relaxed, he let himself lapse into broken English. Sometimes, after spending the morning with him, I'd fall into the pattern of his speech, talking his broken English back at him, an efficient pidgin that I came to respect for its streamlined efficiency and ability to convey nuance.

'I went to dentist yesterday,' Satvik told me. 'She says I have good teeth. I tell her, "Forty-two years old, and it is my first time at dentist." And she could not believe.'

'You've never been to the dentist?' I said.

'No, never.'

'How is that possible?'

'Until I am in twelfth grade in my village back home, I did not know there was a special doctor for teeth. Since then, I never went because I had no need. The dentist says I have good teeth, no cavities, but I have stain on my back molars on the left side where I chew tobacco.'

'You chew.' I tried to picture Satvik hawking a plug like a baseball player, but the image wouldn't come.

'I am ashamed. None of my brothers chew tobacco. Out of my family, I am the only one. I started years ago on the farm. Now I try to stop.' Satvik spread his hands in exasperation. 'But I cannot. I told my wife I stopped two months ago, but I started again, and I have not told her.' His eyes grew sad. 'I am a bad person.'

Satvik's brow furrowed. 'You are laughing,' he said. 'Why are you laughing?'

Hansen was a gravity well in the tech industry – a constantly expanding force of nature, always buying out other labs, buying equipment, absorbing the competition

Hansen labs only hired the best, without regard to national origin. It was the kind of place where you'd walk into the coffee room and find a Nigerian speaking

German to an Iranian. Speaking German because they both spoke it better than English, the other language they had in common. Hansen was always hungry for talent.

The Boston lab was just one of Hansen's locations, but we had the largest storage facility, which meant that much of the surplus lab equipment ended up shipped to us. We opened boxes. We sorted through supplies. If we needed anything for our research, we signed for it, and it was ours. It was the antithesis of most corporate bureaucracy, where red tape was the order of the day.

Most mornings I spent with Satvik. We'd stand side by side at his lab bench, talking and keeping busy. I helped him with his gate arrays. He talked of his daughter while he worked. Lunch I spent on basketball.

Sometimes after basketball, as a distraction, I'd drop by Point Machine's lab in the North building to see what he was up to. He worked with organics, searching for chemical alternatives that wouldn't cause birth defects in amphibians. He tested water samples for cadmium, mercury, arsenic.

Point Machine was a kind of shaman. He studied the gene expression patterns of amphioxus; he read the future in deformities. The kind of research my mother would have liked – equal parts alarm and conspiracy.

'Unless something is done,' he said, 'most amphibians will become extinct.' He had aquariums filled with salamanders and frogs – frogs with too many legs, with tails, with no arms. Monsters. They hopped or swam or dragged themselves along, Chernobyl nightmares in long glass jars.

Next to his lab was the office of a woman named Joy. Like me, she was new to the lab, but it wasn't clear when she'd started, exactly. The others only seemed to know her first name. Sometimes Joy would hear us talking, and she'd swing by, delicate hand sliding along the wall – tall and beautiful and blind. Did acoustical research of some kind. She had long hair and high cheekbones – eyes so clear and blue and perfect that I didn't even realize at first.

'It's okay,' she said to one researcher's stammering apology. 'I get that a lot.' She never wore dark glasses, never used a white cane. 'Detached retinas,' she explained. 'I was three. It's nothing to me.'

'How do you find your room?' It was Satvik who asked it. Blunt Satvik.

'Who needs eyes when you have ears and memory? The blind are good at counting steps. Besides, you shouldn't trust your eyes.' She smiled. 'Nothing is what it seems.'

In the afternoons, back in the main building, I tried to work.

Alone in my office, I stared at the marker board. The great empty expanse of it. I picked up the marker, closed my eyes. *Nothing is what it seems.*

I wrote from memory, the formula spooling out of my left hand with practiced ease. A series of letters and numbers, like the archaic runes of some forgotten sorcery – a shape I could see in my head. The work from QSR. I stopped. When I looked at what I'd written, I threw the marker against the wall. The stack of notes on my desk shifted and fell to the floor.

Jeremy came by later that night.

He stood in the doorway, cup of coffee in his hand. He saw the papers scattered across the floor, the formula scrawled across the marker board.

'Math is merely metaphor,' his voice drifted from the doorway. 'Isn't that what you always used to say?'

'Ah, the self-assuredness of youth. So rich in simple declarations.'

'You have nothing to declare?'

'I've lost the stomach.'

He patted his own stomach. 'What you've lost, I've gained, eh?'

That raised a smile from me. He wasn't a pound overweight; he simply no longer looked like he was starving. 'Isn't that just like us,' I said, 'giving ourselves primacy. Maybe *we're* the metaphor.'

He held out his coffee cup in mock salute. 'You always were the smart one.'

'The crazy one, you mean.'

He shook his head. 'No, *Stuart* was the crazy one. But you were the one to watch. We all knew it. Before you came along, I'd never seen a student get into an argument with a professor.'

'That was forever ago.'

'But you won the argument.'

'Funny, but I don't remember it like that.'

'Oh, you won, all right, if you think about it.' He sipped his coffee. 'It just took you a few years.'

Jeremy walked farther into the room, careful not to step on the papers. 'Do you still talk to Stuart?'

'Not for a long time.'

'Too bad,' he said. 'You partnered on some interesting work.'

Which was one way to put it. It was also Jeremy's way of bringing up his reason for dropping in. Work. 'I got a visit from one of the review board members today,' he said. 'He asked about your progress.'

'Already?'

'It's been a few weeks. The board is just staying on top of things, curious how you're adjusting.'

'What did you say?'

'I said I'd look in on you, so here I am. Looking in.' He gestured toward the formula on the marker board. 'It's good to see you working on something.'

'It's not work,' I said.

'These things take time.'

Honesty welled up. There was no point in lying. To myself or him. A rising bubble in my chest, and just like that, it burst: 'Time is what I'm wasting here,' I said. 'Your time. This lab's time.'

'It's fine, Eric,' he said. 'It'll come.'

'I don't think it will.'

'We have researchers on staff who don't have a third of your citings. You belong here. The first few weeks can be the toughest.'

'It's not like before. *I'm* not like before.'

'You're being too hard on yourself.'

'No, I've accomplished nothing.' I gestured at the board. 'One unfinished formula in three weeks.'

His expression shifted. 'Just this?' He studied the dozen symbols laid out in a line. 'Are you making progress?'

'I don't know how to finish it,' I said. 'I can't find the solution. It's a dead end.'

'There's nothing else? No other research that you're pursuing?'

I shook my head. 'Nothing.'

He turned toward me. That sad look back again.

'I shouldn't be here,' I told him. 'I'm wasting your money.'

'Eric – '

'No.' I shook my head again.

He was quiet for a long while, staring at the formula like so many tea leaves. When he spoke, his voice was soft. 'R&D is a tax write-off. You should at least stay and finish out your contract.'

I looked down at the mess I'd made – the papers scattered across the floor.

He continued, 'That gives you another three months of salary before you face review. We can carry you that long. After that, we can write you up a letter of recommendation. There are other labs. Maybe you'll land somewhere else.'

'Yeah, maybe,' I said, though we both knew it wasn't true. It was the nature of last chances. Nothing came after.

He turned to go. 'I'm sorry, Eric.'

4

That night in my motel room, I stared at the phone, sipped the vodka. A clear glass bottle. Liquid burn.

The cap rolled away across the cheap carpet.

I imagined calling Marie, dialing the number. My sister, so like me, yet not like me. The good one, the sane one. I imagined her voice on the other end.

Hello? Hello?

This numbness in my head, strange gravities, and the geologic accretion of things I could have said, *not to worry, things are fine*; but instead I say nothing, letting the phone slide away, and hours later find myself outside the sliding glass window, coming out of another stupor, soaked to the skin, watching the rain. It comes down steady, a cold drizzle that soaks my clothes.

Thunder advances from the east, as I stand in the dark, waiting for everything to be good again.

In the distance, I see a shape in the motel parking lot. A figure standing in the rain with no reason to be there – gray rain-slicker shine, head cocked toward the motel. The shape watches me, face a black pool. Then comes the sudden glare of a passing car, and when I look again, the rain slicker is gone. Or was never there.

The last of the vodka goes down my throat.

I think of my mother then, that last time I saw her, and then there is this: the slow dissolution of perspective. I lose connection to my body, an angular shape cast in sodium lights – eyes gray like storm clouds, gray like gunmetal.

'It's not for you,' my mother had said on that autumn day many years earlier.

My arm flexes and the vodka bottle flies end over end into the darkness – the glimmer of it, the shatter of it, glass and asphalt and shards of rain. There is nothing else until there is nothing else.

It is a dream I have sometimes. That last time we spoke, when I was fifteen.

She bears many names, most of them apocryphal.

My mother looks across the table at me. She doesn't smile, but I know she's happy. I know she's in one of her good moods, because I'm visiting.

She's back home again – the very last time, before everything went so irredeemably wrong. She drinks tea. Cold, always. Two ice cubes. I drink hot cocoa, my hands wrapped around the warm mug. We sip while the ceiling fan paddles slowly at the air above our heads.

'I'm in mourning,' she says.

'Mourning what?'

'The human race.'

And the gears in my head shift, as I note the change of direction: one of these talks, then. Like a rut her mind keeps falling into – all tracks leading eventually back into the wilderness.

'The Y chromosome of our species is degrading,' she says. 'Within a few hundred thousand years, it'll be whittled away to nothing.' Her eyes travel the room, never resting on one thing for more than a few moments.

I play along. 'What about natural selection? Wouldn't that weed out the bad ones?'

'It won't be enough,' she says. 'It is inevitable.'

And maybe it is, I think. *Maybe all of it is inevitable. This room. This day. My mother sitting across from me with restless eyes and her shirt buttoned wrong.*

Light slants through the windows of the dayroom. Outside the leaves are blowing across the yard, accumulating against the stone wall that Porter put up to keep the neighbor's corgi out of the rose garden.

Porter is her boyfriend, though she will never call him that. 'My Gillian,' he calls her, and he loves her like that was what he was made for. But I think he reminds her too much of my father, which is both the reason he is around and the reason he can come no closer.

'Your sister is getting married,' she says.

And it makes sense suddenly, our earlier conversation. Because I knew, of course, of my sister's engagement. I just didn't know my mother knew. Her active eyes come to rest on me, waiting for a response.

My mother's eyes are called hazel on her driver's license – but hazel is the catch-all color. Hazel is the color you call eyes that aren't blue or green or brown. Even black eyes are called brown, but you can't tell someone they have black eyes. I've done that, and sometimes people get offended, even though most *Homo sapiens* have this eye color. It is the normal eye color for our species across most of the world. Jet black. Like chips of obsidian. But my mother's eyes are not the normal color. Nor are they the blue or green or hazel in which the DMV transacts its licenses. My mother's eyes are the exact shade of insanity.

I know that because I've seen it only once in my life, and it was in her eyes.

'The Earth's magnetic field fluctuates,' she tells me. 'Right now South America is under a hot spot. Those beautiful auroras are just charged particles passing into the visual spectrum. I saw them once on your father's boat, sailing north of the cape.'

I smile and nod, and it is always like this. She is too preoccupied with the hidden to ever speak long on the mundane. Her internal waylines run toward obscured truths, the deep mysteries. 'The magnetic field is weakening, but we're safe here.' She sips her tea again. She is happy.

This is her magic trick. She manages to look happy or sad or angry using only a glance. It is a talent she passed on to me, communicating this way – like a secret language we shared through which words were not necessary.

Earlier that school year, a teacher told me that I should try smiling, and I thought, *Do I really not smile? Not ever?*

Like my mother, even then.

When she finally earned her degree, it was in immunology, after halting runs at chemistry, astronomy, genetics. Her drive as intense as it was quixotic. I was nine when she graduated, and, looking back, there had already been signs. Strange beliefs. Things that would later seem obvious.

Hers was a fierce and impractical love. And it was both this fierceness and impracticality that built such loyalty in her children, for she was quite obviously damaged beyond all hope of repair – yet there was greatness in her still, a profundity. Deep water, tidal forces.

She stayed up late and told us bedtime tales – that line between truth and fantasy a constantly moving boundary. Stories of science, and things that might have been science, if the world were a different place.

My sister and I both loved her more than we knew what to do with.

When my father didn't come back, it was me she woke first, barely getting the words out, collapsing in my bedroom. And I remember so little about that night, like it was part of somebody else's story – but I remember the intake of air, her hitting the light switch, waking me – then it all pours out in words, everything, countless years of it. Lifetimes. A waterfall of words. A slow screaming that would not stop. Has never really stopped.

And I remember the room. The color of the walls. Almost photographic details combined with odd gaps of memory – things I should know but somehow can't see. Old cracks in the drywall. I can see them clearly. The feel of the slick wooden banister as I float down the stairs, picture frames brushing my shoulder. I see a thin layer of dust on the chandelier in the foyer, but somehow my sister is missing – erased from these memories, though she must have been there. Or perhaps that's her, standing in the back, in the shadows.

And then the gravel scrapes my bare feet, and Mother can't walk, collapsing on the sidewalk outside our house. I'm standing in the driveway while red lights spin silently. There are police, but none with faces. Just flashlights and badges and underwater words.

Your father . . .

And she couldn't finish. Couldn't get the words out.

And nothing after that was ever really the same again. For any of us. But for my mother most of all.

Now she sips her tea again, and I see the happiness change to worry in her eyes. Those not-quite-hazel eyes that do not bear names well.

'Are you okay, Eric?'

I only nod and sip.

'Are you sure?' she asks.

Her father was a quarter Cherokee and looked it. She and I have this in common: we both look like our fathers.

'Everything's fine,' I say.

She is tall and long-limbed. Her hair, once brown, is streaked with white. She is now and always has been beautiful.

If we resemble each other, it is in our eyes – not the color, for mine are blue-gray, but in the shape. Our hooded expression. Eyes protective of their secrets.

She never drank. Not once, not ever. Not like my father.

She'd tell you.

She came from a long line of alcoholics – *bad alcoholics*, she'd say. Get-in-fights-and-go-to-jail alcoholics. Her own father and grandfather and brothers. Some of her cousins. So she understood it. Like Huntington's or hemophilia – a taint of the blood winding its way down through the generations. And I wonder if that was a part of it. The strange, alchemical familiarity that draws two people together. She and my father.

Sometimes it is a thing as simple as the way you laugh. Or it's a familiar hair color. Or the way you hold a Scotch glass: casually, fingers sprawled around the circumference of the glass's rim, so the palm hovers above the cool brown liquid. That sense you get when you meet someone new – that feeling of . . . *We know each other. We've always known each other.*

Maybe that's what drew her. Or maybe she just thought she could fix him.

And so Mother never drank, not once, thinking it would be enough to save her.

She told me many times growing up that I shouldn't drink either. Alcoholism on both sides of the family, she said, so I shouldn't even try it. Shouldn't risk that first swallow.

'It's not for you,' she said.

But I did try it. Of course I did.

Not for you.

And nothing had ever been more wrong.

5

Sounds of the lab.

Satvik said, 'Yesterday in my car I was talking to my daughter, five years old, and she says, "Daddy, please don't talk." I asked her why, and she said, "Because I am praying. I need you to be quiet." So I ask her what she is praying about, and she said, "My friend borrowed my glitter ChapStick, and I am praying she remembers to bring it back."'

Satvik was trying not to smile. We were in his office, eating lunch across his desk – the one surface of the room not covered in file folders or books or electronic parts. Light streamed through the windows.

He continued, 'I told her, well, maybe she is like me and she forgets. But my daughter says, "No, it has been more than one week now."'

This amused Satvik greatly – the talk of ChapStick and the prayers of children. He spooned another bite of rice and red peppers into his mouth. This was the simple and searing conflagration that passed for his lunch.

'I'm tired of eating in your cluttered office,' I said. 'We should try something different.'

'Different how?'

'Act like normal human adults. Visit a restaurant.'

'A restaurant? You insult me. I am a simple man trying to save for my daughter's college.' Satvik spread his hands in mock outrage. 'Do you think I am born with golden spoon?'

And then he regaled me with the tragedy of his nephews, both raised in New York on American food. 'They are both taller than six feet,' he said, shaking his head. 'Much too big. My sister must buy new shoes all the time. In my family back home, nobody is that tall. Not one person. But here, same family, they are six feet.'

'And American food's to blame?'

'You eat the cow, you look like the cow.' He took the last bite of his meal and winced, sucking air through his teeth. He closed the plastic lid on his bowl.

'Those peppers too hot?' I asked. The possibility intrigued me. I'd seen him eat food that would have melted my fillings.

'No,' he said. 'When I eat on the tobacco side, it stings me bad.'

When we finished packing up the last of our lunchtime mess, I told him I wasn't going to be hired after my probationary period.

'How do you know?'

'I just know.'

His face grew serious. 'You are certain you are to be fired?'

Blunt Satvik. *Fired.* A word I hadn't used, but accurate, in the only way that mattered. Soon I'd be unemployed. Unemployable. My career over. I tried to imagine that moment, and my stomach clenched into a fist. Shame and dread. The moment when it would all come crashing down.

'Yeah,' I said. 'Fired.'

'Well, if you are certain, then don't worry about it.' He

leaned across his desk and clapped me on the shoulder. 'Sometimes the boat just sinks, my friend.'

I thought about this for a moment. 'Did you just tell me that you win some and you lose some?'

Satvik considered this. 'Yes,' he said. 'Except I did not mention the win part.'

It was during my fifth week at the lab that I found the box from Docent.

It started as an automated e-mail from the Transport Department saying there were some crates I might be interested in. Crates labeled PHYSICS, sitting on the loading dock.

I found them on the far loading bay, huddled together as if for warmth. Four wooden boxes of different sizes. I got out the crowbar and opened them one by one. Three of the boxes held only weights, scales, and glassware. But the fourth box was different. Larger, heavier.

What have we here? I said to myself. I blew the dust off the top and pried the lid open. The crowbar slipped from my hand and clanged to the floor. I stared into the fourth box for a long time.

It took me a minute to convince myself that it might be what I thought it was.

Very quickly, I closed the box, hammered the lid down, and went to the transport computer. The paper trail started with a company called Ingral in New York. Ingral had been bought by Docent, and now Docent had been bought by Hansen. The box had been in storage the whole time, gradually moving between trophic levels of the corporate food web. Who owned it before Ingral was anyone's guess. The box might have been sealed for ten years. Maybe longer. Its original provenance lost to time.

I clicked the PROPERTY RECEIVED button next to the transport number and typed my name into the space provided. My finger hesitated over the keyboard. I hit RETURN.

With that, the box was mine.

I tracked down a hand dolly and with some difficulty managed to wheel the crate outside, then across the parking lot to the main building, where the freight elevator took me to the second floor. The box took up a good portion of my office. Later that day, I scouted for lab space in the adjunct buildings and, after touring several possibilities on the first floor of North building, settled for a chamber on the second floor along the back, room 271. It was a medium-sized space with no windows and bare walls – its only true mark of distinction a patch of darkened floor tiles, marred by some earlier experiment gone horribly wrong. I signed the paperwork and was handed the new key card.

Later that day, I was drawing on my marker board when Satvik walked into my office. 'What is this?'

'This,' I said, gesturing to the board, 'is my project.'

Gone was the old, half-finished formula, erased with the single swipe of my hand. The new diagram was as simple as I could make it, but it still took up most of the board.

Satvik's eyes narrowed as he studied the scrawl. 'You have a project now?'

'Yes.'

'Congratulations!' His smile beamed. He grabbed my

hand and shook. 'How did this wonderful thing happen?'

'Save the congratulations,' I told him. 'Let's not get ahead of ourselves.'

'What is it?' He was looking at the board again.

'You ever hear of the Feynman double-slit?' I said.

'Physics? That is not my area, but I have heard of Young's double-slit.'

'It's the same thing, only instead of light it uses a stream of electrons.' I put my hand on the box that was still resting on the hand dolly. 'And a detector. I found it in the crate, along with a thermionic gun.'

Satvik looked at the box. 'Gun?'

'A thermionic gun. An electron gun. It's part of a replication trial.'

'You are going to use this gun?'

I nodded. 'Feynman claimed every situation in quantum mechanics can be explained by saying, "You remember the case of the experiment with two holes? It's the same thing."' I patted the box, '*This* is that thing.'

'Why are you doing this project?'

'I want to see what Feynman saw.'

6

Autumn comes quick to the East Coast. It is a different animal out here, where the trees take on every color of the spectrum, and the wind has teeth. As a boy, before the moves and the special schools, I'd spent an autumn evening camped out in the woods behind my grandparents' house. Lying on my back in the tall grass, staring up at the leaves as they drifted past my field of vision.

There is a moment, climbing a tree, when you know you should climb no higher. A winnowing of branches the farther you go, like the choices in life.

It was the smell that brought it back so strong – the smell of fall – as I walked to the parking lot. Joy stood near the roadway, waiting for her cab.

The wind gusted, making the trees dance. She turned her collar against the wind, oblivious to the autumn beauty around her. For a moment, I felt pity for that. To live in New England and not see the leaves.

I climbed into my rental. I idled. No cab passed through the gates. No cab followed the winding drive. I backed out and then shifted into drive. I was about to pull away but at the last second spun the wheel and pulled up to the turnaround.

I rolled down the side window. 'Is there a problem with your ride?'

'I don't know,' she said. 'I think there might be.'

'Do you need a lift home?'

'I don't want to trouble you.' She paused. Then, 'You don't mind?'

'Not at all.'

I pulled the handle, and the door swung open. She climbed in. 'Thank you,' she said. 'I'm sorry if it's a bit of a drive.'

'It's fine. I wasn't doing much anyway.'

'Left at the gate,' she said.

The truth was, it felt good to be useful. It made me feel normal in a way that I hadn't in a while. So much of my life was out of control, but this I could do – provide a ride to someone who needed it. She guided me by stops. She didn't use the street names, but she counted the intersections, guiding me to the highway, the blind leading the blind. The miles rolled by.

Boston, a city that hasn't forgotten itself. A city outside of time. Crumbling brick and stylish concrete. Road names that existed before the Redcoats invaded. It is easy to lose yourself, to imagine yourself lost, while winding through the chaotic streets. Outside the city proper, there is stone everywhere, and trees – soft pine and colorful deciduous. I saw a map in my head, Cape Cod jutting into the Atlantic. The cape is a curl of land positioned so perfectly to protect Boston that it seems a thing designed. If not by man, then by God. God wanted a city where Boston sits.

The houses, I know, are expensive beyond all reason. It is a place that defies farming. Scratch the earth, and a rock will leap out and hit you. People build stone walls around their properties so they'll have someplace to put the stones.

At her apartment, I pulled to a stop in a small parking lot. I walked her to her door, like this was a date. Standing next to her, I noticed she was only a few inches shorter than me, long and lean, and we were at the door, her empty blue eyes focused on something far away until she looked at me, *looked*, and I could swear for a moment that she saw me.

Then her eyes glided past my shoulder, focused again on some vista only she could see.

'I'm renting now,' she said. 'Once my probationary period is over, I'll probably buy a condo closer to work.'

'I didn't realize you were still on probation, too.'

'I actually hired in the week after you.'

'Ah, so I have seniority. Good to know.'

She smiled. 'I'm hoping to stay on once my probation ends.'

'Then I'm sure you will.'

'Perhaps,' she said. 'At least my research is cheap. I bought the acoustical software before I came here, so now it's only me and my ears that they're paying for. I'm a small investment. Can I entice you in for coffee?'

'I should be going, but another time.'

'I understand.' She extended her hand. 'Another time then. Thank you for the ride.'

I was about to turn and leave, but her voice stopped me. 'You know, I heard them talking about you.'

I turned. 'Who?'

'Men from the front office. It's a strange thing, being blind. Sometimes people think you're deaf, too. Or perhaps being blind makes you invisible. Am I invisible to you?'

The question caught me off guard. There was something in her expression. A deviousness to her smile. 'No,' I said. I wondered if she knew she was beautiful. She must know.

'Most people are good talkers,' she said. 'But I've cultivated a facility for the opposite. Jeremy said you were brilliant.'

'He said that?'

'I have a question before you go.'

'Okay.'

She brought her hand up to find my cheek. 'Why are the brilliant ones always so fucked up?'

Her hand was cool on my skin. It was the first time I'd been touched in a long time.

'You need to be careful,' she said. 'I can smell the alcohol on you some mornings. And if I can smell it, so can others.'

'I'll be fine,' I said.

'No.' She shook her head. 'Somehow I don't think you will.'

7

Satvik stood in front of the diagram I'd drawn on my marker board.

He was silent as he considered the scribblings. At one point, his hand went to his ear, tugging at the earlobe. I didn't want to prompt him. I was interested in his unadulterated opinion.

'Okay, what is it?' he asked finally. It was already late, and many of the other researchers had gone home for the day.

'The wave-particle duality of light,' I said.

I'd spent most of the day drawing and going over checklists in my head. Part of it was just overcoming inertia, building myself up to actually do it. The other part, maybe, was finding a path to believe it all again. Can you half believe something? No, that wasn't quite right. This was quantum mechanics. The better question: can you both believe in something and not?

Satvik stepped closer to the marker board.

'Wave-particle duality,' he said slowly under his breath. He turned to me, gesturing at the diagram. 'And these lines over here?'

'This is the wave part,' I said. 'Fire a photon stream through two adjacent slits, and the competing waves create an image on the phosphorescent screen. The frequencies of the waves zero-sum each other in a set pattern, and a characteristic image is captured there.' I pointed to the drawing. 'Do you see?'

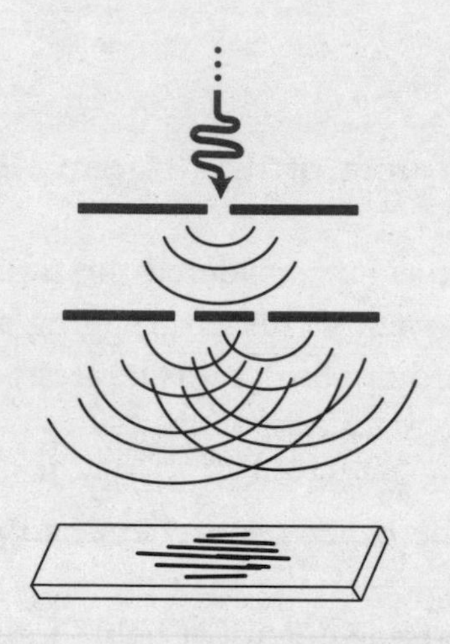

'I think so. The photons act as the waves.'

'Yes, and as the waves pass through the slits, one wave front becomes two, the ripples overlap, and you get the interference pattern.'

'I see.'

'But there's a way to produce a totally different result. A totally different image. If you put a detector at the two slits' – I began drawing another picture below the first – 'then it changes everything. When the detectors are in place, a kind of translation occurs, from the conjectural to the absolute – and when you look at the results, you realize that somewhere between the gun and the screen, light has stopped behaving like a wave and started behaving as a particle series.'

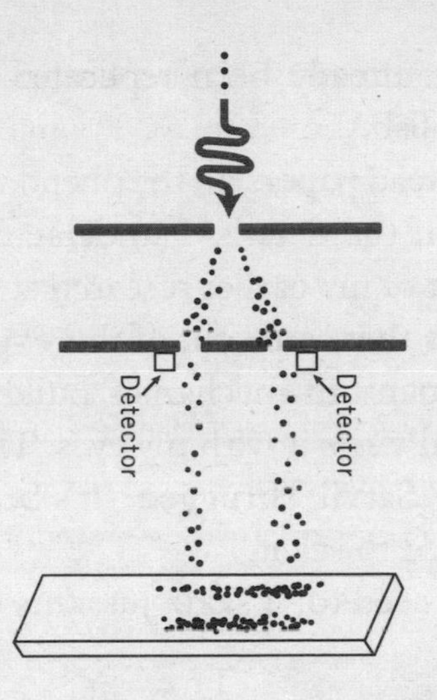

I continued, 'So instead of an interference pattern, you get two distinct clusters of phosphorescence where the particles pass straight through the slits and contact the screen without impacting each other.'

'This uses the same gun?'

'Yes, the same photon gun. Thc samc two slits. But a different result.'

'I remember now,' Satvik said. 'I believe there was a chapter on this in grad school.'

'In grad school, I *taught* this. All those probabilistic implications. And I watched the students' faces. The ones who understood what it meant. I could see it in their expressions, the pain of believing something that can't be true.'

'This is already a famous experiment, though. You are planning to replicate?'

'Yeah.'

'Why? It has already been replicated many times; no journal will publish.'

'I know. I've read papers on the phenomenon; I've given class lectures on the details; I understand it mathematically. Hell, most of my earlier research at QSR is based on the assumptions that came out of this experiment. Everything else in quantum mechanics builds from this, but I've never actually *seen* it with my eyes. That's why.'

'It is science.' Satvik shrugged. 'It's been done already, so you don't need to see it.'

'I think I do need to,' I said. 'Just this once.'

The next few weeks passed in a blur. Satvik helped me with my project, and I helped him with his. We worked mornings in his lab. Evenings we spent in North building, room 271, setting up the equipment for the experiment. The phosphorescent plate was a problem – then the alignment of the thermionic gun. In a way, it felt like we were partners, almost, Satvik and I. And it was a good feeling. After working so long by myself, it was good to be able to talk to someone.

We traded stories to pass the time. Satvik talked of his problems. They were the problems good men sometimes have when they've lived good lives. He talked about helping his daughter with her homework and worrying about paying for her college. He talked of his family *Backhome* – saying it fast that way, *Backhome*, so you heard the proper noun. He talked of the fields and the bugs and the monsoon and the ruined crops. 'It is going to be a bad year for sugar cane,' he told me, as if we were farmers instead of researchers. And I could imagine it easily, him standing at the edge of a field. Like it had only been an accident that he'd ended up in this place, this life. He talked about his mother's advancing years. He talked of his brothers and his sisters and his nieces, and I came to understand the weight of responsibility he felt.

'You never talk of yourself,' he observed at one point.

'There's not much to say.'

He dismissed that with a wave of a hand. 'Everyone has things to say,' he said. 'But you keep quiet. You are alone here?'

'What do you mean?'

'No family? You live alone?'

'Yeah.'

'So there is only this place.' He gestured around him. 'Only work. People forget they are going to die someday. There's more to life than career and paycheck.' Bending over the gate arrays, soldering tool in hand, he changed the subject. 'I talk too much; you must be sick of my voice.'

'Not at all.'

'You have been a big help with my work. How can I ever repay you, my friend?'

'Money is fine,' I told him. 'I prefer large bills.'

'You see? Paycheck.' He tsked me softly and bent closer to his work.

I wanted to tell him of my life.

I wanted to tell him of my work at QSR, and that some things you learn, you wish you could unlearn. I wanted to tell him that memory has gravity and madness a color; that all guns have names, and it is the same name. I wanted to tell him I understood about his tobacco; that I'd been married once, and it hadn't worked out; that I used to talk softly to my father's grave; that it was a long time since I'd really been okay.

But I didn't tell him any of those things. Instead, I talked about the experiment. That I could do.

'It started a half century ago as a thought experiment,' I told him. 'It was about proving the incompleteness of quantum mechanics. Physicists felt quantum mechanics couldn't be the whole story because the analytics takes too many liberties with reality. There was still that impossible incongruity: the photoelectric effect showed light to be particulate – an array of discontinuous quanta; Young's results said waves. But only one could be right. Later, of course, when technology caught up to theory, it turned out the experimental results followed the math. The math says you can either know the position of an electron or the momentum, but never both.'

'I see.'

'You've heard of the tunneling effect?' I asked.

'In electronic systems, there is something called tunneling leakage.'

'It rises out of the same principle.'

'And relates to this?'

'The math, it turns out, isn't metaphor at all. The math is dead serious. It's not screwing around.'

Satvik frowned as he went back to his soldering. 'One should strive to know the world accurately.' A few minutes later, while making careful adjustments to his field gates, he traded his story for mine.

'There once was a guru who brought four princes into the forest,' he told me. 'They were hunting birds.'

'Birds,' I said, tracking his change of subject.

'Yes, and up in the trees, they see one, a beautiful bird with bright feathers. The first prince said, "I will shoot the bird," and he pulled back on his arrow and shot into the trees. But his accuracy failed him, and the arrow missed. Then the sccond prince tried to shoot, and hc, too, missed. Then the third prince. Finally, the fourth prince shot high into the trees, and this time the arrow struck and the beautiful bird fell dead. The guru looked at the first three princes and said, "Where were you aiming?"

' "At the bird."

' "At the bird."

' "At the bird."

'The guru looked at the fourth prince, "And you?"

' "At the bird's eye." '

8

Once the equipment was set up, the alignment was the last hurdle to be cleared. The electron gun had to be aimed so the electron was just as likely to go through either slit. The equipment filled most of the room – an assortment of electronics and screens and wires. A mad scientist's chamber if ever there was one.

In the mornings, in the motel room, I talked to the mirror, made promises to gunmetal eyes. And by some miracle did not drink.

There were pills in my suitcase – a half-finished prescription to ease the shakes. But I'd never liked how they made my head feel. I popped two pills in my mouth.

One day became two. Two became three. Three became five. Then I hadn't had a drink in a week. The ravening thirst was still there, just under my skin. My hands still shook in the morning as I gripped the cool porcelain. But I did not drink.

I have a project, I told myself. *I have a project.*

It was enough.

At the lab, the work continued. When the last piece of equipment was positioned, I stood back and surveyed the whole setup, heart beating in my chest, standing at the edge of some great universal truth. I was about to be witness to something few people in the history of the world had seen.

When the first satellite was launched toward deep space in 1977, it carried a special golden record. The record held diagrams and mathematical formulas. It carried the image of a fetus, the calibration of a circle, and a single page from Newton's *System of the World.* It carried the units of our mathematical system because mathematics, we're told, is the universal language. I've always felt that golden record should have carried a diagram of this experiment, the Feynman double-slit.

Because this experiment is more fundamental than math. It is what lives under the math. It tells of reality itself.

Richard Feynman said this about the slit experiment: 'It has in it the heart of quantum mechanics. In truth, it contains only mystery.'

Room 271 contained two chairs, a marker board, and two long lab benches. The setup itself sprawled across the length of the room, covering the tables. Two slits had been cut into sheets of steel that served to divide the areas of the setup. At the far end, the phosphorescent screen was loaded into a small rectangular slot behind the second set of slits. Where the photons hit the screen, the screen would glow.

Jeremy came by a little after 5:00, just before going home for the evening.

'So it's true then,' he said. He smiled and stepped farther into the room. 'They told me you signed up for lab space.'

'Yeah.'

'What is all this?' he said, looking around.

'Just old equipment from Docent,' I said. 'The

Feynman double-slit. No one was using it, so I thought I'd see if I could get it to work.'

His smile faded. 'What are you planning exactly?'

'A replication trial.'

I could see the disappointment as he weighed his next words. 'It's good to see you working on something, but isn't that a little dated?'

'Good science is never dated.'

'I understand the sentiment, I do, but I have to be honest with you. I don't think this is the kind of thing that will change the review board's mind.'

'That's not why I'm doing it.'

'Then why?'

And how could I explain the need? A thing I barely understood myself – the rightness of that moment when I opened the crate and saw what was inside: the experiment that physics had been living in the shadow of. As if I was meant to see it. The gulf between the quantum world and relativity that physics could not cross.

When I didn't answer, he walked over to a stool and sat. 'Please,' he said, gesturing to a chair. 'I've been wanting to talk to you.' His expression was solemn.

I sat.

'Eric, I don't normally do this, but I wanted you to know that I've made a few inquiries on your behalf.'

So the visit wasn't so random after all. 'You didn't have to do that.'

'It turns out there are projects already in place here that could use a good researcher like you.'

'What do you mean?'

'For the most part, we hire people who drive their own

paths here, as you know, but sometimes a project will grow beyond expectations, and researchers start looking for good team members. There's a small team in South building that could use another body.'

'Who?'

'Dr. Lee. He already has two other researchers working with him.'

'And I'd be the third wheel, is that the idea?'

'Well, fourth, technically, counting him. He said he could plug you right in. He welcomes another set of gloves on the project. His words exactly.'

'He doesn't know me. Why would he say that?'

'Because I lied and told him you were easy to work with.'

'You mean, you asked him for a favor. Did you tell him I was charming, too?'

'My dishonesty goes only so far.'

I took a moment, imagining how that conversation might have gone.

'You don't need to do this,' I said.

'We all need favors from time to time. Favors are what make the world go round.'

And I could see he believed it. Or wanted to. 'I already owe you,' I said.

'It will still be tricky, but there's a chance, if you worked with Dr. Lee . . .' His words trailed off. I realized he couldn't even bring himself to say it.

'The review board might overlook my lack of productivity?' I asked.

'It's possible. Like I said, it's just a chance. I don't want to make any promises.'

'And what chance would you be taking, playing favorites like that? You have bosses, too, isn't that what you said to me?'

'Let me worry about that.'

'I'm not letting you risk your own position to help me.'

'The risk is small.'

I studied his face, looking for the lie. I didn't trust his evaluation of risk. He'd put himself in harm's way before. And it had cost him.

'You haven't even mentioned what Dr. Lee is working on,' I said.

'Does it matter?'

I stared at him.

'Macrophages,' he said.

'You've got to be kidding.'

'You're too good for macrophages?'

'Hardly,' I said. 'I don't know anything about them.'

'What's there to know? Besides, you're a quick learner. He needs assistants, not PhDs.'

'It's not my area. It will quickly be apparent to everyone involved that it's not my area.'

'Then what *is* your area, exactly?' He snapped. He hadn't expected this resistance. It was the outrage of a man who'd just thrown a life ring, only to see the drowning man paddle in the other direction. 'You turned your back on all the work you did at QSR.'

'I had my reasons.'

'What reasons? You still haven't said.'

Because a single unfinished formula can break you. I shook my head. 'It hardly matters now.'

'It matters a lot, unless there's a secondary market for

ex-quantum theoreticians that I'm unaware of. If you won't continue your previous research, where does that leave you?'

'Maybe nowhere.'

'Then *take* the position.'

And I wanted to.

I wanted to say yes. It was on the edge of my tongue. I could picture myself forming the words, telling him what he wanted to hear. I could picture myself learning everything there was to learn about macrophages. Diving into a new subject. *A new start*, my sister had said. Laboratory assistant was a long step sideways, but it would be work. Employment. Some kind of usefulness. I could do it. I wanted to do it.

Instead I said, 'I have a project.'

'This?' Jeremy gestured to the setup, the crazy equipment. 'This won't get you through review.'

I thought of Jeremy's bosses. The ones who might not like him playing favorites. Careers had been damaged by less. A knot tightened in my stomach. 'So be it.'

He threw up his hands. He scowled at me long enough that I knew it wasn't me at the other end of his stare but himself. Or maybe his father – the corporate goon with the giant desk. A man who'd never budged an inch.

When he finally spoke, his tone was measured. 'Eric, you and I go way back. As far back as I go with anyone. I don't want to see your career end like this. What are your plans when you leave here?'

How to answer that one? How do you tell someone that you have no plans? That your plans come to an abrupt end a few months into the future. I thought of the gun, and its name rose up – Panacea – christened one drunken night as I marveled at the slick coolness of the trigger. Maybe that was how this ended. How it was always going to end, since those bad days in Indianapolis.

'Do you want to stay here and work?' he asked.

'Yes.'

'Then *do* that. Take the favor.'

I looked at him, my old friend. In college, during his sophomore year, he'd pulled over in an ice storm to help a stranded motorist. He did things like that. It was on the way back to school after Christmas break. While helping to change the old woman's tire, he'd been struck by a pickup truck that slid on the ice. He'd spent the better part of a month in the hospital – broken bones, a torn spleen. It had also cost him a whole semester of classes, and he'd graduated behind everyone else. Most people would have seen that stranded motorist and kept on driving, but he'd pulled over and climbed out. That's just how he was, always wanting to help. And here he was again. But I knew the feel of ice under my wheels.

'Not like this,' I said. 'I can't.'

He shook his head. 'I want to be clear,' he said. 'If this is your project, I can't save you.'

'It's not your job to save me,' I said. 'This is enough, right here. The double-slit. I *need* to see it. I can't explain it better than that.' And how could I? How could I tell him that I hadn't had a drink in days? How could I tell him of the miracle of that? 'I think I was meant to see it.'

'*Meant?* Now you sound crazy.'

My mother's eyes flashed in my head.

'There is no meant,' Jeremy continued. But there was

resignation in his voice. He'd seen the drowning man slide beneath the waves.

'Once you believe in quantum mechanics,' I said, 'it's hard to rule something out merely because it is impossible.'

He glanced toward the apparatus. 'But what are you expecting to prove?'

'Just one thing,' I said. 'That sometimes the impossible is true.'

9

The day we ran the experiment, the weather was freezing. The wind gusted in from the ocean, and the East Coast huddled under a cold front. I got to work early and left a note on Satvik's desk.

Meet me in my lab at 9:00.
– Eric

I did not give any details. I did not explain further.

Satvik walked through the door of room 271 a little before 9:00.

'Good morning,' he said. 'I got your note.'

I gestured toward the button. 'Would you like to do the honors?'

We stood motionless in the near darkness of the lab. Satvik studied the equipment spread out before him – sheets of steel and the long silver barrel of the thermionic gun. Electrical wiring ran the length of the table. 'Never trust engineer who doesn't walk his own bridge,' he said.

I smiled. 'Okay then.'

It was time.

I hit the button. The machine hummed to life.

We watched it.

I let it run for a few minutes before walking over to check the capture screen. I opened the top and looked inside. And then I saw what I'd been hoping to see. The distinctive banded pattern, an interference signal on the screen – the regular arrangement of dark and light. It was there, just as Young and the Copenhagen interpretation said it would be.

Satvik looked over my shoulder. The machine continued to hum, deepening the pattern by the second.

'Would you like to see a magic trick?' I asked.

He nodded solemnly.

'Light is a wave,' I told him.

I reached for the detector and hit the ON switch – and just like that, the interference pattern disappeared.

'Unless someone is watching.'

The Copenhagen interpretation proposes this fundamental incongruity: Observation is a principal requisite of phenomena. There is nothing that exists until it is first witnessed to exist. Until then there are only probability waves. Statistical approximation.

For purposes of the experiment, the behavior of the electron is probabilistic – its specific path not merely unknown but theoretically unknowable, manifesting as a diffuse probability wave front that passes through both slits at once. Beyond the slits, these waves interfere with each other as they propagate, like two snakes traversing a pond, the ripples crossing and recrossing each other as they expand outward, forming a diffraction pattern on the capture screen.

But what if detection by an observer were possible at the slits? What if you could prove which path the electron took? In this case, its movement would no longer be subject to probabilistic forces. Here probability collapses. Becomes certainty. Becomes measured fact. If a particle is shown to pass through only one slit, then rationality dictates that it can't interfere with its own propagation. And yet it remains, if you shoot light through two slits, the pattern will form. Slowly, photon by photon. A single experimental setup with two different theoretical outcomes. This incongruity would seem self-contradictory, except for one thing. Except that the interference pattern disappears if someone is watching.

We ran the experiment again and again. Satvik checked the detector results, being careful to note which slit the electrons passed through. Sometimes the left; other times the right. With the detectors turned on, roughly half the electrons were recorded passing through each slit, and no interference pattern accrued. We turned the detectors off again – and again, instantly, the interference pattern emerged on the screen.

'How does the system know?' Satvik asked.

'How does it know what?'

'That the detectors are on. How does it know the electron's position has been recorded?'

'Ah, the big question.'

'Are the detectors putting out some kind of electromagnetic interference?'

I shook my head. 'You haven't seen the really weird stuff yet.'

'What do you mean?'

'The electrons aren't really responding to the detectors

at all. They're responding to the fact that you'll eventually read the detectors' results.'

Satvik looked at me, blank-faced.

'Turn the detectors back on,' I said.

Satvik hit the button. The detectors hummed softly. We let the experiment run.

'It is just like before,' I told him. 'The detectors are on, so the electrons should be acting as particles, not waves; and without waves, there's no interference pattern, right?'

Satvik nodded.

'Okay, turn it off.'

The machine cycled down to silence.

'And now the magic test,' I said. 'This is the one. This is the one I wanted to see.'

I hit the CLEAR button on the detector, erasing the results.

'The experiment was the same as before,' I said, 'with the same detectors turned on both times. The only difference was that I erased the results without looking at them. Now check the screen.'

Satvik opened the slot and pulled out the screen.

And then I saw it. On his face. The pain of believing something that can't be true.

'An interference pattern,' he said. 'How could that be?'

'It's called *retrocausality*. By erasing the results after the experiment was run, I caused the particle pattern to never have occurred in the first place.'

Satvik was silent for five full seconds. 'Is such a thing possible?'

'Of course not, but there it is. Unless a conscious observer makes an ascertainment of the detector results, the detector itself will remain part of the larger indeterminate system.'

'I don't understand.'

'The detectors don't induce the phenomenon of wave function collapse; conscious observation does. Consciousness is like this giant roving spotlight, collapsing reality wherever it shines – and what isn't observed remains probability. And it's not just photons or electrons. It is everything. All matter. It is a fault in reality. A testable, repeatable fault in reality.'

Satvik said, 'So this is what you wanted to see?'

'Yeah.'

'Is it different for you now that you've actually seen it?'

I considered this for a moment, exploring my own mind. 'Yes, it is different,' I said. 'It is much worse.'

We ran the slit experiment again and again. The results never changed. They matched perfectly the results that had been documented and written about decades earlier. Over the next two days, Satvik hooked the detectors up to a printer. We ran the tests, and I hit PRINT. We listened as the printer buzzed and chirped, printing out the results – transferring the detector's observations into a physical reality you could hold in your hand.

Satvik pored over the data sheets as if to make sense of them by sheer force of will. I stared over his shoulder, a voice in his ear. 'It's like an unexplored law of nature,' I said. 'Quantum physics as a form of statistical approximation – a solution to the storage problem of reality. Matter behaves like a frequency domain. Why resolve the data fields nobody is looking at?'

Satvik put the sheets down and rubbed his eyes.

'There are schools of mathematical thought which assert that a deeper, harmonic order is enfolded just below the surface of our lives. Bohm called it the *implicate*.'

'We have a name for this, too,' Satvik said. He smiled. 'It is *Brahman*. We've known about it for five thousand years.'

'I want to try something,' I said.

We ran the test again. I printed the results, being careful not to look at them. One from the detector, the other from the capture screen. We turned off the equipment.

I folded both pages in half and slid them into manila folders. I gave Satvik the folder with the screen results. I kept the detector results. 'I haven't looked at the detector results yet,' I told him. 'So right now the wavefunction is still a superposition of states. Even though the results are printed, they're still unobserved and so still part of the indeterminate system. Do you understand?'

'Yes.'

'Go in the next room. I'm going to open my folder with the detector results in exactly twenty seconds. In exactly thirty seconds, I want you to open the screen results.'

Satvik walked out. And here it was: the gap where logic bleeds. I fought an irrational burst of fear. I lit the nearby Bunsen burner and held my folder over the open flame. The smell of igniting paper and a flare of bright yellow light. Black ash. It was over quickly. A minute later Satvik was back, his folder open.

'You didn't look,' he said. He held out his sheet of paper. 'As soon as I opened it, I knew you didn't look.'

'Because I lied,' I said, taking the paper from him. 'And you caught me. I destroyed the detector readout without looking at it. We made the world's first quantum lie detector – a divination tool made of light.' I looked at the paper Satvik had given me. The interference pattern lay in dark bands across the white surface. The wavefunction had not collapsed. I would never know which slit the particle had gone through because those results were now ash. Therefore, the particle had gone through both slits as a probability wave. 'When that result was printed, it meant I was never going to look at those results. So did I really have a choice? Could I have looked if I wanted to? Some mathematicians say there is either no such thing as free will, or the world is a simulation. Which do you think is true?'

'Those are our options?'

I crushed the paper into a ball. Something slid away inside of me – a subtle change – and I opened my mouth to speak, but what came out was different from what I intended.

'I did have a breakdown.'

I told Satvik about the arrest in Indianapolis, stumbling and shouting in the street. My sister's neighbors watching through their blinds. I told him about the formula that I'd been working on to unite quantum mechanics with the rest of physics, like a lost theory of everything. I told him about the drinking and the eyes in the mirror and what I said to myself in the morning. I told him about my uncle coming to me when I turned eighteen: 'I was his brother,' he'd said, 'but you were his son.' As he handed me the evidence box still banded with police tape. Kept for years, the most powerful talisman. 'It should be yours if you want it.'

I told him about the smooth, steel ERASE button I put against my head – a single curl of an index finger to pay for it all.

Satvik nodded while he listened, the smile blasted from his face. I spoke for a long while, pouring it all out in a single rush, paying for all the weeks of quiet, and when I finished, Satvik put his hand on my shoulder. 'So then you are crazy after all, my friend.'

'It's been thirteen days now,' I told him. 'Thirteen days sober.'

'Is that good?'

'No, but it's longer than I've gone in two years.'

We ran the experiment. We printed the results.

If we looked at the detector results, the screen showed the particle pattern. If we didn't, it showed an interference pattern.

After so much talking, we worked silently through most of the night. Near morning, sitting in the semidarkness of the lab, Satvik finally spoke. 'There once was a frog who lived in a well,' he said.

I watched his face as he told the story.

'One day a farmer lowered a bucket into the well, and the frog was pulled up to the surface. The frog blinked in the bright sun, seeing it for the first time. "Who are you?" the frog asked the farmer.

'The farmer was amazed. He said, "I am the owner of this farm."

'"You call your world *farm*?" the frog said.

'"No, this is not a different world," the farmer said. "This is the same world."

'The frog laughed at the farmer. He said, "I have swum to every corner of my world. North, south, east, west. I am telling you, this is a different world." '

I looked at Satvik and said nothing.

'You and I,' Satvik said, 'we are still frogs in the well. Can I ask you a question?'

'Go ahead.'

'You do not want to drink?'

'No.'

'I am curious, what you said with the gun, that you'd shoot yourself if you drank . . .'

'Yeah.'

'You did not drink on those days you said that?'

'That's right.'

Satvik paused as if considering his words carefully. 'Then why did you not just say that every day?'

'That is simple,' I said. 'Because then I'd be dead now.'

10

When I was four, I stepped on a fire ant's nest in the backyard and was stung nearly a dozen times. The ants crawled up my pant legs and got lodged at the elastic waistband where they could climb no higher, and so stung me again and again in a ring around my waist and on my thighs and calves. I remember my mother shouting and stripping me naked in the grass while I screamed – shaking the ants loose from my clothes, crinkly red insects lodged in my flesh.

Inside the house she tore open cigarettes and placed the tobacco on the stings, holding them in place with Band-Aids.

'To draw the poison out,' she said. And I marveled at her skills. She always knew just what to do.

I sat on the couch, watching the old TV until my aunt came to babysit. My mother had a dinner party to attend, and Father was meeting her there after work.

'Go,' my aunt told her. 'He'll be fine.' And so my mother left. I stood in the window and watched her car pull down the driveway. She was gone.

But minutes later, I heard keys in the door. My mother had come back, and though my aunt frowned and shooed her away, she would not leave.

'You need to go,' my aunt said. 'It's a company party.' But my mother only waved her off and sat next to me on the couch. 'There'll be others,' she said. Though there never were. 'I can't leave.'

She held me as we watched the nature channel for the next hour while my stomach cramped, and the pain grew, and my legs purpled and swelled and wept.

Satvik and I left for the night, and I found myself in my car, hesitating at a green light. I idled in the left lane, watching the light turn yellow, then red. I turned my car around. I returned to the lab and climbed the stairs and looked at the machine. Some wounds you cannot leave. My mother had shown me that.

I ran the experiment one final time. Hit PRINT. I put the results in two folders without looking at them.

On the first folder, I wrote the words *detector results*. On the second, I wrote *screen results*.

I drove home to the motel. I took off my clothes. Stood naked in front of the mirror, imagining my place in the indeterminate system.

According to David Bohm, quantum physics requires reality to be a non-local phenomenon. Deep in the quantum milieu, location no longer manifests, every point merging to equivalence – a single, concordant frequency domain. Bohm's implicate order that lives beneath everything.

I put the folder marked *detector results* up to my forehead. 'I will never look at this,' I said. 'Not ever, unless I start drinking again.' I stared in the mirror. I stared at my own gunmetal eyes and saw that I meant it.

I glanced down at my desk, at the other folder. The one with the screen results. My hands shook.

I laid the first folder on the desk.

In the closet, I knew, was a small security box mounted to the wall. I walked over and opened it. I made up a pass code – my mother's birthday, 2-27-61 – and put the folders inside.

Keats said, *Beauty is truth, truth beauty.* What was the truth?

The folders knew.

One day, I would either drink and open the detector results, or I wouldn't.

Inside that second folder, there was either an interference pattern, or there wasn't. A yes or a no.

The answer was already printed.

I waited in Satvik's office until he arrived in the morning. He put his briefcase on his desk, surprised to see me sitting in his swivel chair. He looked at me, at the clock, then back at me.

'What are you doing?' he asked.

'Waiting for you.'

'How long have you been here?'

'Since four thirty a.m.'

He glanced around the room to see if I'd changed anything. The same clutter of electrical equipment. To the rest of us, it was chaos, but Satvik probably had it memorized. I kicked back in his chair, fingers laced behind my head.

Satvik just watched me. Satvik was bright. He waited.

'Can you rig the detector to an indicator?' I asked him.

'What kind of indicator?'

'A light.'

'How do you mean?'

'Instead of a readout, can you set up a light that goes off when the detector picks up an electron at the slit?'

His brow knitted. 'It shouldn't be hard. Why?'

'I thought before that there was nothing to prove with the two-slit experiment, but I might have been wrong.'

'What is left?'

I leaned forward. 'Let's define, exactly, the indeterminate system.'

11

Later that morning, Point Machine watched the test. He stood in the near darkness of room 271. The machine thrummed. He studied the interference pattern – the narrow bands of phosphorescence.

'You're looking at one-half of the wave particle duality of light,' I said.

'What's the other half look like?'

I turned the detectors on. The banded pattern diverged into two distinct clumps on the screen.

'This.'

'Oh,' Point Machine said. 'I've heard of this.'

Standing in Point Machine's lab. Frogs swimming.

'They're aware of light, right?' I asked.

'They do have eyes.'

'But, I mean, they're aware of it?'

'Yeah, they respond to visual stimuli. They're hunters. They have to see to hunt.'

I bent over the glass aquarium. 'But I mean, aware?'

'What did you do before here?'

'Quantum research.'

'Meaning what?' Point Machine asked.

I tried to shrug him off. 'There were a range of projects.

Solid-state photonic devices, Fourier transforms, liquid NMR.'

'Fourier transforms?'

'Complex equations that can be used to translate waveforms into visual elements.'

Point Machine looked at me, dark eyes tightening. He said again, very slowly, enunciating each word, 'What did you do, *exactly*?'

'Computers,' I said. 'We were working with computers. Quantum encryption processing extending up to sixteen qubits. I had a partner with a whole team under us, working at a start-up right out of college. It was all applied theory stuff. I was the theory part.'

'And the applied part?'

'That was my friend Stuart. He was interested in dynamics-based modeling solutions. Packing more polygons into the isosurface meshwork of 3D renders.'

'So what happened?'

'We pushed model fidelity by an order of magnitude but eventually came up against the computational constraints of the system. Near the end, we used the Fourier transforms to remodel the wave information into visuals.'

'Waves to images.'

'Yeah.'

'Why?'

'For me, it was the challenge. To see if it could be done. For the others, there were more practical reasons.'

'Like?'

'Pushing past the system's polygon budget. It was a way to render 3D space efficiently. Stuart was into hardware improvements. Modeling design. Starting his own company. Things that were actually useful.'

'Did it work?'

'The company? Yeah, it's still based in Indiana.'

'No, the computer.'

'Oh, that. Kind of. We reached a sixteen-coherence state and then used nuclear resonance to decode it.'

'Why only kind of? So then it *didn't* work?'

'No, it worked; it definitely worked,' I said. 'Even when it was turned off.'

It took Satvik two days to rig up the light while I built the box.

Point Machine brought the frogs in on a Saturday. We separated the healthy from the sick, the healthy from the monsters.

'What is wrong with them?' Satvik asked.

'Pollutants.'

One frog was spiderlike – a phalanx of pale and twisted legs sprouting from its rear quarter. The legs twitched when Satvik picked it up. Another leg flexed and straightened.

'Pollutants do this?'

'To amphibians, yes. The more complex a system, the more ways it can go wrong. Amphibians are very complex.'

'Poor bastards,' Satvik said. He dropped the frog into the other aquarium with a loud plop.

Joy was next door, working in her lab. She heard our voices and stepped into the hall.

'You working weekends?' Satvik asked her when she appeared in our doorway.

'It's quieter,' Joy said. 'I do my more sensitive tests when there's nobody here. What about you? So you're all partners now?'

'Eric has the big hands on this project,' Satvik said. 'My hands are small.'

'Ah, so you have Eric to blame for your lost day off?' She followed Satvik's voice deeper into the lab, fingers trailing the wall.

'So it would appear,' I said. I hammered the last nail into the corner of the box. It was a flimsy thing of plywood two feet square, into which a small light had been wired – the bulb scavenged from a small chandelier at Satvik's house.

'I'd heard you were going to be leaving here.' The statement was pointed at me.

There was an awkward moment. Point Machine glanced up from his aquariums.

'Not quite yet,' I said.

'Then what are you working on?' she asked.

Satvik shot me a look, and I nodded.

So Satvik explained it the way only Satvik could. It took five full minutes, as he went over every detail, and she never interrupted him.

'Oh,' she said, finally. She blinked her empty eyes. She stayed.

We used Point Machine as a control. 'We're going to do this in real time,' I told him. 'No record at the detectors, just the indicator light inside the box. When I tell you, stand there and watch for the light. If the light comes on, it means the detectors picked up the electron. Understand?'

'Yeah, I get it,' Point Machine said.

Satvik hit the button, firing a stream of electrons. I watched the phosphorescent capture screen while an interference pattern materialized before my eyes – a now-familiar pattern of light and dark.

'Okay,' I told Point Machine. 'Now look in the box. Tell me if you see the light.'

Point Machine looked in the box. Before he even spoke, the interference pattern disappeared. 'Yeah,' he said. 'I see it.'

I smiled. Felt that fine edge between known and unknown. Caressed it.

I nodded at Satvik, and he hit the switch to kill power to the gun. I turned to Point Machine. 'You collapsed the probability wave by observing the light, so we've established proof of principle.' I looked at the three of them. 'Now let's find out if all observers were created equal.'

Point Machine put a frog in the box.

And here it was – the stepping-off point. A view into the implicate.

I nodded to Satvik. 'Fire the gun.'

He hit the switch, and the machine hummed. I watched the screen. I closed my eyes, felt my heart beating in my chest. Inside the box, I knew a light had come on for one of the two detectors; I knew the frog had seen it. But when I opened my eyes, the interference pattern still showed on the screen. The frog hadn't changed the system at all.

'Again,' I said.

Satvik fired the gun again.

Again. Again.

Point Machine looked at me. 'Well?'

'There's still an interference pattern. The probability wave didn't collapse.'

'Meaning what?' Joy asked.

'It means we try a different frog.'

We tried six. One after another. Pulling them from their aquarium and putting them in the box. None changed the result.

'They're part of the indeterminate system,' Satvik said.

'What does that mean?' Point Machine asked.

Satvik didn't answer, just pulled at his ear, lost in thought.

I watched the screen closely, and the interference pattern suddenly vanished. I was about to shout, but when I looked up, I saw Point Machine peeking into the box.

'You looked,' I said.

'I was just making sure the light worked.'

'It worked. I could tell the moment you saw it.'

We tried every frog in his lab. Then we tried the salamanders. None collapsed the waveform.

'Maybe it's just amphibians,' he said.

'Yeah, maybe.'

'What does that have to do with anything?'

'I haven't the slightest idea.'

'How is it that we affect the system, but frogs and salamanders can't?'

'Maybe it's our eyes,' Point Machine said. 'Quantum coherence effects in the retinal rod-rhopsin molecules themselves.'

'Why would that matter?'

'Optic nerve cells only conduct measured quanta to the visual cortex. Eyes are just another detector.'

'It's more than just our eyes.'

'You don't know that.'

'Frogs have eyes. They have a cortex.'

'Can I try?' Joy interrupted.

We all turned to look at her. A brown lock of hair had fallen loose from its place behind her ear and now dangled across her cheek, pointing to her mouth. Her expression was serious.

'Yeah,' I said.

We prepared the experiment again, this time with Joy's empty eyes pointed at the box.

'You ready?'

'Yes,' she said.

Satvik hit the button.

The machine hummed. We let it run for ten seconds. I checked the results.

I shook my head. 'Nothing.' The interference pattern hadn't collapsed. Instead of two distinct points, the screen still showed the intersecting waves.

'It was worth a try,' Point Machine said.

The next morning, Point Machine met Satvik and me in the parking lot before work. We climbed into my car and drove to the mall.

We went to a pet store. I bought three mice, a canary, a turtle, and a squish-faced Boston terrier puppy. The sales clerk stared at us.

'You pet lovers, huh?' He looked suspiciously at Satvik and Point Machine.

'Oh, yes,' I said. 'Pets.'

The drive back was quiet, punctuated only by the occasional whining of the puppy.

Point Machine broke the silence. 'Perhaps it takes a more complex nervous system than amphibians.'

'That shouldn't matter,' Satvik said. 'Life is life.'

I gripped the steering wheel, remembering a dozen late-night arguments back in college. 'What's the difference between mind and brain?'

'Semantics,' said Point Machine. 'Different names for the same idea.'

Satvik regarded us. 'No, it's more than that.'

'It's like the old question about the guitar,' I said. 'Do you play the guitar with your fingers or with your head?'

'Brain is hardware,' Satvik said. 'Mind is software.'

The Massachusetts landscape whipped past the car's windows, a wall of ruined hillside on our right – huge, dark stone like the bones of the earth. A compound fracture of the land. Somewhere to the east was the ocean. Cold, dark water. We drove the rest of the way in silence.

Back at the lab, we started with the turtle. Then the canary, which escaped afterward and flew to sit atop a filing cabinet. Then the mice. None of them collapsed the wave. The final mouse, white with red eyes, the classic lab mouse, moved cautiously across the table, whiskers vibrating, before Satvik caught it by its tail and put it back in its cardboard travel carrier.

'Time for the dog,' Point Machine said.

The Boston terrier looked up at us, googly-eyed, from its spot on the floor. It whined, tilting its head to the side.

'Are its eyes supposed to look like that?' Satvik asked.

'Like what?'

'You know, in different directions?'

'It's the breed, I think,' Point Machine offered. 'A lot of them are like that.'

I lifted the black-and-white puppy and placed it in the box. 'All it has to do is sense the light. For the purpose of the test, either eye will do.' I looked down at man's best friend, our companion through the millennia, and harbored secret hope. *This one*, I told myself. *This species, certainly, of all of them.* Because who hasn't looked into the eyes of a dog and not sensed something looking back?

The puppy yelped in the box. There wasn't much room to spare; the lightbulb jutted into the box near its head.

Satvik hit the button and ran the experiment.

'Well?'

I leaned over, looking down at the capture screen. The interference pattern was clear and steady.

Inside the box, I knew, the light had come on. But from the perspective of the universe, it had not been observed.

'Nothing,' I said. There was no change at all.

12

That night I drove to Joy's. She answered the door. Waited for me to speak. 'You mentioned coffee?'

She smiled then, pretty face framed in the doorway, and there was another moment when I felt sure that she saw me. She stepped back and opened the door wide.

'Come in.'

I moved past her, and the door clicked shut.

'I don't get company often,' she said. 'I apologize if the house is a mess.'

I glanced around, unsure if she was making a joke. Her apartment was small and orderly. I didn't know what I was expecting. Maybe this, exactly. Bare, pictureless walls. A couch. And then later, a bed.

It started with a silence. Then a touch.

A kiss soft, unsure of itself.

On the sheets, she arched her back. Skin like silk.

Living in sound and touch. Covers pooled on the floor. Her hands clutching tightly behind my neck, pulling me closer – a voice in my ear as our slick bodies slid past each other.

Afterward, in the darkness, we lay for a long time without speaking.

When I thought she was asleep, her voice surprised me. 'I usually know them better.'

'Who?'

'The ones who steal the covers.'

'Borrowing,' I said. 'I'm borrowing the covers.' I reached down and grabbed the blanket from the floor and draped it over her naked shoulder.

'Are you good-looking?' she asked.

'What?'

'I'm curious,' she said. Her hand reached out in the darkness and found me. She ran her fingers through my hair.

'Does it matter?'

'I have standards.'

Despite myself, I laughed. 'In that case, yes. Gorgeous, in fact.'

'I don't know about *that*.'

'No? You don't trust me?'

'Maybe I asked around.'

'Then why would you need to ask me?'

'Maybe I was curious what you thought.'

I took her hand and placed it on my face. 'I'm as you see.'

Her hand was cool on my cheek. After a long silence, she asked, 'Why did you come here tonight?'

I thought of the box and the puppy. The light that went unobserved.

'I didn't want to be alone.'

'The nights are hardest for you.' She stated it simply, like a fact. Like fire is hot. Water wet. Nights hardest.

Here is one advantage when talking to the blind. They can't see your expression. They don't know when they've struck bone. 'What is your work?' I asked, changing the subject. 'You've never said, specifically.'

'You never asked, specifically. Call it acoustical fabrication.'

'And what is that?'

'You start with wide, white-frequency tone, and then you remove everything you don't want.'

'Remove?'

Her slender arm curled behind my neck. 'Sound can be a flexible tool. A catalyst for chemical reaction or an inhibitor. Start with a maximum frequency density and then carve away those parts that you don't want to hear. There's a Mozart concerto hidden in every burst of static.'

Again, I couldn't tell if she was joking.

I sat up in the lightless room. At that moment, in the dark, we were the same. Only when I turned the light on would our worlds be different.

'Mornings are hardest,' I told her.

In a few hours the sun would rise. The sickness would come or not come. 'It's time for me to go.'

She ran a hand along my bare spine. She didn't try to get me to stay.

'Time,' she whispered. 'There is no such beast. Only now. And now.' She put her lips against my skin.

The next day, I left a message with Jeremy's secretary, asking him to come by room 271.

An hour later, there was a knock on the door, and he stepped into the room.

'You've made a finding?' he asked. He still had his suit jacket on. It would be a day of meetings for him, I knew. It was how you told the scientists from the managers. The color of their coats. Satvik and Point Machine stood behind me.

'We have.'

His face showed confusion. 'A *new* finding, the message said?'

'Just watch.'

Jeremy observed while we ran the experiment. He looked in the box. He collapsed the wavefunction himself.

Then we put the puppy in the box and ran the experiment again. We showed him the interference pattern.

Again, his face showed confusion. He wasn't sure what he'd just seen. 'Why didn't it work?' he asked.

'We don't know.'

'But what's different?'

'Only one thing. The observer.'

'I don't think I understand.'

'So far, none of the animals we've tested have been able to alter the quantum system.'

He scratched at the back of his neck. A line formed between his eyebrows. A single line of worry on his unlined face. He was silent for a long time, looking at the setup, thinking things through.

I let him get there on his own.

'Holy shit,' he said finally.

'Yeah,' Point Machine said.

'This is repeatable?'

'Again and again,' I said. I stepped forward and turned the machine off. The hum faded.

'Stay here.' Jeremy strode out of the room.

Point Machine and I looked at each other.

Jeremy was back a few minutes later, this time accompanied by another man in a suit. An older man, white haired. Upper management. One of the names behind the quarterly evaluations. One of the names who would be firing me.

'Show him.'

So I did.

Again came the moment of realization. 'Jesus,' the man said.

'We'd like to run more tests,' I said. 'Work our way up through every phylum, class, and order – primates being of particular interest because of their evolutionary connection to us.'

'Of course,' the manager said. His eyes went far away. It was the face of shell shock. He was still processing.

'We may need more resources.'

'Then you'll have it.'

'And a budget.'

'As much as you want,' the manager said. 'As much funding as you want.'

It took ten days to arrange. We worked in conjunction with the Franklin Park Zoo.

Transporting large numbers of animals can be a logistical nightmare, so it was decided that it would be easier to bring the lab to the zoo than the zoo to the lab. Vans were hired. Technicians assigned. Point Machine put his own research on hold and appropriated a lab tech to feed his amphibians. Satvik's research also went on official hiatus.

'I don't want to interfere with your work,' I told him when I found out.

Satvik shook his head. 'I must see this through.'

It was a Saturday morning when we set up the experiment in one of the new exhibits under construction – a green, high-ceilinged room that would one day house muntjacs. For now, though, it would house scientists, the zoo's strangest and most transient tenants. Blocking out the light was the hardest part, with canvas deployed over the broad glass entryway. The working floor itself was still unfinished and recessed below the level of the entrance; so three short stairs had to be assembled that led down to the wide octagon of bare concrete on which the tables were set up. Satvik worked the electronics. Point Machine liaised with the zoo staff. I built a bigger wooden box.

This box was six feet square, reinforced on all sides with two-by-four studs every twelve inches. It was large, strong, and lighttight.

Satvik noticed me with the electric saw. 'Be careful,' he said. 'Shortcuts lead to long cuts.' As he walked away, I wondered if that was one of his expressions, or if he'd made it up special.

The zoo staff didn't seem particularly inclined to cooperate until the size of Hansen's charitable donation was explained to them by the zoo superintendent. After that, they were very helpful.

Setup continued through the weekend until everything was up and running, just like at the lab. As a control, I put Satvik in the box and ran the test. He saw the light. The interference pattern collapsed into two distinct points on the capture screen.

'It works,' Point Machine said.

The following Monday we started the experiment. We got to the zoo early, and the keepers let us in the gates.

To corroborate our earlier work, we'd already agreed to start with frogs.

Satvik checked the light one final time, and then Point Machine put one of his frogs in the wooden box.

'You ready?' I asked.

He nodded. I looked over at Jeremy, who'd arrived with an entourage a few minutes earlier and now stood off to the side, near the wall. His face was set in concentration. Behind him, two managers in suits sweated in the muggy darkness. They were here to see the machine work. Point Machine stood by the capture screen, along with a handful of technicians.

I hit the button. The machine thrummed like a guitar string.

'How's it look?'

Point machine checked the screen. He gave a thumbs-up. 'Just like at the lab,' he said. 'No change.'

We ate lunch in the zoo cafeteria among the milling crowds. A thousand visitors, kids in tow. Balloons and ice cream. A double stroller jutted into an aisle while families came and went. No one had any idea about the experiment that would take place behind the construction signs just a few dozen yards away.

Point Machine ordered pizza but couldn't finish.

Across the table, my own stomach twisted, appetite gone.

'Which ones will it be?'

'There's no way to know.'

'If you had to guess.'

'It'll happen somewhere between class and order,' Point Machine said. 'The primates for sure.'

'What do you think, Satvik?'

He looked up from his paper plate. 'I don't know.'

Point Machine drained the last of his Pepsi.

'I'm telling you,' he said. 'Somewhere in Primatomorpha. That'll be our first hit.'

We ran the first experiment just after noon. Satvik hit the button. The interference pattern didn't budge.

Over the next three hours, we worked our way through representatives of several mammal lineages: Marsupialia, Afrotheria, and the last two evolutionary holdouts of Monotremata – the platypus and the echidna. The zookeepers walked or wheeled or carried the animals to us in cages. One by one, the animals were placed carefully in the wooden box. The machine ran. The interference pattern never changed.

The next day, we tested species from the Xenartha and Laurasiatheria clades. There were armadillos, sloths, hedgehogs, pangolins, and even-toed ungulates. The third day, we tackled Euarchontoglires. We tested tree shrews and lagomorphs. Hares, rabbits, and pikas. None of them collapsed the wavefunction; none carried the spotlight. On the fourth day, we turned finally to the primates.

We arrived at the zoo early that day. Zoo staff escorted us through the gate and up the hill. They unlocked the muntjac house and turned on the lights. Satvik provided the zookeepers with the day's list, which they then discussed among themselves for several minutes.

We began with the most distantly related primates. We tested lemuriformes and New World monkeys. We put them in the box, closed the door, hit the button.

Then Old World monkeys. Subfamilies Cercopithecinae and Colobinae. The red-eared guenon and the Tonkean macaque.

Then a single Sumatran surili, which clung to the zookeeper's arm, face like a little gremlin doll. A stuffed animal that blinked. Finally, we moved to the anthropoid apes. All failed to collapse the wave.

On the fifth day, we did the chimps.

'There are actually two species,' Point Machine told us while the zoo staff prepared the transfer. '*Pan paniscus*, also called the bonobo, and *Pan troglodytes*, the common chimpanzee. They're congruent species – hard to tell apart if you don't know to look. By the time scientists caught on in the nineteen-thirties, they'd already been mixed in captivity.' Zoo staff maneuvered two juveniles into the room, holding them by their hands like parents leading a child. 'But during World War II, we found a way to separate them again. It happened at a zoo outside Hellabrunn, Germany. A bombing leveled most of the town but, by some fluke, left the zoo intact. When the keepers returned, they expected to find their lucky chimps alive and well. Instead, they found a massacre. Only the common chimps stood at the bars, begging for food. The bonobos lay in their cages, dead from shock.'

The zoo staff led the first chimp toward the box. A juvenile female. Its curious eyes met mine. They closed the door, and Satvik secured the latch.

'You ready?' I asked.

Satvik nodded.

We tested both species. Chimp and bonobo. The equipment hummed. We double-checked the results, then triple-checked.

The interference pattern did not budge.

Nobody wanted to speak.

'So that's it then,' Point Machine said finally. 'Even chimps don't cause wavefunction collapse.'

I toggled the power switch and turned the machine off for the last time. The hum faded to silence.

'We're alone,' I said.

Later that night, Point Machine paced the lab. 'It's like tracing any characteristic,' he said. 'You look for homology in sister taxa. You organize clades, catalog synapomorphies, identify the out-group.'

'And who is the out-group?'

'Who do you think?' Point Machine stopped pacing. 'The ability to cause wavefunction collapse is apparently a derived characteristic that arose uniquely in our species at some point in the last several million years.'

'How do you know that?'

'It's the most parsimonious interpretation. None of our sister taxa have it. This is a uniquely derived trait. An apomorphy. It must have arisen after our split from the other primates.'

'And before that?' I said.

'What?'

'Before that. Before us.'

'I don't follow.'

'Those millions of years. Did the Earth just stand dormant as so much uncollapsed reality? What, waiting for us to show up?'

13

Writing up the paper took several days. I holed up in my lab, organizing the data, putting it into a clear structure that could be read, digested, submitted for publication. The shakes were bad in the mornings, so I took my prescription, washing it down with coffee and orange juice. Once the paper was complete, I wrote the abstract. I signed Satvik and Point Machine as co-authors.

SPECIES AND QUANTUM WAVEFUNCTION COLLAPSE

Eric Argus, Satvik Pashankar, Jason Chang. Hansen Labs, Boston, MA

ABSTRACT

Multiple studies have revealed the default state of all quantum systems to be a superposition of both collapsed and uncollapsed probability waveforms. It has long been known that subjective observation is a primary requirement for wavefunction collapse. The goal of this study was to identify the higher-order taxa capable of inciting wavefunction collapse by act of observation and to develop a phylogenetic tree to clarify the relationships between these major animal phyla. Species incapable of wavefunction collapse can be

> considered part of the larger indeterminate system. The study was carried out at Boston's Franklin Park Zoo on multiple classes of vertebrata. Here we report that humans were the only species tested that proved capable of exerting wavefunction collapse onto the background superposition of states, and indeed, this ability appears to be a uniquely derived human characteristic. This ability most likely arose sometime in the last six million years after the most recent common ancestor of humans and chimpanzees.

Jeremy read the abstract. We sat in his office, the single sheet of paper resting on the broad expanse of his father's desk.

Finally, I spoke. 'You said you wanted something publishable.'

'Serves me right, telling you something like that.' The crease between his eyebrows was back again. 'This is what I get.'

'Not so bad, is it?'

'Bad? No, it's incredible. Congratulations. This is amazing work.'

'Thank you.'

'Still,' he said. 'It's going to start a shit storm. You must know that.'

Jeremy looked down at the paper I'd written, his blue eyes troubled. I could see him as a boy, eighteen again, sitting in the university library where I'd first met him. His face smooth and young. The ice storm and sliding truck still two years in his future. The paper that would complicate his life still more than a decade from his desk.

He looked up from the paper. 'But what do these results *mean*?'

'They mean whatever you think they mean.'

Things moved fast after that. The paper was published in the *Journal of Quantum Mechanics*, and the phone started ringing. There were requests for interviews, peer review, and a dozen labs started replication trials, all with a keen eye toward finding the flaw in the procedure. And always it was assumed there *must* be a flaw. Outside the research community, it was the interpretations that got crazy, though. I stayed away from interpretations. I dealt with the facts.

Like this fact: there is exactly one liquor store on the shortest route between work and the motel. I took the long way, trees lining the road – and I didn't drink. Some nights I didn't trust myself to go home at all, didn't trust that I'd take the long way, so I stayed the night, bathing in the safety shower of the chem lab on the first floor of North building, a flagrant violation of lab protocol and all things holy. Around me were bottles of every chemical known to man – potassium sulfate, antimony trioxide, caustic potash, nitrogen sulfide, ferric ferrocyanide – every chemical, that is, except alcohol in a form that wouldn't poison me.

Satvik's office was still back in the main building, though he could be found, more and more often, only in his lab space, a small room he'd acquired on the second floor of South building.

Satvik, for his part, worked on perfecting the test itself. He worked on downsizing it, minimizing it, digitizing it.

Turning it into a product. He was an electronics guy, after all, and the big, awkward setup at the zoo had cried out for improvement. It became the Hansen double-slit, and when he was done, it was the size of a loaf of bread – a small dark box with an easy indicator light and a small, efficient output. Green for yes and red for no. I wonder if he knew then. I wonder if he already suspected what they'd use it for.

'It doesn't matter what you know,' he said as we stood in his office after that first demonstration of the new machine. He touched the small, magic box he'd created. 'It's about what is *possible* to know.'

He abandoned his gate arrays. So, too, was his easy smile abandoned, and I wondered at the price he'd paid to work on the project. Gone was the talk of his daughter and the complaints about the crops back home. Now he spoke only of the experiment and his work on the box. Above his workstation I found a quote taped to the wall, torn from an old book.

> *Can animals be just a superior race of marionettes, which eat without pleasure, cry without pain, desire nothing, know nothing, and only simulate intelligence?*
>
> – *Thomas Henry Huxley, 1859*

14

That Friday night, I swung by the motel office before heading up to my room. Pink flamingos on the front lawn. I never understood that. The property wasn't themed as far as I could tell. The name, generic: The Blakely Motel. It was brown and rectangular, nearly featureless, two squat levels with an outside walkway that ran along the upper floor. It looked like any of a dozen other old motels that dotted the seaboard in this part of the world – a certain well-worn shabbiness – but there were those two pink plastic flamingos on the front lawn. Or maybe that was the point. Maybe a featureless brown motel needs those two flamingos.

The clerk at the front desk saw me coming and waved a stack of envelopes.

'Mail here,' she said. Her name was Michelle or Marla.

I took the mail from her outstretched hand and then paid for another month in advance. I got the feeling that they liked the long-term tenants. The once-a-week cleanings. I took the mail up to my room and threw it on the table.

Two letters. One, neat and businesslike. The other hand-scrawled.

The first was from work. I tore it open, and inside I found a single folded sheet of paper:

Eric Argus
Employee 1246
Direct deposit confirmation

Dear Mr. Argus, I'm happy to inform you that you've passed your probationary hiring period and have been converted to full-time employment. Enclosed please find a $1,000 bonus check as appreciation for your hard work. A 15 percent increase in salary is rendered effective immediately. Welcome to Hansen Laboratories.

I put the letter down and stared at it. I read the first sentence over and over. Full-time employment. I wasn't sure what to do. A part of me wanted to jump into the air. Or call somebody. What was the expected protocol? Full-time employment; I realized then that I'd never really expected it. Not even after the paper.

I took out my checkbook. I wrote five hundred dollars on the line. Dropped it in a new, fresh envelope. I wrote my sister's address.

I owed her more than that. Much more. The doctor bills alone.

I thought about calling her – the push of a few buttons on my phone. I wanted to tell her – tell somebody. I wanted to talk and get it all out. The experiment, the zoo, the paper. I pulled the phone out of my pocket and held it in front of me, but I couldn't make myself hit the button.

It wasn't enough, I realized. The two months sober. The five hundred dollars. It wasn't enough.

And how to explain the paper? Jeremy's voice still in my ear, *what does it mean?*

Instead of calling, I closed my phone. *Soon enough*, I told myself. When I had another month of sobriety. When I could call her and tell her that I'd done something worthwhile. Then I'd call. I folded the letter and slid it into my pocket.

Only then did I look at the second piece of mail that I'd received. The writing scribbled and hurried. I looked at the name on the return address. A street in Indianapolis. It meant nothing to me. The name, though, was one I knew well.

I tore open the envelope.

Inside was a single sheet of paper.

Handwritten. A single line.

> *We need to talk.*
> *– Stuart*

I looked at it for a long time. I wondered how he'd gotten my address. Science could be a small world. He could have read about the experiment. Or maybe the timing was coincidence. Maybe some new fire had arisen phoenix-like from the ashes of our previous work, and he was reaching out. A darker thought occurred: maybe he was in trouble.

We need to talk. Just that single sentence.

I crinkled up the paper and threw it in the trash.

15

Over the course of the next month, there were other letters from other sources, gradually filtered through official channels at work. A medical doctor named Robbins made his interest in the project known through carefully worded correspondence.

Those letters turned into phone calls. The voices on the other end belonged to lawyers, the kind that came from deep pockets. Robbins worked for a consortium with a vested interest in determining, once and for all, exactly when consciousness first arises during human fetal development.

Hansen Labs turned him down flat until the offer grew a seventh figure.

Jeremy tracked me down that morning while I was changing the coffee filter, presumably because he knew my defenses would be down. 'He wants you to be there.'

'I don't care,' I said.

'Robbins asked for you specifically.'

By then the negotiations had been going on for some time.

'And I'm specifically saying no.' I poured the coffee grounds into the filter and slid the plastic receptacle into its slot. 'I don't want any part of it, and you can fire me if you want to.'

Jeremy gave a weary smile. 'Fire you? If I fired you, my

bosses would fire me. And then they'd hire you back. Probably with a raise. In fact, they'd probably give you my job.'

'I'd be terrible at your job. My first order of business would be to hire you back, so maybe it would all work out.'

The coffee machine percolated. Brown liquid drained into the pot while Jeremy pulled a clean mug down from the cabinet. 'So you're sure you won't go?'

'I'm sure.' I'd seen what Robbins was proposing. It was ingenious in its own way, I had to admit. An application of the test that I'd never considered. But I wanted as far from it as I could get.

'All right then,' he said. 'I'll pass that along.' Which wasn't the same as letting it go. He poured himself a steaming mug, then leaned against the counter. When he spoke again, the boss part of him drained away – and he was just Jeremy, my old friend. 'This guy Robbins is a real prick, do you know that?'

'Yeah, I know. I've seen him on TV.'

'But that doesn't mean he's wrong.'

'Yeah,' I said. 'I know that, too.'

Hansen provided technicians for the procedure. I stayed clear of the contract talks, but it was obvious that Hansen was taking a nuanced approach to the situation, positioning itself as neutral expertise while trying to divest itself, as much as possible, of the messier ramifications that might come out of the test results. It would be a difficult tightrope to walk.

Satvik was the primary liaison on the project – a duty that seemed to particularly weigh on him.

Late one morning, I found him in his office. He sat

hunched over a snarl of fiber optics, thin shoulders pulled up tight around his ears. Strapped to his forehead on a delicate pivot was a light and tiny camera. The flat-screen monitor next to him displayed the image in extreme close-up – wires thick as bridge support cables, fingers like tree trunks.

'How's the prep work going?'

The soldering tool pulled back, and the image spun as he turned to look at me. 'Almost time for the final smoke test,' he said.

I saw my face on the monitor, huge and alien. 'Smoke test?'

He turned back toward the bridge cables again. 'You start it up, hope you don't see smoke.'

'You gonna be ready for this?'

'The box is ready. I'll be ready. What about you?'

'That's the best part. I don't need to be ready.'

'More than you think,' he said. On the video feed, his soldering tool slipped deeper into the machine. 'This is your test now. You might end up famous.'

'What? How's that?'

'If things go wrong.' He bent closer to his work. 'Or if things go right.'

'I don't want to be famous.'

Satvik seemed to agree, nodding his head. 'In that water, you would drown, my friend.'

'Wait a second. What if I wanted to be famous?'

He glanced at me. 'It would go badly.'

Blunt Satvik.

I left him to his work.

*

A few weeks before the tests were going to occur, I got the call. I'd been expecting it. Robbins himself. The phone cool against the side of my head.

'Are you sure we can't get you to come?'

His voice was different than I'd expected. Softer, more conversational. I'd only heard him on TV – his voice either booming from the pulpit or broadcast through the media bullhorn of various talking-head cable shows. Doctor turned pastor turned media figure. But this was a different Robbins. More subdued.

I took a moment to answer, carefully considering the man on the other end of the line.

'No,' I said. 'I don't think that will be possible.'

'Well, your presence will be sorely missed,' Robbins said. 'Taking into account your role in the project, we would surely love to have you there. I think it would be a great benefit to the cause.'

'I think your cause will get along fine without me.'

'If the issue is monetary, I can assure you – '

'It's not.'

There was a pause. 'I understand,' he said. 'You're a busy man; I can respect that. All the same, I wanted to personally thank you.'

'For what?'

'It's a great thing you've accomplished. You must see that. Your work is going to save a lot of lives.'

I was silent. The silence became a void – an area of negative pressure meant to draw me in. I pictured him as I'd seen him on TV. Tall, square-jawed. That certain variety of good-looking that some kind of men grow into, while others are busy growing old and plump. I pictured the phone next to his ear. I wondered if he was alone in an office somewhere, or if he had people around him. A whole team of lawyers, hanging on every word. He waited me out, and when I spoke again, so much time had elapsed that we both understood we were having a different conversation.

'How did you get the mothers?' I asked.

'They're committed volunteers, each one. Special women, to be sure, who felt they were called for this important task.'

'But where did you find them?'

'We're a large, national congregation, and we were able to find several volunteers from each trimester of pregnancy – though I don't expect we'll need more than the first one to prove the age at which a baby is ensouled. Our earliest mother is only a few weeks along. We had to turn some volunteers away.'

Ensouled. The same word that he'd been using in the press releases. A word that put me on edge. 'What makes you so sure that's what you're testing?'

'Mr. Argus, how else might we define the difference between man and animal? If not the soul, then what?'

While I stumbled for an answer, he went on, 'Call it the spirit, if you will, or use another name, but it is unquestionable what your test has found. That thing that marks us out. A thing that the world's religions have for so long told us was there.'

I spoke the next words carefully. 'And you're fine with them taking the risk? The mothers, I mean.'

'We have a whole staff of doctors attending, and medical experts have already determined that the procedure carries no more risk than amniocentesis. The diode inserted into the amniotic fluid will be no larger than a needle.'

'It sounds like you have everything worked out.'

'Every precaution is being taken.'

'One thing I never understood about this, though . . . a fetus's eyes are closed.'

'I prefer the word *baby*,' he said, voice gone tight.

I thought about the way my view of Satvik changed when I'd first heard him speak. I heard change now, in the voice on the phone. A slight shift in the temperature of the words. I was becoming something different to this man on the other end of the line.

'A *baby's* eyelids are very thin,' he continued. 'And the diode is very bright. We have no doubt they'll be able to sense it. Then we have merely to note wavefunction collapse, and we'll finally have the proof we need to change the law and put a stop to the plague of abortions that has swept across this land.'

I put the phone facedown on my desk. Looked at it. *Plague of abortions*.

There were men like him in science, too – ones who thought they had all the answers. Dogma, on either side of an issue, has always seemed dangerous to me. I picked up the phone again. It seemed to weigh more than it had just a few moments earlier. 'So it is as simple as that?'

'Of course it is. When is a human life a human life? That is always what this particular argument has been about, has it not?'

I stayed silent.

He continued, 'In a just society, our rights end where the

next person's begin. All would agree. But where is that beginning? When does it start? There's been no answer. Now we'll finally be able to prove that abortion is murder, and who could argue?'

'There'll be a few, I suspect.'

'Ah, but you see, now the science will be on *our* side. This will change everything. We're all possessed of the same miracle. A consciousness unique to humanity. I sense that you don't like me very much.'

'I like you fine. But there's an old saying, "Never trust a man with only one book."'

'One book is all a man needs if it's the right book.'

'That's the problem though, isn't it? Everybody thinks their book's the right one. Have you considered what you'll do if you're proven wrong?'

'What do you mean?'

'What if wavefunction collapse doesn't occur until the ninth month? Or the magic moment of birth? Will you change your mind?'

'That's not going to happen.'

'You sound sure.'

'I am.'

'Maybe,' I said. 'Maybe you're right. But I guess now we find out.'

PART II

All great truths begin as Blasphemies.

– George Bernard Shaw

16

When I was a boy, there were two things my father liked to do. Sail and drink. He'd met my mother in college, when they were both juniors and poor as dirt. She was still a chemistry major, he economics. The story of their meeting was family lore.

'The foundations of economics are genetic,' he told her, when she finally deigned to speak to him in the park outside the university library. He'd noticed the helix on the cover of the book she carried.

Later, she would talk about the day he proposed: their senior year, a walk on the beach and in the distance, heeled over in the bay, a white sailboat like a breaching whale. They watched it for an hour, and my father told her, 'Someday I'll have one.' He might have been telling her that he'd be president one day. Or an astronaut.

My father graduated and, while my mother switched sciences, he went to work for the biggest corporation that would hire him. The world was a machine into which hours were invested, and out of which money flowed. He was good at his job, and soon there were cars and a house and a baby and then another – and my mother later talked about those years often. The way scholars might talk of a lost golden age. Untrue in its parts, but true as a whole. For no golden age is truly golden. But for my mother, reality was always abstract art – a pattern of color on canvas, a collection of brush strokes.

And maybe there was this truth: it was golden enough.

I was seven years old when he first took me out on the bay. My father's boat was a thirty-six-foot Catalina. The *Regatta Marie*, a medium-sized cruiser that carried four hundred square feet of sail. His work had by then made millions for his employer, and there were bonuses paid, promotions, partnerships. I never understood any of it. I understood only that my father was good at what he did. Special somehow. Gifted.

For seven days the *Regatta Marie* was our whole world, sailing up the rocky coast, just the two of us. The wind blew from the south, and the ship heeled, sprinting into the waves, sails snapping like prayer flags. We kept the shore in sight that first trip. At night, we got out the binoculars and watched the city lights twinkle in the blackness.

The next day, my father shouted in joy at the spray, while the harness held me in place, and the chop disintegrated against the hull in a million shiny droplets. He clung to the helm, soaked to the skin – one leg steadied against the side of the cockpit as the boat heaved along on its side. We ate soup cooked on cantilevered pots, cold saltwater sluicing periodically across the starboard windows. From the safety of my harness I watched my father in his element.

He was drinking almost every day by then, but the water kept him honest. He never drank beyond the harbor if he had passengers aboard. 'Too dangerous,' he'd say. Because even he understood the sea wasn't to be trifled with.

After that summer sail, school started for me, and my father started going out alone, each time venturing farther and farther out. His first blue water solo voyage, I checked over his supply list, written on a large yellow legal pad.

- Check lines
- Buy new halyards
- Check through hulls for rot
- Set sail Sept 6th
- Don't die

Later, when I was twelve, I checked his lists again, looking for that last item, and it wasn't there. Somewhere along the line, it had fallen off the list.

Since he never drank when he drove or worked or sailed with crew, he did all these things less often as time went by. Our excursions beyond the harbor grew fewer. And then there was that last time. That last time we ventured out into deep water.

I guided the ship by pointing. 'There!' I shouted. 'Let's go there!' Pointing to a bit of blue no different from all the other bits of blue, the rise and fall of dark waves, and I handled the ropes while we tacked, and the great sail above us shifted as he steered into a beam reach. The canvas filled and the lines creaked, while the whole large and mysterious machine leaned over on its side, and we were off.

The ocean is vast. A tiny vessel against the expanse of a world. And he loved that point where you couldn't see land anymore. Seventeen miles on a clear day. Sometimes sixteen or fourteen or ten, depending on the weather. He'd stare out over the horizon. 'There,' he'd say. And I'd look. And I'd see he was right. There was no land. Only the ocean. And no point going farther. Beyond here, everything was the same. The ocean was one thing. And the ship would rise and fall like breathing. A spaceship in the darkness as we moved across the waves.

When the wind comes from the east, the storms can sneak up on you. Catch you unaware. The way life can catch you unaware.

I watched the unnamed marina in the distance as the airport shuttle rounded the curve. I looked past Point Machine's shoulder while he dozed, black hair against the glass. I could see the sailboats and the masts swaying. The highway curved again as we approached the city, driving parallel to the water. Buildings loomed. I nudged him. 'We're almost at the hotel.' But he did not wake.

I looked out through the glass at the small slice of ocean, never forgetting the water was cold and the water was deep, and the things you love most can hurt you.

I could smell the salt when I climbed off the shuttle. Point Machine and I grabbed our bags as we stood beneath the front awning of the conclave hotel, a plush Ramada not far from the water. We decided to make a pass through the commons before checking in.

Already, the crowds were gathering.

'Quite a turnout,' Point Machine said.

I switched the strap of my duffle bag to my other shoulder. 'Now I remember why I don't come to these.'

The trip was mandatory, a decree handed down from bosses whom even Jeremy was afraid to disappoint. I'd refused to help with Robbins, so this was the alternative.

The lesser of two evils. Still, I'd dragged my feet until higher-ups were invoked. In the end, I did it for Jeremy. 'They want a representative from Hansen to attend,' he told me. 'Preferably someone high-profile, and right now, that's you guys. Satvik is already committed elsewhere.'

That 'elsewhere', of course, being Robbins.

So when the date arrived, I'd packed my bags and met Point Machine at the airport.

In truth, it was the last place I wanted to be. Three days earlier, the first threatening letter had arrived at the lab. The police were called.

When I'd asked, Jeremy only said, 'You don't want to read it.'

Eventually, he showed me the xeroxed copy. Ten words in black magic marker. Enough to remind me that the world was a dangerous place.

Marble gave way to thick carpet as we entered the central commons, weaving our way through the flow of bodies, and I was struck by the aural wave of a hundred simultaneous conversations. It had been a long time since I'd been to one of these, but you never really forget them. The milling crowds, both postgrad and undergrad. The never-grads and PhDs. The science bloggers rubbing shoulders with editors.

In the best cases, it brought future collaborators together. Forged new systems of understanding the world. I thought of the famous 1961 conclave where Feynman met Dirac. Just two men sitting across the table from each other.

In the worst cases, these things could be cliquish and exclusionary – but still with one silver lining. Always, for those so inclined, it was a great excuse to drink. I'd packed my prescription of nalmefene and popped two pills before I got on the plane.

We found the check-in desk. After a short wait in line behind a group of German-speaking researchers, we showed our identification to the staff and received name tags and small plastic lanyards, along with plastic bags stuffed with conference literature. We leafed briefly through our new provisions. Somewhere in the little booklet, I knew, would be a short description of our experiment, along with dozens of other studies that were being highlighted. We'd managed to avoid having to give an actual talk, but only because I'd put my foot down. Still, that didn't stop other researchers from discussing the experiment. Point Machine's name tag used his real name. I turned mine around so that it faced my chest.

After stowing our luggage in our rooms, we headed down to the main floor armed only with our booklets. I scanned the map for the most vital piece of information.

'This way,' I said.

Three minutes and two asked questions later, we found the hospitality suite, a rather elaborate affair, now crowded with all forms of attendees. A cheese spread competed for space with brownies on a narrow table along one wall. We grabbed our complimentary juices and then, able to put it off no longer, headed for the talks.

The first talk was on quantum crystal dynamics. The speaker lectured eloquently on the crystalline substructure of carbon. The talk droned on. I glanced at Point Machine.

'I pick the next one,' he said. And did. Hidden phylogenetic substructure among endangered amphibians.

This one had slides and so was far superior. We watched the researcher wave at the screen with a long pointer. She spoke quickly in that perfect, accentless Midwestern of news anchors and people from Ohio: 'Molecular analysis was performed on specimens sampled from across a wide range of threatened habitat.'

At one point, a frog appeared on the slide, and Point Machine seemed to perk up beside me, while the news anchor voice droned on: 'The presence of hidden, cryptic species nested within populations of tree frogs highlights the need for ex-situ conservation.'

The PowerPoint presentation continued – a series of graphs and slopes, one kind of tree frog living hidden among another. My attention wavered.

Applause indicated the end of the session, and we stood and filed out with the rest.

Later that night we had a dinner scheduled, arranged through the home office. An address and two names: Ken Brighton and Gershon Boaz.

Point Machine and I found them already waiting for us at the restaurant – a place called the Zoco Chophouse. Dinner so fancy the salad didn't have lettuce. That's how you knew. That's how you knew it was serious.

Both men were tall, in suits and ties. Brighton was the broader of the two, large across the shoulders in a way that promised custom tailoring. It was hard to place his age. He might have been forty, but something about his stride made me suspect he was younger. His hair was a bright, golden blond, cut short. The second man, Boaz, was just as tall but without the extra mass. His hair was a bit longer and gone silver-white, though his face was smooth and unlined. They were a striking pair, and I noticed eyes tracking them as they approached from across the room. They might have been catalog models in other lives, if models looked like lawyers, and lawyers terrified you.

The hostess placed us at a table in the back. I had assumed there was some unstated quid pro quo with the bosses back home. The dinner a professional courtesy. But now that I'd seen them, I wasn't so sure.

'There are two men you should meet' was all that Jeremy's voice mail had said, along with their names and a time for the restaurant. The rest was a mystery. I began to wish I'd asked a few more questions as I faced the two strangers.

'Gentlemen,' Brighton began the introductions. Hands were shaken. 'Thank you for joining us.'

'Call me Eric,' I said.

Point Machine and I took our seats across the table from the men, and when the waitress arrived a moment later with a basket of steaming bread, Brighton spoke for the group. 'What's your finest red?'

'We have a fine Château Lafite Rothschild, 1989,' the waitress said.

'A bottle for the table, if you would.'

'I'll be okay with a Coke,' I interjected.

'Nonsense, just one drink. You're not on the wagon, are you?' His smile broadened.

That took me aback for a moment, until I realized it was a joke.

'No,' I lied. 'But I – '

'Well then, it's settled.'

And for him it was. He was past it already, sending the waitress off with a smile and a nod of his head – a man so used to getting his way that it came as second nature.

Brighton, it came as no surprise, was the talker of the pair, guiding the conversation with practiced ease. A golden tongue to go with his golden hair. He spoke of wines while we scanned the menus. Boaz, for his part, remained silent.

At one point, after waxing eloquent on the myriad subtle complexities harbored within the bouquet of a properly aerated 1990 Auslese, Brighton seemed to catch himself, and he leaned forward as if to engage.

'But enough about wine,' he said. 'I want to thank you again for agreeing to meet on such short notice.'

'It's our pleasure,' I said. 'It's nice to see a bit of the city.'

'Crowds can be exhausting. I know you've had a long day, and your time is valuable, but I just had to meet the team responsible for the experiment that I've now become so interested in.'

'So you've read the paper?' Point Machine asked.

'Oh, yes. With great interest.'

'Do you often read the scientific periodicals?' Something about this struck me as unlikely – this man of wines and custom suits, reading back issues of the *Journal of Quantum Mechanics* in his spare time.

'Only occasionally, I will admit,' he said. 'I am a dilettante – nothing more. An interested amateur. We do have eyes in the industry, though, and they alert us when something of particular interest presents itself.'

'And your work is certainly of particular interest,' Boaz

added, speaking for the first time. His voice was gravel to his companion's smooth butter. There was something odd in his expression as he looked at me. Something I couldn't put my finger on.

Brighton continued, 'I've always considered quantum mechanics to be an obstinate theory. Even in those edge cases where a normal, reasonable theory would have the good sense to break down, we find quantum mechanics stubbornly adheres to theoretical expression. It is a prediction machine.'

'Like no other,' I said.

At that moment, the waitress arrived with the bottle of wine. She smiled and took our orders. Brighton ordered duck; Boaz the blackened chicken. Point Machine and I were steak men, it turned out. I asked for salad on the side.

When the waitress left, the conversation shifted away from quantum mechanics, picking up again where Brighton had earlier put it down, as he guided us through wines and into art. Brighton spoke of his years in France and Germany, and his visits to Berlin. 'There is a museum in Solingen, the Deutsches Klingenmuseum, that is dedicated to the "perspective of the blade". I loved that wording, when I came across it in their brochures, as if a piece of steel can have its own particular view of the world. But who could doubt it must be true? The museum curators claim that you can tell a great deal about societies by the kinds of edged blades they create. Ornate butter knives, crude bayonets, bastard swords of blackened iron. There is a sword there, the *Richtschwert*, that was used as a beheading sword.' Brighton poured himself a glass of wine. 'Now there is a blade with a perspective.'

The salads arrived, and Brighton reached across the table and filled my empty wineglass. 'A toast,' he suggested.

Point Machine flashed me a concerned look as I reached for the glass and raised it with the others.

'To discovery,' Brighton said.

'To discovery.'

We clinked glasses. I lifted the wine close to my face. From the corner of my eye, I saw Point Machine watching me. I breathed deeply, taking in the fruity aroma. I felt my pulse quicken, the choice rising before me. I set the glass back on the table without drinking.

Brighton's eyes met mine over the top of his wineglass. He smiled and extended his toast, lifting his glass higher: 'May we learn something new every day.' He drank.

The main course came steaming and popping, brought in on circular trays.

We were halfway through the meal when Brighton's banter shifted gears again, and he spoke between bites. 'So, tell me about the experiment that has brought us together.' And here at last was our reason for meeting.

'The test was designed to detect quantum wavefunction collapse,' Point Machine began.

I let him do most of the talking while I chewed my steak. He went over the experiment in detail. The frogs and the puppy.

'Fascinating,' Brighton said when Point Machine mentioned the chimps. He pushed his empty plate away. 'So it is much as I've read. You left nothing out?'

'The paper captured most of the details.'

'What I'm interested in,' Brighton said, turning now toward me, 'are those details that the paper *didn't* capture.'

'Such as?'

'Why you ran the experiment in the first place.'

'Why does anyone run any experiment?' I said. 'To see what will happen.'

'What did you hope to accomplish?'

I contemplated what remained of my salad, wondering what the green leafy stuff was, exactly, if not lettuce. A small crouton held a dime-sized blob of what looked like caviar. I considered the possibility that I'd been eating vitamins that my body wasn't used to. Certainly, a fifty-dollar salad contained nutrients not found in its cheaper brethren. For the price, it should.

'Accomplish?' I asked.

'Yes,' Boaz cut in. The silver-haired man leaned forward. His voice was tight. That same strange expression back again. 'What were you trying to prove?'

And then it hit me. Anger. That expression was anger.

I placed my fork on the table. 'Curiosity, nothing more.'

'About a decades-old experiment? There's more to it than that.'

'Meaning what, exactly?' I let the slightest chill seep into my voice.

Boaz opened his mouth to speak, but Brighton silenced his companion with a flick of the hand – a subtle gesture, but it was enough. Boaz's mouth snapped closed. Brighton seemed to gather his thoughts for a moment before he spoke. 'Forgive my friend,' he said. 'He pushes forward when he should stop. He can't help himself. It will be the ruin of him someday, no doubt.' Brighton leaned back in his chair and tossed his napkin on the table. 'You are a learned man, Eric, but I wonder how familiar you are with the classics?'

'I've read my share.'

He paused for a moment and then continued. 'Human understanding began with superstition. Then came the great thinkers – Plato, Aristotle, Galileo, da Vinci, Newton – each one doing his part to bring us out of the darkness, adding another layer to the integument. In the wake of this new wave of rationality, all the old superstitions fall away. Then there was Cantor and Poincaré, math and physics rising toward a new golden age. Until the cracks started showing.'

He leaned forward again, and his voice softened. 'What Gödel did to math, Heisenberg did to physics. Incompleteness. Uncertainty. Even matter is indeterminate. Our new beliefs falling like towers. And then *you*,' he said. 'You go bring an old belief back from the dead.'

'And what is that?'

'The soul.'

And then I suddenly understood the other half of this strange equation. The reason we were sitting there. This meeting was all about Robbins.

Brighton's smile faded. 'Tell me, how do you like working at Hansen?'

'I like it fine,' I said.

'It's a long way from Indianapolis.'

That caught me. 'What?' I was no longer sure what conversation we were having. The sand was shifting under my feet.

'A long way from your work at QSR. You don't consider the two-slit to be a distraction from your real work?'

'How do you know about my work at QSR?'

'As we said, we have eyes in the industry.'

I stared across the table at him. 'A dilettante, you said.'

'In a matter of speaking.'

I glanced at Point Machine. A crease had formed between his eyebrows. He knew it, too: something wasn't right here.

'You have me at a disadvantage,' I said. I looked between the two men in turn. 'I just now realized, after all this time talking, you've never mentioned what it is that you actually do.'

And there was the true artistry of a golden tongue. To be able to speak for an hour without revealing anything. To speak without leaving the impression that your words, by the hundreds, were full of empty air.

Brighton seemed amused by this direct approach. 'We're a holding company,' he said. 'Very small and specialized. Investments and research. Buy and sell. Also, there is a certain private endowment. We keep a low profile, while we keep our ears to the ground.'

'And how do you know Jeremy?'

'Who?'

'Jeremy. Our manager who arranged this dinner.'

'Ah, Mr. Bonner, you mean. We don't know him. At least, not on any personal basis. This is a detriment, certainly, when one wishes to make the acquaintance of another firm's star employee, but it isn't an insurmountable obstacle. We can be very persuasive when need be, and it is amazing what a simple telephone conversation can facilitate in the right hands.'

'It is amazing, yes.'

Brighton sipped his wine. 'A call was made to your employer – an introduction proffered on our behalf, and here we are. We're pleased for this opportunity to congratulate you. And to offer you encouragement.'

'Encouragement?' I couldn't keep the incredulity from my voice. They hardly seemed encouraging.

'To pursue *other* work.'

It could have been a threat if spoken by another man. Or if we weren't sitting in a crowded restaurant, with smiling waiters coming and going, and soft music playing in the background. Or it could have been a threat if I let it be one.

'I'm fine where I'm at.'

The smiles at the table faded. Brighton stared at me. 'I can see that you're right. There is a place for every man, I firmly believe that. And you are in yours, that's easy enough to see.'

'Why did you call this meeting?'

'To congratulate you, as I said.' Brighton placed his napkin on his plate and signaled for the check. He looked back at me. 'In 1919,' he said, 'there was an Englishman appointed to a professorship in Peking, and his only opportunity to study the circulatory system came in the form of cadavers. The police at this time produced endless corpses, usually by hanging or beheading, which could be purchased. When the anatomist complained about the mangled quality of the necks he was seeing, the authorities responded by sending his next batch of cadavers to him still alive, hooded and pleading, and with instruction to please put them to death by manner that better suited his needs. Would you like to know what he did?'

I nodded. The slightest movement of my chin.

'The professor returned them. He lacked commitment, I think.' A smile peeled back from Brighton's teeth. 'How committed are you?'

I considered the man sitting across from me. The five-thousand-dollar suit. The predatory smile. I wasn't sure what game he was playing, but I knew when I was out of my league. I slid my chair out and stood. 'Thank you for the dinner, gentlemen.' Point Machine rose to his feet beside me.

'Thank *you*, Eric,' Brighton said. 'It's been a pleasure.' He stood and extended his hand. When I shook it, he clasped his other hand over mine, holding it in place. 'Before you go, one question. Robbins's experiment is in a few days; what do you expect will happen?'

'I couldn't venture a guess, either way,' I said.

'You say "either way" as if there are only two possibilities.'

'Aren't there? Either he finds wave collapse, or he doesn't.'

I felt his hands tighten on mine. 'I think, Mr. Argus, that you've set in motion a series of events that you can't begin to understand.'

His expression shifted, and for a moment it looked as if he were deciding whether he should say more. His grip loosened. 'But I guess we'll all see soon enough.'

'I don't have an ax to grind either way,' I said and I pulled my hand back. 'I'm staying out of it.'

'I'm afraid you're already in it about as far as anyone can go.'

At that moment, the waitress arrived with the check.

Brighton motioned, and the waitress set the leather folder on the table and left.

Brighton took his seat again. 'We all have our axes to grind,' he said. 'Anyone who claims otherwise is lying.' He opened the folder and signed the bill in a series of jagged slashes. 'It's all in the perspective of your blade.'

17

The next day Point Machine and I skipped the afternoon lectures and left for the airport early. We spoke little on the taxi ride.

In the airport, once we were past security and nearing our gate, I saw a familiar face on one of the televisions that hung from the ceiling. Robbins. Face animated. Hands moving while he talked. He was like a politician in a debate, laying out his platform one plank at a time.

I slowed as I passed the TV, catching just a bit of his monologue. Something about deontological ethics and deprivation. The words lacked context, and without context lacked meaning, but there was no mistaking the ecstatic look on his face. A pause to smile, and then the smooth voice: 'The testing tomorrow will prove it.'

Another talking head flashed on the screen, the obligatory counterpoint, face just as earnest, Harvard credentials captioned below. 'He's overreaching,' the counterpoint said. 'The science doesn't support that interpretation.'

A dozen people watched the TV from where they sat. Others played with their phones. Others slept. The airport was half-empty, midday, midweek. Midlife.

I thought of what Jeremy had asked. *But what do these results* mean?

They mean whatever you think they mean.

And that's why it was so dangerous.

I thought of all the Scotch in the world.

I kept walking.

The night when I got back to my motel, I called Point Machine at his house. It was call or drink. And I didn't want to drink. Because I knew if I drank again, even a single sip, I'd never stop. Not ever.

He picked up on the fifth ring. Faraway voice.

'What's going to happen tomorrow?' I asked.

There was a long pause. Long enough that I wondered if he'd heard me. 'Not sure,' he said. The voice on the other end was coarse and weary. It was a voice that hadn't been sleeping well. 'Ontogeny recapitulates phylogeny.'

'Meaning what?'

'Look early enough in gestation, and we've got gills, a tail, the roots of the whole animal kingdom. It's all there, like a little time machine, starting with a tadpole and working your way up. You climb the phylogenetic tree as the fetus develops, and the newer characteristics, the things that make us human, get tacked on last.'

'How will that impact the test?'

'What Robbins is testing for is only found in humans, so my gut tells me he's wrong, and wave collapse comes late. Real late.'

'You think it works that way?'

'Eric, I have no fucking idea how it works.'

The day of the experiment arrived, and we went to work like it was nothing. We waited for the press release – something on the TV or radio. Some announcement.

The first hint that something went wrong came in the form of silence.

Silence from the Robbins group. Silence in the media. No press conferences. No TV interviews.

Just silence.

The announcement wouldn't come out till later.

Satvik rejoined us at the lab, but when we interrogated him, he had no answers to share. He'd helped them with the equipment but hadn't been present for the testing.

'How could you not know?' Point Machine asked.

'They didn't let me watch the testing,' Satvik said. 'They kept me away.'

One day turned into two. Two into three.

Finally, a terse statement was issued by the group, which called their results inconclusive. Robbins came out a few days later, saying bluntly that there had been a failure in the mechanism of the test.

Satvik scoffed. 'Failure? What failure?'

We sat in his office and watched the news link on his desktop, forwarded from Jeremy. *You probably want to see this*, the e-mail heading had read.

'The box was perfect,' Satvik muttered. 'If there had been failure, they would have asked for my help.'

I clicked the PLAY button. In the video, Robbins stood at a lectern of some kind, microphones in array. The link was a press conference. 'The test itself is flawed,' Robbins said. He wore a neat suit. Camera flashes lit up the blue screen behind him. His expression was confident, his tone measured. 'The procedures required to perform the testing on pregnant women made accurate evaluation impossible. We weren't able to get meaningful results.'

He opened the floor up to questioning. Reporters asked questions, but the answers were all the same.

'The test was flawed.'

'The mechanism failed.'

'Meaningless.'

I clicked the link closed.

'There was no flaw,' Satvik said. 'He didn't get the answer he wanted.'

'Yeah,' Point Machine said. 'I think you're right. He's lying.'

But the truth was something stranger, of course.

And, of course, that came out later, too.

18

In the following weeks, Satvik buried himself in work. I'd find the lights on in his lab, the electronic debris field of his tabletop skewed in new configurations. His slot in the mail room filled, then emptied, then filled again.

I woke at 7:00 a.m. Shaking hands, cold porcelain. A bad morning. The worst in a while, after a night of bad dreams: A dark unfurling. A vision from childhood.

I drove to the lab at 8:00.

I found Satvik already in his office. He'd let his hair grow in the previous weeks. The roots were salt and pepper, the ends mostly dark. It gave him a disheveled appearance that he hadn't had when I'd first met him. The old Satvik was gone, replaced by this thin man with haunted eyes.

He was packing up a box, folding the cardboard flaps across the top.

'Going somewhere?'

His head jerked up. I'd startled him. 'I'm packing equipment. I'm going to be on the road.'

'For what?'

'A project.'

I stepped farther into the room, remembering when I'd first said those words to him. Words that had started it all. 'What project?'

'Something I must check,' he said, finishing up the

box. He picked up a roll of duct tape from the table. 'I will tell you about it when I get back.'

'Why not now?'

'Because I'm probably wrong, and nothing will come of it.'

'Does Jeremy know you're going?'

'I sent him an e-mail. He'll know when he reads it.'

'You're working too hard. Do you remember when you told me that?'

'I remember,' he said.

'People forget they're going to die someday.'

He smiled. The first smile I'd seen since before the Robbins experiment. For a moment, I saw the Satvik I'd met that first week at the lab. 'This is different,' he said.

'How?'

'This is something I must do.'

I nodded, accepting his answer, though I didn't like it. For some reason, the story of the princes rose up in my head.

At the bird.

I was struck again by how much he'd changed. The experiment had done that. I'd done that. I glanced around the room, and I could see that some of his electronics were missing. It was hard to guess what he'd packed up.

'You need any help with that?'

He shook his head. 'No, it's fine.' He yanked a strip of duct tape from the roll and plastered it across the top of the box. 'I'll be back in a week.'

'Why are you doing this?'

'Because Robbins was lying,' he said. 'The test didn't fail.'

'That has nothing to do with you. You can just let it go.'

'I cannot,' he said.

I stared at him. Satvik was that fourth prince and always had been. *At the bird's eye.* He was never going to just let it go.

He picked up his box and headed for the door.

'Be careful out there.' I watched him go.

'You as well, my friend.'

The truth, when it came out, came in waves. It hit the news the next day, like a slow tide Robbins couldn't stop. It was only later that I'd realize that Satvik must have known. Must have seen some hint on the Net.

The truth was that some of the fetuses *did* pass the test. Just as Robbins had hoped. The video surfaced on YouTube. Uploaded anonymously. A leak from Robbins's inner circle. The mothers smiled, while the doctors hovered – the little diode trailing away from the distended abdomen. Robbins himself was in the shot for certain frames, waiting for the results.

Some fetuses *did* cause the green indicator light to go on. Some did trigger wavefunction collapse.

But others didn't. And those videos surfaced, too.

The same doctors. Different patients.

Heated voices.

'Try again.'

'Again.'

The mother's worried face. And a light that would not change, would not turn green, no matter what.

'What does that mean?' the mother asked, voice rising to a panic. 'Is my baby okay? What does *this mean*?'

Video after video. A dozen abdomens of various degrees of distension. Two very different results. Most fetuses did collapse the wavefunction. But some didn't.

And gestational age had nothing to do with it.

Satvik wasn't back in a few days. Or a week.

Ten days later, I received the call in the middle of the night, waking me from a nightmare.

'I found one in New York.' It was Satvik.

'What?' I rubbed my eyes, trying to wake up. Trying to make sense of the words coming through the cell phone.

'A boy. Nine years old. I tested him with the box, and he didn't collapse the wavefunction.'

'What are you talking about?'

'He looked in the box, but he didn't collapse the wave.'

I blinked in the darkness. Satvik had seen it first, before any of us. What was true of the fetuses would be true of others.

At the bird's eye.

'What's wrong with him?' I asked.

'Nothing,' Satvik said. 'He's normal. Normal vision, normal intelligence. I tested him five times, but the interference pattern didn't budge.'

'What happened when you told him?'

'I didn't tell him. He stood there staring at me.'

'Staring?'

'It was like he already knew. Like he knew the whole time it wouldn't work.'

Days turned to weeks. The testing continued. Satvik found more of them. A lot more.

He traveled the country, searching for that elusive, perfect cross section and a sample size large enough to prove significance. He collected data points, faxed copies back to the lab for safekeeping.

I imagined Satvik on the other end of the line, sitting in some dark hotel room, fighting a growing insomnia, fighting the terrible loneliness of what he was doing.

Point Machine sought comfort in elaborately constructed phylogenies, retreated into his cladograms. But there was no comfort for him there. 'There's no frequency distribution curve,' he told me. 'No disequilibrium between ethnographic populations, nothing I can get traction on.' He pored over Satvik's data, looking for the pattern that would make sense of it all.

'Distribution is random,' he said. 'It doesn't act like a trait.'

'Then maybe it's not,' I said.

He shook his head. 'Then who are they, some kind of empty set? Nonplayer characters in the indeterminate system?'

Satvik had his own ideas, of course.

'Why none of the scientists?' I asked him one night, phone to my ear. 'If it's random, why none of us?'

'It's self-selecting,' Satvik said. 'If they're part of the indeterminate system, why become scientists?'

'What do you mean?'

'Lots of species are capable of ordered behavior,' he said. 'It doesn't mean they have consciousness.'

'We're talking about humans,' I said. 'This can't be right.' Even as I said it, I wanted to pull it back – reel it back onto my tongue, the thing said over and over in quantum mechanics. *It can't be right. It can't work that way.*

'Data is data,' Satvik said. 'Your eyes are two slits.'

'Do they even know what you're testing them for, when they look at your little light? Do they know they're different?'

'One of them,' he said. He was silent for a moment. 'One of them knew.'

And then days later, the final late-night call. From Denver. The last time he'd call me.

'I don't think we're supposed to do this,' he said, voice strangely harsh.

I rubbed my eyes, sitting up in bed. 'Do what?'

'I don't think we're supposed to build this kind of thing,' he said. 'The fault in reality that you talked about . . . I don't think we were expected to take advantage of it this way. To make a test.'

'What are you talking about?' Light from the parking lot slanted beneath the curtains, drawing a pale line across the floor. Around me, the room had grown cold in the night.

'What happened?' I asked.

'I saw the boy again.'

'Who?'

'The boy from New York,' he said. 'I saw him today. He came to see me.'

My mind wasn't working yet. I tried to process what he was telling me. 'The boy,' I said. I was still half-asleep. I needed coffee. 'What did he want?'

'I think he came here to warn me.'

And then Satvik hung up.

19

I called him several times over the next few days, but he never answered. It was as if Satvik had fallen off the face of the Earth, along with his special little box. The calls went straight to voice mail. I spent the nights in the lab, sleeping on my cot. I was at the lab when I got the call from his wife.

'No,' I said. 'Not since Monday.'

She was crying into the phone. 'He calls home every night. He never misses.'

'I'm sure he's fine,' I lied.

When I hung up, I grabbed my coat and keys and headed for the door. The rental glowed under the parking lot lights.

Do they know they're different? I'd asked him.

One of them, he'd said. *One of them knew.*

I punched the gas as I hit the main road, accelerating through a yellow light.

The more complex the system, the more ways it can go wrong. Point Machine had said that.

And things go wrong. That spotlight. Little engines of wavefunction collapse. Can a spotlight sense the darkness, when it sees only light?

I hit the highway two minutes later.

A knock on the door.

Her face filled the narrow gap.

'Joy,' I said.

She let the door swing open as she turned and walked deeper inside. There were no words. Not until later.

On her bed, she rested her warm cheek against my shoulder. I told her about Satvik. The call from his wife.

She lay silently and did not speak. In the darkness, she was a shape. The curve of a hip.

'The nightmares come every night now,' I said.

'They will pass.'

'What do you know about dreams?'

She heard it in my voice, the real question. 'Sound and touch,' she said. 'But I remember dreaming in sight. It was so long ago that I'm not sure if I remember seeing or only the dream of seeing. Or maybe they are the same.'

'Maybe they are,' I said.

'There was another threat today,' she said. 'A letter at the lab. I overheard Jeremy in the hall.'

The shadows moved. I couldn't see her, but I felt her arm across my chest.

'So what do you dream?' she asked.

'I never remember.'

'Keep your secrets,' she said. 'I don't blame you.'

'Do you think he's okay?'

She didn't answer for a long while. 'He'll be back. I think he's just lost his way.'

'Come in.'

Jeremy sat behind his desk, pen in hand, papers spread out before him.

I'd been considering all morning what to say, but now that I was there, I wasn't sure how to begin. 'I think something's happened,' I said.

Jeremy set his pen down. 'What do you mean?'

'To Satvik. Nobody can get in touch with him; his cell goes straight to voice mail.'

'Have you talked to his wife?'

'I spoke to her last night, and she hasn't been able to reach him either. She's concerned.'

'Does he usually fall off the radar like this?'

'A few days, here or there, but he usually returns calls.'

'Not mine,' he said. His face showed irritation. 'Do you know what he's been working on?'

'He faxes reports.'

'That's more than I've been told. I don't like being kept in the dark.'

'I thought he was keeping you informed.'

'He hasn't kept me informed of anything. He asked for time away from the office to explore new avenues of research – I think that's how he put it – but it's been long enough. He needs to come in.'

'That's the problem; we can't reach him. And I heard there has been a new threat.'

He waved that off. 'Letters. E-mails. It's sporadic.' He opened his desk drawer and pulled out a stack of envelopes. He slid them across the desk. 'Robbins's group really opened up a can of worms. Now that he's backed away from it, we're getting it from both sides.'

I picked up the stack and leafed through a few of the letters. They were a strange mix. Long handwritten screeds and short declarative threats. The short ones had the most pop.

I hope you have good insurance.

'Have you gone to the police?'

'Several times. Most of the letters aren't actionable, and the few that are didn't exactly leave a forwarding address. But the police are looking into it.'

I flipped through several more, each one stranger than the last. One in all red marker. Another neatly typed. And finally, the last one, which didn't seem like a threat at all: *Beware the flicker men.*

I handed the letters back. 'I don't like that nobody's heard from Satvik. Do you think we should file a report?'

That raised his eyebrows. 'A report? You mean a missing-person report?'

'Yeah.'

'I think it's a bit premature for that. At least from us, anyway. If his wife wants to register a report, that's certainly up to her, but I don't want to jump to conclusions.' Jeremy picked up his pen again.

It was his nature, I knew. He never saw the harsher possibilities. It was hard for him to imagine.

'He's probably lost his phone,' he said. 'He'll turn up, and when he does, have him call me.'

'Okay.' I stood to leave, but I stopped at the door. 'One more thing,' I said. 'Something that's been bothering me. Those two men you had us meet for dinner. Brighton and Boaz. Do you remember?'

'Yeah, I was going to ask you about that.'

'How much do you know about them?'

'They run some kind of endowment. Well connected, apparently.'

'Endowment?' A magic word in certain circles. A word that could open doors. No wonder they'd been able to make the dinner happen.

'Part of some kind of exploratory committee,' Jeremy said. 'Or that's what their people told us. Why, did something happen?'

'Something Brighton said.' *You say 'either way' as if there are only two possibilities.* 'I think they knew something about Robbins's test.'

'Knew what?'

'That he wasn't going to get the results he expected.'

His face grew puzzled. 'How can that be?'

'I don't know.'

I turned to go. My hand was on the doorknob when he said, 'If Satvik calls, and there *is* some kind of trouble, let me know. Whatever it is.'

As the sun went down, I dialed the number. Point Machine picked up on the second ring. 'No,' he said. 'I still haven't heard from him.'

I told him what Jeremy had said about Satvik, and about our business dinner at the symposium.

'I don't like this.'

I considered for a moment. 'You have contacts across the industry, don't you?'

'Yeah.'

'Do me a favor. I'm going to be busy the next few days.

See what you can find out about Brighton and Boaz. Find out about this endowment.'

'Do you think they have something to do with Satvik?' He sounded skeptical.

'I don't know,' I said. 'But they seemed to have done their homework on me. Now I want to return the favor.'

20

Night fell as Satvik approached the state line, so he rolled his window down, feeling the air on his face.

He'd driven Highway 93 to 89. Over the hills and into Vermont, across the White River, and then across it again, as the highway and waterway zigzagged each other through the lowlands. He headed toward the green country. Away from the city. Away from the lab.

It could have been like that. I could imagine it.

Satvik's trunk full of equipment. Like a stone around his neck. A burden he carried. Perhaps he was tired of all the testing. Tired of the reports. Tired of chasing things that couldn't possibly exist: those who walked among us but weren't us. His phone rang on the seat next to him. He was tired of that, too. He ignored the call.

Now there was only the wind and the dark and the white lines of the highway.

I tried to believe in the idea of it.

Satvik cutting loose. Stepping back.

Perhaps he wanted his gate arrays, with their logical simplicity. Or he was tired of the questions that had no answers. Or it may have been the boy who had done it. The final straw. The boy from New York; the one who'd tracked him down.

One of them knew.

Thirty miles later, the ringtone came again. Satvik

checked the number. Another call from the lab – the light from his phone casting a green-white glow across the front seat of the car. He wanted to answer. And not to answer. He just needed time, he decided. A few days. Space to clear his head. In a few days, it would all make more sense. He felt it intuitively, the way he felt when his gate arrays weren't right and he wasn't sure why. Sometimes the harder you looked, the less you saw. He was too close to the problem. He took his phone and tossed it out the window onto the highway. An impulsive choice for a man who had never been impulsive, but he felt better immediately. Better than he had in weeks. Better than he had since before he'd seen Robbins's press conference.

He drove on, leaving his phone behind as mile stacked upon mile. He'd buy a new phone later, once he'd had a few days to rest.

It might have been as simple as that.

Or he could have been on the road, trunk full of equipment, as a car came up behind him.

A dark stretch of highway.

Satvik continued on at fifty-five miles per hour, as the other car approached.

Three men inside. The same men who'd written letters to the lab. They were angry. Disturbed.

As the car behind him sped to pass, a gun came out, unseen. Satvik was listening to the radio, thinking of home. He'd been too many days away. He would call his wife tonight, he'd promised himself. Call the first moment he could. He'd accidently let his cell battery run low, and once it was charged, he'd found he had no reception. It was the edge of nowhere, wilderness on both sides.

He was done with the road. Done searching for a bottom when there was no bottom to see.

The car sped alongside.

He was reaching for the knob on the radio when out of the corner of his eye he saw it: the barrel coming up and out of the other vehicle as it passed.

And Satvik's face went slack for a single instant before the trigger was pulled.

The blast lit up the space between the cars, and Satvik's vehicle continued on for several hundred feet as if nothing had happened before drifting to the right, onto the shoulder, never slowing. His car hit the berm at fifty-five miles per hour, continuing to drift, now pulling harder, until the slope of the grass fell away steeply into a deep woods, and the car rocketed downward, out of sight, into the trees and wilds below, and was gone. The darkness was an envelope that sealed up behind him.

It could have been like that.

Or it could have been that he'd lost his phone, like Jeremy said. Or he'd lost his charger.

He might have been in New Jersey or New York. Or across town in Boston. In a motel room no different from this one.

21

'I'm here to see Mr. Robbins.'

The receptionist smiled. 'Do you have an appointment?'

She was young and bubbly, with very straight, very white teeth, and her whole being seemed to give off an air of neat precision. Even her hair was exact – not a strand out of place.

I almost hated to disappoint her. 'No.'

'I'm sorry,' she said. 'He's booked for the day. You'll have to make an appointment. We usually schedule a few weeks in advance.'

'I need to see him now,' I told her. 'I've driven a long way.'

Her smile never wavered. 'Unfortunately, that's not going to be possible.'

The room we were in might have been the reception area of the Oval Office. The carpet was lush and blue. Paintings graced the walls. The vaulted ceiling rose to the sky. No fewer than five people currently sat waiting in the plushly appointed surroundings for their chance to spend time with the great man.

'He's in there?' I asked. I took a step toward the ornate double doors just behind her.

'I'm afraid he won't be able to see you.'

I'd considered just walking past her and opening the doors, but something about her lack of concern and the retention of her gleaming, confident smile made me suspect I'd find myself facedown on the lush blue carpeting if I tried to touch those doors without permission. Perhaps paratroopers would descend on me from the vaunted heights. Or perhaps she'd lay me out herself.

I decided diplomacy was in order. 'My name is Eric Argus, and – '

'Oh, I know who you are.'

That stopped me. Her smile still hadn't budged.

I glanced around the room. All eyes were watching me now. Time to take a different tack.

'What if you told him I was here, and then he could decide for himself if I needed an appointment?'

'He only takes meetings scheduled in – '

'I drove two hours. Please, it'll take two seconds to ask.'

The slightest crack appeared in her armor. A moment's hesitation. I pressed the gap. 'If he learns that I was here, and he wasn't told . . .'

Her smile dropped by a micrometer at the left corner of her mouth.

'Please,' I said. 'Two seconds.'

She stared at me for what seemed like a very long time and then reached across to her intercom. There was a click of a button. 'Sir,' she spoke into the intercom, 'I'm sorry to interrupt you, but Eric Argus is here. He doesn't have an appointment.'

The intercom was silent for eight full seconds during which the receptionist never took her eyes off me. Just when I began to think there would be no response, there was a crackle, then, 'Send him in.'

She hit another button, and the double doors swung

open. Her smile was back at full force. 'You may step inside.'

I felt the glare of the other patrons as I walked past. I was that guy in traffic who zooms by the line of cars, only to merge at the front.

Robbins sat at his desk facing two men seated across from him. The two men turned. Sharks in suits.

'If you'll excuse me,' Robbins said to the sharks. They nodded and rose to leave. 'And close the doors behind you, if you would.'

The doors closed with a whisper. What followed was the silence of a bank vault.

'Eric Argus,' Robbins declared triumphantly when we were alone. 'How many times did I try to get you to see me?'

He was smaller than I expected, less polished and perfect without the TV makeup, but otherwise the same man I'd come to envisage from the cable shows. 'Twice, I think.'

'And now here you are, out of the blue, when it can do me not the slightest worldly good. I'm a busy man, Mr. Argus. To what do I owe this honor?' His face was cool and expressionless. He hadn't asked me to sit. Perhaps I wouldn't be staying long enough to warrant it. His office was as enormous as it was opulent – decorated to within an inch of its life. There were several overstuffed chairs, paintings on the walls, a single formal bookcase of serious-looking leather tomes. Behind him, French doors looked out into a small, closed courtyard.

I decided to get right to the point. 'I was hoping that you might have information about a friend of mine.'

He didn't even blink. 'Who?'

'Satvik Pashankar. The tech who worked with you on the box.'

'Oh, I think I remember him. Satvik was his name, you say? I haven't heard from him. Why do you ask?'

'Because he's missing.'

'Missing.' For the first time, his face registered emotion or some facsimile of it. 'When did our friend go missing?'

'A week ago.'

'Sometimes people need to get away. I expect he'll turn up.'

I looked at him closely. I wanted the truth from him, even if he didn't speak it, but either he was very good, or he really didn't know anything about Satvik. I decided the direct approach would be best.

I pulled the folded piece of paper from my back pocket and tossed it down on his desk. The paper sat there for a moment before he reached for it.

'We've been getting these at the lab,' I said. 'Some of your followers perhaps.'

He unfolded the paper. He looked at what was written. His wide-set brown eyes lifted to my face. He folded the paper again and slid it back across the desk toward me.

'What possible reason would any of my followers have for doing that?'

'The experiment,' I said. 'These kinds of threats have been coming in for the last month or so. Some worse than that.'

He gestured to one of the two chairs facing his desk. 'Please, sit.'

I sank into plush red leather. Like sliding into a sports

car. The chair probably cost a month's salary. 'In the interviews you gave, you said there was a failure in the mechanism of the test.' I said.

'Yes.'

'There was no failure, was there?'

'Is that what you came here for, a confession? Do you really need one? You saw the videos that were leaked.'

'I saw them.'

'Along with the rest of the world. *Failure* is the word we used when describing the experiment, but there's another word for it, of course – *disaster*. The truth is, I wish I'd never heard of your little box. It's caused nothing but trouble.'

'So maybe one of your followers decided to take that out on Satvik. Or maybe you did.'

Robbins laughed. 'Why on earth would I do that? What would I have to gain?'

I shrugged. 'You didn't like what the box had to say.'

'Well, you're right in that regard, but there's nothing to be done about it now. The cat's out of the bag, so to speak. And your technician friend disappearing won't put it back in. Truth is, if anything does happen to your friend, it will only draw attention to this whole sad episode, which otherwise is best soon forgotten. I'd much prefer to just close the book on this.'

I remembered the last time he'd spoken to me of books. This wasn't the confident, headstrong Robbins whom I'd spoken to on the phone months ago. This man was humbled. In retreat. Things had changed.

'You told me all you needed was one book, if it was the right one.'

His professional smile faded. 'Sometimes, the creator denies us answers in order that we might better demonstrate faith. Or so we must suppose.'

'An interesting supposition.'

'And yet it is the one we are left with. Sometimes, though, in my darkest hours, I wonder if we aren't the unknowing beneficiaries of some kind of a joke.'

The cool, professional smile was totally gone now. Cracks had appeared in the skin near the corners of his eyes, which were puffy, as if he hadn't slept.

'This isn't a joke,' I said. 'My friend is missing.'

'I even wonder, from time to time, if *joke* is too kind a word. Maybe *trick* is a better word. In a lot of ways, I have you to thank for the soul-searching I've found myself so distracted by this past month.'

'Me to thank?'

'After the experiment, I had a crisis of conscience,' he said. 'I wondered, why would God create children who have no souls? What possible purpose could there be? And there is this question which has kept me awake some nights: what would such children grow into?'

It was a question I'd been trying hard not to think about. The same question, perhaps, that had kept Satvik out on the road.

'I didn't come here to discuss theology with you.'

He waved that off dismissively. 'Everything is theology, or nothing is. Tell me, do you think it is odd that free will is a focus of both religion and physics?'

When I didn't answer, Robbins leaned back in his chair. 'This is a Montese,' he said, gesturing to the painting that hung on the wall opposite his desk. On the wide canvas was painted a scene in reds and browns, a girl sitting on the lip of a stone well, a great cathedral rising in the background. From the top of the steeple, a crucifix cast a long shadow across the town. The painting was beautiful. The girl, haunting and sad.

'Eighteenth century,' Robbins said. 'The artist killed himself at age twenty-eight. That's part of why his paintings are so valuable; there aren't many of them. Being creative can be hazardous, which is one reason I've stayed away from the arts; but what of the ultimate creator? I wonder. Why is it, when men ponder divine motivations . . . why do they always assume that God was sane?'

At first I assumed the question was rhetorical, but he waited for an answer. I had none to give. There were no answers, not to any of this.

'So perhaps it's foolish to question why our creator does anything,' he went on. 'Perhaps there is no underlying logic to it. Maybe the ancient Eastern philosophers were asking the right questions all along. Not *why*. But only *what is*. What is beneath the glossy patina? Can anything in this world be truly relied upon? Even atoms are an evanescent haze – emptiness stacked upon emptiness which we've somehow all willed ourselves to believe in.'

It wasn't what I expected. He was drifting, so I brought him back. 'In regard to Satvik, there must be something you can do.'

His eyes snapped to attention. 'Like what?'

'Talk to your congregation.'

Robbins laughed. A deep baritone that went on and on. 'So you think if some member of my congregation *was* involved, they'd simply turn themselves in because I said so?'

'Maybe.' I shrugged.

'Churches are made in our image as sure as we are made in God's. From a church, the congregation takes what teachings as suits them, and they leave the rest. For a member of the flock to be so . . . extreme in their views, it makes me suspect that there's not much I could say one way or another to sway that person's mind. What does your employer say about your missing friend?'

'They're taking a wait-and-see attitude.'

'Well, perhaps they know their business.' He paused, and his brown eyes searched my face. I could see him come to a decision. 'Still,' he said. 'It couldn't hurt, what you're suggesting. A sermon on the evils of taking the law into our own hands? That sort of thing?'

'It'd be a nice start,' I said. I decided to play a hunch. 'Is the security new or have you always been this paranoid?'

A joyless smile crept to his lips. 'The security is new. As is the guard out in the courtyard.' He gestured toward the French doors, but if there was anyone out among the trees and bushes, they were hidden.

'Why the sudden interest in security?'

'Circumstances change. The world moves on.'

'Oh?'

'We stare into that little box you made, and we collapse the wave. What is true at one scale is often reflected in another. Even fame, it seems, follows the rules of quantum mechanics. The eye of the public changes what it observes.'

'So you're getting your own letters.'

'Let's just say that all attention isn't good.' The smile faded. 'These are the costs we face to live in pursuit of the big questions.'

'Speaking of questions,' I began – and here I paused, choosing my words. There was only one more card to play. I watched him closely. 'Have you heard of a man named Brighton?'

His face froze at the mention of the name – just a momentary lapse, so subtle that I could almost pretend I hadn't seen it. He shook his head. 'No,' he said. 'Never heard of him.'

I stared him down. It was the first thing he'd said that I didn't believe.

'Before you ran your experiment,' I said, 'I talked with this Brighton, and he seemed to know more than he should have. He seemed to know that you were going to find something unexpected.'

He watched me and said nothing.

'So how did he know?' I prompted him. 'Who is this Brighton to you?'

'I don't know anyone by that name.'

I could see the lie all over his face. I pushed again. 'How could anyone know what you were going to find?'

'Perhaps it was a guess. Or maybe you misinterpreted him.'

'Maybe,' I said, though I didn't believe it for a second.

'If someone *had* known,' he said, 'I wish to God they would have warned me. I could have avoided the news conferences.'

Unexpectedly, Robbins rose to his feet. For a moment, I thought he was going to bring our little meeting to a close, but instead he turned and stepped toward the French doors. He didn't open them but stood in the pie-shaped slice of sun that arced through the glass. He looked out through the windows, arms crossed.

With his back to me, he spoke. 'You know, until recently, I've never sought to avoid what was difficult. I've always sought to apply rigor to my beliefs,' he said. 'This is why your test was so alluring. I thought it was the answer.'

'The answer to what?'

'The oldest question of all. Maybe the only one that matters. Are we this body? I've made myself an expert on disparate subjects that would not, in some men, comfortably occupy the same mind, and I have done these things, I now realize, because my faith is weak. I can say that now. I can admit it.' I saw his eyes move to my accidental reflection in the glass. 'As a boy, did you ever wonder how life arose?'

'I was a math kid.'

'In medical school, I learned the endocrine and circulatory systems – all the valves and levers of the organism – and I saw no meaning there, no purpose, other than the purposeless functioning of cells in service to their own continuation. Ordered into a complex architecture, certainly, but without any evidence of spirit. There was no light in the husk.' He nodded to himself slowly, as if he were reliving some particularly dark part of his life. 'And what was true on that scale is true of the world. Just as all cells come from pre-existing cells, you can look at the larger universe and see an endless unbroken chain of events, linking back toward some original first cause – Aristotle's theorized unmoved mover. Is there any meaning to life, any overarching purpose to it? I look around me, and I ask, where is God in all this – the cause without cause? Is he even necessary?'

'You're talking religion, not science.'

Again his eyes found mine in the reflected glass. 'There was a scientist, Steven Weinberg, who famously said, "The more the universe seems comprehensible, the more it seems pointless."'

'I'm familiar with the quote.'

'Don't you see that this is what your test has given us.'

'And what is that?'

'The light in the husk,' he said. 'The point of it all. It has been there the whole time.'

He turned away from the window and stepped back to his desk. He sank into his leather chair. 'Did you know I was a twin?' he asked. 'No? It's true.'

I tried to picture a world with two of him.

As if reading my mind, he said, 'My brother died at birth.'

'I'm sorry to hear that.'

'As a boy in Catholic school, I wondered how ensoulification might have worked in our case, as my brother and I were of one body. Did that body have one soul that split? Or, for that brief time when we were one, were there two souls contained in the armature of that single blastocyst, which by their presence *caused* the divide that cleaved two bodies? Twinning is a mistake, of that there is no doubt, but of which kind? Perhaps the presence of two souls is the *cause* of twinning, not a by-product. Or perhaps there was merely one soul between us, my brother and I. Did I get it, or did he? Or did we share a soul together?'

And it began to make sense then, the demons that

drove him. The kind of childhood that might shape a man such as him. Doctor become pastor become whatever he was now, sitting in front of me.

'And what of the people who have no soul at all?' he continued. 'Like the Calvinists believe, saved and unsaved, preordained before you are ever born. Maybe they had the truth of it.'

'I didn't take you for a Calvinist.'

'I never was one.' He said. 'I'm reminded of other times in my life when I have pondered the differences which divide us. Where do killers come from? I've looked into eyes of men and seen no remorse, no repentance, no thought at all for the lives of others. Who can look into the face of our fellow man and not question if there might be those among us who lack some spark of humanity?'

'So will that be your next experiment?' I asked. 'A test for sociopaths?'

'In trying to arrogate to ourselves that privilege which is only God's to wield, we invite disaster.'

'What privilege is that?'

'True sight, of course – into the nature of a man's conscience or its lack thereof.' His expression darkened. 'I'm not interested in further experiments. You aren't the only one who's lost people.'

It took a moment, but those words struck with the force of a freight train. 'Who did you lose?'

By his expression, I knew he'd said something that he hadn't intended to. He smiled slowly but remained silent.

'Why did you lie about Brighton?'

'I told you, I don't know anyone by that name.'

As I looked at him, it struck me. 'So that's who the guards are for.'

He chuckled softly. If his eyes looked tired before, they now looked exhausted. 'Some mysteries we chase. Others we flee from. How did non-life beget life? Are we the tissue or the spark? And the final mystery. The one we all will one day learn the answer to.'

'And what's that?'

'Where does the light go the moment after death? It's not an answer I want to find out just yet.'

'Nor I.'

'In order to believe in God, Mr. Argus, you must also believe in the devil. Ask yourself, which one is likelier to seek you out? I was an unbeliever at certain points in my life. It is the ultimate irony, that by meeting the devil, one can be brought around to God.'

His hand shifted under his desk. A slight movement. 'But sometimes,' he said, 'I wish I could go back to not believing.'

A moment later the doors opened. I realized then that he'd hit a security button. With that, our meeting was adjourned. 'I'll make your little sermon for you, as you requested,' he said. 'But now it's time for you to go.' Four large men came in. Two bald heads, two crew cuts.

He turned to the men. 'See Mr. Argus out, will you?'

The bigger crew cut put a hand on my shoulder.

I considered resisting, an instinctual response. I stood. 'You'll be hearing from me again,' I said.

'Mr. Argus, I'm sad to say I truly doubt it.'

22

It was four days later when I got the call. A Saturday afternoon, just as the light was beginning to grow long outside my motel room window. The buzz startled me – a sudden glow from the table where I'd set my phone.

It buzzed exactly twice and then went silent. I eyed the screen. Missed call.

I didn't recognize the number at first. Local area code. The number looked familiar but didn't show up as a contact.

And then I realized why. I stared at the number.

It was a number I was familiar with but never called. It was my own number from work.

I stiffened, suddenly very much alert.

I called the number back, but there was no answer. My own voice on the service, recorded once and then forgotten: *I'm not in my office, but if you leave a message, I'll get back to you.* I called again. Then again. Five times over the next minute or two, while I dressed, but there was never an answer. Just my own voice on the other end.

I'm not in my office, but if you leave a message –

I'm not in –

I'm not in –

I began to hate the sound of my own voice. I considered calling Jeremy, but what would I say? That I'd received a call from work on a Saturday afternoon? A mysterious hang-up? What would he do about that? People often were at the lab over the weekend. It wasn't exactly the kind of thing you called the cops about. Or maybe it was, considering everything that had happened. Most likely, he'd just drive to work himself and check on it.

I splashed water on my face, trying to clear my head. I tried to picture who could have been at the other end of that telephone, sitting in my chair, dialing my number, and only one person came to mind. And he'd called me, not Jeremy.

But why call from the lab? Why not use his cell? After all the silence, why call from the work phone? It didn't make sense. Unless he didn't want to be traced. Or maybe Jeremy was right, and he'd just lost his phone. Maybe the work phone was just the one he happened to have convenient. But then why hang up?

A third option was that it wasn't Satvik at all.

I opened the duffel bag, rooted inside, and pulled the gun out, weighing it in my hand. There are some things you do, you can't undo.

I checked for a round in the chamber. The weapon was loaded.

But you had to trust yourself. I caught a glimpse of myself in the mirror over the dresser. Brown hair wild. My square face thinner than it had been in a long time. My eyes restless.

I wrapped the gun in an old pair of blue jeans and put it back in the duffel. Then I put the duffel in the security box in the closet.

I found my shoes and headed out the door.

*

I drove to the lab as the sun went down, my phone on the passenger seat next to me. It had rained earlier in the day, and the roads were still wet. I hit the wipers to beat away the spray kicked up by other cars. I arrived at the lab just as dusk fell, and the small yellow light clicked on in the visitor parking. I continued on, taking the curving drive around to the back.

When I saw it, my heart beat faster. Satvik's car sat parked in the middle of the lot. His gray sedan. I almost shouted.

I parked next to him and climbed out. I walked to the old Subaru and felt the hood, as I'd seen on an old cop show once. The hood was still warm under a few beads of water.

I headed into the main building and swiped my badge to open the security door. I crossed the lobby and took the stairs to the second floor.

The front halls were well lit, but deeper in, I had to rely on the last of the setting sun.

'Satvik!' I called out. 'Are you here?'

There was no answer.

He'd called from my office extension, but I decided to check his office first.

The only sound was the clicking of my shoes.

As I got closer to his room, I saw that his light was off. Not a hopeful sign. At his door, I flicked the switch. The office was empty. It looked exactly as it had for the past few weeks. No sign that Satvik had been there.

I left the light on and continued down the hall, heading for Satvik's lab space. This, too, was empty.

His equipment lay spread out across his lab bench

much as it had every other time I'd visited. I was about to leave, but I stopped.

Something looked different. I studied the room.

It took me a moment to place it.

The diagrams were gone. Pulled down from their place on the wall. One corner of paper still flapped against the wall where it had been torn. The diagrams hadn't been so much taken down as ripped away.

My nerves on high alert, I left his room and took the hall around the corner.

I stopped. Here, at last, a light was on.

My office.

I saw the light pouring out through my door.

'Satvik!' I called out.

I waited. There was no answer.

'Satvik, is that you?'

Only silence greeted me. I walked to my office.

It was empty.

I stepped inside, studying the small room. Not a piece of paper out of place. Not a thing disturbed. I sank into my swivel chair, trying to decide what to do. The phone sat on my desk. I picked up the receiver and called Satvik's cell, thinking maybe he'd answer if he saw I was here, but I got the same result as the previous week. Straight to voice mail. His phone was either turned off or dead.

I thought about calling his house, but something held me back. What if he still hadn't contacted his wife? I didn't want to disturb her. This was looking more and more uncertain, and I didn't want to call until I had something solid to tell her. And if Satvik hadn't gone home yet, he might have a good reason. No, better to wait and sort things out. There would be time enough for that phone call once I knew what was happening.

But what *was* happening? A mysterious hang-up. A familiar car in the lot. I laid my forehead on the desk. The surface was cool and solid.

If his car was here, it meant that he had to be here somewhere. Though not necessarily in this building.

My head snapped up.

I stood, crossed to the window, and pulled the blinds. Through the glass, across the rear parking lot, I saw the out-labs, and just beyond them, nestled at the far end of the lot, I saw the old warehouse – W building. The front door was open.

I moved quickly.

I took the stairs at a run and hit the glass doors. Cool evening air. Across the back parking lot, I followed the sidewalk up to the entrance of the warehouse and passed through the open doorway. The storage facility was larger than the main building and more open. But there was the same silence. In here was kept all the old equipment. A series of offices and small storage units took up the front of the building. The back was a grid of larger storage cubicles, piled high with the castoffs of a dozen closed facilities. An equipment grave yard.

'Satvik?' I called out.

I passed down a long hall of darkened offices and then pushed open a door leading to the interior. I hit the lights.

Nothing. The great room was empty. I walked the line of cubicles just to be sure, looking down the long rows as I went. I stopped at the far end.

It didn't make sense. Where the hell was he?

Against the far wall was a workstation with a pen and clipboard. I tore off a sheet of paper, flipped it over, and wrote:

Satvik, call me.

I'd leave the note on his car, I decided. If I didn't hear anything by morning, I'd call Jeremy, the police, his wife. I'd call everyone. Or better yet, I'd just pull my car around near the gates and watch and wait. If anyone came to Satvik's vehicle in the next few hours, I'd confront them. I put the clipboard back and made my way toward the front.

As I crossed the room, I was so focused on my thoughts – the note and the car – that I didn't notice the light at first. A glimmer out of the corner of my eye.

I turned my head.

One of the offices near the entrance. Light poured through a half-open doorway.

It hadn't been there moments earlier. I was certain of it.

I stopped.

The note fell from my hands and wafted to the floor.

'Satvik,' I said.

There was no response.

Somebody had turned that light on. I wasn't alone.

'Satvik, is that you?' Louder this time. I took a step toward the open door, a single step. It was the silence that stopped me. The utter, total silence.

I stood frozen in place. I'd spoken loud enough to be heard, but there was no response. And there wouldn't be one. I suddenly knew, somehow, that whoever was in that room, it wasn't Satvik.

I took a slow step backward.

And then the entire world came apart.

A thump I felt in my skeleton.

The shock wave moved through me, lifting me off my feet.

I hit, and then there was no sound. None at all. Not even a ringing, as my face rested on the cool tile floor –

My bathroom. Morning light pouring in – a smooth, hard surface on my cheek, like a dream. I tried to lift my face to the porcelain bowl to puke again, but I couldn't seem to do it. The floor felt so good and so cool, and the air was so hot – and the ringing started. My ears rang so loud I couldn't think.

My eyes opened to a glow. Pieces of missing wall. Orange flare in the background. I tried to think, but nothing made sense. I was in the storage building, not my bathroom. I coughed – a wracking gasp – as pain shot through my chest. At first, I assumed my ribs were broken. There is a moment after a bad fall when the body tries to discover if it will live or not. The first few gasps of air. A heart that keeps beating or doesn't. Bones that move smoothly or grate against their own parts.

It happened to me lying on the floor as the fire bloomed around me.

My eyes blurred – a glow like halos fuzzing my vision.

I winced and closed my eyes. When I opened them again, the fuzziness was still there.

I tried to roll, and my body moved – the pain no better and no worse, and so I lay my hands on the tile, trying to stand up, trying to get some purchase on existence – and the light seemed to grow and spread. Bright orange flames. And above it, and out of it, billowed dark smoke.

And then the coughing came again, as the smoke rolled across me, and all I could think was *fire*. Jesus, *move*. But my body didn't seem to work.

The smoke grew thicker as the fire sizzled and popped. At that moment, the sprinklers went off. It seemed to make no difference.

I tried to stand again, and this time I got to my knees as the water came down, soaking my clothes, while the air filled with a choking cloud. I climbed up on one leg. My lungs burned. My eyes burned. I couldn't see at all, tears streaming down my face.

I stumbled toward an open office, slamming the door behind me, sucking air. I stripped off my shirt and stuffed it under the door, trying to keep the smoke out. I wiped at my eyes with the backs of my hands, but the burning was still there. What was that burning? What kind of accelerant had they used?

I went to the window, but it didn't open. It was a single pane of glass – no hinges, no latch.

'Fuck.' Safety glass.

I took a deep breath, trying to calm myself. I needed to think. Around me, I could feel the air growing warmer. I flung the door open and sprinted to the right, driven by the flames. At the far end, through blurry eyes, I spotted a door marked UTILITIES. Or it might have said that.

My hand found the doorknob, and I dove inside. Here, at last, the air was cool and fresh. The only sound was the sound of my ragged breathing. I pulled my cell from my pocket and opened it for light. Its green face lit up the darkness.

I was in a narrow access corridor that ran behind the offices. It seemed to run the length of the building. I moved fast. Although the air was better here, I could still smell the smoke. Even in the sealed corridor, the temperature was beginning to rise. Sprinkler or no, the building was going to burn.

I passed a long bank of fuse boxes. I ducked around water pipes and electrical cables. When I got to the far end, there was another door. Beyond it, I could hear the fire, like distant surf, crackling and crashing, a rising static.

I put my hand to the steel door and yanked it back. There was no going that way. The fire was moving quickly. Far more quickly than I would have expected.

I glanced around, searching for some answer, some way out, and that's when I saw the ladder connected to the wall. I pointed the dim glow of my cell upward, and the ladder lost itself in darkness over my head. A narrow tube leading up.

Without much choice, I climbed.

At the top of the ladder was a platform and a short stairway leading to a steel hatch in the ceiling. I put my shoulder against it and pressed. Nothing.

I pressed again, putting every ounce of strength into it. Sweat poured from my face. The hatch didn't budge.

I collapsed back on the platform, breathing hard. Smoke was rising up from below, choking me so I pointed my cell at the hatch, and that's when I saw the handle – a simple steel latch. I cursed my stupidity and pulled, and the hatch came free with a loud clang, pushing up and over, and I was suddenly out under a dark sky, and the air was so clean and sweet that I could barely believe it.

I got several feet across the roof before I fell to my knees, gasping. The in and out of air through my burning windpipe. I could feel the exact shape of my lungs.

When I stood, the world swayed a bit, and I staggered to the edge of the building to look down. The reality of the situation struck home. I was on the roof of a burning warehouse. The roof was maybe twenty-five feet from the ground. Too far to jump, unless there was no other choice.

Another explosion shook the structure beneath me, a deep rumble like a growl from a dragon. I thought of all the equipment below. Who knew what materials were burning? At least the electron microscopes were safe in the main building. And Point Machine's frogs, the dozens and dozens of offices. The warehouse unit might be a loss, but Hansen would go on.

I turned, and behind me smoke curled up from the open hatch through which I'd just climbed. The fire was growing.

A third explosion shook the roof, like a baseball bat under my feet, and this time I went down. There came the sound of falling glass, and now smoke was billowing along the outside of the building, too, through shattered windows below. The heat grew. I rose to my feet and crossed toward the far side, feeling the tar under my shoes grow slick as it began to melt. A gentle sag began to form in the center of the rooftop, so I changed course, moving to the edge.

In the distance, sirens warbled.

The sag deepened. It was all happening too quickly. As I watched, the center of the roof seemed to slide down into itself, just a few feet wide at first, then growing – a black sinkhole through which shimmering heat and dark smoke rose – and I realized that waiting for the Fire Department might take longer than I had.

I sprinted along the outside edge, trying to put distance between myself and the central part of the roof. And then I remembered the grounds shed. I'd seen the maintenance crews park the lawnmowers there – a small shed that abutted the warehouse in the very back.

At the far back of the roof, I leaned over the edge.

There.

It was a silver rectangle below me. A slanted roofline. Still more than a full-story drop but survivable.

I studied the drop. Adjusted expectations.

Probably survivable.

Beyond the rectangle was a cement pad, wooden pallets, dumpsters.

I turned and scanned the rooftop, looking for anything I might use.

The sirens warbled louder now, pulling onto the property. Flames lit up the sky through the broken windows below. The Fire Department would have no idea I was up here, and there was no way I was going to risk crossing the sagging roofline to approach the front of the building, where they might see me.

This wasn't just a fire; it was an inferno. A blazing oven. The heat baked up through my feet. Time was running short.

I leaned over the edge of the roof.

I studied the drop, looking for handholds – anything I

might use to get myself a few precious feet closer to the ground.

There was nothing.

Sheer cinder-block wall on this side of the building.

Light bloomed in the darkness behind me, and I turned my head. A new hole was forming in the roof near the front. The heat surged. I was out of time.

I slid over the side of the wall and lowered my body out over the edge.

I kicked out into nothingness.

The slant of the tin roof below is what saved me, transferring my momentum into circular spin.

I struck feet first, legs slightly bent, and my knees buckled immediately. My butt slammed next as I rolled backward along the slope of the roof – then my shoulders and head, bouncing off the tin, and I saw stars as my feet came up and over, and I was tumbling backward into open air, with just enough light to see the stack of wooden pallets rising up to meet me. I hit hard – arms first, saving my skull – and then my right hip came down with a loud crack, splintering the wood, impact juddering along my entire body, knocking the wind from my lungs as I rolled and twisted and came to rest.

I baked in the glow of the fire.

A cool hand on my forehead. I didn't understand it.

The sirens warbled louder. Above me, the flames rose to the heavens. The warehouse. *What was I doing at the warehouse?* My thoughts were jumbled. I remembered the parking lot. Satvik's car. 'Where is Satvik?'

'Shhh' came the voice.

'Where am I?'

'Lie back.' It was a woman's voice. 'The paramedics are coming.'

There was blood on her face. She was younger than me. Late twenties. She wore a gray rain slicker with a hood that partially covered her sandy blonde hair. An old scar neatly bisected her eyebrow. Another younger scar showed pink on her chin. Blood came from her nose, smeared across her cheek by the swipe of a hand. It dripped to her slicker.

The heat was growing.

She stood, grabbed me by my ankles, and *pulled*. I lifted my head as I felt the cement slide beneath my shoulders. She dragged me along, pulling me behind a dumpster, away from the heat, the roar of flames. She collapsed next to me.

'What happened?' I asked.

She gave no answer.

She put her cool hand on my forehead again, and I saw she was missing two fingers. Her left pinky was missing from the second knuckle. Her ring finger was missing from the third. Old wounds, long ago healed.

'Where is he?' I asked her. 'Where's Satvik?'

'No good place,' she said.

And the dizziness came again, and pain, like a white-hot knife to my temple, and the world went black.

'Hey!'

I rolled over, lifting my head. Voice in the distance.

'Hey you!'

The voice came from a fireman rushing toward me. Big body. Young face.

I looked around, and the woman was gone.

'You okay?' the big man asked as he kneeled beside me.

I said nothing at first. Finally, I mumbled, 'My head.'

'Are you burned?'

I didn't answer. Instead I rose to my feet and let him guide me around the other side of the building.

A dozen firemen fought the blaze. Two fire trucks crouched at a safe distance in the parking lot, hoses snaking across wet, steaming pavement, their water lines drenching the structure. The red spinning lights made everything move. I saw another night, years earlier, outside my house. Red lights. Police without faces and underwater words.

Other than the fire trucks, mine was the only vehicle in the lot. Something was missing, but I couldn't place it.

I glanced back at the warehouse, and the flames were twenty feet high now, roaring out of the top of the roof.

'Are you burned?' The fireman asked again.

I looked down at myself, and that's when I noticed my shirtsleeve was blackened. The edges of the sleeve a jagged snarl of burned fabric.

'Oh,' I said. The world spun with the lights. I sat.

The man turned, shouting over his shoulder, 'Hey, let's get some help over here!'

23

A light shone in my eyes.

'What's your name?'

It was a Fire Department medic. I had the feeling he'd asked me that a few times already, but I couldn't be sure.

'Eric Argus,' I said.

'How are you feeling?'

The question didn't register as words. Just sounds without meaning. I tried to concentrate.

'Do you have any pain?' The face loomed closer. He was pale, with a round face and a thick goatee. His skin a craterscape of old acne pits.

'I'm fine,' I said.

'Do you think you can stand?'

'I'm fine. There's nothing wrong.'

'How old are you?'

I thought for a moment. The number wouldn't come. 'Twenty-eight,' I said. 'Or maybe twenty-nine.'

'You have a concussion.'

'No, I'm fine,' I said. 'There's nothing wrong with me.' I tried to get up.

'You're not fine.' The hand stopped me again.

'Where's my friend?'

'Who?'

'I'm fine,' I said. I looked around. The burning

warehouse. I tried to make sense of it. Something horrible had happened.

'Twenty-eight or twenty-nine,' I told him.

The next memory was the ambulance.

Stethoscopes hung from the wall above my head.

The sirens blared, a steady warble I'd heard a hundred times, though never from the inside.

I was on my back, looking up at the ceiling, feeling the movement of the vehicle through space. When the ambulance took a corner, the stethoscopes swung out from the wall like gravity shifting off the vertical – silver dollars at the end of thin black tubing. They swayed in unison, hovering over my face as the ambulance rounded a corner. The slow dance of stethoscopes. It was a phenomenon. I bore witness.

The third time it happened, the medic swayed, too, nearly losing his balance. 'Hey!' He shouted to the driver. 'Take it easy. He's not going anywhere.'

'I'm fine,' I told him.

It was happening this way:

Or had already happened. Or would happen. The sound of sirens. A jumbled memory that did not cohere. Satvik's car in the lot. The heat of the fire.

There were stethoscopes. I saw them clearly as they swung in synchrony.

I tried to sit up.

'You're awake.' The paramedic's face was round and pale and cratered. An alien moon. Phobos. Deimos.

The moon spoke. 'Just relax, we're almost there.'

'Where?'

'The hospital.'

'Is Satvik going, too?'

'Who?'

'Satvik.'

The stethoscopes swung out over my face again, as a long arm braced itself against the side of the ambulance. 'I don't know who you're talking about,' the moon said.

The dream.

My mother, in her blue-white gown.

'Every time there's been a jump in brain size, it's been correlated with fluctuations in the Earth's magnetic field.' She's animated, speaking quickly, trying to get it all out. 'The poles flip, and right now South America is in the hot spot.'

The sound of running water filters in from the kitchen. The bang of pots and pans as my sister tries to take control of the chaos. Light streams through the windows. The place is cluttered; it is our first time here in weeks. Medication bottles litter the table.

'That's not how it works,' I tell her. My polymath mother. 'You know that. You *must* know that.'

'But if I'm right and direct feeding of mitochondria will lengthen the life span by even fifty percent, what would be the implications for the world?'

I backtrack, trying to follow the train of thought, but there's no path to find. It's her wilderness, and I cannot follow her there.

'I'm going to try to market the weight loss part of this, but not the age-defying part, because the government would step in. Einstein is wrong. I just need you to help me prove it. I've thought about it since yesterday, and light and time are hooked together. If light can be slowed passing through an atmosphere, then it should be able to speed up, too. Newton said that for every action there is an equal and opposite reaction. If we are able to prove that time is separate from light, then it means that the speed of light can be broken. A photon uses all its energy for motion, so it experiences no time and has no mass, right? A black hole is mass only, no time, no motion, so there has to be some phenomenon that is time only, with no mass and no motion and – '

'Mom.'

'And they don't want people living to be two hundred or three hundred years old. I'd end up in jail if they found out that it worked.'

'Mom, please.'

'I lost ten pounds and my hair turned brown. I found a way to force-feed mitochondria. Look, my hair is almost brown. Two ingredients. Calcium and folic acid.'

'Mom, stop.'

But she doesn't stop. Can't stop. Any more than any of us can stop being what we are.

'Most of the universe is missing,' she says. 'Scientists know this, so they invented dark matter, but dark matter is a cheat.' And now I see anger rising up in her, genuine outrage in those hazel eyes. 'It's like assigning lethals to your Punnett squares to make the numbers come out right.' Her arms flail. 'The gene frequencies don't make sense, so you invent lethals to explain why the math doesn't follow. All that missing heritability.'

I reach for her hand across the table.

'Dark matter is just a way to equal your equal signs,' she says. 'A hack. A fix.' She leans forward. 'Black magic.'

'Mom, I miss you.'

I startled awake, feeling my gorge rise. My head hurt. The room spun around me. A hospital room. I saw the doctor enter. I saw him smile.

I opened my eyes. There was no doctor.

No room. I was just confused.

The stethoscopes swayed. I was still in the ambulance. I felt it come to a stop.

'Am I here?'

The moon only shines down on me and says nothing.

'I washed my hair in calcium and folic acid.'

She's across the table from me but a million miles away. My sister is behind her, watching us.

'The wet nurse of Tutankhamen was named Maia,' my mother says. 'That's no coincidence. The Mayans built pyramids, too. I want you to take two petri dishes and put eucalyptus in one to see if it kills the bacteria. This could work, Eric.'

She talks more, and I let the words wash over me like a river. A babbling brook. White noise. Pyramids. Folic acid.

'When your father gets back, we're going sailing again. Your father will take us out past the cape.'

I nod at her. I hold her hand.

Eventually, I stand, Marie tugging on my elbow.

'It's time to go,' my sister says, but my mother's eyes are on me.

'Don't forget the eucalyptus. With that West Nile out there, this could save a lot of lives. Do you hear me, Eric?'

'I have to go, Mom.'

'Do you hear me?'

'Yeah, I hear you.'

'I don't like living here alone,' she says, and her eyes are suddenly clear and sharp, and that is the worst thing. Worse than all the other things. 'I want him to come home.'

The bang of doors. A judder across my backbone as the gurney crosses the threshold.

Ceiling lights roll past. I'm in a white hallway.

A man with a beard leans over me, and the penlight shines in my eyes. An emergency room doctor. 'Pupils dilating normally,' he said. 'No bleeding.' He looked down at me with a reassuring smile. 'And how are we doing, sir? Any pain?'

'My head,' I told him.

The hall opened up to a nursing station. 'Put him in number six,' someone called out.

The bed wheeled in a new direction. There was suddenly a curtain on one side, a wall on the other. The bed stopped. 'Here we are,' one of the nurses said. A television monitor hung from the ceiling.

'I think you have a concussion,' the doctor said.

I thought of Satvik. Without me, he would have been working on his circuits. I thought of his daughter's ChapStick.

'How old are you?' the doctor asked.

'Thirty-two.'

'Birthday?'

'January ninth.'

'What day is today?'

'Saturday.' The answers came quickly.

'So what happened?'

'I don't know.' I thought of Satvik again, his car parked in the lot. 'I really don't know.'

They started fluids and took X-rays. 'You're lucky,' the doctor said as he wrapped my hand in white gauze. 'These burns will hurt, but it's mostly first degree, so you should heal without much scarring. The big risk is infection, so keep it clean and take your antibiotics.'

'Did anyone else come in?' I asked.

The doctor looked down at me as he noted something on my chart. 'It's been a busy day.'

'No, I mean from the same fire. Did any other ambulances come in from the fire?'

'No,' he said. 'Just you.'

24

They kept me in the hospital overnight for observation. A raft of pain drugs, along with a prescription for more.

The next morning, two stone-faced detectives came by and grilled me on the previous night's events, so I told the entire story while they recorded the conversation. They never used the word *arson* but mentioned that the fire was officially suspicious – at least until the fire investigators finished their evaluation.

'They burned it down,' I told them.

'Who?'

'Whoever called me from the lab.' I told them about the call. I told them about the explosion, and the ladder, and jumping from the roof. I told them about the woman.

They perked up. 'Did you know this woman?'

'I'd never seen her before.'

'Describe her.'

They wrote it all down and then shifted into questions about Satvik. I told them what I knew, which wasn't much. After five minutes, they seemed to have what they needed. 'You've been very helpful. We'll be in touch.'

My burned hand throbbed. My head pounded. I still felt slow, like my thoughts were coming single file, and the ones in front couldn't get out of the way. It was all jumbled.

Jeremy called shortly before visiting hours. He wanted

to drive up right away, but I made him wait until the doctor gave me the all clear. 'I'm going to need a ride out of here,' I told him. Approximately a million feet of red tape later, the doctor signed me off, and I was allowed to go.

A nurse wheeled me down to the front entrance, and when I complained, she said, 'Sorry, hospital policy.'

'What is?'

'We wheel you in; it means we wheel you out.'

'Why would that be a policy?' I asked.

'Just the way it is.' From her weighty tone, she might have been addressing one of the deeper mysteries of the universe. How are two particles entangled? That's just the way it is.

'The point of a hospital is to arrive sick and leave well,' I said. 'From a marketing standpoint, wheeling patients out doesn't inspire confidence.'

The nurse mumbled something under her breath and left me in the wheelchair near the front doors. I checked my phone and saw a half dozen voice messages that I wasn't in the mood to listen to. I turned the phone off.

Jeremy's car pulled up a few minutes later.

'Jesus, Eric' were his first words. His face a dull red. I'd never seen him so worked up. 'We're gonna find out who did this.'

I climbed into his car and shut the door. He spoke quickly, filling me in on everything that had been happening. His words came in a steady stream – he'd already talked to the cops, already been on the phone with the insurance and the fire marshal and had been in meetings with the big bosses. 'We're hiring a new security contractor for the lab,' he said. 'Twenty-four seven. This shouldn't have happened. We should have had better security after that first threat came in.'

He had already connected the two events in his mind. The threatening letters and the fire. And why wouldn't he? It seemed an easy leap to make.

He asked about the call from the lab, so I told him the whole story from front to back.

'You actually jumped from the roof?'

'Yeah.'

'Jesus.' He shook his head. 'The police report had said that, but I thought maybe there'd been some confusion. That's two stories up.'

'Only one story to the roof of the shed.'

'And this woman, the one who pulled you away from the fire, you'd never seen her before?'

For some reason, my mind flashed to the rain slicker and another night a few months back. A shape in the parking lot outside my motel. 'I don't know,' I said. 'I don't think so.'

'And you never actually saw Satvik? Just his car?' Same questions as the cops. I felt my heart sink.

'Just his car,' I said. 'So I take it that means he hasn't shown up?' I'd been hoping Jeremy was holding out on me, saving the good news for last. But even before he answered, I realized there was no good news.

'I haven't heard from him,' he said.

'What about his wife?'

'As far as I know, no one has heard from him.'

Jeremy drove in silence after that. His last words sank in slowly. If Jeremy hadn't been worried about Satvik before, he was worried now.

*

As we neared the city, Jeremy asked, 'So where am I taking you? I forgot to even ask.'

'Homeward,' I said, and then I gave him directions.

Several miles ticked by in silence. As the car neared the turn-in, I saw the flamingos.

'You're still living in this shithole?'

'I like it.'

'You like this place.' He didn't look convinced. 'The rats don't like this place.'

'I keep my costs low.'

'Why the hell am I paying you so much then?'

'I wondered that myself.'

Jeremy pulled into the half-empty lot and parked.

I looked up at the door of my room – second story at the far end, near the stairs, but when I reached for the handle of the car door, I hesitated. I didn't feel like getting out, facing that room alone.

Jeremy seemed to sense this. 'And what about you?' he said.

'What about me?'

'The fire. How are you dealing with all this?'

'I'm fine.' I knew what he meant, though. What he was asking underneath it all. Would I snap like in Indianapolis, drink too much, do something crazy?

'You know, it wasn't supposed to be like this,' he said. He stared out through the windshield. 'It was supposed to be easy, like old times. Instead, they burned a building down.'

'I'm sorry,' I said. And I meant it. I'd brought it all down on him. The questions. The attention. I thought of snowy roads. The feel of ice under spinning wheels.

He looked over at me. 'That's not what I meant. You've nothing to be sorry about. You should take some time off. As much as you want.'

'I don't need – '

'Paid leave,' he interrupted me. 'At least a week or two. Maybe longer. That reminds me.' He reached in the backseat and grabbed a small stack of papers and envelopes. 'I took the liberty of cleaning your mail slot for you.' He handed me the stack of mail.

I looked down at the stack of papers in my hands. Junk mail. Newsletters. Various envelopes.

'That paid leave is an order, by the way. Came from the top down. Just a few weeks, until we can get our hands around this.'

I nodded. A few weeks. That could mean a couple of different things. I wondered if he regretted hiring me yet.

'What did your sister say when you called her?' he asked.

'Not much,' I said. Which wasn't a lie. Suddenly, the car was too confining. I reached for the handle and pushed the door open. 'Thanks for the ride.'

He gave me a look. 'You didn't call her, did you?'

'I didn't want to worry her.'

'You should call her,' he said. He turned the ignition and started the car. 'She already worries.'

25

My sister. So like me, yet not like me.

It's amazing, sometimes, the things you lose. Other memories stay, like a burr caught in your mind. The sound the furnace makes when it kicks on in a darkened house. It's a feeling you get – like a trance, family sleeping down the hall – and it's like everything at that moment is right, and always will be – one random moment when everything is good.

And other memories, too. The mirror in your parents' bedroom, constructed of foot-wide rectangles glued to the wall, and when you look it is a broken boy looking back. A child of edges, a dozen discrete boxes, all slightly out of alignment, and you can move your feet slightly to adjust the angle at which you're viewed, so that your face is neatly in one mirror and your shoulder in another and your arms another, a complete compartmentalization of your being.

And another memory: Sitting up at night by the window, waiting for your father to walk through the door. Your mother coming in. 'What's wrong?'

And having no words to explain it. Just inarticulate fear. The worry that someday your father might not return.

But Mother never worried. Never remembered the bad times.

Her memory was of her own making. Like a superpower.

A flex. And she could believe whatever she needed. Like an eye dilating the shape of reality – controlling her memories the way that some Tibetan monks could control their heartbeats. Yet she could say things that would stop you in your tracks – startle with their insight. 'Osteoporosis is adaptive,' she declared one afternoon. 'Life expectancy drops for each inch above six feet. As you age, osteoporosis shortens the distance that your circulatory system travels and thus helps the ailing heart.'

Years later I'd look that up and find nothing in the literature. Her own idea.

She invented words. They spilled off her tongue like golden coinage. Words that should be. Words like *circulous. Sarcasmic. Englatiate.*

'*Englatiate?*' I asked.

'To encase your enemies in ice,' she explained.

And I could only nod. Of course.

And another one, after the teachers gave her my test results. She reached out and touched my hair. 'My smart boy. My *mathemagician*.'

My sister would only shake her head. The good one. The sane one.

In the motel room, I picked up the phone. Dialed the numbers – all but the last one. My finger hovered over the button.

It's late, I told myself. Marie was probably already in bed. And what would I tell her? After everything that had happened in Indy, would she even believe it?

I could hear her question – her voice rising higher, 'What do you mean a building burned? Eric, what did you *do*?'

What did I do?

I tried imagining what I might say to that. I put the phone down.

The file was hidden midway through the stack of papers and envelopes that Jeremy had brought me. He probably hadn't even noticed it – just grabbed it with the rest of the mail in my box.

The file was thin. A beige folder. I recognized the sloppy handwriting scrawled across the face of the folder: *That info you asked for on Brighton.*

It was from Point Machine. I'd actually forgotten. Had it only been days ago that I'd asked him to find out what he could?

Inside was a note, along with a few pages of photocopy.

– Eric

I couldn't find much, but I made some calls and pulled some favors, and this is all I could pin down.

The short answer: Brighton's a ghost. No d.o.b. No last known address. The name doesn't start showing up in databases until '92, and that's only in regard to incorporation documents. A consulting company called Ingram. Buy and sell, a corporate investment group, just like he said. But a lot more funded than you might expect. Nothing particularly interesting, other than one thing, and this I had to dig for. They're the controlling officers of the Discovery Prize. You might have heard of it? Sorry I couldn't find more.

I'd heard of it all right. Ingram was one of several groups that offered prize money to researchers who answered long-standing problems in math and science. Like the XPRIZE in aeronautics and the Millennium Prize in math, the Discovery Prize and its ilk were considered a way to drive innovation.

I turned the page, and there was a list of rules and criteria. A hundred thousand dollars paid out to a wide variety of research subjects. Mostly physics and computer science. Three winners in the last seven years. On the next page was a tally of names who had won. Below that was a census of research subjects that had been under consideration. Unease crept up my spine.

Sometimes after returning from a day sailing with my father, I'd find my mother in the dining room, writing on her paper. Her paper, she called it, like a singular thing, though it seemed always to grow, and the subject to change.

'Did you see any whales?'

'No,' I said. 'We watched the coastline.'

And she nodded and went back to writing – that time on the subject of lipid systems.

Measuring a coastline is a cartological impossibility. All the ins and outs and incongruities. But you can measure its roughness – its specific frequency of irregularity. That was my mother. A wavy line. Understandable only in approximation. Her name was Gillian, but that never seemed quite right. When I thought of my mother, it was the name Julia that would, more and more, come to be her name. The Julia sets. Her appellation that even she didn't know.

Mother wasn't disappointed that I hadn't wanted to

follow her into immunology. 'It's an incursive field,' she once told me, by way of explanation. 'And besides,' she added, 'natural science and physics are both the same thing, aren't they?'

'What do you mean?' I was twelve at the time, already enraptured with physics and numbers. Turning my back on her madness.

'One has Darwin, the other, Einstein. But when it comes down to it, it's all just religion.'

'It's the opposite of religion.' I said, a little too brusquely.

She shook her head. 'It comes from the same drive. The need to understand.' Her eyes gave back nothing. 'The only question becomes, how bad do you need to know?'

I picked up the phone. How bad did I need to know?

I dialed Point Machine's number. The phone rang twice. 'Hello.'

'I got your report,' I said. 'Where did you get the research list?'

There was a pause on the line, followed by an explosion of words. 'Jesus, Eric, are you okay? I heard about what happened. I called and left messages, and I – '

'The research,' I pressed him.

'Uh . . .' He seemed to flounder, trying to catch up. 'The research? So you got the file then. A contact at the university put it together. But how are you doing? I heard about the fire.'

'And this is all public record?'

'Yeah, it's all public, if you know where to dig.'

'There are no dates attached.'

'I'm not sure of the dates. Why are you calling about this?'

I scanned the paper. The research I was interested in was listed halfway down. 'How far back does this go?'

'Seven years.'

'And it's up-to-date?'

'Yeah, probably. I'm not sure. Listen, what's this about?'

'There's a term on the list that's very specific.'

'What do you mean, specific?'

'*Branching transforms* – the meaning's not important. It's just a mathematical function.'

'I'm not following you.'

'I made it up,' I said. 'I coined the term just after college. There were only a few of us working on it.'

There was a pause on the line. 'And that term is on the index of research that's been looked into for this prize.'

'Yeah.'

'When were you working on it?'

'With my old partner. Before Hansen.'

'But that was . . .' His voice trailed off.

'Way before we met Brighton,' I said.

There were a few more seconds of silence. 'Why were they interested in this work?'

'That's a very good question.'

Before Einstein there was Gaston Julia.

The dictionary describes a mathematical function as a kind of system. In truth, functions are transformative – they are the if/then at the heart of computation.

I hung up the phone and placed it down on the table in front of me. The silence of the room was complete. I walked to the mirror.

The first time my mother described a ribosome to me, I'd recognized the principle. A nucleotide sequence enters one side of a ribosome, and a polypeptide chain comes out the other – a simple and ordered transformation of data. A mathematical function if ever there was one.

At the end of World War I, a French mathematician named Gaston Julia was the first to map the behavior of complex numbers under multiple iterations of a function f. Apply any number z to function f to obtain an output. Then apply function f to the output, resulting in a secondary output. Then apply function f to the secondary output, resulting in a tertiary output, and on and on in endless procession. Like a ribosome that ate its own product in a never-ending loop.

Graphed in three-dimensional space, these Julia sets produce complex, beautiful structures. The Julia sets. Mandelbrot fractals. Pathological curves. And stranger things, too. Things that mathematicians call monsters.

Thoughts can be monsters, too.

'I'm not going back,' I said to the darkness in the room.

I looked in the mirror and tried to believe it.

26

The flight to Indiana took off at 8:00 a.m. I ate bad airport food while I waited to board. Hours later I landed, rented a car, and was on the highway by midday.

The city traffic, I found, was a sieve through which some cars flowed, and others were caught. I didn't have the knack for the local grid. Progress was slow.

I thought about Satvik's gate arrays – evolution dictating the most efficient designs. If only city planners could have modeled the roads with the same technique.

Once off the highway, I navigated through the sprawl of an old residential neighborhood. One of the oldest parts of the city.

The homes were low and powerfully built, like short, stocky wrestlers. They looked well-nigh indestructible – row upon row of squat tract houses, brick and stone. Front fences crowded the sidewalk. The people on the street here were monochrome, a sign that something was working against diffusion.

Farther out, the neighborhood changed abruptly, as if I had crossed a line in the sand. Shopping malls and pharmacies and gas stations and hotels. There must be a word for this kind of neighborhood. A special zoning ordinance known only to those public officials who gerrymander these things. Then another transformation, like a final phase shift. Large box structures. Open space.

Tall buildings. Small, neat office complexes built at some distinguished remove from the roadway and moated all around by a lake of parking. I checked the GPS on my phone one last time and turned left at the sign.

It was just before 2:00 p.m. when I put the car in park and turned off the engine.

I'd arrived.

The office complex itself was shorter and wider than the others. Aside from that, there was nothing about the structure that stood out. A typical commercial building that might house dozens of companies. Gold-tinged windows, lots of concrete. It's the parking that strikes you, when you've been away from the Midwest for any length of time. The luxury of open lots. Asphalt pads like salt flats – an embarrassment of parking. The coasts don't understand. In the Midwest, it can sometimes be considered rude to park next to another car. Like sitting next to the only other person in a midday matinee.

But even by Midwest standards, this lot was unusually bare. A dozen cars occupied a space that could have accommodated a high school football game. Near the front I saw a BMW parked in one of the reserved spots. Green. Stuart's favorite color, I remembered, though the car I'd last seen him drive had cost less by an order of magnitude.

I looked at myself in the rearview mirror, remembering his letter, which I'd thrown away: *We need to talk.*

I climbed out and walked up to the building.

Stuart hadn't started out wanting to run a company. For him, it was always about the tech. Building the better mousetrap. Pushing the polygons. And the company was just how you funded that. He'd been good at the tech, but his heart was never in the corporate side of things. At least not back then. He'd never aspired to run an empire. I looked up at the squat building in the heart of the corporate bramble and wondered if he'd gotten what he'd really wanted.

I made my way through the front doors.

Inside was eerie. A big, open space that echoed like a mausoleum; stunted trees in wood planters – an inside courtyard meant to seem like an outside courtyard, themed vaguely Asian. There was no foot traffic. I walked across the empty anteroom and stopped in front of the placard that listed the names of the companies in the building. On the first floor were a handful of insurance and marketing companies, along with a couple of companies with names that sounded like vitamins. The second, third, and fourth floors were empty. The fifth floor listed only one company, a name I remembered well: High-throughput Technologies.

Despite myself, I smiled. I still remembered the first time he had said the name aloud.

'You can't name a company that,' I'd told him.

But he'd proved me wrong. And now here it was listed on a directory a dozen years later. High-throughput – a name with one foot in screening, the other in informatics. It was all big data when you got down to it.

I took the elevator to the fifth floor. The elevator dinged, and the doors opened to a hallway. Unsure what to do, I stepped off the elevator and followed the hall to a set of French doors on which the word HIGH-THROUGHPUT was glazed in small black letters. I pushed the door, and it opened.

The walls were beige. The carpet gray and industrial – the kind of dense, low carpet used in high-traffic areas like doctors' waiting rooms. But there was no traffic here. There were no chairs. No coffee table with the latest issue of *Scientific American*. I expected a receptionist. Something. There was a desk, but no one behind it. Beyond the desk, another hall.

'Anybody here?' I called out.

After a moment's hesitation, I followed the hall to where it came to a T, and then I took a right. Thirty feet later, the hall opened up, like the end of a train tunnel coming out of a mountain, and I suddenly found myself in a larger expanse. *Where were all the people?*

Here, I realized, was the workspace. The room for the technicians and designers – the employees who actually made the company run. A cube farm that extended to the horizon. Empty. Abandoned. I kept walking.

Beyond there, the floor space was divided into a series of smaller rooms, mostly empty. Carpet, the same high-traffic gray, gave way to tile, then farther in, raw cement. The entire set of rooms had the air of a place that had once been something but was now vacant.

I continued on, exploring further. There were more desks, filing cabinets with their drawers left open, telephones, and computer monitors. In the corner I saw a photocopier with its paper tray removed. Paper sprawled around it like the guts of some disemboweled beast. I saw coffee mugs and a small trophy on which #1 DAD was inscribed. Second and third place were not in attendance. Here were the accoutrements of thousands of working hours. An office that had run its course, like a civilization. In the distance, I thought I heard a sound. A faint drilling.

'Hello!' I called out. 'Is somebody there?'

The drilling went silent. I continued on, moving deeper into the maze.

I found him in a side room, faced away from the door, standing near an apocalypse of integrated circuitry splayed out across a huge lab bench where a dozen technicians might have once worked. But now there was just him. A small drill rested on the flat surface.

'Stuart.'

His shoulders straightened. He turned. He had a shotgun in his hand, now pointed at my chest.

'You came,' he said. 'I knew you would.'

27

'He showed up two weeks ago.'

I followed Stuart as he led me past rows of empty offices. He carried his shotgun on his shoulder with practiced ease.

Some rooms were empty. Others still held furniture. One office was bare floor to ceiling except for a single swivel chair stationed like a sentry in the middle of the room. I wondered what had happened here. It was like walking through an Old West ghost town, everything abandoned when the gold dried up. *No*, I thought, when I saw a half-eaten sandwich moldering on a paper-strewn desk. *This wasn't an Old West ghost town; this was Chernobyl. Its inhabitants hadn't left; they'd fled.*

'Satvik was here?' I said. I tried to keep my voice level, but the shock of this news seeped in.

'Yeah.'

'Nobody has heard from him.'

He nodded but didn't slow. I couldn't see his face. 'That explains it,' he said.

'Explains what?'

'I expected you sooner.' The shotgun switched shoulders as he walked. 'He seemed to think somebody was following him,' he said.

'Did he say who?'

'To be honest, a lot of what he said didn't make much

sense. At least not at the time. He was jumpy. Seemed a bit troubled.'

He hadn't started out that way.

We came to a steel door, and Stuart hit a series of numbers on the punch pad. There was a chime, the door clicked, and Stuart pushed it open. More empty offices. Half-finished spaces. Dozens of barren cubicles.

I stared at the emptiness, then at Stuart and his gun. He'd always had a menacing profile – bony and projecting, like he carried a percentage or two more Neanderthal than average and it had all landed in his face. If anything, the years had served to exaggerate the tendency. His wide shoulders cut in front of me as we passed into the next room. 'What the hell happened here?'

'We grew quickly the first few years,' he said. 'Maybe too quickly. We needed the room, so I leased this place. We had a hundred and thirty employees at one point.'

'Where are they now?'

'Beaches, I hope. Lord knows I paid them enough.'

'Paid them?'

'Buy-out packages. They shouldn't have to work another day unless they want to. You remember Lisa and Dave?'

'Yeah.' Two faces flashed to mind. College seniors who'd been a part of the original team.

'They both took their cuts and headed east. All the way east.'

I looked around at the chaos. This didn't look like early retirement to me. It looked like mass exodus. People running for the lifeboats.

I tried to think of other names. Other people I might

have known from the early days. I tried to imagine the company ballooning to 130 people. Boom then crash.

'How is your wife?' I asked.

'I wouldn't know.'

There was no bitterness in his voice. Just a simple statement of fact. I might have asked him about the weather on a day he hadn't been outside.

'Sorry to hear that,' I said. 'How long?'

'A year. Maybe a bit more. The lawyers finalized everything a few months back. I made it easy for them. She got everything else, and I got this.' He waved an arm at his abandoned kingdom. 'And how's your sister and mom?'

'My sister's doing well. Mom passed a few years back. A stroke.'

'My condolences.' He turned to face me. 'Listen, Eric, I'm sorry about the way things ended between us. I said some things . . . it was a difficult time.'

'It's fine.'

'I mean – '

'Seriously, Stuart,' I interrupted him. 'It's fine.' I hadn't come to pick at old scabs. I glanced around, wanting to change the subject. 'When did you shut down?'

'We haven't.'

Reading the confusion on my face, Stuart continued, 'Oh, you thought – '

'The place looks a bit . . . over the edge.'

He laughed. 'That's one way to put it.'

'What happened?'

'Here,' he said. He slung his shotgun over his shoulder again and motioned for me to follow. 'Let me show you.'

*

We took a staircase down.

'How did Satvik find you?'

'It wasn't hard,' he said. 'He said he tracked down the address from the corporate listing. It's not like we're off the grid.'

'He never mentioned that he was coming here. He never said a word to me about it.'

'Do you tell your friends everywhere you go?'

'He also never told his wife.'

I glanced at Stuart's gun again. It occurred to me that I might be talking to the last person who'd seen Satvik. I decided to shift the conversation back toward the reason I'd come.

'You heard of a company called Ingram?'

'Sounds familiar. Can't place it.'

I stopped. I pulled out the paper and handed it to him. 'The Discovery Prize ring any bells?'

'Ah, I remember now,' he said. He scanned the paper and then handed it back. 'Interesting lineup, I see.'

'Past winners.'

'Ingram runs the awards, right?' He kept walking, and I followed behind.

'That's them,' I said. 'And that's why I came. I saw they were interested in our branching transforms.'

'Yeah, they were here. That was four years back, and it didn't go well. An odd situation, really. They came in, a whole team in suits and ties, saying we were short-listed for an award we hadn't applied for. Asked a lot of questions about what we'd been working on.'

'Short-listed?'

'Yeah, that's what threw me off. Short-listed by who?

Our work was private – or at least it was supposed to be. It was never really clear how they'd come to hear about it. After a while, it occurred to me that an award would be a great pretext to get vision on a competitor's tech.'

'You mean espionage.'

'Maybe.'

'So what happened?'

'We went along at first, but I drew a line on what we'd show them. They weren't happy about it. In the end they went away.'

We exited the stairwell and crossed an empty floor to the back of the building, where we came to a second stairwell. This one had the look of a recent modification – a crude metal spiral that had been dropped through a hole cut in the floor. I followed him down to the next level. It looked much like the last.

'How many floors do you own?'

'We're on four floors now. We bought out the leases from most of the other companies.

'All those floors empty?'

He nodded. 'Well, mostly. There are still other companies on the first floor.'

'Why buy out the other floors if you're leaving them empty?'

'We needed a buffer.'

'For what?'

'For this,' he said.

We passed through a short hallway before crossing through a black door into a darkened room. There were no windows here – only the blue glare of monitors and electronics along the far wall.

'He came just like you did,' Stuart said. 'Your friend, Satvik. He took the elevator up and introduced himself. He said he knew you, so I let him talk.'

'Why did he come?' My voice took on a hollow sound, and I realized that the room I was in was much larger than I expected.

Stuart smiled in the faint glow of the computer screens. 'The same reason as you,' he said. 'Only he didn't know it.' He hit a switch near the door, and the lights came on. 'To see the sphere.'

'The breakthrough happened when we figured out how to read electron spin states in real time,' Stuart said. 'It's not just about charge anymore. This preserves coherence. We have nanospin circuits and the archival of process data. The process scales like you wouldn't believe.'

Stuart led me deeper into the room.

The space was vast. Nearly the entire floor of the building. Along the far wall ran two parallel banks of hardware, eight feet tall, grated for airflow. Opposite that, against another wall, spread a control panel to make a jet pilot sweat – buttons and dials and diodes, screens gone black and dead, snaking across the concrete. Wires poured from empty sockets. Equipment sprawled over every surface. It was impossible to take in – too much, too chaotic, and then I noticed the glass. Shards spread across the floor like a million tiny diamonds. If the rest of the building felt abandoned and neglected, here it seemed a bomb had gone off. My feet crunched on glass as I crossed the room, until my eyes caught what was at the far side, and then I froze in place. Suddenly, I recognized what I was looking at. I'd seen the plans on the back of a napkin a dozen years ago.

'You built it, after all.'

'Did you think we wouldn't?'

At the far end of the chamber, mounted atop a steel pole, was a large glass sphere, sixteen inches in diameter. Above the sphere, suspended from the ceiling, hung an enormous dish from which a single electrical cord drooped, trailing toward the wall.

'Did you get it to work?'

'Depends on your definition.'

'Using your definition.'

His eyes seemed to grow smaller beneath his meaty brows. His version of scowling. 'Then it doesn't work.' he said. 'Not really.' It was a confession, I realized. Perhaps even to himself. 'But it does do something. That's why I wrote you that letter and asked you to come. I read your paper.'

'My paper?'

'I think it's connected somehow.'

I stared into the glass sphere. A crystalline opacity. White particulate fog. The closer I looked, the more I sensed a pattern inside. I moved my head slightly, and light refracted at a different angle. Suddenly, inside the sphere, a pattern appeared, multifaceted, arising from inner fault lines in the glass. Like a lightning strike but more complex and symmetrical.

'There's a pattern,' I said.

Stuart nodded. 'A shatterplex,' he said. 'Complex geometry in higher dimensions. An illusion, really, made from fissures inside.'

I shifted my head slightly, and the image inside took on new, complex facets – like a cut gemstone, internally organized.

'You manufactured this?'

'The sphere, yes, the refraction pattern, no. It's not really glass but a kind of quartz machined to a tolerance of micrometers. The pattern formed the first time I used it – some kind of emergent property associated with the realignment of interior molecules.'

I moved my head again, and the interior gem disappeared, those inner fault lines hidden as I looked at the sphere from a slightly different angle. I was staring through it again.

I circled slowly, trying to see it from other angles. 'You said it doesn't work, but it does do something.'

He hesitated before he spoke. 'It takes a picture.'

I looked at him. 'A picture. Of what?'

'Of space. Three-dimensional space. Perfect imagery. That's all it can do.'

'Three-dimensional space? So it's kind of a camera?'

'That's one way to think of it.'

I moved closer and lifted my hand to the sphere. It was cool.

'What kind of fidelity?'

He laughed. 'Even reality doesn't bother with this many polygons.'

Just out of college, I had found it a freeing experience to design tech that would never be sold to the public. To me, it had been theory.

I didn't have to worry about good user interface or cost

per unit. We could dump excess heat with bigger fans or water cooling. The solutions could be big and ugly. The question became only, do the right materials exist?

Stuart stepped toward the sphere and stood next to me, shotgun still on his shoulder.

'When we first started this,' he said, 'I thought we were about two years away from science admitting that quantum mechanics was magic.'

'If you study magic, does it become science?'

'You learn it's all science.'

I stared into the clear quartz, looking for the flaw. 'It was just an idea.' I'd been exploring the logical limits of the theory, exploiting its loopholes. A thought experiment – nothing more. The way the two-slit test was a thought experiment. Like a tongue finds a sore tooth, I was drawn to those places where theory breaks down. Pinpointing those places where things can't really work the way they seem to.

I heard my own words in my head: *The math is dead serious.*

'What do you call it?' I asked, looking at the sphere.

He waited a long time to answer. 'The sphere is the sphere. The shape inside is the gem.'

The inspiration, I remembered, had come from breakthroughs in photography.

Ramesh Raskar's femto-photography, to be exact – a way to record light on a video feed. Images slowed to millionths of a second until even photons could be seen to crawl. And I'd wondered whether the same principles could be put to work breaking down reality into discrete packets of information. Was it possible to find the grain resolution of reality itself?

Raskar's genius had been to use his femto-photography to see around corners. By capturing light, slowing it down to a measurable quantity, you can analyze its bounce. You can record photons as they ricochet off solid objects, finding their way back to the sensor. The time interval is key. The farther away an object, the longer it takes for light to bounce back to the source. In the same way bats create three-dimensional landscapes with reflected sound, you can assemble maps of reflected light.

I had seen the images. A light shines down a hall while a computer records the data. On-screen, around a blind corner, a shape resolves slowly from the static field. The return bounce of one photon in a million, or a hundred million, building an image a nanosecond at a time.

Certain quantum messenger particles have been theorized to travel in time as well as space. By tracking a particle's path in time, you could get a certain 'bounce' pattern; and, just as with Raskar's camera, seeing around corners, reconstructing images by timing the bounce of light, you can get a bounce pattern of a moment ago. You can reconstruct it.

Theoretically, with a strong enough particle cannon, and enough computational power, you could project all the way back to the unifications of the four forces in the universe – the big bang and everything forward of it. Being able to measure the time interval was key. Just as a good timepiece had once been required for sailors to calculate their longitude, all that was required to pinpoint your precise location in space-time was the right bit of automata. In this case, a timepiece that tracked messenger particles.

Stuart lowered his shotgun from his shoulder. 'Shall we kick the tires?' he asked.

'Please.'

Stuart went to the wall of dials and knobs. 'Watch the sphere,' he said. Then he leaned his shotgun against the console and sank into a swivel chair.

I watched the sphere. I stared into it. Clear as an empty Scotch glass, until you shifted your head, and then the shape appeared.

'You ready?' Stuart called out. 'Touch it.'

'What?'

'Touch the sphere.'

I placed my hand on the smooth surface.

'Here goes nothing,' he said.

A moment later there was a flash – a pulse of light that was more than light, and my head started to throb. For a moment, I felt a twinge, a slight glow to my vision, like a migraine halo, but it faded quickly and was gone.

'You okay?' Stuart asked.

'My head.'

'The side effects only last a second,' Stuart said.

'Side effects?' But it was true. My head cleared, and fuzziness faded. My vision returned to normal.

'Now look,' Stuart said.

I turned and saw myself in the sphere. A crystal clear image, like high-def TV. My hand frozen, reaching forward to touch the surface.

'Holy shit.'

'It's a perfect re-creation,' Stuart said. 'Right down to the threads in your socks.'

'So that's a 3D picture?'

'Watch,' he said.

And then I saw the scene shift – the perspective changing, as the image in the sphere rotated, getting smaller, as if the camera had pulled back. I turned and looked around the room, looking for the lens that could have taken such a shot, but there was none.

'Are you looking for the lens?' Stuart asked.

'Where is it?'

'There is no lens. Just the sensor.' He pointed to a white dish in the ceiling.

'I don't understand.'

'It's created a 3D model of the entire room. Like a video game. And you're in it. We can adjust the angle of the image to see the scene from any direction. The perspective is controlled over here.'

He worked his hand on a small roller control, and the scene in the sphere changed, shifting to a new perspective.

'This is amazing.'

'This is nothing. Watch this.' He bent to his keyboard and hit a series of commands. There was a sound like static, and for a moment the scene in the sphere twitched. And then it started to play backward. I saw my own hand retract slowly from the sphere. I saw my own face turn back toward Stuart, as if I'd heard something. And then the image went gray.

'It moves.'

'Hell yes, it moves, and that's not even the amazing part.'

'So you recorded this?'

'No, it's not like that. Here, let me show you.' He walked to the center of the room. He reached up to the electrical cord hanging from the ceiling. 'This is the sensor's power source.' He yanked the cord, and it came out from the wall. 'The sensor is off, unplugged. Nothing is being recorded by anything. Now put your hand back on the sphere.'

I did as he asked. This time I spread my fingers as wide as they'd go. The quartz was warmer now. Body temperature. The few seconds it had run had heated it a dozen degrees.

'You ready?'

'Yeah.'

He plugged the cord back into the wall. 'Now the sensor is powered. Remember, your hand was already on the sphere when I plugged it in.' He touched the controls, and the light pulsed again. A sound I felt in my bones. That same touch of pain. That same fuzziness in my vision. It faded quickly.

In the sphere, an image flashed into existence. Me standing at the sphere, hand on the quartz, like a perfect mirror.

'Keep your hand there,' he said.

'Okay.'

'Now watch.'

He hit the dial, and the image shifted. I saw my sprawled fingers slide, saw my hand retract as I backed away and turned my head. The image stopped.

He played it again. Again I watched, searching for the error. But there was none. It was me, played in reverse. Three seconds – the image of me reaching my hand out to touch the sphere. He played it again and again.

'But the sensor was unplugged when I did that,' I said. 'How can it have recorded me moving?'

'There are a lot of limitations,' he said. 'Don't get me wrong. The length is different every time, but usually less than five seconds. And the range of the image is highly constrained. It'll only record within a certain circumference.' He turned the knob on the control, and the image panned out a dozen feet before fading to gray. He spun the knob, and it zoomed back again. 'With minute adjustments of the sensor, I've been able to increase the radius of the read. It started out just a few feet – an area not much bigger than the sphere itself, but now it's expanded to fill most of the room.'

'But I still don't see how the sensor recorded something before it was turned on?'

'The sensor didn't record the state of the photons,' he said. 'It recorded the bounce.'

I looked at him. And then I understood. I understood what he'd done. The enormity of it. 'Holy shit,' I said again. He hadn't recorded a moving sequence at all. He'd taken a snapshot; the rest had been assembled from the messenger particle bounce data.

'You're able to play images that happened before you started recording.'

'That's why I sent them all home,' he said. 'All the people who helped to build it and designed the algorithms to analyze the data. And that's why I wrote to you. This is only a prototype, but this tech is a game changer. It's a camera that can look at anything. Anything.'

'Even back in time.'

He nodded.

'If the world found out, there are people who might not be happy about this kind of tech.'

'Anybody with a secret to keep.'

'Criminals,' I said. 'Governments.'

'Things worse than that, Eric.' He walked to the cord and pulled it from the wall again.

'You said it records five seconds.'

'Usually,' he said.

'But not always?'

He smiled. 'If you study magic hard enough, does it become science?'

Something about the way he said that gave me pause. 'What did you see?'

'It went back eight seconds one time. And one time farther than that.'

'How much farther?'

'Far enough. I think . . .' Here he seemed on the edge of stopping himself but instead continued. 'I think sometimes it can get confused.'

'Confused about what?'

'About what it sees. Which past it's looking at.'

He walked back to the controls. He picked up the shotgun from where it leaned against the console. 'Sometimes I see things that didn't really happen,' he said.

I waited for him to explain.

Stuart put his shotgun on his shoulder and crossed the room to the sphere. He stood next to me. 'I see it in the sphere but never in real life.'

'What?'

'I'm not sure. It's always at the edges.'

I looked around the room. The chaos. The sheer weight of what he'd been dealing with. His company shutting down. It was easy to imagine that a man could break under such pressure.

'Maybe you're seeing reflections,' I said.

Stuart nodded. 'Yeah,' he said. 'That's what I thought the first time.' His expression was tired. 'That's probably what I'd still think, but I have it recorded. Would you like to see?'

Stuart walked back to the control panel and manipulated the toggle.

The sphere lit up. I moved closer, and in it I could see the room. I saw Stuart, shotgun in his hand.

'This image was taken a few months ago,' he said. 'There was something at the very edge of the render where I couldn't get a good look.'

I squinted and looked close. There was nothing unexpected in the image. Just Stuart. An image of Stuart, standing near the sphere.

Stuart continued, 'If you run the scene twice, in quick succession, you can bridge it longer. You can zoom in to see yourself watching, looking into the sphere. And then you zoom in on the sphere inside the image. That's how I saw it the first time, by accident. Later, I went looking.'

I wondered at the side effects Stuart talked about. I wondered about the pain in my head when he'd started the machine. What would that do if you used it over and over? What would it do if you used it a dozen times a day? Would you see things that weren't there?

'There it is,' Stuart said.

I looked. My mouth dropped. In the sphere, I saw a shape – a subtle irregularity. A shadow at the edge of perception. It could have been anything or nothing, until it moved. When it moved, my understanding shifted.

'Now here's where I can bridge the scene,' Stuart said.

Suddenly, the image zoomed out and began to play,

and I wasn't seeing the shadow anymore, but the entire scene, until I saw the image of Stuart as he approached the sphere, carrying his gun. The scene zoomed in closer, and the sphere itself became clear and bright, itself an image. Like a TV that showed the image of a TV.

I glanced toward the real Stuart, who stood at the controls. I turned back to the recording.

I watched the image-Stuart peer into the sphere. I saw him see what we saw, the strange shadow in the room inside the sphere – a shadow in the shape of him. Another version of him, standing where he hadn't stood. And then the image-Stuart pulled the shotgun from off his shoulder. He took three steps back. He raised his gun and fired.

The quartz exploded, and the sphere went dark.

Stuart left the controls and stood next to me. 'I thought I could fix it,' he said. 'I thought starting over might correct the irregularity, but it didn't. Replacing the quartz took two months, and when I ran it again, I saw the shape at the edges. Like a parallel version of myself. I know it's there. Somewhere.' He gestured around the room. 'Or maybe it's in here.'

I glanced down at the floor, and I suddenly understood the glass all around, not glass at all – a perfect ballistic pattern across the dark gray cement, radiating outward from the central dais. I turned to look at that spot in the room where the shadow had stood.

A perfect ballistic pattern across the dark gray cement, that is, except for two spots. Two distinct foot-size gaps in the quartz, where it looked as if someone had been standing.

28

What was Satvik hoping to get from coming here?'

We stood on a courtyard that wrapped around the second floor of the building. The first two floors were slightly wider than the floors above, producing a terrace that circled the building in a ring. There were a series of picnic tables and small trees. As a neat and ordered little park, it stood in stark contrast to the chaos of the interior. The wind periodically made Stuart's hair dance around his head, while his wrinkled shirt flapped open, and I wondered how many days he'd been wearing the same clothes.

Stuart carried his shotgun over his forearm. He looked like a lost hunter.

'He wanted to see the other work you'd done.'

'Why?'

'At first, I wasn't sure. Then I realized it had to do with the test. The two-slit.'

'Do you know where he is now?'

Stuart shook his head. His dark eyes looked out over the terrace as the light faded. 'He seemed scared, though. Something had him scared.'

'Why do you carry the gun?'

'Because I think he was right to be scared.' We watched the sun go down for several minutes. Night came on. 'Let me see that paper again,' Stuart said.

I handed it to him. He scanned the paper. 'Look at the

type of research that's on here. What does it all have in common?'

'It's all over the place.'

'That's because you're not looking. The winners are red herrings. If you only look at who actually won the prize, that research has just been skirting at the edges.'

'The edges of what?'

'The real questions. You don't see it? It's the *other* research they're really looking into. The research that didn't win.' He frowned. 'I think I knew some of these researchers. Or at least I knew guys working in the same areas.'

'Who are they?'

'Warnings,' he said. He handed the paper back. 'Two of them are dead.'

'Recently?'

'In the last few years. A car accident. Another one jumped from a building. It's dangerous having research on the Discovery Prize short list.'

He turned away from me and leaned against the railing. 'It gets quiet up here at night. So peaceful.' He looked in the distance. 'We didn't build that gem in the sphere; we discovered it. That's how it feels, like it was always there. An artifact buried in the ground. The tech is just the shovel that digs it out.'

'When was the last time you were home?'

'Weeks,' he said. 'I have everything I could want here. There's food stockpiled. Electricity, water, and plumbing.' He glanced down at his weapon. 'My shotgun.'

'Spoken like a man under siege.'

He turned toward me, eyes suddenly focused. 'I was

impressed by your paper. The experiment was elegant and simple. And then what happened afterward. That doctor.'

'Robbins,' I said.

'Bad business, that.' Stuart shook his head and chuckled. 'And there's the rub, isn't it? Just your luck. You find the soul, and then you stumble across the soulless.'

'There's no proof it means that.'

'Proof? Do you think people need proof?' He pointed. 'Look over there. You see that church parking lot?'

I could see where he was pointing. A building in the distance, two blocks down, barely visible from where we stood. I would have taken it for a sports complex or some kind of small arena.

'I can see that church parking lot on Sundays, and these last few weeks it's been fuller than I've ever seen it. All this talk of souls and strange scientific tests. Your man Robbins and those videos that came out. People might not be sure what that test of yours found, exactly, but they know it found something.' He looked up at the sky. 'But it's all just six quarks and six leptons, right? All the matter in the universe. The twelve particles that make up everything. Six quarks and six leptons.' He leaned out over the railing. 'Do you think it's quarks and leptons in that quartz?'

'It's an image,' I said.

He waved his arm again. 'It's all an image. All of it. It's not even a question anymore, is it? The math's been going that way for years. When you drill down into it, it's mostly just empty space, and nothing really touches – just the illusion of touching, the experience of touching. Call it quarks and leptons if you want. The only true argument left is what it all means.'

'And what do you think it means?'

'Damned if I know.' He laughed. 'That pattern in the quartz is telling us something, burned like an afterimage. The first time I used the sphere, those imperfections were left behind, and yet when I used it again, there was no image distortion. I've thought long and hard about what that has to mean.'

'Come to any conclusions?'

'There's only one thing it can be,' he said. 'I think that pattern in the quartz is a negative of sorts.'

'A photographic negative? Of the room?'

'Of reality.' He shrugged. 'Three-dimensional space-time. Somehow it's all coded inside that single shape, right down to the Planck length. Didn't you used to talk about trying to unify quantum mechanics with relativity?'

'And you think that pattern does that?'

He shrugged. 'Reality does it. We just don't know how.'

We were silent for a long time after that, looking out at the night sky.

'So what happens now?' I said finally.

He turned toward me. 'There are no investors anymore. The money dried up. It's over.'

'There must be something you can do.'

'No,' he said. 'Look around you. The intellectual property is worth something, but it'll be parceled out like everything else. I thought I'd be able to raise the capital I needed, but I was shut out. The investors fled. But at least I got to see it first. And I got to show you.' He stood up straight. 'Why is it you left?'

'It was a decade ago.'

'And you've still never said. You ran away from the work. Later, I heard about you getting arrested, acting crazy.'

Crazy. A word that had loomed since childhood.

'I was drunk.'

'Something about your sister's hand.'

I watched his face in the fading light. There was no recrimination. Just puzzlement.

I stepped away from the railing. It was almost full dark now. The lights had come on in the parking lot. 'That was another life,' I said. 'I've moved on.'

'Whatever you have to tell yourself.'

It was time to go. I saw that now. Some things were best left in the past. We both looked out at the growing dark, and neither of us spoke for a while. When he did speak, it was on another subject.

'Your friend Satvik didn't tell me where he was going, but he did mention a name – Vickers. He asked me if I'd heard it.'

'Have you?'

He shook his head. I racked my brain, but the name meant nothing to me, either. 'Was there anything else?' I asked. 'Anything you can think of?'

'One strange thing, just before he left. He told me to be careful.'

'Careful of what?'

'He said there was a boy. He told me to be careful of the boy.'

29

On the plane, I closed my eyes. The red-eye back to Boston.

Pills to sleep, but sleep didn't come. Instead, a disconnected hum: a sense that everything that happened was happening to someone else. I was an observer of myself – of what I was about to do or was doing still. Observing myself into existence as I held out my hand in front of me.

'Don't believe your eyes,' I heard myself say to the darkness.

I wanted a drink so bad.

The darkness came.

And with it, forgetting.

I was thirteen when it started. Movement at the edge of perception. The space felt but not seen. A gaping, looming maw. And I could not explain it, did not have the words.

And my grandmother held me and rocked me as the dark thing revealed itself and spread – a wave cresting above that would crash over me and sweep me away, and I cried sometimes and called it the *feeling*, though it was not a feeling at all but a thing seen when my eyes were closed. And later, my grandmother's face grew concerned, then scared for her only grandson. A boy who had by then seen too much, and lost too much.

So I stopped telling her when the dark thing happened. I no longer cried and told her when the feeling was back. And in my room I felt it grow. A surge of madness.

I'd face it, this churning darkness that I could not quite see – and it was like I was standing too close to a train whistle, so loud you can't stand it; only it wasn't sound but something else. Something bigger.

And then I, too, became scared and clenched my hands over my eyes and screamed numbers at it, two, three, four, five, and on, because it was all I had – and I learned something that I did not expect. I could drive it away, this craziness, this dark nothing.

I could make it go away with numbers.

The plane landed. Bright airport lights.

In the parking garage, I found my car. And on it, wedged in my windshield wiper, a note.

I thought it was a ticket at first, until I opened it:

Soon.

In the car I took two more pills.

A long, winding drive. In the city darkness, streetlights were the new constellations, and I queried my father about where he'd gone, whispering to the void, but there was no answer. Only death. Like Satvik might be dead. And the dead are always silent to the living.

I turned the wheel.

In the middle of the night, I startled awake, arm jerking to catch myself, as if I'd tripped and fallen from some height.

I woke sweating, heart hammering in my chest.

'Shhh,' she whispered. She ran a hand across my sweating brow. 'Go back to sleep.'

'I felt like I slipped.'

'It happens to everyone,' she said. 'That was just your soul falling back in place.'

I sat up. 'I need to go.' I'd driven to her apartment hours earlier. I'd needed to feel solid, to feel something, in order to climb outside my own head, but it had been a mistake. My head had followed me here.

'Stay,' Joy whispered. 'You're fine.' Her hands were on my bare shoulder.

'How do you know?'

'Everything's going to be fine.'

I thought of her words to me months earlier. 'No,' I said. 'Somehow I don't think it is.'

In the morning, I woke sick.

Cold tile floor. I puked in the toilet.

The nightmares had been bad. A rising fire.

In my sleep my lungs had burned, and I snapped awake, realizing that I'd been holding my breath.

I washed a pill down with milk.

'Are you sure that's a good idea?'

She was standing near me in the kitchen darkness. She'd heard me fumble with the pill bottle.

I kissed her on the forehead and left at first light. Outside her apartment door, the sky was falling – the rain coming in sheets. I ran through the puddles to my car.

Near my motel, through the rain, I saw the unmarked cruiser. So obviously a cop, I wondered why they bothered. Or maybe that was the point. The kind of vehicle that screamed official business. Black midsize sedan. Tinted windows. Step away from vehicle, nothing to see here. Rain pounded the glossy paint.

Here to question me? I wondered. *Another interview about the fire?*

I passed the car without looking, but instead of pulling into the motel parking lot, I continued on and pulled into the gas station across the street.

I thought of the note on my windshield. *Soon.*

As I approached the gas station doors, I glanced up the street toward the parked car. Although I couldn't see anyone through the tint, I noticed the windshield wipers cycled every few seconds, wiping away the deluge.

I bought a loaf of bread. Peanut butter. A six-pack of Coke. Dinner of champions. I was inside only a few minutes. When I came out, the car was gone. I glanced around, scanning the traffic; I couldn't see it anywhere.

I climbed back in my car and crossed the street to the motel. I was out of my car and hustling toward the staircase when I heard the gunning engine and the tires splashing through puddles. I didn't bother to turn.

At that moment, a man in khaki pants and a dark polo shirt stepped from around the side of the staircase and stopped in front of me. He was big, blocky, midthirties. He looked like an ex-college wrestler or maybe a small safety – thick neck straining the polo's middle button.

'Eric Argus,' he said.

I stopped. I looked at him as the rain came down, soaking us. For a moment, I considered lying, but what would be the point? He obviously knew who he was looking for.

'Yeah.'

'There's someone who'd like to speak with you.'

As I was trying to decide how to respond, I heard the car door open behind me. I turned to look. The same car from earlier. Black tint. Not a cop car after all, unless Polo Shirt was a cop, and that didn't seem likely. They'd been waiting for me. I dropped my bag to the pavement.

'Who'd like to speak to me?'

'We'll be happy to introduce you.'

'You mean now.'

'If you please.' He took a step closer. And I almost bolted. I could do it. The guy was too big to have much stamina. All those oxygen-hungry muscles working against him. If I got the jump, stayed out ahead . . .

As if reading my mind, the driver's door opened, and another man stepped out. This one taller, thinner, a few years younger. The runner of the pair, if a runner was needed.

I turned back toward Polo Shirt. 'And if I don't want to?'

He raised an eyebrow. Answer enough.

I glanced around, but they'd picked their time and location perfectly. We were around the corner and out of sight of the main office. The staircase blocked the view from the road, and the rain kept most people inside.

'I made this easy for you, didn't I?'

Polo gestured toward the open car door. 'It was always gonna be easy,' he said.

In college I'd seen bouncers roll drunks through double doors, rolling them like tumbleweeds. It would go like that if I resisted. Or I could still sprint left, take my chances on foot.

I glanced up toward my motel room door, and that decided it. A dark room. Unanswered questions. Whoever had set this up had gone through a lot of trouble. They must have reasons to see me. And where there were reasons, there might be answers.

I let myself be ushered into the car. Polo Shirt climbed in after me and shut the door. The car pulled away.

We drove thirty minutes. South, toward the city.

'Who am I meeting?' I asked. Then a few minutes later, 'Where are we going?'

If either man had a tongue, he chose not to reveal it. Eventually, we rode in silence.

The rain had stopped by the time we took the off-ramp. Five minutes later, we came to a parking garage entrance, and the wooden arm rose automatically. We took the curve down, tires protesting, and second thoughts began creeping in. I thought again about running – opening the door and making a dash. At this speed, I could jump free and roll.

Before I could make up my mind, the car pulled through a small set of doors and parked nose against the wall. There were walls to the left and right as well. The men didn't get out. Instead, the doors closed behind us. For a moment I was confused; then I felt the floor begin to move. We were rising. An elevator for a car? I'd heard of such a thing but never seen one in real life. It was an experience reserved for the super-rich. Those who wanted to keep their Aston Martins close. The elevator rose quickly. There were no glowing numbers above the doors. No ding as we passed different levels. This was an elevator with one stop.

My stomach lurched slightly as the elevator came to rest. The heavy doors opened, and beyond, through the windshield, I could see a grand entranceway. Bright lights and a chandelier.

The two men climbed out of the car, and I followed. They led me wordlessly into the penthouse. High ceilings. Marble floors. It wasn't just rich but a different thing entirely. A multimillion-dollar flat. I'd never seen anything like it. There was a step down into another room, and the men led me deeper into the home, crossing a racquetball court-sized swath of white shag carpeting. A red ball, the kind a child might play with, sat in the center.

Through the open veranda doors, I could see a large patio and beyond that, other towers rising against the dark blue sky. We were twenty stories high, I guessed. Maybe thirty.

'Eric.'

I turned, looking for the voice.

Standing near an enormous mahogany table was Satvik.

30

'Satvik!'

I crossed the room as Satvik's boyish features spread into a wide smile – a cherub's face beneath graying hair.

He held out his hand to shake, but I grabbed him and pulled him into a hug.

'What are you doing here?' he said.

I clapped him on the back. 'You're alive.'

'Of course I am alive. What did you think?'

'I didn't know what to think.' I glanced around. We were in a grand lounge of some kind. Two large couches. A white-brick fireplace. A sitting room perhaps, but I wasn't sure. I lacked the vocabulary. No house I'd grown up in had a room like this.

'Do you have any idea . . .' I was at a loss for words. The shock was too much. 'Where the hell have you been?' I tried to keep my voice down, but relief was quickly turning into something else. Anger. Outrage.

Satvik shook his head. 'Two weeks I've been here. What's going on, I still cannot say.'

It was then I noticed the cut over his eye. The wound had healed – or was healing. It was deep, just between his hairline and eyebrow. It looked as if it had probably needed stitches but hadn't gotten any.

My anger ebbed. 'Your forehead . . .'

'And you,' he said, gesturing to the bandage that was still on my hand. 'What happened?'

I glanced down at my own hand. I'd forgotten the bandage. 'There was a fire,' I said.

'Fire?' His brow furrowed.

'At Hansen,' I said. 'The warehouse burned down.'

His eyes widened. 'Burned down? Was anyone hurt?'

I shook my head. 'Just me.'

'What happened?'

Where to even begin? Everything I thought to say seemed dependent on some earlier detail. 'A lot has happened,' I said. 'But we have to call your wife first. And then Jeremy. People are worried about you. We need to let them know.'

His face changed then. 'I'm sorry, Eric.'

'Sorry about what?'

'This place is not what you think.'

At that moment, a pair of doors opened with a bang, and a small group filed out from a study, talking noisily among themselves. When I saw who led the way, I felt my stomach drop. It was Brighton. A smile slid across his face as he approached us. 'Look who is here,' Brighton said.

He was dressed in a dark turtleneck that stood out in contrast to his golden hair. Two men and a woman followed behind him, but kept their distance. The men were probably bodyguards of some kind, but the woman was harder to place.

She wore a dark business suit and carried a briefcase. A lawyer or an accountant perhaps. She was in her midforties, too sharp-cornered to be beautiful exactly, but striking nonetheless. Her eyes a pale, liquid green.

'Mr. Argus,' Brighton said as he extended a hand. 'It's good to see you again.'

I let his extended hand hang in the air. 'Why am I here?'

The smile changed shape, tightening to a thin slit. His hand lowered. 'Right to the point,' he said. 'I like that. It lets us bypass the usual niceties. I can see that we're beyond them now anyway.' He turned to the woman. 'If you'll excuse us.'

The woman nodded and left without a word. The two guards stayed.

When she was gone, Brighton turned toward me. 'Apologies if I kept you waiting, but business responsibilities beckon,' he said. 'I thought it was time that you and I had another chat.'

A chat. Was that what this was going to be? 'I'm listening.'

'Alone.' He gestured to his men, and the guards moved to stand near Satvik. One of them placed a casual hand on Satvik's shoulder. Like a familiar friend might. Satvik gave no resistance.

'Come,' Brighton said, gesturing for me to follow. He walked toward the veranda doors at the back of the room.

'You are a difficult man to pin down, Eric,' Brighton said, as we stepped outside. The patio was enormous. White marble flooring, glass railings. The air was cool, and the sound of traffic wafted up from the street below. Thirty floors, I decided, as I took in the view.

'Not so difficult,' I said. 'You found me easy enough.'

'Well, a difficult man to understand, then. Nothing with you is ever simple, is it? Which is why I wanted a chance for us to speak.'

'So you kidnap me?'

'Kidnap?' He chuckled. 'You came willingly. You were politely asked, and you complied. Or am I mistaken?'

He was right, of course. In a court of law I wouldn't have been able to say otherwise. 'And what about Satvik?'

'He wasn't so politely asked, I will admit. But it couldn't be helped in his case. He is a fighter, that one, though you might not know it by looking.' He glanced at me. 'You, though, not so much. You are an avoider of fights, aren't you? A runner.'

I pulled my phone out of my pocket. I lifted it, hit DIAL, and then put the phone to my ear.

I expected him to rush me. Instead, his smile came again. 'Who would you call? What would you say?'

He hadn't moved. No guard ran in to jerk the phone away.

After three seconds of silence, I pulled the phone away from my ear and looked at it. The call had failed.

'It's a simple thing to block calls,' he said. 'Better that I have your undivided attention, without the distraction of phones, so that we may talk this out and come to a meeting of the minds.'

'So then talk.'

I slid the phone back into my pocket.

He laughed. 'You look at me like I'm your enemy. I'm not so bad as you imagine. It is a common fallacy, to imagine the worst of those whose motives you don't understand. We like to paint things in good and evil, but rarely are things so easily divided. In truth, it's all a matter of perspective. There is only the arrow of the universe to consider. The rest is just . . . unnecessary filigree. Ornamentation.'

'And what about the Discovery Prize? Ornamentation as well?'

His eyes narrowed momentarily. I'd caught him off guard. 'In some ways. But not in others. As I said, there is no good or evil but merely the arrow. But there *are* those who work against that arrow. And there are those whose goal it is to help it along. Which are you, I wonder?'

'I don't have any idea what you're talking about.'

'Sure you do. You know more than you might expect.' He paced the white marble. 'How *is* your sister, by the way?'

The threat was implicit. 'What do you want?'

'I want to know your opinion on something. It's a question I have about a subject in which you have a particular expertise, it seems.' He glanced at me while he continued to pace. 'If you're drinking, and you do something in a blackout, does it count?'

I stared at him.

'Certainly, the question must have crossed your mind,' he said. 'Consciousness is such a finite resource, after all. So if you slam a door – break your sister's hand while drunk – break it so bad that it takes surgery to fix the bones . . .' He let the question trail off.

I felt my face grow hot.

'It must be some consolation – that uncertainty,' he said. 'That *excuse*. Are you still there, behind your eyes, when you're blackout drunk? Are you still responsible for what you do?' He came up beside me and stopped pacing. He spoke softly near my shoulder. 'Does it still count against you?'

My hands clenched and unclenched. I opened my mouth to speak but didn't trust the words.

He chuckled softly. 'Ah, so there is something behind that calm exterior, after all. I was beginning to wonder. Tell me, in your professional opinion, would you still collapse the wave while blacked out? We could test it, you know. We have good bourbon right here. Special reserve, double oaked. You just have to drink and drink, and then we'll use Satvik's little box to see what happens. Absolve you of your sins, or not.' Brighton stepped to the railing. The wind gusted. From the distance came the sound of a car horn and then another. The sounds of the city. He leaned out over the handrail. I thought about rushing him. Grabbing his legs and lifting. He turned back toward me as if he'd read my mind. 'When you drink until you black out, where does consciousness go, I wonder?' He looked at me as if expecting an answer. 'That weight that you feel so strongly,' he continued. 'Such a gift, this consciousness, yet some find it unbearable. They work hard to blot it out. What are you afraid of?'

He stepped closer. 'They say that to know somebody, you must learn what they fear. What's your worst fear, Eric? Is it that you won't be remembered?' He seemed to read my face. 'No, that's the fear of other men, not you,' he said. 'Perhaps you fear not being able to finish your work?' His searching eyes seemed to find something in my face. 'Ah, that's it, isn't it? It must have been hard on you, what happened in Indianapolis.'

'Why am I here?'

'You ask a question, and yet the answer is before you. Tell me, what use are you to me? What use is Satvik?'

'I don't know.'

'These are strange days we live in. For in all of recorded history, it has never been possible to reconcile the husk with the spirit. And yet now here we find ourselves.'

I looked at him sharply. *Husk with the spirit.* It sounded familiar.

'You've talked to Robbins.'

He nodded. 'I've whispered in his ear. Whispered enough to know that he won't be a problem. But you' – he gestured in my direction – 'what a world of problems you have created.'

He turned and looked out over the city again. 'What kind of world have you created, Eric? Have you ever stopped to think? Your little test, you and Satvik, and all the nosy scientists who will come after you, checking and rechecking, until they find what you have found – that there exists a segment of the population who can't collapse the wave. Do you think that information can be stopped now? Do you think a discovery can be undiscovered?'

'No.'

He shook his head. 'Not easily, anyway. Civilizations have lost knowledge before, but not without pain. Once your paper was published, it was all doomed, I think. The world spins on its axis, but it has more axes than you can see. Even now there are labs out there, setting up equipment, applying for funding. Even now there are people who have taken notice. The machine is in motion. If I close my eyes, I can hear the gears turning. They will push forward; they'll find what you found, and then what will happen?'

'What do you mean?'

'What will happen to the human beings who are different? You must have considered this.' He turned his face toward me. 'Robbins called it a soul, and others will, too, but no matter what name it goes by, the fact remains that your test has drawn a line. Exposed the paradox to the dissector's scalpel.'

'What paradox?'

He cocked his head to the side in puzzlement. 'The paradox of free will. Do you really not see?'

I didn't see. Brighton's face shone pale in the dim light. His expression solemn.

'Will people demand that their politicians be tested? Their judges? Their potential spouses? The process is already incubating – spurred by Robbins's findings. The question is being asked, in churches, in mirrors. And where will it take us? These people who aren't people . . . what happens to them? Can they be trusted? Are they fair game for work camps? Fair game for genocide?'

'You're crazy.'

'These are extreme responses, I will admit, but consider. What about humankind makes you suspect that they are disinclined toward extreme responses? People kill each other over differences in religion, differences in culture, differences in race. What divides one tribe from another? Is it anything so significant? People look for any reason to believe in the inhumanity of their fellow man, and you've provided the ultimate justification. Villages will burn, if not here, then elsewhere. If not this year, then next. An old story writ anew, like the witch trials of Salem – tying stones to the backs of innocents just to see if they float. It's in our nature. Do you even realize what you've started, Eric? You broke the world. You broke the illusion.'

A chill climbed slowly up my neck. 'Who are you?'

'Ah, *now* you ask the question. I am one who has lived long enough to know.'

'And who are they?' I asked. 'The ones you speak of. The ones who can't collapse the wave. What are they?'

'They have a name. You haven't guessed it yet, Eric?'

'What name?'

He turned his face away from me, looking out over the city again. 'They're born, they live, they die.' He turned toward me. 'We call them the fated.'

Brighton led me back inside. He walked leisurely, keeping me beside him as we crossed the suite. The lights seemed bright after the darkness outside. We passed a library, where I saw Satvik sitting in a high-backed chair, two guards standing near the open doorway. Satvik sensed the movement and looked up. Our eyes made contact briefly before I passed the doorway. It was hard to read anything in that split second, but I thought I'd caught fear in his eyes. Fear for himself. Or perhaps for me. It was hard to tell.

At the far end of the hall, Brighton led me through a set of doors and into a large and dimly lit room. 'Do you play?' Brighton asked.

In other penthouses this might have been called a bonus room. It might have held a big-screen TV, a full bar, several couches and stools. In Brighton's version of luxury, the room held four pool tables. The windows were blacked out with dark paper. The pool tables themselves were ornate works of art. Leagues of plush green felt. Delicate woodwork. Against the wall was hung an assortment of pool cues. And here, at last, I saw the drink bar, set up tastefully at the far end of the room. That bourbon that Brighton had spoken of, along with every other kind of spirit. Glass bottles on thin glass shelves positioned in front of a long mirror.

On the pool table nearest the door, a strange assortment of equipment had been set up. I looked at it closely, trying to make sense of it. What looked like an audio speaker was lying on its back, with a white plate of some kind attached above. It was then that I noticed the stains on the second pool table. Leagues of plush green felt, yes, except for those places where the felt was darker. I tried to imagine the stains were something benign, but my mind kept filling it in. Huge, dried pools. A large circular stain at the far end of the table. Two smaller stains in the center. Another near the side pocket. As if a man had been laid out, bleeding from a dozen wounds.

Brighton noticed me staring. He walked past the stained table and stopped in front of the table with the equipment.

He motioned to his guard near the door. There was a click, and the light over the first table suddenly came on, and I could see the equipment clearly. It wasn't a speaker exactly, I now saw, but something else. A black box with several knobs and some kind of mesh surface along the top. A handful of pool balls were spread out randomly across the table. Above the box, held by a metal bracket, was the small white plate – a flat disk of hard plastic. A two-pound bag of black sand lay tipped over near the box, splaying black specks across the table, ruining the felt.

'All great discoveries have their martyrs,' he said. 'There's always a price to pay for revelation.' He grabbed the cue ball off the table. 'Wernher von Braun created the V-2 rocket. It killed tens of thousands in World War II, but it also led directly to NASA's Mercury capsules.' He held the white cue ball up and then placed it on the table. 'The moon,' he said and rolled the white ball. It bounced against the rail and hit the six-ball before coming to rest. 'Before von Braun was Niccolò Tartaglia, the father of ballistics. Poor, stammering, smash-faced Tartaglia, who invented the parenthesis in mathematics and proved that trajectories had curves.' Brighton put his hand on the two-ball. 'And here's a parenthetical aside for you – all those people who died because of those trajectories.' Brighton rolled the two-ball across the table, where it clacked into other balls, which bounced off the rails. A ball hit the black box in the center of the table and got mired in the sand. 'And then there was the discovery of fission, first detailed theoretically by Lise Meitner, who wondered what kind of chain reaction might be possible. A few years later, we got our answer, didn't we? And so it always goes; the discovery of steel leads inexorably to the blade, and the martyrs bleed.'

He leaned forward and rolled the seven-ball away from its resting place near the box. Then he picked up the bag of sand and poured it on the white plate. 'This is called a tone vibration plate. An old device, perhaps you've heard of it?'

'No'

He reached toward the black box. 'This is the frequency modulator.' He turned the knob until it clicked, and I could suddenly hear a soft hum. He turned the knob a little more, and the hum grew louder – the pitch higher. On the white plate, the sand began to vibrate and dance, shifting and flowing as the plate vibrated. Slowly a shape formed. A pattern. Like a child's rounded, looping scribble, an alien kaleidoscope. The sand gathered itself into curving black lines, while other parts of the plate were left pale and bare.

'The space around us seethes with waves,' Brighton said. 'Around us, through us. Sound waves, radio waves, light waves. The waves of matter itself. They are mostly invisible to us, except where our consciousness pulls them into physical existence. Like the sand pulls the waves into physical existence.'

He turned the knob, and the hum grew higher. The sand on the plate responded to the new frequency by changing the pattern again, shifting from a child's scribble to a series of concentric circles. Black dots on a white surface. These were mathematical shapes. Fractal dream catchers. Mandalas. Shifting, roiling, like a living, animated thing. Phasing from one shape into another as Brighton slowly turned the knob – first a honeycomb, then a series of parallel, wavy lines, like an abstract hieroglyphic. 'These wave patterns extend upward,' he said. 'The sand only captures a planar slice.' He turned the knob further – a tone like wasp wings, and the pattern shifted into a series of circles – like the face of a revolver, six small rings held in array around a larger, central circle. The black eye of a gun barrel.

Brighton removed his hand from the knob and picked up the bag. He poured more sand onto the plate – too much – pouring until it overwhelmed the pattern, spilling over the sides, making a mess on the table. He tossed the empty bag to the floor. On the plate, the sand vibrated and roiled, interfering with itself, struggling to organize, but there was no pattern. Nor room for one. Only shifting, featureless black.

'It's all just waves and waveforms,' he said. 'A vibrational tone – and it just takes a trick to see it. To cut that horizontal slice.' He straightened and looked at me. He wasn't talking about the plate anymore. 'Not a certain kind of eye but a certain kind of heart. That strange spark in your chest that pins you to this reality. That's what makes all of this manifest. Everything around you. Are you a religious man, Eric?'

'I keep an open mind.'

'Have you ever wondered why the universe is constructed as it is? Gravity, electromagnetism, the various internucleic forces – their relative and absolute strengths and ranges, all balanced on a knife blade. Shift just a little, and all is vacuum.'

'The anthropic principle,' I said.

He nodded. 'Those forces are as they are, or we wouldn't be here to calculate them, sure. But there's another way to look at it, subtly different; the universe must be just as it is, or it would remain unobserved.' He leaned over the table. 'If unobserved, would it really exist at all?' He turned the knob on the box, and the tone rose in pitch, like a wasp near my ear. 'Perhaps the universe needs us as much as we need it. A great collaboration. And without us' – he looked down at the plate of vibrating black particles – 'it's just a churning, writhing mass.' Without warning, he slammed his hand down on the table, and the whole apparatus shook.

The sand bounced off the plate, spilling everywhere, and what remained settled slowly into a new pattern, now clear and sharp as the white plate showed through. A series of gentle curves, like the wings of a butterfly.

'Do you think the universe wants to be observed?' he asked.

'The universe can't want anything.'

'You're so sure?'

'If you're talking about some kind of awareness, then – '

'If the universe had awareness, it wouldn't need you. No,' Brighton said, 'I'm talking about something more elegant than that.' He moved around the table and turned off the black box. The hum went quiet, and the sand stopped moving, the pattern now frozen in place. He seemed to contemplate the pattern. 'Heisenberg spoke of particles as potentialities rather than fact, yet here they sit.' He picked up the cue ball again. 'I've found that when physicists talk about reality with precision, they do it with formulas; when they discuss it in general, they sound like monks.'

He was silent for a moment and then placed the cue ball back on the felt. 'There is rock art in Australia thirty-eight thousand years old. More in Europe, separated by thousands of years, and yet of a common theme. Like there was a template.'

'What's your point?' I didn't understand the shift in subject.

'There are single caves that show continuous habitation for twenty thousand years. Shell middens with twenty-seven feet of strata, built up generation after generation for longer than civilization has existed, without a single new kind of artifact, a single new innovation. Can you imagine it? An unchanged village like Plato's theory of Forms. Not just a village but the Platonic ideal of a village, with pictures on the wall no different in style from images painted eighteen thousand years earlier.'

He was losing me. 'What does that have to do with any of this?'

'Things are moving more quickly now. Speeding up. There were people born into homes without electricity who had grandsons who walked on the moon. Now we have nuclear power, the microchip, wireless worldwide connectivity that fits into your pocket. So what's changed? Look around you, and you can see it. It's all broken open now. If you listen closely, you can almost hear it.' He closed his eyes, face serene.

'Hear what?'

He opened his eyes. 'Gabriel's horn.' He stared at me, and his smile broadened. 'You asked why you were here, Eric, and that is your answer. The time of the eberaxi is upon us.'

31

The guards led me down the hall. We passed the library where Satvik had been sitting, but now his chair was empty. In the front room, we crossed the white shag carpet again, and this time I noticed the red ball was missing. I glanced around, but it was nowhere. They led me down another hall and around the corner from the kitchen to a heavy wooden door with a steel latch. The taller guard used a key to unlock the door, and then he shoved me inside. Behind me, I heard the click. I turned and kicked the door hard enough to rattle its hinges.

'Eric' came a voice.

In the near darkness, I could only see a shape.

'Satvik?'

'Afraid so.' The shape moved. 'This is where they keep me at night,' he said. 'My room. Now yours, too. I knew you were coming.'

'How?'

'They put an extra mattress on the floor. Who else could it be for?'

I felt my way through the darkness until my foot hit something soft. I bent and felt the mattress with my hand, then took a seat. The only light came through a small brass grating in the base of the door. A vent for air flow, I assumed.

'What is this room?' I asked.

'It was a pantry, I think, before they took out the shelves.'

'Explains the lack of windows,' I said. 'And it's in the center of the flat, so no one can hear us shout.'

'There was shouting last night,' Satvik said. His voice was low. 'We're high enough, I don't think they care.'

'What shouting?'

'From the other room. I never saw him, though. They never brought him in here.'

I thought of the stains on the pool table. I decided not to mention it. 'So what happens now?' I asked.

'We sleep.'

'No, I mean, what happens to us? What are they going to do with us?'

'I don't know. They don't tell me.'

The darkness felt suddenly claustrophobic. The air hot and stuffy. Even with the vent, I wondered if the air was enough for two, or would they find us blue and suffocated the next day. I pushed the thought away – useless paranoia. 'How did they get you?' I asked.

'Off the street. I tried to run. They took my car, too.'

The car. That explained that night at the lab.

'And they used the boy,' he said.

'The boy from New York?'

'He's with them now. One of them all along, I think. Brighton had me test him; he wanted to see.'

'What happened?'

'The boy didn't collapse the wave, just like before. There have been others like him. I tested Brighton, too, though he didn't notice at first. I thought I was tricking him, but maybe he was tricking me.'

'Is he like the boy?'

'No,' Satvik said. 'Brighton is something else.'

'What do you mean?'

Satvik paused. 'It's hard to say. He only looked for a few moments, so I couldn't be sure.'

'Sure of what?'

'It was like he could choose,' Satvik said. 'Like he could choose to collapse the wave or not.'

We were quiet after that, sitting in the darkness. Eventually, he told me of his trip across country, trying to understand what the two-slit was testing.

'But why go to High-throughput? I still don't understand.'

'It was a message,' he said. 'A note on my car, along with the address. Google showed the connection to your old research.'

'A message from who?'

'Just a name. Vickers. I thought I would learn more, but I learned nothing. I think it was part of the trap. They caught me the next day.'

After another long silence, I spoke. 'We have to find a way out of here.'

'The guards are fast,' he said. 'That's what happened to my face.' I felt his body shift in the blackness. 'Did you talk to my family?'

'No,' I said.

'I miss my daughter,' he said. 'I worry what will happen if I don't come home.'

'It'll be okay, Satvik.'

'This is what I miss most – reading to her at night. When I was on the road, I did not do that.'

'You'll read to her again.'

'I hope you're right. She likes the stories. I tell stories, and she lies in bed and listens.'

'Did you ever tell her your story of the four princes?'

'She knows all the parts.'

'There's more than just what you told me?'

'Much more.'

'So the fourth prince, the one who shot the bird's eye, what happened to him at the end?'

'It is a long story.'

'And what happens?'

Satvik was quiet for a moment. 'He dies.'

In the middle of the night, a sound woke me. For a moment I forgot where I was, and then it all came back. A sound like a bouncing ball. I put my face to the vent, and I could see into the kitchen. I saw short legs crossing the room. The red ball bouncing on the floor. It was the boy.

'Psst,' I called out.

The ball stopped bouncing. The boy turned. Ten years old maybe. Dark, curly hair. He bent into my field of vision, looking at me through the vent, and I could see his face. He stared at me, his face expressionless. Not the slightest surprise.

'Can you open the door?' I whispered.

The boy cocked his head slightly. His face never changed. A normal boy, a typical boy. A boy in blue jeans and T-shirt. No different from any other boy you might see in a park.

I waited, but he didn't respond. 'Can you – '

He flung the ball, and it struck the vent in front of my face. I flinched back. I saw his legs walking away.

The next day the guards woke us with a bang on the door. I rolled out of bed and climbed to my feet as the door swung open. They let us take turns in the bathroom, while one of the guards waited outside the door.

'So where's Brighton?'

The guard just looked at me and said nothing. He wasn't one of the guards I'd seen the night before. He was tall, dark-skinned. Wore a thin sports jacket, open at the front. They must work in shifts, I realized. How many men did Brighton have working for him? The boy, if he was still around, was nowhere to be seen.

'Any chance of breakfast?'

'You can grab whatever you want.' The man pointed toward the kitchen. 'You've got five minutes.' I crossed the suite and stepped onto the kitchen tile. It took me a moment to find the fridge, so perfectly hidden in a secret panel beside the six-burner stove. I scrounged inside the Sub-Zero and grabbed a carton of orange juice. Then I pulled out a drinking glass from one of the upper cabinets. The glass was heavy. I wrapped my fingers around it. Heavy enough to use as a weapon. If I broke it against the marble, I'd have an edge that could slice a jugular. The guard took a few steps into the kitchen, eyeing me closely. He put his hands on his hips, opening his jacket slightly, and I saw the gun holster. I filled the glass with orange juice, drank it down, and then put the glass in the sink.

A few moments later, Satvik came down the hall, Polo Shirt and another guard following close behind.

'Grab your shoes,' Polo said. 'We're leaving.'

'Leaving for where?'

'The street. We're dropping you off in a park.'

'Dropping us off?'

'Yeah, letting you go.'

I blinked. Stared at him. It didn't make sense. Not after everything that had happened. 'Just like that?'

'I'm not gonna repeat myself.'

Polo shoved me toward the room where I'd spent the night. I followed Satvik around the corner and inside the room. We stooped to pick up our shoes. Satvik looked dazed. His face unreadable.

I glanced behind me, and Polo was still around the corner.

I leaned close to Satvik and whispered, 'I don't like this.'

Satvik's face broke into a smile. The dazed look faded. 'They are letting us go.'

I shook my head. 'Why would they do that?'

'I don't know,' he said. He slipped his shoes on. Black loafers. 'They are done with us, maybe.'

'Satvik, this doesn't seem right.'

Satvik stood. 'I was working too hard. When I get home, I will be different. Too many hours. For what? Fertilize to cut, fertilize to cut.'

'What are you talking about?'

'It is like lawns. You put fertilizer, and the grass grows faster. But why? There is no outcome.'

'Satvik, I need you to focus.'

'I am focused. I have been here two weeks. Today I go home.'

'You believe him?'

'He said he's letting us go.'

I thought of my mother then. Her ability to believe what she needed to. Like a superpower. Maybe we all had that in us. Maybe we could all draw from it when we needed to.

The other guard came and got us and ushered us toward Polo, who stood by the private elevator. The doors opened, and I expected to see the car, but the elevator bay was empty. Just a blank metal floor and four steel walls. As large as a one-car garage.

'In,' the guard said.

The four of us stepped inside. I stood next to Satvik, and Polo pulled the metal gate closed. Then the exterior elevator doors closed slowly. I could smell the grease of the elevator cables.

Satvik was still smiling. 'Things will be different now.'

'Yeah,' I said.

Polo hit a button, and the elevator jolted into movement.

'I have been too long away. I'll see my daughter tonight.'

I could only nod.

'She will be happy to see me.'

'Happy,' I said.

The man in the polo shirt raised his arm in a fluid movement and shot Satvik in the head.

32

I didn't scream until after.

The splash of blood against the wall – and then I flung myself at the shooter, but he was expecting it. He spun away, using my own momentum against me, as he grabbed my arm and slammed me into the gate. My face mashed against the hard steel, and I felt my nose break. Stars swam before my eyes. Dark spots. I turned and swung my fist blindly, but there was only air, and then a chipping jab to my jaw that sent me to the floor.

I shook my head, trying to clear my vision. When I moved to stand, a kick smashed me in the ribs, sending me onto my back – the wind knocked out of me so that I couldn't grab air. I gasped like a fish. Then another kick came. And another. I curled into a ball, protecting my vitals. Consciousness winnowed to a fine white point, slipping away, and then the kicks stopped.

The elevator lurched to a halt. I felt the jolt beneath my hip. Then the vibration as the elevator doors opened. Men stepping out, the murmur of voices.

It had all happened in the course of an elevator ride. Satvik dead. Me on the floor, smashed and bleeding.

A white Range Rover was backed up to the opening of the elevator bay. Beside me, Satvik lay on his face, a pool of blood expanding across the metal floor. I became aware of movement then, coming closer. Polo and the other guard, stepping back inside.

They wrapped Satvik's body up in a tarp.

I wanted to kill them.

I wanted it so bad I cried. Cried in rage as I tried to pull myself to a sitting position. The one who'd pulled the trigger only looked down at me.

'Watch those eyes,' Polo warned.

I stared at him, wanting to take him apart. Wanting to bite out his throat.

He kicked me in the face then.

My head snapped back, and I felt my lip split. Blackness swam.

'I said watch those eyes.'

When I looked up with blurry vision, Polo was standing over me. I didn't look away. Instead I reached for the wall. I pulled myself forward, glaring up at him. The guard's face went flush with anger. He pulled his gun and pointed it at my face. I thought of the pattern in the sand. Six circular chambers. But this was no revolver. Instead, a semiautomatic. I kept coming, wobbling to my knees.

He cocked the hammer back.

'Not yet.' The other guard reached out and put a hand on Polo's wrist. Pushed the gun down. 'Unless you want to do the digging.' The anger in the guard's face was still there, but he seemed to get himself under control while he holstered his gun.

He looked down at me. His arm flexed – so fast that I barely saw it, the crunch of bone, and the world went dark.

*

'Up.'

The word came from nowhere as I felt myself being yanked by the arm. It might have been seconds later or minutes.

I tried to fight, but my head swam – body not responding as I was dragged across the elevator floor. I rolled, trying to get my knees under me. The grip on my arm released, and I collapsed onto my stomach. Blood from my broken nose drained down my throat. The floor of the elevator was silver-gray, a smooth steel. I could see my hands on it, but they felt like somebody else's. My stomach heaved. I puked blood across the clean surface, splashing blood and bile across the man's shoes. It was some consolation at least. The only blow I'd landed.

'Get him in the fucking Rover already.'

The two guards jerked me by the arms, opened the hatch, and threw me in the back. The zip ties were at the ready. Polo cinched my wrists behind my back and pulled them tight enough to cut off blood flow. I'd lose my hands if they left me that way for long. It didn't seem likely to matter.

They threw Satvik on top of me and then slammed the hatch closed.

His dead weight pressed down on my legs as the vehicle circled through the parking garage. I could feel his arm against my back – his legs draped across my calf. The blood from his head wound spilled out of the tarp and soaked my shirt.

Up front, the men talked low and steady, but I couldn't make out their words. That suited me. I didn't want to hear them. Satvik was dead. I was about to die. I thought of my sister. My father and mother. Satvik's words, *People forget they are going to die someday.* I felt the laugh rising like madness. And there was a reason, I realized. You *have* to forget. Because you can't hold that in your mind. You can't contain it. Your own extinction. The end of it all. Does the world wink out of existence? Or is there something more? Something after.

The Range Rover came to a stop. A moment's pause, and we were moving again, rounding a bend, the light suddenly bright and yellow. Daylight streamed through the glass. We were outside the parking garage and on the city streets.

The Rover accelerated. I thought of what Polo had said in the penthouse. *Letting you go*, he'd said. Sometimes there was a bit of truth to a lie. *Dropping you off in a park.* I could imagine Satvik and I buried there deep and dark, where no one would ever find us. It wouldn't be hard.

The drive continued, the sound of the road. It was several minutes later when the low talk from the front seat cut off abruptly. Sudden silence.

I noticed it without even being aware of it at first. It wasn't the silence that came at the end of a conversation. It was something else. Cut off, like their attention had been snagged. Cut off like they'd *seen* something. I could feel the vehicle start to slow.

Polo's voice came, 'The fuck is this?'

'Tell her to get the fuck out of the road.'

'What's she doing?'

'Hey – '

The squeal of tires.

'Look ou – '

And then the crash came, and the world turned on its side.

The impact was deafening – a violent jerk that slammed me against the hatch, and then I was rolling, bouncing off the walls as broken glass rained down in a glittering cascade. The vehicle skidded on its side, pavement scraping past, throwing sparks inches from my face where the window used to be. When the movement finally stopped, I was on my back, knees pressed against my own head. But that wasn't right. It was Satvik's knees, not mine. Our bodies entangled by the crash. I shifted my weight, and my arm came free – snapped loose from the zip tie by the force of the impact. I pulled my arm out from under me, blood pouring from my wrist. Satvik was still draped over me, his face turned away as if in shame. I was screaming. I didn't realize it until my voice gave out. A high-pitched crackle that seemed to choke itself.

I crawled out through the rear window. We were on a city street. Warehouses on one side, chain link on the other. Construction zone of some kind – the location too isolated to be accidental. Only one pedestrian stood gape-mouthed on the sidewalk. An old woman with thin plastic grocery bags in each hand. The car that had hit us was a dozen feet away, a brown sedan. After the crash, it had continued on and now sat crumpled against a light pole. Our vehicle was on its side, twisted wreckage littering the street.

The pop of sheet metal drew my attention, and the driver's door of the brown sedan jerked open. A shoe hit the ground, but I didn't wait to see. I turned and pulled myself across the pavement. The smell of gasoline assaulted my nostrils as glass drove itself into my hands and knees. I got a dozen feet before there was a sound behind me, and I turned. Polo was sliding out of the vehicle now – coming through the shattered windshield, trailing blood. His leg moved at a funny angle, and he cried out. Twenty feet up the sidewalk, the old woman dropped her grocery bags and ran. A six-pack of Coke hit the pavement and burst, fizzing across the cement. And that's when I saw the other man.

He crossed from the wreckage on the other side of the street. Tall and pale and bearded. Scalp buzzed to stubble. He carried a gun in his hand.

The scars were what you noticed. They crisscrossed his flesh, deep and puckered. Like a bomb maker too intimate with his craft. Our eyes locked then – almost a nod. He approached the wreckage, smile curling back from his teeth. The sound of sirens rose in the distance.

He raised the gun toward the spidered windshield. He didn't speak. *Pop, pop, pop, pop.* It happened so fast. The bullets striking meat and metal. The driver never had a chance. The adrenaline dumped into my system like a sizzle. I kept crawling, putting as much distance as I could between myself and the carnage. I looked back to see if the tall man followed. He'd moved around the side of the vehicle where Polo lay. Polo still moved, leg bending strangely from a dozen joints. The man used his foot to flip him over on his back, and I could hear the ragged breathing, red bubbles frothing from his lips. Broken ribs, a pierced lung. And then a shoe came down on Polo's throat, pressing him into the pavement. His eyes rolled in their sockets. A moment later, a loud snap. The breathing stopped. The scarred man's eyes moved to me, and I froze. I dared not move. He circled around to the back of the vehicle. He crouched near where Satvik lay, half in, half out of the broken hatch, still wrapped in the tarp. He pulled the tarp back from Satvik's face, almost tenderly. Or maybe I just saw it like that.

Satvik's dark eyes far away. Focused somewhere else. I hoped it was somewhere good.

'Already dead,' he said.

'And the other one?'

I turned my head but couldn't see her. The other voice. The scarred man looked down at me. Made eye contact again. The sirens were louder now.

'Still alive,' he said. 'Hurt, though.'

I saw his hand flex on the gun, adjusting his grip, but he didn't raise the weapon. A thin runnel of smoke rose from the barrel.

'Quicker to end it,' he said.

'No,' the woman's voice came again. A familiar voice, I realized. And then I saw her as she stepped from around the side of the wreckage. Saw the scar that bisected her eyebrow. The woman who had saved me from the fire.

'Vickers says we take him,' she said. 'So we take him.'

PART III

To go in the dark with a light is to know the light.
To know the dark, go dark.

– Wendell Berry, 'To Know the Dark'

33

Sirens passed the old panel truck going in the other direction. It was the kind of old truck used to haul furniture – a square box on wheels. The woman and I were in the back. The scarred man up front driving. I sat behind him, leaning against the wall. I could feel the vibration against my spine.

I stared at the woman sitting across from me. 'Who are you?'

'Friends,' the woman said.

'Don't lie to the man,' the driver said. 'That's no way to start out.'

She grunted. It could have been agreement. It could have been a laugh. At that moment, up the street, another police car came around the corner, lights spinning. I watched through the front windshield as the cop flashed by.

'Okay, not friends,' she said. 'Not exactly.'

'Then who?'

It was the man who answered. 'We're less likely to kill you than the other guys.'

I braced myself with my hands as the truck wove its way through the streets.

Occasionally, the driver craned his neck, checking the mirrors while the engine whined. The woman's mouth drew a grim line. I looked at her left hand, the missing fingers – most of her ring finger and part of her pinky. The flesh pink and gnarled.

Through the windshield I saw traffic and buildings and houses – pedestrians with their heads turned in our direction, frowning at the reckless driver. But no more cop cars.

No one chased. At least not that I could see.

She seemed to follow my thoughts. 'The cops,' she said, 'are the least of our worries.'

I thought of the stethoscopes as we rounded a corner. When we had straightened out again, the woman rose to her feet and moved to the front. She leaned over the passenger seat and picked up something from the floorboard. The scarred man turned his head, and the top of his left ear was missing – pink scar tissue carving an ellipse across the side of his skull, a curving line where hair no longer grew.

She turned and moved toward me. 'Come here,' she said, grabbing hold of the back of my neck. I let myself be pulled forward. The bag descended over my face.

'Why bother?' The scarred man said.

Less likely to kill you than the other guys.

'Just in case,' she said.

'In case what?' he said. 'You think he's walking away from all this?'

The bag was scratchy and dark, some kind of woven cloth. From the front seat, the driver's voice came softly. 'There ain't no walking away.'

When we arrived at our destination, I heard the doors open. I felt my arm being pulled, so I swung my feet out and stood. I let myself be pulled along.

'Watch your step.'

It was night. I couldn't see, but I could tell by the air and the sounds of crickets in the distance.

The ground under my feet changed from soft earth to something harder. We were inside. Our footsteps made slight echoes as we walked. Wherever we were, the room was big, I decided. *An airport hangar? Was I about to be whisked away to another location?*

After walking for a few minutes, the voice came again. 'Another step.'

I lifted my leg higher, and there was a six-inch rise. Now the sound was different. The echo gone. Rough hands jerked my shoulders around.

'Sit.'

I reached behind me, feeling the cool wood of a chair. I sat. There were murmurs and the shuffle of feet. I heard talking but couldn't make out what was said.

Footsteps circled. Heavy. They stopped.

'Search him.'

Hands groped at my body. My pockets, my legs, my crotch. They took my phone but left my wallet.

'No weapons.'

The bag was pulled off my head. A single mechanic's light hung from a hook in the corner of the room, blinding me. We were in an old warehouse of some kind. No, an old factory, I decided. The room was a manager's office – a large window of mesh-reinforced safety glass looked out on a continent of cement flooring – the dimensions like an artist's study of perspective. The glass was spidered, held together by wire. There was no door. The far side of the building was corrugated steel, bowed and rusty. The whole place looked as if it had been abandoned years ago and left to rot.

The man and woman now stood in front of me.

'He's younger than I expected,' the scarred man said.

I glanced up. Large. Six foot two by the look of him. His scars and unruly beard made him look like a pirate who'd been too long out at sea. Not the pirates of cartoons and summer comedies. Instead, the pirates who followed ships into international waters, boarded them at night, and killed everyone aboard who didn't seem likely to draw a ransom.

'Where am I?' I asked.

Without a word, the scarred man swung a huge fist into the side of my head. I went down hard, chair and all. The world faded and then came back.

'Stop!' the woman snapped. The man's arm was pulled back for another blow, fist cocked near his right shoulder. She pushed him hard in the chest. 'Enough.'

The push seemed to snap him out of his anger, and he smiled at the woman. He held up his hands, palms out. 'Fine, fine,' he said

His smile faded when he looked down at me. He lowered into a crouch, one elbow on his knee.

The woman tried to pull him back to his feet, but he shook her off with a jerk of his arm. 'I'm not going to hurt him,' he said. His eyes turned back toward me. 'But he needs to know his place here.'

His eyes crawled over me.

'I could say I hit you for speaking out of turn, but it wouldn't be true. The truth is, I thought I should set things straight here at the beginning.' He bent closer, speaking right into the side of my face. 'I don't like all the trouble you've caused. You're going to do what we say, or we're going to kill you, do you understand?'

'Enough,' the woman said again.

'No, I want him to answer.' His eyes bore into me. 'Do you understand?'

I pulled myself up to an elbow.

I looked around for something to grab. Anything. Something to hit him with. My ears were still ringing. My nose throbbed in pain. I felt the chair, and my fingers curled around one wooden leg.

'Stop,' the woman said. She had seen my hand on the wood.

She turned toward the man and reached behind her back, and that's when I saw the knife. Her damaged fingers curled around the handle.

'I said, *stop.*' And this time her voice was different. Low and slow and deadly. Almost quiet. They were words said in a way that meant there would be no more words.

He turned to look at her. He seemed to consider her stance, turned sideways to him, one hand out of sight.

'We'll let Vickers decide,' he said.

He turned back toward me. 'Stand up.'

I did my best to do as he instructed, but my head still wasn't right. My balance was shit, but I managed to gain my feet.

The woman lifted the chair from the floor and righted it.

'Sit down,' she said.

I sank onto the chair. The scarred man walked around me.

'There will be people looking for me,' I said.

'More than you know. They're probably watching your motel as we speak.'

Motel. It meant they knew where I lived.

'Where do you think you'd be right now if we hadn't come along?' he asked.

He seemed to expect an answer. 'Dead, probably,' I said.

'That's right. So whatever else happens, we don't owe you anything. Even life. Do you understand?'

'Who are you?'

'Oh,' he said, softly. 'That's really gonna depend.'

34

Dinner was a mix of beans and bread. Night had fallen, and we sat around a small fire in another, deeper part of the warehouse, beneath a high ceiling, among a confusion of splintered crates that had been piled into a barricade against the greater expanse of the room. One wall of our makeshift encampment was an old semitrailer, missing the wheels; another wall was lost in the shadows. They had pulled the panel truck around to the back of the structure and thrown a tarp over it.

Above our heads sprawled vast leagues of sheet metal and steel I beams, below which hung sporadic, empty trays that might have once held fluorescent bulbs but now held only empty air. Occasional gusts of wind entered the room through distant gaps in the walls, fanning the flames of the campfire. I listened carefully and could hear only crickets and the sound of spoons on plates. No highway noise. No sounds of the city. Wherever we were, we were out in the boonies.

I watched them while they shoveled food into their mouths. First the woman, thin and anxious. Her eyes active. She ate quickly, like she was starving, but it was more than hunger that drove her – like food was an unwelcome diversion of her attention. The man who'd hit me ate slower, eyes focused on his plate. The woman called him Hennig. A fitting enough name for a pirate, I decided. He took his meal in big bites, chewing slowly. *Hennig the half-ear*, I thought to myself. When the fire began to dim, he rose and grabbed several large scraps of wood from a nearby stockpile to feed the flames. He didn't look at me. Didn't speak. He was already finished with his meal, and had now turned his attention to his handgun. The air smelled of beans, wood smoke, and gun oil. He cleaned the weapon while I stared into the fire.

They bound my wrists with duct tape – a rhythmic *pull, wrap, pull, wrap*, as the tape wound up and over and around. My injured hand throbbed. The hair on my arms would be a lost cause, I knew, when that tape came off. *If* that tape came off. There was always a chance I'd die with it on. A possibility that I overheard discussed after they taped my feet and carried me across the room to the broken-down trailer. With no arms to catch my fall, I hit my head on the steel and cried out.

'Quiet,' Hennig said. 'Or we'll tape your mouth next.'

His unpredictability I feared. But it was a reasoned fear. One I could control. When he mentioned taping my mouth shut, there was nothing reasoned about it. The thought of it made my arms tremble – the shakes always just under the surface. I thought about puking in the morning, tape still on my mouth, gagging and drowning on my own vomit.

I was silent as vacuum.

They took shifts over the next few hours, walking the grounds.

From my position against the trailer, I watched them come and go, until they both sat by the fire.

When the fire had nearly burned itself out, the woman rose and spoke to Hennig, who was cleaning his gun again. Or a different gun. She leaned close, speaking into his missing chunk of ear. In the fire's glow, I saw Hennig's eyes move to me. They seemed to argue, and then Hennig nodded.

He crossed the room toward me, while she stood and watched.

There was a knife in his hand. It was a hunter's knife, gleaming orange in the last embers of the fire. It was a wicked piece of steel, curved slightly, tapering to a point. I imagined the blade sliding neatly between my ribs, slicing skin and muscle and pleura, digging for my heart.

Hennig didn't speak. He crouched next to me. He was quick about it. There was a jerk and then a quick *snit* sound, and my ankles pulled free.

'Stand,' he said. 'I'm not dragging you.'

I used my elbows to roll myself onto my side, trying to get my feet under me. A strong arm yanked at my bicep, pulling me upward, and I was on my feet again. I held my bound wrists out to him, but he shook his head.

'That tape stays on,' he said. He pointed inside the trailer. 'You sleep there. I want you against the far back wall of the box.' He motioned with his head toward where the woman sat. 'She's going to sleep at the front of the box, meaning you can't get out without stepping over her. You're her problem, do you understand?'

I nodded again.

'I'm sleeping out here.' He gestured toward to the floor around the fire. 'Even if you get by her, you can't get out of this room without stepping over me.' He leaned forward. 'Don't become my problem tonight.'

He motioned me toward the steel box, and I retreated inside. It was the kind of box you saw on highways, pulled behind semis. It was thirty feet long, eight feet wide, nine feet tall. A hundred thousand Pokémon dolls might have fitted inside. Or one luxury living-room set, shipped special, all the way to Malibu. Tonight it would be my bed. Near the back, where there was no ventilation or light or heat.

I walked to where the blackness was absolute. I felt the back wall with my hands then sat. Although the walls of the box were steel, the floor was lined with wood and mushy with rot. I stretched my legs and looked out toward the front, and it was like sitting in the small end of a telescope, watching the world from a little spot of darkness.

A few minutes later, the woman gestured for me to come closer. I ventured out of the box again, and she handed me a blanket. It was thick and warm and didn't smell too bad.

'The box is just for tonight,' she said. 'Vickers will be here tomorrow.'

'This Vickers is in charge?'

'You could say that.'

'You were the one who saved me at the lab. You pulled me away from the fire.'

'The fire.' She nodded. Her dirty blonde hair swayed. 'Not our handiwork.'

'Brighton's?'

'He was sending a message.'

'Hell of a message.'

She smiled. 'You should have run that night and not come back. You might have had a chance.'

'So who is he?'

'Not who he seems,' she said. She was silent for a moment. 'His kind lives by hiding.'

'Funny, he doesn't seem the hiding type to me.'

She shook her head. 'He's hiding in the same place that his kind have always hidden. In plain sight.'

This seemed fitting to me. Like the way you can know a particle's location or its velocity. Never both. The universe is built of secret knowledge.

'And what is your name?' I asked.

She was turned away from the fire, lost in shadow, so I couldn't read her expression. 'That's the last thing you need to be worrying about.' She went silent again after that, and I began to think that she wasn't going to say more. But whatever inner argument she waged blew itself out. 'Mercy,' she said. 'You can call me Mercy.'

35

In the morning, the sound of voices woke me. Then a distant sizzling. I opened my eyes, and light streamed through a thousand holes in the roof. They might have been bullet holes. Or rust holes. In a rainstorm, this place would leak like a screen door.

I sat up. At the front of the trailer, the blanket was folded into a neat square. Mercy was already gone, talking with Hennig. I could hear them but not see them – voices drifting from outside the box.

I summoned the will to move and rose to lean against the steel. My shoulders screamed in pain, but I didn't let myself make a sound.

Mercy returned. She eyed me from around the corner. 'You're up. How are you feeling?'

Alive, I could have said. My stomach twisted but not from hunger. For three seconds I thought I'd puke, and then I did puke, bringing up bile and acid until my eyes stung and my nose throbbed. I tried to breathe through my nose, but it was still caked with blood. I felt moisture on my hand as I propped myself up.

'You okay?'

I let her ask twice before the nausea passed and I felt I could speak.

'Fine,' I said. Not yet trusting myself to longer conversation.

'You sick? Got the flu or something?'

'No,' I said, voice burned and awful. 'Mornings are hardest.'

She approached, careful to step around the vomit, serrated steak knife in hand. 'The rest of this tape can go,' she said.

When you are being approached by a knife-wielding stranger at 7:00 a.m. after being bound all night, there are worse things to hear spoken.

'Hold out your arms.'

'Thank you,' I said.

I sat up straight and did as she asked while she considered the task before her. She held the knife up to the tape, trying to visualize the angle least likely to accidentally slit my wrists.

'Don't thank me. He's letting me cut you loose mostly because I mentioned you'd need to use the bathroom. I told him I wasn't gonna hold it, so it'd be up to him.'

If it was in me to smile, I might have. 'Good thinking,' I tried to say, but the words barely came out. My voice was getting worse, not better. I needed water. I must have been quite a sight, sick and bedraggled after a night in the box.

The knife pierced the tape, and she sawed slowly while I tried to pull my hands apart. I felt the cold steel brush my skin.

'Careful now,' she said. 'No sudden movements. The only thread we have for stitches is your shoelaces.'

With a final jerk of the knife, the tape was severed and my arms came apart. My stiff joints took a moment to believe it. I still had tape attached to my forearms, but at least my shoulder sockets were mobile again. I stretched my arms slowly, raising them over my head.

'Sorry about having to tape you up,' she said. 'Just a precaution. Come on, breakfast's for you, too.'

I followed her out of the trailer, stepping onto the filthy cement floor. Sunlight wasn't doing the place any favors. It was far more derelict than I'd realized last night. What I'd thought was some kind of rubble pile in the corner was actually a small bush, grown up through cracks in the floor. This place hadn't just been abandoned for years, I realized, but decades. None of the windows held glass, and the wind whistled through. Outside were more buildings, visible across a narrow divide that might have once been a causeway. Everywhere outside the windows, I saw long, low rectangular structures of steel and concrete. It looked like an old factory grounds or maybe an old army base of some kind.

I followed her to the fire and sat.

The breakfast was far better than the dinner. Eggs and bacon, cooked on an iron skillet over an open fire. It was like camping but under the confines of a tin roof that loomed high overhead. When I finished the eggs, I spoke. 'The bathroom?'

'Show him,' Mercy said.

Hennig stood and led me through a narrow hole in the wall, past a strange assortment of old boilers and into a third room, vastly larger and partially open to the elements. Here, sunlight poured through skylight-sized holes in the roof, and entire trees grew in the middle of the floor. Pipes ran everywhere in various sizes and shapes, some three feet across at their openings, sliced in half by long-forgotten welding torches. It didn't seem like the kind of thing you'd see in an old barracks, so my understanding of the place shifted. Definitely an industrial complex of some kind, though its original use was a mystery.

We followed a wall of crumbling red brick until we approached a door with a faded sign, MEN, stenciled across the warped wood, but Hennig passed that by and kept walking. 'No water,' he said. 'That'd get ripe pretty quick.'

We continued along the wall for another hundred feet until we came to an open doorway. I followed him outside, sun shining down, and on the other side of a neglected gravel roadway, a small building had completely caved in on itself. It had no roof at all, though three walls still stood.

'There,' he said. We stopped at a barrier of cement. 'Number one on this side of the wall, number two the other.'

'Number one,' I said.

He gestured to the wall. 'Well, have at it.'

I glanced around while I peed, trying to get a lay of the land. From where I stood, the buildings seemed to sprawl in every direction, variations on a theme. The place was a maze; I could see why they liked it. If it came to conflict, home court advantage would be important.

Three minutes later, we were back at the fire, where I found breakfast cleaned up. There were jugs of water and a scrub pad.

I saw guns on a table. A rifle. A shotgun. Two pistols. These people, whoever they were, suddenly seemed less homeless than paramilitary. Hennig picked up the last of the wood and placed it on the fire.

I fiddled with the tape still stuck to my arms, giving an experimental tug. The pain confirmed what I'd already suspected.

'Best to just do it quick,' Mercy said. 'Like a Band-Aid.'

I yanked hard – a flash of pain. The tape came away, along with the hair on my forearm. I checked the skin. No blood at least. I yanked the other side free.

Hennig leaned against the table and stared at me while he picked his fingernails with his knife. He let the knife drop to the table, where it stuck straight up. 'The tape may be off, but that doesn't mean you have the run of the place.'

I said nothing.

He looked at his watch. A diver's watch with a big dial face. Thick leather band to go with his thick wrist. 'Vickers will be here soon.'

'Come on, let's find some more wood for the fire.' Mercy motioned to me to follow.

I followed her through the building. We walked outside by a different exit, and here the waist-high grass moved like waves. The breeze was picking up. Mercy led the way. I thought wood might be hard to find, but once we were some distance from the building, it was everywhere. Stunted, dried-up bushes, perfect for kindling. There were larger trees, too, still green, and Mercy pulled the branches down, snapping them off, stripping their leaves. Around the corner we found a pile of old planks.

'Here, help me break this.'

She lay the board across a nearby cinder block. 'You're heavier,' she said, motioning at the board. I stepped onto the wood, and it broke with a loud crack. She grabbed the longer piece.

'Again,' she said. So I did.

I thought about running.

I might have been faster than her. I outweighed her by sixty pounds, so I was probably stronger. Other than the knife, she didn't seem to be armed. A gun was hard to conceal without a bulge of some kind, but it wasn't impossible. She could have had a derringer strapped to her calf beneath her loose jeans. I let my eyes wander over the surrounding landscape. I saw tall, swaying grass and bushes and the upward slope of a hill, leading up into trees. Bombed-out buildings all around. In the distance, at the top of the hill, I saw a chain-link fence that might have once been topped with barbed wire but now only trailed dangling crimson strands – either snipped intentionally long ago or rusted through and fallen. Only the brackets at the top of the fence stood as a reminder that the protective walls of the citadel had once had teeth. I could make it to the fence, and then up and over, and she'd likely never catch me. Not unless she was fast. Not unless she was armed. Not unless she was willing to kill me.

Her shouts might rouse her friend, I knew, but he was still thirty yards away, inside a building, back at the dying fire. So I'd have a head start.

She looked at me as if she knew what I was thinking.

'A mile of woods that way,' she said. She pointed to the fence. 'A big hill and a drop, and then you'd come out on the tide flats. If the tide is in, you'd hit the canal and cold water. Maybe some current – enough to suck you out to sea – or maybe not. If you're lucky, and the tide isn't in, you'd hit a mudflat, three quarters of a mile – a dangerous crossing but doable – and then beyond that a rise and woods and then a town at the top. Roads. A dock. Civilization.'

It wasn't a dare. Not even that.

Because the math had an escapable calculus. If I did get free from them, then what?

Sailors have died abandoning ships they should have stayed on.

She looked at me. 'So?'

I gave a last, lingering look at the fence and the woods. 'Not today,' I said.

We gathered wood until our arms were full, and then we started back. She took a different path through the ruins. 'This place used to be a smeltery,' she said. 'God knows how long ago. Then it was a gasworks for three decades. Then a storage lot for ingots. Then empty. Maybe someday it'll be bulldozed and turned into condos. It's amazing how something can be built for one purpose and then transform into something else.' We ducked as we passed through another hole in the wall. This building was smaller but empty as the rest.

'Did you guys put these holes in?'

'Tactical retreat is what Hennig calls it. The holes give us the short path if we need it. As long as we stay out of the line of sight, then whatever's following might miss the holes and have to take the long way around.'

'And if you can't stay out of sight?'

'Then we better be faster.'

'Faster than what, exactly?'

'Same thing everyone needs to be faster than,' she said. 'What's coming for you.'

We walked across a pile of corrugated steel roofing that clattered under our feet. I lost my balance on the slick tin but caught myself.

'We call these places hides,' she said. 'This one is better than most. Private and out of the way. The cops patrol the exterior sometimes, but they never come inside. Keeping the bums and vagrants away is the hardest part. They wander in. Hennig makes them go away.'

'I bet he does.'

'Not that kind of away. Nothing permanent. He's not a bad guy.'

'Easy for you to say. You didn't get punched in the face.'

She shook her head. 'You don't even understand what you don't understand.'

'Then enlighten me.' My arms had begun to ache from carrying the wood.

'That'll happen soon enough.'

Something about the way she said it made me uneasy. I took a guess. 'Vickers,' I said. 'When?'

'Oh, Vickers is already here.' She stopped.

We were outside the building where we'd spent the night. I realized then what the walk might have been about, besides the wood. If Vickers had second thoughts about what to do with me, then they'd be inside waiting. No need to discuss it with me standing there.

Mercy cocked her head toward the hole in the wall. 'After you,' she said.

Either way, I didn't have much choice. I walked toward the hole, bent, and stepped through to the other side. She followed close behind. Maybe too close.

My vision took a moment to adjust.

We were in at the edge of the encampment. I saw the trailer and the fire. I looked for Hennig, but he was nowhere to be seen. Hiding behind the cargo hold, waiting to pounce? Or sent away?

I stepped farther in. The camp was deserted.

But I didn't have to wait long.

A moment later, I heard voices approaching from the other room. Hennig came through the doorway first, followed by Vickers. Or who I assumed must have been Vickers.

She was still partially in shadow. Tall, with short brown hair. She wore dark slacks, and a long sleeve button-up. White collar. Gold bracelet on her left wrist. By her clothes, she might have just stepped out of a boardroom somewhere or been impaneled on a grand jury. Whoever she was, she wasn't dressed like a person hiding in the woods.

Because there was nothing else for it, I walked around to the other side of the fire and dumped my cache of wood on the floor. The stranger glanced over at me as she approached the fire, taking note of my presence for the first time. Her pale green eyes lifted to my face.

And it was then that I recognized her.

It was the woman from Brighton's penthouse.

Confused, I glanced at Mercy. But she offered no explanation.

The new woman appraised me, face expressionless.

She could have been angry, or disappointed, or just evaluating.

Since I wasn't sure what to say, I said nothing. Just let her eyes move over me while she worked over whatever decision she was coming to. Or maybe she'd made the decision already, and she was just coming around to the way she'd let me know. Mercy walked around the fire and sat at the open mouth of the trailer.

'We were never formally introduced,' the woman said. She stuck out her hand. 'My name is Vickers.' I took a step forward and shook. The hand was delicate, long-fingered.

'Eric Argus,' I said.

Vickers turned toward Mercy. 'Hennig didn't do that to his face, did he?'

'Some of it,' she said.

Vickers looked at me. 'Walk with me,' she said. 'We have a lot to discuss.'

36

'A long time ago, there was a woman who crunched corporate budgets and filled in spreadsheets and made careful, prudent assessments of risk versus gain; then something terrible happened.'

'And what was that?' I asked. We were outside the building, walking an old roadway. Here tire tracks beat twin paths through the tall grass that carpeted the landscape.

'She found that all her assessments were wrong. The world was more dangerous than she'd realized.'

We came to a particularly deep rut in our path and avoided it by stepping over the strip of grass and into the other track. Above us, the sun angled down through great upwellings of white, cauliflorous cloud. A postcard day. 'Accurate assessments can only be made when one has all the information,' she continued.

'And you lacked that information, is that where this is going?'

'We all lack it to some extent. I've always been a cautious person, but this world has turned me into something I never thought I'd be.'

'And what's that?'

'A gambler.'

'So that's why I'm here,' I said. 'A gamble.'

She nodded. 'In some ways.' She opened her suit jacket while we walked, and she pulled out two glossy four-by-six photos. She handed them to me. 'I know you've met Brighton, but is there a second man in this photo who looks familiar?'

I recognized him immediately. 'Boaz,' I said.

'When did you first meet them?'

'At a conference a few weeks back.'

'What did you talk about?'

'That night? Swords, mostly, as I recall.' I studied the photos in my hand. They looked like security camera footage. Brighton was with a group of men walking into a building. An old bank or an office building of some kind. Boaz was at his side. A phalanx of businessmen striding toward or away from some high-powered corporate meeting.

'Ah, the sword talk. He really must have liked you.'

I handed the photos back. 'I didn't get that impression.'

'These are a few years old.' She slid the glossy prints back into the inside pocket of her suit jacket. 'They're more careful now. It's harder to get close to them.'

'You seem to manage,' I said. I thought about what she'd said. Corporate budgets. Spreadsheets. 'You work for them.'

'In a manner of speaking,' she said. 'More specifically, I work for the foundation. I only see them occasionally at the offices, but I have no illusions. All the directives are handed down directly by them. I'm a good little corporate drone, or was, anyway. They hire straight from the Ivy Leagues mostly, though they'll pull talent where they find it. Certain kinds of minds, good at synthesizing data from a wide range of sources. It's a specialized talent, but I'm better at it than even they know. Better than they ever expected, and that's what has led us to this place. I was a little too good at my job.'

'So I take you've quit?'

'You don't quit,' she smiled. 'No one who works for the foundation ever quits. You run,' she said. 'You close out your bank accounts, and you run, and then they catch you. That's how this goes. How it always goes.'

'So there have been others.'

She nodded. 'Just a few that I've found evidence of over the years. They demand loyalty, but if they can't get that, they'll settle for silence. The permanent kind.'

'If it always goes that way, then why run at all? Why not stay and play the good corporate drone?'

'Because I learned something the others didn't. I learned who they really are.' She stopped in the trail and looked at me. 'The foundation is where I first saw your name.'

'Because of the experiment.'

She shook her head. 'It goes back further.' She turned away from me and continued walking. 'I was a part of the foundation's inquiry and evaluation team, running the groundwork for the Discovery Prize, and there was a lot of research that we watched. A complex weighting system, trying to evaluate whose work deserved special attention. There are always hundreds of projects on the list. Thousands of names. I thought at first that we were trying to find those who were worthy, but over time I realized something different.'

'And what was that?'

'The foundation's stated goals were a lie. We weren't trying to reward achievement. We were trying to predict it.'

'Predict it?'

'Yes.'

'For what purpose?'

She didn't answer. Instead, she turned her face toward the trail and changed the subject. 'When Brighton talked to you at his penthouse, what did he speak about?'

'A lot of what he said didn't make sense,' I said.

'Try me.'

'He talked about waves. The anthropic principle. Gabriel's horn.'

'Ah, the horn,' she said. 'He does have a penchant for the classical. Was there anything else?'

I tried to recall. The elevator flashed to mind. The feel of the metal on my face. I shook it off. 'Something called the aberis or abrex.'

'The eberaxi.'

'Yeah. That was the word.'

'So then it exists after all. What did he say about it?'

And here it was. The gamble. The point where I would pay off or go bust. I saw it in her eyes, the way she waited for the answer. I stopped in my tracks. Vickers took two more steps before she realized that she was walking alone.

She turned and looked at me. There is a moment in any negotiation when you have to draw a line in the sand. This was mine. Vickers was smart enough to see that. Negotiation is about give-and-take. It was my turn to ask questions. Her face was passive, waiting for me to speak.

'Why does Brighton want me dead?' I asked. 'Why did he kill my friend?'

Her face didn't change, but her eyes grew weary – the eyes of a defeated general. 'The world has its secrets,' she said. 'And those who want them kept. Your box tells a story that shouldn't have been told.'

I thought of Satvik. Minimizing it. Digitizing it. Turning it into a product. I thought of him wrapped up in a tarp.

'No,' I said. 'There's more than that. The paper is already published. Brighton talked about the ones who can't collapse the wave. He called them the fated.'

'A name as good as any.'

'What did he mean?'

'You're the physicist,' she said. 'What do you think he meant?'

'I don't know.'

'Then it's because you're looking at it backward. *They're* not the mystery, after all.'

It was something in her expression. The way she looked at me, as if I had only to consider the obvious. 'You mean, *we're* the mystery.'

She smiled. 'Of course.'

It was always there, that incongruity. Free will in a determinant universe. Because the math was dead serious. It was only in us that it failed. The mystery wasn't those who *couldn't* collapse the waves. The mystery was those who could.

'Consciousness itself,' she said. 'That has always been the mystery, hasn't it?'

'And what about the fated? Who are they?'

'Think of them as the connective tissue of the world,' she said. 'They work and raise families. They vote in countries that vote and riot in places that riot. They are behind coups or lose their heads to coups or swing close elections. They are a silent minority, functioning within a complex set of parameters. They stabilize the social order, so that societies can grow and flourish.'

'I don't understand.'

'The anthropic principle requires the universe be just so to produce life, but let's extend that further. Must it not be just so to produce culture? Certain roles all in proportion. The fated help guide things just so.'

'They have intent, you mean.'

She shook her head. 'No, they can't intend anything. Their behavior is prefigured, they can only do.'

'Toward what end?'

'Their influence aids civilization. Consider them the grease that keeps the wheels of societies turning. Without the grease, metal grinds against metal. The apparatus seizes. Melts down. The great engine stops turning. But the fated don't invent anything. They can't create. For that, people like you are required.'

'Required by who?'

She blinked. 'By the world, of course. That first time you met Brighton, you ate a meal with him.'

It took me a moment. My own gears ground against themselves. 'Dinner, yes.'

She turned slowly and started walking again. I realized that she expected me to follow, so I kept close behind on her right. Her shoes made small imprints in the soft soil. She glanced toward me. 'What must that have been like to sit across a table like that? I never ate with the man. We've spoken only about business. Even before I learned what he was, I sensed there was something terrible in him. Philosophers write that evil exists so that good might reveal itself.' She looked at me. 'Do you think that's true?'

'I wouldn't know.'

'It's all written down, if you know where to look. Little hints in the documentation, and then it all suddenly makes sense. Always there are different sides. Pick any religion, and you'll find warriors in the oldest stories. The names don't matter. I was never a believer, so imagine my surprise when I learned that all the old stories are true.'

Nothing would surprise me, I realized. Not anymore. 'And Brighton is one of these warriors? Is that what you're saying?'

'Yes.' Her green eyes were flat and expressionless. 'One of the oldest.'

'What does he want?'

'What their kind have always wanted. To halt advancement. To impede progression. To delay the advent of post-Malthusian growth. They sow chaos. They are an enemy of the world. Their goal, quite simply, is to stop us from achieving the next level of societal development.'

It sounded insane. The kind of paranoid delusion made for little white rooms.

'The opposite of the fated, you mean?'

She waved that off. 'No. The fated are just a tool of the world and, like any tool, can be broken. Mere pawns in the game. No, Brighton and his kind are the opposite of what *you* are – the ones who push things forward. They're the ones who hold things back. They're enemies of civilization itself.'

'You said, "his kind". Mercy used those words, too.'

She looked at me closely. 'They've used different names in different languages.'

'And you? How do you name them?'

Her face was solemn. 'The ones who've seen them in action all use the same name. We call them the flicker men.'

I stared at her. A name I'd heard before. A name from a letter.

'Do you know how crazy this sounds?'

'Even after everything you've seen?'

'But why? None of this makes sense. These flicker men . . . even if they are what you say, what possible motives could they have?'

'You doubt me. That's good. It's the scientist in you, demanding evidence.' At that moment, we came to a crossroads in the trail and a fresh tread pattern in the mud. This trail was the way in and out of the facility. Thirty years ago, this was probably a road, with a neat, white dotted line. Now it was layered over with dirt and grass – the asphalt broken up and buried. She led me down the track to the right. 'Tell me what you know about Brighton,' she said.

I followed behind her. 'He's rich,' I answered. 'He's insane. He – '

She interrupted me. 'Runs an awards organization that tracks advancements in the field of mathematics and physics.'

'The foundation,' I said. 'Yeah.'

'A cover,' she said. 'By controlling such an organization, he gains early access to research. It gives him a foothold on new discoveries. After that, there are several options. There's the carrot, so subtle you'd never see it – luring researchers into high-salary, dead-end positions. A carefully cultivated career path that makes rich, incompetent administrators of brilliant bench scientists. If that doesn't work – and it often doesn't – there's the stick. They choke off funding. Sometimes they purchase new technologies outright, only to shut them down. And then there's patent trolling – legal sleight of hand that makes war zones of courtrooms, while wasted careers and technologies pile up like cordwood.'

I thought of Stuart's corporation. *The funding dried up.*

'They are an enemy of civilization,' she continued. 'Always working at cross-purposes to the larger good. There's a wide range of tactics they employ, and if those all fail, there's always the final tactic. The one they save for a last resort.'

'And what's that?' I asked. Though I knew the answer before she spoke it.

'Researchers go missing,' she said. 'Brighton is careful and selective. Sometimes it looks like an accident. And usually it happens *before* the research goes public.'

'But why Satvik and I? We've already published. Even if what you say is true, it's too late. Our work is out there.'

'It's not just the work you've done already,' she said. 'It's also the work you might do in the future. Brighton is afraid of something you're working on.'

'That's crazy. I'm not working on anything.'

'Your name was on a list *before* your work at Hansen. It must be some research you've started. Something you were on the cusp of.'

'You worked for them; you don't know what it is?'

'I didn't have access to all the files. There were other analysts watching other names. Meetings and directives that I wasn't privy to. All I know is that he thinks you were on the edge of something big. Some discovery that could advance things. That's why you have to die.'

My head was spinning. It was all too much. Too crazy. 'You're talking about a secret conspiracy to kill scientists?' I said. 'They can't just make us disappear. There will be questions. We have laws and investigators and reporters.'

She shook her head again. 'You have no idea how powerful he is. His money and influence are only the beginning.'

'I'm a witness to a murder. I saw Satvik killed. They shot him in the head right in front of me. I'd testify – '

'If you went public with this, you'd be dead by morning.'

I tried to read her face, searching for the truth. Was it just a threat to keep me cooperative? Or did she really believe it? I thought of Robbins behind his security doors. *You aren't the only one who's lost people.* Whatever Robbins knew, he hadn't gone to law enforcement. Maybe there was a reason for that.

You run, and then they catch you.

'You seek evidence,' she said and pulled something else out of her jacket. A newspaper, I realized, folded open to the middle. She handed it to me. 'Today's issue,' she said. 'That's why I wasn't here when you arrived yesterday. I knew you'd want proof.'

It was an article halfway down the page. I read the heading: 'Man Dies in Car Accident.' I saw Satvik's name. My heart sank as I scanned the paragraph. There was no mention of a shooting. No mention of the other dead men. No mention of foul play at all. The newspaper said he died from blunt trauma.

'But he was shot,' I said. 'I saw it.'

'Not according to the paper.'

Twenty yards ahead, we came to the final building. A large warehouse of cinder block and steel. I saw her car parked against the wall. A gray sedan like a million other gray sedans. A vehicle that would get lost in the crowd.

She turned her face into the sun, her visage so hard and sharp that it looked chipped from stone. 'Come,' she said and motioned me through a gap in the wall. If the old structure had ever had a door, that was long ago.

She led me down a narrow corridor. It took my eyes a moment to adjust to the dark interior, but I followed her down a dim hall.

She glanced at me as we walked, and her face was impossible to read in the shadows. 'The eberaxi, too, has gone by different names,' she said. 'Eberrin. Eberex. Axierra.' She turned away as she continued walking. 'And another name. Errant axis. A thing named for its own result.' She approached a doorway. 'Come.'

Her words sparked a memory. 'Brighton talked about the world's axis.'

'What did he say?' she asked.

'That the world had more than you can see.'

We stepped into an open room, and it took me a moment to make sense of it. 'Yes,' she said. 'He's right. And here we trace one of them.' Against the wall were tables and a workstation. Reams of paper and charts. If this place had once been a warehouse, it was now something else.

Sudden movement caught my eye. Quick-gray, near the floor.

My eyes tracked motion in the shadows – a change of direction, too regular to be an animal. More like a machine. And then I understood. Suspended in the center of the room, a huge weight swung from the end of a long wire.

'Welcome to the pendulum room,' she said.

37

The weight swung from the end of its tether thirty feet long. A ball of iron dangling from a single thin wire.

'It's big,' I said. The first words that came to mind. So big that the arc of movement seemed to skim along the ground in a straight line before rising.

'The wire needs to be thirty feet for it to work well,' Vickers said. 'Though it can be shorter if you correct for air flow. There's no correction for air flow here, though, so we went big. The weight is almost ten pounds.'

'I take it that it's not just a pendulum.'

'That's the beauty. It is. And any pendulum on Earth could do what this one does.'

'Which is what, exactly?'

'Describe an arc through three-dimensional space.' She walked farther into the room. 'And while it swings, it maps out the procession of the Earth. These pins here mark out the movement.'

She pointed at the neatly swept concrete floor, and I could see the simple nails standing on their heads, forming the outline of a large circle, like the teeth of some tremendous bear-trap mechanism hidden in the floor. Stonehenge if Stonehenge was nails. I stepped closer and saw that a dozen of the nails had been knocked down, presumably by movement of the pendulum. Six on one side of the circle, and six on the other.

'So it shifts over time.'

She shook her head. 'You're looking at it wrong. The pendulum stays true, like a navigator's compass. It's not the pendulum moving around the room; it's the other way around, the whole Earth moving beneath the pendulum – describing an arc within the spiral arm of the Milky Way; just as the spiral arm is moving, too, in relation to . . . what, exactly? Call it the larger interstellar background. Or maybe the fabric of space-time if you believe such a thing exists. Have you ever wondered if there are hidden ley lines in the universe? Some location against which you can measure all other points?'

'No such location exists.'

She gestured toward the iron bolus as it swung past, a gray blur. A *whoosh*, and a rush of air. 'You think a deterministic universe is a paradox, try to explain a universe where this pendulum somehow knows how the universe is aligned. Einstein bemoaned spooky action, yet here it is, right in front of us.' She gestured to the pendulum. 'The truth is, nobody has the slightest idea why this happens.'

'Brighton spoke of waves,' I said. 'This implies some directionality.'

She nodded and walked to the workstation. A table and charts. 'Waves, yes, but of what medium? It's easy to talk of waves, but when we look at matter, what are we looking for exactly? There is a reason that when physicists talk in unguarded moments, they eventually speak of the universe as a kind of information.'

From atop a stack of paper charts, she picked up a book. Heavy and large. She tossed it to me.

I caught it. Saw the bookmark and opened the book to the marked page.

It wasn't what I expected. 'Renaissance art?'

On the page was an image of the angel Gabriel, blowing his trumpet, all the angels of heaven lined up behind him, forming a ring that seemed to disappear into oblivion. There was something fractal and beautiful in the circle of wings – like a cryptic mandala hidden in the pattern.

'Gabriel's horn,' she said. 'To be blown on judgment day, when all will answer for their sins.' She turned to look through the books again. 'I've always liked that image. The horn and the angels. But there is another.'

She picked a second book up from the table. A dog-eared volume. This one on mathematics. She lay the book on the table before me and leafed through the pages.

'This, too, is Gabriel's horn,' she said. 'A paradox.'

I moved closer and looked over her shoulder. I studied the image on the page. The graph of *f*: *x* as a function of 1/*x*.

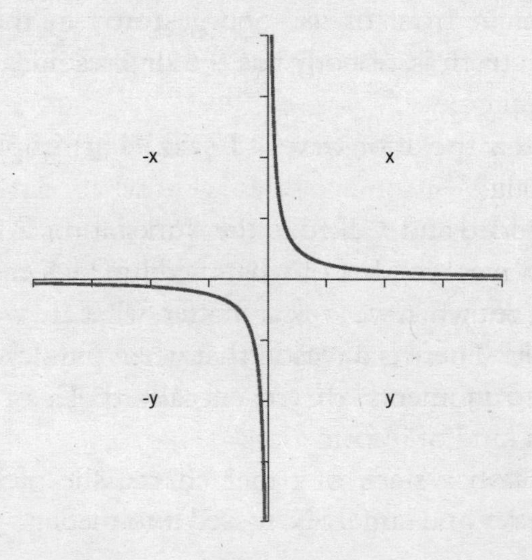

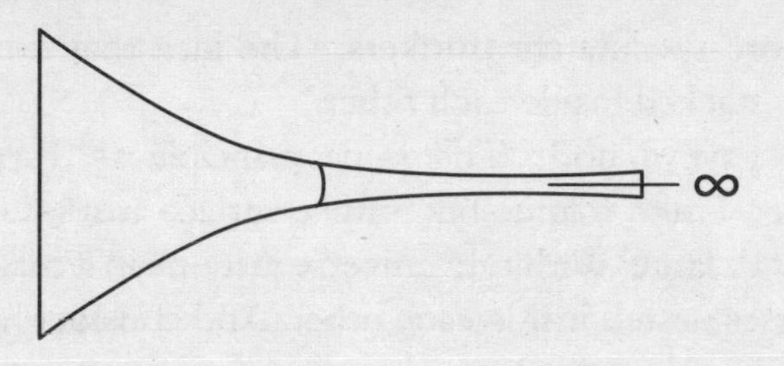

'The reciprocal of *x*, spun around its axis,' Vickers said. 'An object that is bigger on the inside than the outside.'

'A mathematical monster,' I said. I knew the figure well. 'The graph has no end. Gabriel's bottomless horn. It's also called Torricelli's trumpet,' I said. 'Finite volume but infinite surface area.'

'It's a metaphor for the universe. A thing Evangelista Torricelli could never have guessed when he described this figure in the 1600s.'

'A metaphor how?'

'The universe isn't a sphere; it's a funnel. Though even that isn't quite right, is it? A metaphor for a metaphor that doesn't quite track.'

I stared at her. It was like listening to string theory. Not even wrong, just somebody's idea of what could be. 'Just words,' I said, more sharply than I meant to. It reminded me of my mother's stories – things that had no intersection with reality.

'Words,' she agreed. 'And data. Here's a different metaphor if you'd prefer. Have you ever heard of a Matryoshka universe?'

'The Russian dolls, you mean.' It was a cosmological theory kicked around for the past few decades by some of the more speculative thinkers. 'The idea that universes can be stacked inside each other.'

She gave a nod. 'The same principle as Torricelli's trumpet. Finite volume but infinite surface area – Gabriel's horn writ large. With our universe just one in a cascade of universes nested inside each other. And consider humanity's unique perspective.'

'Meaning what?'

'What is humanity's niche in all this? Why are humans different? It is our ability to observe and to reflect what we observe. It is our ability to recapitulate the world around us. First in paintings and books, and now using technologies, the reproductions growing ever more sophisticated.'

I thought of the cave paintings that Brighton mentioned.

'It is an impulse in our nature,' she continued. 'First we see, and then we reflect. Imagine a painting of a bicycle; then imagine the bicycle cast as a sculpture. Finally imagine a sculpture so perfect in every detail that it is indistinguishable from what it reflects. Imagine that you might ride upon this perfect sculpture. Is it not, in fact, just another bicycle? As civilization advances, and we improve our ability to transcribe the universe, at what point does the effigy *become* what it is representing? And what if inside this vastly complex counterpart, a civilization arose which itself spawned its *own* counterpart?'

'Counterpart?' I said. 'You're talking about constructed realities.'

'All realities are constructed in one way or the other, are they not? Either through the work of some will or rising as an emergent property from a system's own underlying laws. There's an Oxford scholar, Nick Bostrom, who calculated the odds that we're in such a nested system.'

She pulled the bookmark from the book and unfolded it – a ragged sheet of paper on which a series of numbers and letters had been scrawled. She spread the paper flat on the table. 'His formula,' she said, pointing to the last line:

$$f_{sim} = \frac{fpNH}{(fpNH)+H}$$

'There could be an infinite number of universes in such a cascade. Existence is not cyclical but seriesmatic.'

I shook my head. I'd seen the formula before. A fascinating exercise in deduction, but like so many theoretical cosmologies, untestable. 'There's no evidence,' I said. 'This is all just speculative.'

'On its surface perhaps, but there is a certain mathematical inexorability to the idea, is there not? If secondary or tertiary realities are possible, then why would those living *inside* those analogues not unleash analogues as well? And then the ones inside *those* analogues. There is no upper bound to the number of iterations, so what are the odds we're living in the prime universe? How many worlds might live upstream from us in worlds stacked upon worlds?'

I shook my head. *Finite volume but infinite surface area.*

She approached from the other side of the table. 'The math is fairly clear: there could be a nearly infinite cascade of universes in such a system, but only one prime world. So either subsequent realities are impossible, or, by the law of averages, we're likely already in one of them.'

I stared at her.

'And if we are in the cascade,' she continued, 'then we know which universe we must be.'

'How?'

'One very special universe,' she said. 'Because we're not yet advanced enough to unfurl our own realities.'

I was about to speak but stopped. I saw it then. Saw where she was leading me.

She seemed to study my face. 'In all of the limitless universes that could exist in such a cascade, ours could be only – '

'The terminus,' I said cutting her off. 'The last universe.' The only one that hadn't yet spawned successors.

She nodded. 'The edge of the spear.'

I thought of the microscope, falling down into the image. *There is no bottom to see.*

I turned and watched the pendulum, considering her words. 'So you're saying this is all some kind of artificial construction?'

'No, not all. You're not even asking the right question. Isn't it obvious now?'

'Nothing is obvious,' I said.

'Even after everything, you're still blind to it.' She shook her head. 'The universe is an object – a collection of waves, just as all matter is a collection of waves. You know this already from your understanding of physics.'

'So?'

'So where does that take you?'

'I . . .' My jaw clenched. I didn't see what she was getting at.

'The universe is just the medium through which the waves propagate. We're not in some kind of simulator.' She shook her head. 'We *are* the simulator.'

I stared at her, trying to comprehend.

'We are creators.' She studied my face. 'Consciousness,' she said. 'That is the magic.'

I opened my mouth to speak, but nothing came out.

'This seething nest of waves is just pattern. The ability to collapse that pattern is what consciousness is. The soul. Whatever you want to call it. Each wave an action potential, which we translate into physical existence by force of experience.'

'You're saying that the universe is an object – a wave medium.'

'Yes.'

'And we construct existence from the pattern of those waves.'

'Yes.'

'Then who made the pattern?'

She smiled again. 'You're assuming it had to be made. Maybe each universe in the cascade is not created but discovered. An emergent property that must be unlocked.'

'And what about the fated?' I asked. 'If they don't collapse the waves, then what do they see when they look around themselves?'

'You're asking if the fated see the world as it really is.'

'Do they?'

'They don't see the world at all. They *are* the world. Or an aspect of it, possessing no part that isn't the world.

They see nothing because there is nothing inside them from which a vantage can be obtained.'

I felt the need to sit.

'They are bound by what they are when they were created. The good sheep of the world, there to keep the balance.'

'What balance?'

'Imagine a world where everyone was like you. Or me. Or like any one of us. Would it function? Would civilization exist? Societies take a balance, easily upset. We are unpredictable by nature, and the fated are an answer to that. They are whatever the world needs them to be.'

'You sound like him,' I said. 'Brighton talked about the world as if it were a thing with needs.'

'Isn't it?'

I ignored the question. 'And if it didn't need them? If the world didn't need the fated, what would they do?'

She shrugged. 'Then they'd probably cease to exist at all.'

I was silent for a long time, taking it in. Letting myself . . . if not believe it, then at least become familiar with it. 'There is a boy who stays with Brighton. He didn't collapse the wave.'

'The fated are the good sheep, mostly, as I said, but they can be turned. If you start young, their predispositions toward suggestibility can be hijacked, trained against the common good. They lack consciences. They lack everything. Imagine a sheep raised on meat. That's our boy there. As Brighton's guards all were boys once.'

'So that's where he gets them.'

She nodded. 'Yes.'

'If those who can't collapse the wave are called the fated, then who are we? What name do you give us?'

'We are the lost,' she said. 'As we are in all the old stories. Awaiting our redemption or our judgment. It's not just space that dilates between worlds, but time as well. As one world lives inside another, a single moment can live inside a thousand years.'

'And these flicker men, I still don't see where they fit. Who are they in all this?'

Here she paused. She looked toward the pendulum, watching it swing. 'They come from higher in the cascade. Not of this world, nor the next, but higher.'

I stared at her. 'And why did they come?'

'Something happened far upstream from us. Something terrible. The bright ones came long ago. And others who fought the bright ones.'

'Others,' I said.

'What one side sought to build, the other side sought to destroy. We were their battleground.'

'What happened?'

'They killed each other. The builders lost, their battles recorded in hieroglyphics. The Indus River valley. Teotihuacán. Peru. Other places, too. The boldest of them died first – then the rest, one after another; their struggles reflected in the rise and fall of civilizations. The two sides annihilated each other until only a few of the old ones remained. The most careful. The most cunning. The ones who could most easily hide.'

'Ones like Brighton, you mean.'

She nodded. 'One of the last.'

'And what of the others?'

'Gone. Dead.'

'Do you understand how impossible this sounds?'

'What is impossible on the time scale of a universe? Or a thousand thousand universes?'

'So if all that is true, and you learned this working for Brighton, then why help me? Why step in front of that?'

'Philosophers may think that evil exists so good may reveal itself, but I think sometimes evil can sneak up on you, too, so that you don't even realize that you are a part of it. And then when you do realize, it's too late, and so you continue on, doing evil because you are scared or because you must, and in this way it is possible to betray your whole life, your whole existence, one decision at a time. I've been a Judas. Scientists have died because of me. The best and the brightest. I decided not one more. I tried to save Satvik, and I failed. Maybe you have a chance.'

She stopped and looked up at the pendulum, and the gray mass of iron swung past in a *whoosh* of air.

'A little more than a year ago, this pendulum shifted,' she said. 'The pins are supposed to drop on a regular schedule. Steady as any clock. But last year, the pendulum left a pin standing. A small detail. Hardly noticeable unless somebody was watching.' She lowered into a crouch near the ring of pins. 'The balance has shifted. Something has changed.'

'What does that mean?'

The pendulum swung past Vickers again, going in the other direction. It disappeared into the shadows.

She turned to look at me. 'It means time is against us now.'

38

Vickers led me back to the encampment. It was early afternoon and the camp was a bustle of activity. The fire was nearly out. Sleeping bags packed away. I had the sense that there was a procedure being followed – like practiced soldiers breaking down their bivouac. Mercy paused when she saw me, relief washing across her face. I realized that she hadn't been sure I was coming back. I wondered if that happened much. Did people often go for walks with Vickers and not return?

Vickers spoke to Hennig in hushed tones near the trailer. A few minutes later, they climbed in the panel van and left.

Mercy and I fed the fire. The flames crackled. 'So it looks like you're staying,' she said.

'What makes you say that?'

'You're still alive.'

Mercy tossed the last of our wood on the pile, and over the next minutes the fire grew. I watched her face, but she never looked at me. Eyes on the flickering heat.

When the others still hadn't returned an hour later, I spoke. 'Where did they go?'

'They'll be back,' she said. Which wasn't really an answer.

While I watched the burning embers, I considered what Vickers had said, trying to wrap my head around it.

Nested universes. Infinite surface area. The flicker men from somewhere higher. Their souls burning their way down through layers of reality like hot stones through ice.

Outside the wind blew, and I heard branches scratching on the sides of the corrugated building. It was full dark when the fire started dying again, so I followed Mercy out for more wood. We were only gone twenty minutes, but when we returned, the panel van was back, parked near the wall, its engine ticking like it had been driven hard. Hennig and Vickers were nowhere to be seen. Off somewhere deeper in the ruins.

Mercy and I nursed the fire back to life. Half an hour later, there was a scream of pain in the distance. A man's voice crying out. It seemed to hang on the night air, fading slowly.

Mercy didn't react. Didn't even look up from the fire. Like she'd known it was coming.

'What was that?' I asked.

'You'll see soon enough,' she said.

Another hour passed before the others returned. They entered the encampment without a word, Hennig's shirt bearing new spatters of red. I didn't ask where they'd been. We ate our dinners from cans, the clink of forks on tin. No one spoke. Just the mesmerizing flicker of the fire, until sometime later even that seemed to fade as the flames sank to a dull glow in the shadow.

I slept by the warm coals, and this time my arms were blessedly free of tape. They trusted me not to bash their heads in while they slept.

In the morning a boot woke me, a firm shove against

my shoulder. My eyes unpeeled to Hennig looking down. 'Get up,' he said.

Mercy and Vickers were nowhere to be seen. I was apparently last to wake.

'This way,' he said.

He led me back through the hole in the wall through which they had come the previous night. A sharp right turn, and I followed him through a doorway and down a short flight of stairs into a kind of cellar.

Here Mercy and Vickers stood, waiting – Vickers, in her business casual suit, seeming out of place.

I stepped closer to Mercy, her back to me. 'What is this?' I whispered.

Mercy gave no answer, but Vickers had overheard me. 'A quiet room,' she said. 'Come.'

I followed them farther in. The basement was dank but well lit; a lantern hung from exposed conduits. In the center of the room was a man tied to a chair. Blood crusted the floor around him in a dry smear. *Not quiet enough*, I thought, remembering the scream I'd heard the night before.

The man was dead. His face battered.

I had a sudden flash of myself in a chair much like this one – Hennig's fist smashing into my head. A bad way to die.

Vickers looked at me as if expecting a reaction.

'Who is it?' I said.

'You don't recognize him?'

I tilted my head, looking closer. My blood ran cold. 'I've seen him,' I said. One of the men from Brighton's penthouse.

'A member of their security team,' Vickers said. 'Well, ex-member now.'

It was the guard who had stayed behind. The guard from the kitchen. His sport jacket now caked with dried blood. I took a step backward, and my feet stuck to the floor. The tacky pool was six feet wide.

Vickers walked around the body. 'He had a few internal injuries when we picked him up. Then a few external ones. Before he died, he gave us information.'

I looked at the body and wondered what methods of persuasion had been used. No obvious signs of torture beyond the battered face. No lumpy kneecaps. Just a face turned to hamburger.

'What information?' I felt sick. I thought of Satvik, wrapped in the tarp. I thought of him in the elevator – his last few moments of life, when he thought he was going to see his family again. I looked at the body in front of me now, and I couldn't feel pity. I couldn't feel anything.

'About the eberaxi,' Vickers said. 'Brighton's done an admirable job of keeping the information hidden, but there's always a weakness. A security detail hears things, sees things. It's hard to keep secrets from those whose job it is to protect you.'

'Did you learn that while working there?'

'Among other things,' she said.

'What is this eberaxi?'

'We don't know for sure,' Vickers said. 'A weapon perhaps.'

'Like a bomb?'

'Perhaps. Or something more subtle. The aberrant axis. A thing mentioned in their oldest archives. A thing they've been watching for. Waiting for. The change in the pendulum was supposed to be a sign. All we know is that it is important to them.'

'What does it look like?'

She was silent, looking at me.

'You don't know that either,' I said. 'It sounds like you didn't learn much.'

She gestured to the dead man. 'We learned that you're a part of it.'

'I'm not part of anything.'

'It would seem Brighton disagrees. Which is why he was so angry that you'd gotten away.'

Heavy boots clomped their way from the shadows, and Hennig stepped near Vickers. He seemed to take up all the empty space.

Vickers turned toward me. 'And we have you to thank for this information.' She turned to look at me. 'Without you, we never would have been able to catch this one. He was out looking for you. We caught him near your motel.'

39

Mercy came to me later that evening, bearing two cups of coffee. One for her, one for me.

The sound of Vickers and Hennig drifted in from around the corner. Their voices rose and then grew quiet. A low murmur.

The darkness of the camp was beaten back by the dying fire. I sat wrapped in a blanket, leaning against the wall of the trailer.

Mercy crossed through a slant of dim starlight that angled through a hole in the roof.

Other than her name, I still didn't know anything about her.

Hennig, too, was a mystery. Perhaps he was a pirate, truly, with long experience in kidnap and robbery. Mayhem off the Madagascar coast. Perhaps he had sent a dozen yachts to the bottom of the sea.

And Mercy. A name that was more than a name.

Mercy held the mug out to me. 'Careful, it's hot. Fresh brewed over the fire.'

'I didn't know you could brew coffee over a flame.' I reached out to take the offered cup.

'The word *brew* is perhaps a bit generous,' she said. 'Now my grandmother was dangerous with her coffee. I'm not saying her hands shook, but she never had more than half a cup by the time she crossed the kitchen. I learned not to walk beneath her. I hope you like creamer and sugar.'

'I do. Where are the others?'

She shrugged. 'Walking the grounds. Making plans.'

She stood next to me.

I thought of asking her what plans, but before I could, she said, 'I don't think any of it will matter.'

'Why not?'

'Because the plans will fail,' she said. 'Now drink.' She watched me sip. 'How is your coffee?'

I pulled the warm cup away from my lips. 'It's good.'

'You sound surprised.'

'I am.'

'It's the cheap shit – boiling water, crushed grounds. It's only technically coffee. Vickers always brings fresh supplies from town, so we'll have good creamer for a day or two before it goes bad. The creamer is what makes it drinkable. Good Karma, hazelnut. That's the name. A ridiculous indulgence I picked up from a boyfriend in college. His name I can barely remember, but this damn coffee? Etched in my heart. Now, wherever I go, I have to seek it out. It would make tar taste good, I think. Usually I don't drink it this late, though, since the caffeine keeps me up.'

'Well, don't risk insomnia for my sake.' I tried to picture her in a normal life, going to college, dumping boyfriends. The image wouldn't come. Her pink, shattered hand clutched at her ceramic cup.

'No, it's fine. Tonight I'm in no hurry to sleep. Puts off the bad dreams.'

I looked at her fingers wrapped around the mug. Raw,

pink flesh. Six months healed, maybe longer. I wondered how it had happened. Nothing about the injury looked clean. No straight edges. Just missing bits of flesh, as if a firecracker had gone off in her hand.

'So you think their plans will fail?'

'I think we're going to die. Every single one of us.' She sat down next to me, legs stretched out in front of her, pointing at the fire. 'Like this world is gonna die. Like all worlds die. Over a long enough timetable, nothing escapes entropy.'

'But that's the key, isn't it? The timetable.'

She didn't respond. Instead we sat silently for a while, and I waited for her to say more. She didn't. She sipped the coffee and watched the fire.

'How did you get pulled into this? What happened?'

'*They* happened.' She stood and walked a few steps into the darkness. She bent and pulled something large from the shadows, and when she returned to the glow of the dying fire, I saw it was a tattered cardboard box. A scrap hoarded from the yard.

'The flicker men,' I said.

She nodded and tossed the cardboard box on the fire. At first, all light died from the world – snuffed out, the blackness complete. Then a yellow flare bloomed at the cardboard's lower bottom corner as the fire caught, growing larger by the second until the whole box was aflame. She warmed her hands. Now the fire lit up the room, and I could see rust peeling off the rafters overhead and the dark rectangles on the walls where windows had once been, and I could see her face. Pale and angular.

'The first time I saw them . . . later, I couldn't even remember how it all happened. Still can't. There are gaps.'

'Gaps?'

'Things I can't remember.'

'I don't understand.'

'She didn't even tell you, did she?'

'Tell me what?'

'What they're really like. The reason we call them the flicker men.' She tossed a twig into the fire. 'I don't think your mind can even process it, what happens when things go bad. You fill it in later yourself. For a long time, I thought I was going crazy, but if you're crazy long enough, it just begins to feel normal. Maybe you know a little about that.'

'Maybe a little.' I wondered then how much she knew about me. Or maybe she just saw it in my eyes.

'I mean, what kind of thing does that to you?' she asked. 'What is so awful that you can't even see it, and you have to fill it in?'

'I don't know.'

'You can sometimes choose not to see them at all if you work at it. And I think that's how most people see them. Or don't see them. Most people just see them in the way that they can handle. In the way that they want to see them.'

'What about you?'

'It's not always a choice.'

I thought of my mother. Belief like a superpower.

'Their pets are even worse.'

'Pets?'

'Hunters,' she said. 'You don't ever want to see those. Some things are more than they seem.'

'What about me?'

'Don't feel special. Some people, it's like they get pulled into this just so they can die. I've seen it before.' She was quiet for a moment, but then added, 'Though you do seem to have the knack.'

'What knack?'

'For surviving.'

I took another sip of my coffee. 'Vickers said that she used to work for them. Did you work for them, too?'

She shook her head. 'No. Some of us . . . it draws us in. Pulls us like we were a part of it somehow, even if none of it seems connected. For me, I thought I was just at the right place at the wrong time. But it was more than that.'

'More?'

'Maybe I've got a knack as well.'

There was a sound behind me. I turned my head, and Hennig stood at the doorway, watching us. I wondered how long he had been there. Maybe he'd been there all along. He had a rifle barrel clasped loosely in his right hand, wooden stock resting on the floor. His face looked wooden in the warm glow of the embers. He lifted the rifle and faded back toward the darkness

When he was gone, Mercy whispered, 'Be careful of that one.'

'What do you mean?'

She waited a moment to answer. 'He used to be one of their guards.'

'One of Brighton's guards?' The news shocked me.

Mercy nodded. 'They were done with him. Thought

they'd killed him, but Vickers brought him back from the edge, stashed him away, sewed him up. Now he's her bulldog.'

I stared into the darkness.

'He's loyal to her,' she said. 'Other people, though, he bites sometimes.'

My hand trailed absently across the cement in front of me. I picked up a flat, thin piece of steel from off the floor. Just a piece of scrap. I checked its flex. I folded it in half, corner to corner. I folded it again. Bringing it to a fine point.

40

I woke at dawn.

It was a sound that woke me, a low reverberation at the edge of perception. The sickness already rising in my stomach. Sleep was a fragile thing, easily broken. That's why I heard it first.

I opened my eyes. Mercy was a few yards away, face turned to the shadows. I rolled onto my stomach and slid toward her across the filthy floor. I felt the shiv of folded steel in my pocket.

'Hey.' I shook her arm. 'Where's Vickers?'

Her eyes fluttered open, confusion showing. 'What?' She sat up, rubbing her eyes.

'Where is Vickers?' I repeated.

Across the burned-out ashes of the fire, Hennig pulled himself upright. He'd heard it, too.

The engine sounds grew louder, closer. 'Cars,' Hennig said. 'More than one.'

Color drained from Mercy's face.

'Here?' she said.

'Where the fuck is Vickers?' Hennig snapped.

At that moment, in the distance, Vickers spoke. 'Two vehicles.' She was standing in the shadows near one of the smashed-out windows, looking outside.

For a moment, no one moved. Then Hennig sprang to

his feet and crossed the room. He stood near Vickers, craning his head through the gap in the wall, looking out. When he turned back toward us, his face was pale. 'It's them,' he said. Hennig turned and sprinted for the weapons. 'This is going to be ugly,' he said, his voice a snarl.

Mercy was silent. She only crouched on the filthy floor, trembling like she was freezing, though the room was near seventy degrees.

'What do we do?' I asked.

They ignored me. Vickers crossed the room and pulled a plastic tub out from beneath the table where the guns were kept. The tub was heavy, and it scraped a path in the dust. She bent and pulled the top off it.

'Bug-out bags,' she said. She tossed one to me.

I pulled the pack over my shoulders. It was old army surplus by the look of it. Maybe ten pounds, half-empty. I saw my phone at the bottom of the bin. I grabbed it and stuffed it in my pocket.

'We need to move quick,' she said. 'We stay together. If we can't stay together, we regroup at the other hide.'

Hennig grabbed a pack and opened it, scrambling to fill it with ammo from the table.

'And where is that?' I asked.

'No time,' Vickers snapped.

I snatched the last handgun from the table, expecting them to stop me. Hennig eyed me close, but said nothing. Mercy shouldered her pack while Vickers headed for the hole in the wall. 'Follow me,' she said. She glanced toward me. 'Stay close.'

*

We ran. Single file, keeping low. We moved quietly, keeping our heads down, moving through the building, crossing from room to room.

We came to another hole in the wall, but instead of diving through as before, Vickers stopped. She bent and peered through the hole.

'So what's the plan?' I asked.

'Don't look back,' Vickers said.

'And if they catch us?'

'You don't want that to happen.'

Hennig had his back to the wall, scanning the room behind us while Vickers looked forward through the hole. Her face was a mask of concentration. She crept farther through, looking both ways. She pulled back.

'I don't like the look of this.' She stood. 'Come on.' She crouched low and led us across the building in the other direction.

We passed through another empty room and through a door that funneled us down a long corridor. Metal paneling covered the walls. The dust on the floor was an inch thick. Nobody had walked here in decades.

We came out of the corridor and into another large room – a place that might once have been a factory floor, but which had long since been gutted to serve as another warehouse. We were halfway across the room when we heard it.

Just outside. The thud of a car door. Then barking. Though there was something strange in the sound. The tones deeper than normal. Vickers froze. The rest of us came to a halt behind her.

'Too late,' Hennig whispered.

The barking grew louder.

'Dogs,' I said.

Mercy shook her head. 'Worse than that.'

'The hounds,' Hennig said. He glanced down at my gun. 'You might be tempted to shoot me with that,' he said. His eyes met mine. 'If that's your plan, then I suggest you wait until *after* what's coming.'

I nodded. 'I won't shoot you.'

At that moment, outside, I heard a sound – the clatter of metal, something large running across a fallen section of corrugated siding.

'Come on,' Vickers said. 'This way.'

We followed.

We ran through the building, leaping over a pile of bricks and passing through a man-door into a smaller room filled with pipes and large steel tubs. Hennig stopped, then turned and made a *shhh* sign with his finger and lips. We flattened ourselves to the wall, keeping in the shadows.

From behind us came the sound of heavy feet, then a moment later, a loud crash. It came from the room we'd just left. There were several voices, and then I heard what sounded like the snort of an animal. The heavy in-and-out breathing of something large.

From where I stood, I could see through the doorway into part of the other room. A moment later, light footsteps. Then a soft chuckle and an answering murmur.

'They're here,' Hennig said.

At the far end of the room, a figure stepped into view.

41

As a boy I had played on the old breakwater near where my father moored his vessel. Out on the water, an old rotting log floated in the shallows – immense and barnacled, bound to pilings. To call it a pier was too kind.

From where I sat on the breakwater, ripples crossed the water in bands, except at the edge of the old log. All around the log the ripples were different. Unaligned. There the currents were disturbed and the shine moved differently. It wouldn't have stood out in photographs, but it stood out as you watched, the glints coming quicker – a place that didn't behave like the rest.

For just a split second, that's what the figure looked like as it crossed through the shadows. A man but something else, too. A perturbation. An area of irregularity where the ripples were busier.

He followed our tracks across the filthy floor.

Hennig was the one who broke first.

He shouldered his shotgun and fired, and the figure looked up – those ripples unfolding like runnels of flame – a seething aurora, and the shape was suddenly crossing the room, eating up the distance in long, lunging strides. I froze, unable to move, unable to think, while Hennig bellowed and fired, and Mercy screamed.

'Go!'

I ran.

Blind panic.

Leaping through a hole in the wall, I sprinted across the empty warehouse and then down a hall, running full blast. When I crossed through another hole, coming out the other side into open air again, my foot caught on something – and I sprawled in the dirt, scraping my face on the ground. Pain shot through my broken nose. I breathed and opened my eyes.

The sun cast a harsh shadow across the path. I climbed unsteadily to my feet, as I felt something warm running down my face. I rubbed my nose with the back of my hand and it came away red. Bleeding again.

I headed for the nearest building, entering through a hangar door. Once inside, I aimed for the darkest shadows, hoping to lose myself. *Where was everyone else?* I felt faint. My head was spinning. When I could run no more, I collapsed near a pile of rubble and wedged myself against the wall.

My vision seemed to retreat, like I wasn't getting all the information from my eyes. Like the concussion from the fire. I heard a gunshot. Then another. Screaming in the distance. Through the open hangar door, I watched Hennig cross between buildings. His face was streaming blood. Eyes wild.

The hound caught him. Or what must have been the hound.

Huge, like a pale rottweiler, but even larger, like no dog I'd ever seen – a thing I couldn't understand. But Mercy was right, the mind fills in.

And I could see it different ways. Just a split second. Something like a hyena – spotted and wild – as it tore his arm. Blood sprayed the ground – and then I saw it the other way. Just a huge muscular dog.

I remembered the gun then – the gun I'd picked up from the table. But when I checked my hands, they were empty. I turned, and it wasn't out on the floor next to me either. I remembered the fall. When I'd tripped, I must have dropped it.

Hennig's screams changed – a sound I did not know a man could make. A sound I wish I hadn't heard. Then silence.

I closed my eyes. I listened and waited.

When I finally looked up from my place in the shadows, several minutes had passed. The clearing beyond the hangar doors was empty, save for a small red shape in the grass that did not move.

I climbed to my feet and moved out, keeping to the edges. I saw a hole in the wall ahead and crossed into another room. And then another. The holes made a path through the ruins. Ahead of me, the wall split; I took the corridor on the right. There was a sound ahead, and I froze in place, heart beating wildly. Something was coming. I saw a doorway to my right, so I ducked inside. It was a small room – a foreman's office of some kind, walls stained black. Windows bashed out. A single wooden desk had collapsed itself into the floor. Thirty years ago, it might have rivaled Jeremy's desk, but now it was rotten and broken, the legs knocked off.

As the footsteps approached, I ducked behind the desk, trying to make my body as small as possible. The footsteps grew closer, and I pressed my face to the floor, one eye searching through a split in the back of the desk. A gap in the water-swollen wood where I could see into the other room.

There was movement that my eye couldn't follow. A pair of legs crossed in front of me, the ghost of fabric.

Where was Mercy?

The legs disappeared behind a column momentarily, and I shifted my position for a better look, and then I saw him. A familiar man.

A man I'd had dinner with. A man who spoke of wines and museums. A man who'd had my friend killed.

It's all in the perspective of your blade.

Brighton crossed the room, and I got a good look at him. He wore a dark hunter's jacket, caked black at the sleeves by dust and dirt. His pale gleaming eyes searched the shadows but found no reason to pause. He disappeared around the corner.

When he was gone, I waited for thirty seconds before I stood and crossed the hall in the opposite direction. As I ran, I kept my eyes open for Mercy, hoping to catch a glimpse. Outside the air was fresh and clean. The sky was blue. I felt exposed – visible from a hundred angles.

In the distance, shots rang out again. Somewhere up ahead.

I turned and ran the other way – cutting back through the building. Heart hammering. I ran blindly, wanting to put distance between myself and the sounds. I ran until my lungs burned and my legs cramped.

I nearly tripped over Hennig.

He was a man of halves. Half ear, half body, lying just beyond the hangar door. Looking down at him, I was again acutely aware that I didn't have a gun. I stooped and picked up his shotgun from the mud. The barrel was covered in blood, but it still looked functional. I gripped the weapon with both hands and ran.

I crossed the threshold of another building without stopping or slowing – I simply held the gun vertically as I sprinted through the doorway. Another warehouse. Another empty expanse. I didn't stop until I found myself in a narrow alley between buildings, blue sky overhead. I crouched with my back to the wall. My breath came in gasps. More shots rang out. Hennig was dead, so the sound meant Vickers or Mercy.

I cracked open the chamber of the shotgun, and I saw only a single round.

It crossed my mind that a single bullet could end it all. I pushed the thought away. I willed my heart to slow and tried to calm my breathing. I'd need to think clearly if I was going to get out of this. I waited. Minutes passed while I watched the gap in the alley, and then I heard a rattle in the distance. Feet on corrugated steel – the tread light and quick. I bolted off the wall at a dead run, threading my way between structures.

Two minutes later, I found her. It was Vickers. I saw her hiding against a wall at the edge of the clearing. The sun threw short shadows behind the buildings, so I moved behind a pile of rubble, trying to stay out of sight. The ruins around me looked familiar, and I realized where I was – the place where we'd gathered wood. The fence was a hundred yards across the tall grass, up the hill. All the running, and I was nearly back where I'd started, a hundred yards from the encampment.

Up ahead, something moved along the rutted track.

Vickers still had her back to the wall, crouched low. She was bleeding from the nose. Bleeding from her head. Her eyes moved to scan the buildings, flitting in my direction, and I opened my hand to her – just a slight movement, but she caught it. She started to step out from the wall, and I waved her back.

Brighton was coming.

She stayed.

Brighton moved slowly between the buildings, pale eyes scanning the shadows.

My eyes watered, and I blinked in the angle of the sun as the grasses waved in the wind. Behind Brighton, a second man was coming up the trail. '*Boaz*,' I heard myself whisper.

I realized they would cross right in front of where Vickers was hiding. There was no way she'd be missed.

As the men came closer, Vickers pressed herself tighter to the wall, face expressionless. She couldn't see them from her vantage, but she heard their shoes on the gravel.

Thirty feet away.

I waved her a warning, but she did not see. And anyway, there was no place for her to go.

Twenty feet. I could see Brighton's eyes searching – looking left then right, as he moved up the road.

'*Turn around*,' I whispered to myself. '*Go another way*.'

Ten feet.

'Shit,' I said.

I stepped out from my place behind the rubble and took three steps into the clearing. I raised the shotgun, forcing myself to see the thing I was aiming at – to *really* see – runnels of black light flickering around his body like the wings of a thousand buzzing wasps. I pulled the trigger.

The gun lurched. The sound was deafening.

The slug clipped the edge of Brighton's left arm in a snarl of fabric, and a moment later, a cloud of dust burst from a wall behind him.

He looked down at his own shoulder in surprise. Then he turned toward me and roared – an inhuman sound of rage and pain.

I dropped the empty gun and ran.

I sprinted for the holes.

My only hope was to get ahead and stay ahead. I hit the first hole at full speed, entering the building. When I looked back after ducking through the narrow gap in the wall, Brighton's eyes locked on mine.

I leaped over a pile of rubble and saw a stray piece of rebar jutting from the concrete. I yanked hard; the steel bar came loose. It felt good to have a weapon again. Any weapon. I crossed the room, and when I ducked through the next hole on the far side, I spun around.

I timed my throw carefully.

You hear stories of incredible feats of strength – people lifting cars off victims when their adrenaline is pumping. I flung the bar with all the force in my body, aiming for the narrow hole through which the man would come, and I saw Brighton's eyes go wide as the steel bar approached, saw the shock and pain – rebar striking center of mass – while he tried to twist away, but forward momentum carried him on, and his shoulder clipped the wall hard and he went down.

It was enough, and I was sprinting out of sight and around the bend, then around another bend, and another, losing myself in the maze of hallways. Ducking left, then right, utterly lost, until I came to a large loading bay.

A metal staircase ran upward along the wall, and I didn't hesitate. I took it two stairs at time, surging upward. Here the building was higher, and the staircase took me up by the rafters.

The catwalk shook with every footstep, so I stopped. I turned. Held my breath. I looked down at the main floor and waited, hoping that my pursuer would pass the staircase by. Hoping he would not look up.

Several seconds passed, and then Brighton entered the room below.

There was a moment of silence as he looked out across the empty loading bay. The stillness seemed to confuse him. He scanned the corners of the room. Slowly, he turned his face upward. He smiled.

'There you are,' he said.

I ran along the catwalk to the far door and crossed into another room. Here was a room of pipes and boilers, with huge empty vats and twisted metal railings.

At the far end of the small room was a doorway and another staircase – a way down, and I almost took it. But I knew I'd never outrun him. He'd catch me and kill me if I kept running. Instead, I moved to the shadows. When you have reached the limits of fight or flight, there is another, final option. *Hide.* I wedged myself behind one of the large vats – a huge steel tank that sat in the corner. One foot nudged into a large drainpipe that disappeared between two pieces of equipment.

I waited.

The sound of running. Heavy footfalls entered the room and crossed to the other side.

Keep going. Take the stairs.

At the far side, the footfalls stopped.

Please. I closed my eyes. I cut myself off from myself. I wasn't there.

Seconds passed.

Then the footfalls continued on, going down the stairs, growing more distant.

Finally, I let out my breath, chest still hammering. Brighton had gone.

I waited to hear something. Anything. I wondered if Mercy had made it. I wondered if she'd gotten away.

There was another sound then, soft, from the other direction. I could almost imagine it hadn't happened. I began counting. The sound didn't come again. *Three, four, five, six* . . . After a ten count, I inched forward. I craned my neck, hoping for a better view of the room, but there was nothing. No one.

I inched farther. Dreading the rasp my knees made on the floor.

The room was dim and grimy; I couldn't see much from behind the vat in the corner – the only light diffuse, filtering in through the open doors and down through rust holes in the ceiling.

Twenty-five, twenty-six, twenty-seven . . .

I was still counting. I counted to sixty in my head before I moved, taking comfort in the familiar rhythms. Throwing numbers at the darkness, like when I was a child.

I crawled along the floor on my hands and knees, keeping close to the vat. My hip scraped something – a sound that seemed loud in my ears. When I chanced a look, my heart rose up in my throat.

Although Brighton was gone, a different man stood in the doorway.

A second familiar face.

Boaz's active eyes searched the shadows. 'Come out, come out, wherever you are,' he said.

It was the same voice from that night in the restaurant. A voice like gravel.

I backed slowly around the vat until I couldn't see him anymore. Boaz's shoes crunched across the floor while I pressed as close to the wall as I could go, making myself small. It was only a matter of time, though. I realized that I might not leave this room alive.

'Eric,' his voice came. 'I know you're in here.' The footsteps moved into the middle of the room.

I backed farther into the corner, and that's when I felt something catch my foot. The edge of the drainpipe, jutting from between a vat and a large pump housing. Two feet wide. The radius of a car tire. A *small* car tire, maybe less. In other, less ruinous times, it had been connected to the vat, draining whatever industrial processes were incubated there. But now the vat was out of position, empty and partially disassembled, and the pipe was exposed. I eyed it critically, doing the math. It would be a tight squeeze, but I could fit. I moved quickly and turned, almost going in head first, but the horror of that stopped me. The hellish blackness. Instead, I twisted myself into position and backed in feet first, making as little noise as possible. There was just enough room for me to shimmy inside. The pipe's interior was smooth and coated with muck, and I wondered what substance it had once carried. On second thought, it was probably better that I didn't know.

Boaz's footsteps came again.

Had he heard me?

I dared not move.

The steps came closer, moving around the vat.

'I watched you go up,' he said, 'but you did not come down.'

I saw his legs, clad in slacks. The shoes were leather mountain boots. The legs moved closer, bringing him around the side of the vat and into the corner.

'By process of elimination, that means you are still here.'

He leaned into the corner, hand brushing past the drainpipe, inches from my face.

'Why are you hiding, little mouse? Your friend Stuart did not hide as you do.'

I felt myself go cold inside. *Stuart.* From where I crouched, Boaz was close enough to touch.

'He took his medicine bravely,' he said.

His hand swung past the opening to the pipe again. It was a large hand. Pale. Manicured. The hands of a businessman.

'You should have seen him on that pool table. All that blood.'

The pipe pressed in all around me. *Was he lying?* I felt sickness rise up. It was too much. First Satvik, now

Stuart. I was responsible. Everything I touched, I destroyed. I held my breath again. I reached backward along my own body, feeling for my pocket, feeling for the cold metal.

The pale hand swung past and was gone. The legs stepped away. I could no longer see him.

My heart still hammered.

There were three seconds of total silence. The darkness of the pipe.

Then sudden movement, and Boaz's head loomed into view. 'There you are!'

I stabbed him in the face with my shiv of folded steel.

42

He howled and unfurled from himself – a sound like a thousand wasp wings buzzing at once – my eyes sliding off what I couldn't understand.

I jerked backward, but his outstretched arm caught my hand, yanking me, so I twisted and stabbed with the shiv, and then the weapon was gone. Pulled from my grasp. I jerked backward, deeper into the pipe.

A clawing hand whipped past my face, brushing the hair off my forehead as I pushed myself backward with my elbows. Boaz screamed in rage and followed. He was larger than me but still not too large for the pipe – as I pushed backward as fast as I could, feeling the pipe slide beneath me; and it occurred to me that it would be a terrible way to die – stuck and suffocated around some bend in the pipe that I wouldn't be able to come back from. I tried to turn my head and look behind, but there was barely room to see around my body. Only blackness. Boaz pressed forward, getting his shoulders past the lip, and the light was eclipsed. He struggled and pressed, scrambling forward, his breath a ragged locomotive in the enclosed space. Abrupt silence, then the rasp of movement as he lowered himself onto his stomach – the inside of the pipe lit from behind. There was a momentary silver flicker in his eyes, like the eyes of a cat at night.

We were twenty feet apart.

He smiled. Hands distended – the shadows playing tricks – long fingers like blades. I imagined those fingers sinking into my face, piercing my eyes, opening my throat. Then I saw it wasn't blade fingers but my steel shiv gripped tightly in his hand.

'Got you now, little mouse,' Boaz hissed.

This is what madness felt like. Concentrated down into its perfect diamond-hard essence. A piece of coal with the weight of all existence bearing down on it.

I pressed backward, moving as quickly as I could, trying not to think about how this ended.

Boaz's smile grew wider, and his body rose up, filling the gap – plunging us back into darkness.

I was half crawling, half sliding now, the inside of the pipe tarry and smooth. Time ceased to have meaning in the darkness.

The scrape of flesh on steel. Ten feet. Twenty. My own ragged breathing.

My legs hit something solid, and my heart banged in my chest as I realized what I had come up against. A bend in the pipe.

I kicked my legs out, feeling for a gap. And found it.

I thought the pipe might bend to the right or left, but I wasn't so lucky.

It was a bend going down.

I angled myself as best I could, arching my back as the skin came off my shins, and I felt my hips move past the bend – a moment of panic. A moment when I felt gravity begin to take hold, and I pressed against the sides of the pipe with my forearms, stopping myself. There was no telling how far the pipe went down. It could be a drop of ten feet or a full story or even farther if it connected down into a subterranean line. The thought made my skin crawl. There'd be no coming back up. My arms slipped, and I heard myself gasp as I pressed harder against the steel to hold my position.

The scrabbling sound in front of me went silent. Boaz had stopped moving.

'What's wrong, little mouse?' In the pipe, his voice oddly distorted. A sound like madness. 'Did you come to the end of the line?'

His eyes seemed to flicker in the darkness again. The distant light behind made a dark, shifting silhouette of him.

He was only ten feet away now. He had been gaining on me. Big as he was in the confines of the pipe, he'd still been gaining. He shifted his position, and the light changed, coming over his shoulders. I saw something in his eyes then – a narrowing. As if he suddenly understood.

He surged forward.

In the blackness, I felt his arms reaching.

There was no time to think. I relaxed my shoulders and let myself go. My belly scraped across the bottom as my legs dropped out from under me – and I almost made it. Almost.

An iron-strong hand clamped onto my forearm.

I screamed and twisted, but the grip was too strong, and I felt myself pulled upward. I kicked my legs out, trying to grip the pipe, while the iron fingers sank into my flesh. The other hand came down, armed with the shiv, jabbing at my face – going for my eyes – so I ducked my chin to take the wounds on the top of my head, using my knees to brace myself. I felt the shiv strike bone. Boaz pulled, and I was a difficult thing to get leverage on, to pull upward – a grown man lodged in a pipe – but his strength was too much, and I felt hot blood raining down on my face from where his grip on my arm had split the skin – and it was like being pulled upward into a fan blade, as he slashed at me with the steel, slicing my scalp open, shrieking in rage. I pressed my knees as hard as I could, but the pull only increased, and with a quick yank, I was drawn upward and felt my arm dislocate from its socket.

The bend in the pipe was suddenly under my stomach, as I was pulled up and forward, and I knew this was the end – I was about to be ripped open from the head down in this filthy dark hell, and then the iron hand loosed my arm to grab my shirt, yanking me closer.

I kicked then, at that exact instant, and I pulled back with all my strength, and I felt my button-down shirt come off over my head, while the curve of the pipe slid past my stomach, raking my T-shirt up to my chin. And then I was falling.

43

The fall was three seconds. Maybe less.

There was a sense of distance sliding past my body, my skin coming off against the rush of metal, and then I struck with bone-jarring force.

I hit with my feet, which slid out from under me along the curve of the pipe – while my shoulder flared white agony, and my head banged the steel. Everything went quiet.

When you're trapped in utter darkness, the line between conscious and unconscious can be a matter of degrees.

I wasn't sure how long I was out. Seconds maybe. Or a minute. The first sound I heard was a scrabbling above me. I tried to move, and something popped in my shoulder – the grind of bone on bone as my dislocated shoulder popped back in place. I cried out, and the scrabbling above me stopped.

I heard him breathing. Then scrabbling came again.

I listened carefully, trying not to believe it.

It couldn't be.

He was coming down.

No.

Even muddled as I was, I knew it was insane. In the tight confines of the pipe, there was no way he could have turned around. That meant he was coming down head first. There's no way he'd risk that. Even if he killed me, there'd be no way to climb back up – not backward. And with me dead in the pipe, blocking the way, there'd be no way forward. He would be trapped. As I was now trapped.

The scrabbling sound grew louder.

I had to move quickly. I shimmied myself along on my stomach as my skin burned. I wondered how much I'd lost to abrasion. I used all the strength in my arms, pushing myself along, backing along the pipe, steel sliding past my knees. Time dilated, moments into centuries.

An eternity later, I paused. I wasn't sure at first, so I concentrated. It took two full seconds to convince myself it was true. A glimmer of light. The faintest possible glow. Even the air was different. Less stagnant. I wasn't sure how much farther I had to go, but somewhere beyond my feet, I was sure the pipe was open.

Please, I prayed, *don't let there be a grating.*

I could imagine it. A steel mesh that my feet would strike first. No way out; no way back. The thing that was Boaz still coming down at me headfirst, shiv in his hand. I pushed the thought away. It did no good to think of it.

The pipe clattered louder. Boaz was coming.

A dozen more feet of grimy steel slid past my stomach, as the light grew brighter from over my shoulder, until I could see my own fingers in front of me, caked black with grime and spattered with blood as I pushed myself backward. I saw deep wounds in my arms, but they didn't bear close inspection. There was no point.

Suddenly, the light was brighter, and my right leg kicked out into open space. There was no steel under my right knee, and then my left, and I was sliding out, gripping the pipe, and it did not occur to me until that moment to wonder how high I was. And then I was out and falling. I slammed to the ground, looking up at the pipe. A fall of five feet.

I sucked air, unable to believe I was free. When I stood, the pipe was face-high, a two-foot-wide hole of blackness. My legs cramped, and I collapsed in a heap, tripping over a small length of steel scrap. I looked around, and I was in a partially disassembled part of the building – as if demolition had been halted midproject. Steel pipes of various sizes and shapes were piled on the floor, along with concrete blocks. High above me, the sheet metal had all been partially stripped away, leaving the skeleton and open sky. I'd read once of corporations that stripped the roofs off old buildings to avoid taxation. Perhaps that process had started here, before the whole issue of taxation had become moot.

There came a sound, and the entire structure above me shook. My legs cramped again as the scraping grew louder. Boaz was almost here. I couldn't run. And there was nowhere to hide.

My hand fumbled for the closest thing – a three-foot length of pipe. It had once been attached to the wall; now it was heavy in my grip.

I climbed to my feet.

First a hand emerged – long and red, soaked in blood – clasping at the edge of the pipe. Then the other hand, still gripping the bloody shiv. The top of his long head came next, as he pulled himself forward, birthing himself from the hell of his confinement.

His face, when he turned it toward me, was contorted in rage, coated with filth. His eyes wheeled toward mine.

I had the pipe raised high – a headsman's stance. He tried to react, but I gave him no time. I brought the steel down on the top of his skull with everything I had.

The pipe struck with the sickening sound of breaking bone. I hit him again, and he jerked – body spasming, blood jetting from the strike; I hit him again and then again and again.

I hit him until the length of steel in my hand was soaked with blood.

I hit him until his pulped body was limp and boneless, sliding out of the pipe in a heap. And then I hit it until I could no longer lift my arms, and the world swam in my vision.

I stared down at him. Skull crushed. Neck broken. No trace of whatever else he might have been. No wasp wings. No aurora flicker.

My vision cleared.

I hadn't killed a living thing since fishing with my father. I waited for it to hit. I waited to feel something for killing this man. Nothing came. I dropped the length of steel in the dirt. I realized then that I didn't believe it was a man that I'd killed. It had been something else.

44

I used the holes in the walls, moving silently through the buildings. A particle passing through slits. My lungs burned from all the dust I'd breathed, so I stopped and coughed softly into the crook of my arm, hacking up a thick black film. I pushed onward. How much time had passed? I wasn't sure.

I nearly stepped on Hennig's body again, red mud spreading beneath him. His eyes looked up to heaven, unconvinced. A dozen feet up the road, I found his pack. I kept moving, listening for any sound.

I slid silently through another hole and crossed through a building. Light slanted through gaps in the roof, creating golden pools on the debris-covered floor. I chose my path carefully, avoiding the fallen strips of sheet metal.

It took me a moment to realize where I was.

The lead weight hung motionless from the end of its wire, inches from the floor. The pendulum now still. All the pins knocked over. I approached the weight and looked up toward the rafters where the wire was lost in darkness.

I kept moving.

At the far side of the building near the gap between the bay doors, I stopped and looked out. Here were great hangar doors a dozen feet high, twenty feet wide. They were open in the center – a slit exactly the width of a man.

Beyond the doors was a gravel track, curving off to the left. To the right was an expanse of grass and bush, the fields where we'd gathered wood. Beyond there was the hill, and the fence in the distance.

I moved fast, covering the open ground as quick as I could. Farther out, amid the grass and the brambles, I stumbled over the foundation of an older building that I hadn't known was there. One wall was missing altogether; the others three feet high, no taller than the grass. I put my back to the crumbling brickwork and caught my breath. There came a growl. In the distance, Brighton stood in the gap between buildings. His jacket was filthy.

For a moment, he seemed to flicker in the sun, trying to be two things at once. Behind him, I saw the hound sniffing the air. Its spotted fur bristled across the shoulders like no breed I'd seen before. Its feet seemed to shimmer with a baking heat, my eyes playing tricks again. I'd gotten lucky with Boaz, but there'd be no getting lucky with the hound. If it caught me, it would tear me apart, as it had Hennig.

I stayed low, heading for the fence, hoping I was downwind. When I got to it, I crouched and looked up. A rusted segment of barbed wire drooped harmlessly to the grass. I'd be exposed if I went over the top. Up on this hill, anything that crossed the fence line would stick out like a sore thumb. Along the bottom, the woven wire hugged the ground, buried deep in weeds and soil. There'd be no going under. Not without digging, and I didn't have time.

I stuck my head up to see where Brighton and the hound might be, but they were suddenly nowhere in sight.

They might have moved into one of the buildings, or they could have been crouching in the grass, eyes alert, waiting for movement. They could have been anywhere.

There was no point in delaying. It wasn't going to get better than this.

I tossed my pack over the top of the fence and then started to climb. Rust flakes stuck to my hands as I pulled myself up and over, and I chanced a look back. In the distance, between buildings, I saw a feral head turn as the hyena-thing caught my movement just as I swung my leg over and let myself drop.

I picked up my pack and ran.

The downslope was steep, and I followed the ravine, leaves and twigs cascading down. I forged a path with my body. Half running, half sliding. At the bottom of the ravine was a dry streambed, lined with stones, and I followed it down. I ducked under a log and dropped to a lower level of the stream, where I came to what would have been, in wetter times, a six-foot waterfall but was now only a stony shelf. I lay my stomach on the stone and swung myself over, continuing onward. The streambed had nearly leveled out when I heard the hound at the top of the rise. There was the sound of an impact as something hit the fence. I wondered if the fence held. I wondered if the hound could climb.

I leaped another log in the ravine and almost stepped into a hole. The sun was high now, but the shadows were still long this far into the cut. Here in the ravine, it was nearly twilight – the shadows deep and impenetrable.

The smell hit me first, before I saw it. The smell of fish and salt and ocean.

I thought of what Mercy had said, *If you're lucky, and the tide isn't in.*

I pushed through dense foliage that had overgrown the creek bed.

Above me, I heard the fence rattle again. Something trying to get up and over. I prayed the fence held. Or that the hill itself was an obstacle.

When I was a boy, my grandparents had owned a huge dog, an Irish setter that I'd played with in the backyard. Out in the yard, it was no contest; four legs were faster than two. But going down the stairs to the basement was another story. And I'd learned this strange truth: going down a steep slope, four-legged creatures were no faster than humans. Sometimes they were slower.

I climbed over a small boulder and sprinted along the streambed until I burst through a thick mass of foliage, pushing it aside with my arms. A final drop of three feet to the sand, and I blinked and came to rest, looking all around, and was suddenly out on the edge of the tide flats – a vast and glossy plain of dark, sandy mud.

My feet made deep gouges on the smooth surface. I was out.

Hours from now there'd be ten feet of water where I stood, but for the moment the shallow seafloor spread out before me, the bed of an inlet exposed to the air. In the distance across the mud, a green bank rose into a tree-lined hill, the reciprocal image of the hill I'd just come down. I set off toward the other side.

The inlet was a half mile across, a narrow lowland between hills where the ocean insinuated itself at high tide.

Runnels of water connected shallow pools, and I was mindful of my step as I picked my way across the slippery muck. I splashed across a series of runoff streams – some deeper than others, wider than others, crisscrossing each other in complex patterns made anew at each low tide. I had to choose my path carefully, or find myself wading knee-deep in cold water, fighting a current. The water was freezing. The sea-salt smell overpowering.

I trudged along the edge of a particularly deep stream, searching for a place where it widened and flattened, so that I might cross, and that was when I saw the footprints. Funneled to this place by the same geography – a single set of smallish prints gouging their way across the silty bottom.

I looked close. They'd filled in with water and had lost their definition, but I judged them about the right size. A woman's prints or a small man's. They could have been a minute old or an hour, but up ahead, nothing moved. I saw no one. The tide plain was empty.

I crossed the stream where the footprints had gone over and followed the tracks for another hundred yards until they came to a place where the sand leveled out, and a wandering trickle of seawater had smoothed the flats as clean as an eraser. I continued on until a sound caught my attention. Something behind me.

I turned, and at that moment, in the distance, the hound burst free from the tree line and leaped onto the flats, bounding across the mud. Its rear legs kicked up huge rooster tails of sand with each long, loping stride, white puffs of steam rising from where its front legs made contact with the wet muck. If it had been no faster than a man while descending the slope, then this terrain was what it was made for. It would reach me quickly.

I turned and ran. Up ahead, several streams converged, and I didn't have time to find a safe crossing. I waded out into the flowing water – up to my knees at first, then my hips, the current pushing me downstream. The cold took my breath away. Like a vice around my chest, squeezing my heart. I pressed on fifteen feet more, then twenty, halfway across – until the water hit my shoulders, salt-water stinging my wounds like fire, and I felt the bottom fall away, and my head went under – and then I was swimming. The cold water was a shock against my face. An involuntary gasp, and the salt taste is something you never forget, once you've been in the ocean, and each time brings it back.

I swam for my life. The current was strong, draining the endless upland tide pools, and it sucked me along, threatening to take me out to sea. I wondered if it had happened that way to Mercy. *Was she out there now, lost in the deeps? Or had she found safe crossing?*

My shoes kicked bottom, sliding past rocks, and I lunged and swam harder, until my feet were suddenly under me, and I waded forward. When I reached the other side, I dragged myself out of the water and collapsed, hands scraping painfully against the rough sand as I pulled myself up the bank. My body shook with cold and exhaustion. When I turned to look, my heart stopped.

Across the stream stood the hound. It stood perfectly still, steam rising from its damp coat. It leveled me with a predatory glare.

But it did not cross.

I stared at it.

Its mouth pulled back from long, curving teeth.

'Don't like the cold?' I said. My voice cracked when I spoke.

It growled low in its throat and stepped to the water's edge. Its pale front leg made a hissing noise as it entered the water – a cloud of white steam. The beast stepped back.

Some things are more than they seem, Mercy had said. Whatever this hound was, it didn't like the sea.

Best not to tempt it, though, I decided. I climbed slowly to my feet, no sudden movements, while its eyes bore into me.

I backed slowly away as it watched. Suddenly, the hound's ears perked up. As if they'd picked up a sound that only it could hear. It froze. A moment later, it turned and bolted, heading back in the direction it had come, sand flying from its feet.

I turned and sprinted for the slope.

The overgrowth was thick and green and without a trail. I broke my way up the slope for the first twenty yards, until the low brush thinned out and the trees began in earnest. Beyond there, the slope steepened, a muddy, slippery, leaf-covered rise, so I climbed at an angle, grasping at the trunks of trees as I went. It was a difficult climb, but two hours later, I reached the top, and the land flattened into a gentle woods, which continued to thin. Another half mile, and I came to a clearing of mowed grass, and then a park with a swing set and monkey bars.

Civilization. I almost fell to my knees, but the thought of having to get up again stopped me.

Afternoon had come to the uplands, and the park was empty. I crossed quickly.

At the edge of the park, a road.

And beyond there, a town. Lights glowed up ahead.

I smoothed my hair and checked my clothes, hoping, at least, not to attract stares. My button-down shirt was gone, and my blue T-shirt was frayed. My khakis sported matching rips at the knees. Looking down at myself, I was suddenly thankful for the swim, because at least the worst of the blood and filth was rinsed away. I was still dirty and stained, but it was a diluted, washed-out kind of dirty that might only attract attention if the person made more than a cursory glance.

Beyond the park, a house-lined side street led me toward a main stretch of road – markets and restaurants and knick-knack shops. People coming and going. Places selling real estate and ice cream and custom clothing.

I kept my eyes peeled as I walked the main drag, looking for a familiar face. Could either of them have made it this far?

If Brighton knew I'd crossed the canal, he might not be far behind. With my current position hemmed in on two sides by water, there weren't many places I could be.

Farther on, the main drag began to slope, and I got a view of the street as it descended toward the water and an enormous wharf. This was a tourist town, and the waterfront was its lifeblood. A hundred yards ahead, amid the walkers and the shoppers, I saw a woman with wet blonde hair. I craned my neck, trying to get a better look, but she was gone. It could have been Mercy, or just wishful thinking. I picked up my pace, wanting to be sure.

A few minutes later, as I got closer, I saw a familiar vehicle pull onto the main road from one of the side streets.

There are plenty of vehicles like that, I told myself.

White Range Rover. The same kind that Brighton's men had shoved me into on the day that Satvik died. The driver of the vehicle had a phone to his ear while he scanned the crowds. He was midthirties, dark hair. I didn't recognize his face, but that could mean anything.

I ducked into a shop and let the Range Rover pass. Bead necklaces and knick-knacks; I tried to look interested. When the vehicle had gone, I stepped back out into the crowd, moving as quickly as I could without attracting attention.

I found the alley that the blonde woman had ducked into, but she was nowhere to be seen. I passed through to another street, closer now to the water and the wharf. I walked slowly, scanning the traffic.

Up ahead, I saw her. Still wet from the crossing. It was Mercy. A wave of relief washed over me. Her arms were crossed in front of her, and she looked cold. But she was alive; she'd made it.

Now that I'd seen her, I considered letting her go.

Maybe it was enough. We'd both gotten free. I could slink away. *And go where? Do what?* I thought of the article on Satvik's death. A car accident, it had said.

In the street traffic up ahead, I saw the vehicle had circled around again. Same driver. Same cell phone to his ear. On her current course, Mercy would walk right past him.

I walked casually through the crowd, keeping my face

turned away from the street until I came up behind her and put my arm over her shoulder. She startled at first but recovered quickly, opening her mouth to speak, but I cut her off.

'They're close.'

'Where?' She did not turn her head, but her eyes darted through the crowd.

'Up ahead, in traffic.' I slowed our gait. We were passing a broad cement staircase that led down toward the wharf.

It was then that I noticed her limp.

'You're hurt,' I said. 'How bad.'

Her eyes were distant. Her face pale.

'I'll survive.'

'Turn here,' I said, guiding her by the shoulder.

We took stairs down toward the water as the Rover passed by. At the bottom of the stairs, we found ourselves at a ticket booth. I looked at the sign.

'Two, please.'

Reaching into my pocket for my wallet, I felt my phone, now wet and dead. Mercy slid a wad of wet bills through the window. Moments later, we crossed through the turnstile and followed a narrow walkway leading down to the ferry. A line of cars trailed all the way up the hill, but the walk-ons had no line.

Once aboard, we climbed the stairs to the passenger level and made our way to a booth by the windows. We sat.

Electric lights and the hum of the engines.

I looked out through the glass toward the entrance ramp, waiting to see Brighton's face among those who boarded. Or maybe the driver's face. If he'd seen us and followed, there'd be no escaping him here. No place to go.

But no face appeared in the walkway.

Mercy laid her head on my shoulder. She was wet and exhausted and cold. I wrapped my arm around her. Her pant leg was torn. One shoe stained red. She saw me looking, so she raised the tattered material. She had a gash on her calf.

'It's not too bad,' I said.

She shook her head. 'It came from the hound. It's worse than it looks.'

'What was that thing?'

'One of their hunters.'

'Where is Vickers?'

'She made it to her car.'

'She got away?'

'Yeah.'

'How do you know?'

She was silent for a moment. 'I saw it. She was hurt, but she made it to her car.'

'Hennig is – '

'Hennig is dead.'

She closed her eyes.

Suddenly, the engine noise grew louder. Boat workers threw off the lines, and the ferry started moving. And just like that, we were off. No one new could enter the boat. The great wooden pylons slid by the window, seagulls alighting.

For the moment, at least, we were safe.

I took a long breath and released it.

As my adrenaline eased back, exhaustion hit me. A bone-weary fatigue. I felt the rough texture of my clothes, still cold and damp. My pants stiff with salt. A coarseness that I knew wouldn't leave until they'd been washed in fresh water. I felt myself begin to shake. I clenched the muscles in my arms and legs, willing myself to stop.

'How did you get away?' she asked.

We were alone in this part of the ship, near the back. It was still an hour before the evening commute, and the crowd was thin. There were a dozen people on the entire level, none of them close.

'I killed Boaz,' I said.

She lifted her head from my shoulder, and her eyes searched my face. 'You killed him.'

Maybe she expected insistence. I was too tired for that. I simply looked at her.

'How?' she asked.

'I hit him.'

'Hit him.'

'With a piece of steel.'

She said nothing for a long time after that. She put her damp head on my shoulder again and turned her face toward the window.

The ship eased away from the shoreline, heading for deeper water. The lights of the town spread out all along the shore.

'You hit him,' she said finally. 'That's all.'

Again I said nothing. Waves splashed against the side of the boat as we sliced through the water. We were traveling at eight knots, I guessed. Maybe ten. Not fast by powerboat standards, but faster than many small sailboats could go. It is counterintuitive that a longer waterline produces a faster sailing vessel. It seems that a longer waterline should mean more drag, more friction, a slower boat. But this isn't true at all.

Whitecaps frothed in the wind, and the ship heaved as it encountered the first big waves.

'They die,' I said. 'Same as us.'

'Not the same,' she said.

I told her about the pipe in the darkness and the shiv of steel. I told her about Boaz's pulped skull, like a shattered jar of jelly. 'I didn't stop until he was dead.'

She nodded, as if she finally understood. 'The pipe kept him confined.'

'He was coming out, and I hit him.'

I leaned back in the seat. I didn't want to talk anymore. The exhaustion was bone deep. I turned away from the window and let the familiar rhythm of the ship overtake me. It was the first time I'd been out on the water in many years, I realized. The first time since my father died. The ship rocked against the waves.

Mercy closed her eyes. As the minutes passed, I wasn't sure if she was sleeping. Her face was turned toward me, a smooth mask of repose. A perfectly angelic face. I wondered what she dreamed of. Her past? Dark angels, strange monsters?

I looked through the window as the ferry rocked in the waves. The wind was stronger this far out. The lights on the opposite shore were visible now. Another bayside town.

A few minutes later, her voice surprised me. 'They're going to keep coming,' she said. 'They're going to keep coming, and coming, and they'll hunt us down.'

The wind rattled the glass. I closed my eyes, and tried to clear my head. Exhaustion descended like a clinging fog. After a time, I slept.

45

There are truths you learn while sailing. You never want a smaller boat while out on the water. You never want a bigger boat while in a marina. Our own struggles were legendary – the *Regatta Marie* swinging wide as my father guided it into our slip.

Most people liked fair weather. Sunny days, light breezes. My father loved the storms. Driving rains.

There is talk among sailors about the one that gets you. The wave with your name. Like the old man who helped us tie our lines one day – and he intoned the story of the *Northern*, his first ship, lost when he was young. The seas were rough but manageable, he told us, until the big one hit. A broadside mountain, conceived in a gale a thousand miles away – and then crossed an ocean until it found him, rolled him, sheared off the mast. The wave with his name.

When a sailor goes missing, there are procedures that the Coast Guard follows. A specific checklist. Some ships go missing and wash up on shore. Other times, boats go straight to the bottom. Never to be seen again. Erased from the world.

The old video is too painful to watch.

A video of my father when he was a boy, running along the sand. Small and brown-haired and unrecognizable. Until he smiled. And in that smile you could see him.

It was that very same beach. The stones like pieces of shipwreck, unchanged, like they'd been there forever and would be there forever. Like my father had been a boy just yesterday, running in the sand with that wide, crooked grin. The video a time machine. And a lie. Because you couldn't go back.

That spark now gone from the world.

When my father went missing, the Coast Guard launched a search. They set up a perimeter, established a grid.

They finally made contact a hundred miles out. Both sails raised in the storm, drunk for days.

He was trying, I think. To lose himself. But the sea would not take him.

By then the cirrhosis was bad. His liver failing, as was his vision. A night drinking rubbing alcohol under a sink. 'There are no blind sailors,' he told me.

And my mother secure behind the protective walls of her denial. 'He's getting better,' she said while he sailed off alone.

There are things I can remember about that last day. The way his skin looked, sickly and blotched. Like a wax model. The doctors had told him that if he drank again he'd die, but some part of him must have suspected what was more probably true: He was dying already. And nothing could stop it. The cirrhosis already too far gone.

So he left for the day, heading to the office.

And later I'd hear fragments of the rest. Small dollops of information spread over the coming years.

I think she might have been okay if she hadn't been the one to find him. I think everything might have been different. It was just bad luck.

He'd left his briefcase at home, and when he didn't return, she'd decided to drive it to his office to drop it off. Or it was some strange premonition that guided her. And I've never been told all the details. Just bits and pieces. And one word – *gun* – repeated over and over.

She'd caught a glimpse of his car as she drove down Western Avenue. She could have driven right past, and ninety-nine times out of a hundred, she would have. There was no reason for her to glance in that direction unless it was to see the water. But her roll of the dice was that hundredth time, so instead of driving past, she looked out toward the water and saw his car parked near the sand. A parking lot with a view of the ocean.

The ferry bumped into the pier with a flurry of bow thrusters. I started awake. 'Come on,' Mercy said. She sat up straight and rubbed her eyes. 'We need to go.'

The other riders were already rising to their feet. We followed the stragglers out of the doors and down the ramp. We walked the sidewalks into the rain. I turned my face up to the sky.

It was raining when my mother parked next to his car in the sandy lot.

It was cold that day, a drizzly October, so perhaps my mother pulled her jacket collar up as she stepped out of the car. Perhaps she turned her face into the rain. I can see her walking around the back of his red Chevy Cavalier. Perhaps she was formulating what she was going to say. She'd tease him for being forgetful, or she'd ask why he was parked there near the sand.

I can see her reaching for his door, her fingers curling slightly in anticipation of the handle. And then I see no more.

It was a passerby in another car who finally stopped and helped a few minutes later. An old dockworker who pulled my mother from where she stood screaming in the middle of the street. She'd tried to stop other cars, but they swerved away, wanting no part.

The police found him in the front seat, gun in his lap. The note read only, *It was the wave with my name.*

As we walked into the town, we found most of the businesses already closed for the night. Another tourist district at the edge of the water.

Farther down the street, I spotted a hotel, but when I pointed to it, she said, 'Not that one.'

'Why?'

'Not the first one we come to.'

A bit farther out, another hotel sign glowed red in the rain. VACANCY. CABLE TV.

We paid with cash.

'Ice maker's at the end of the hall.'

The room was clean and no frills. A floral pattern on the blankets. I turned the heat up as far as it would go. The double beds were soft.

I slept like the dead.

When I woke in the morning, Mercy was already up and dressed, sitting at the tiny round table in the corner. She had coffee and a doughnut put aside for me.

'Continental breakfast,' she said. 'I was afraid you would miss it.'

I noticed a small plastic bag on the bed.

'Toothbrush and toothpaste,' she said. 'A razor. They sell them at the little store just up the road.'

She put the news on the TV – the steady drone of international politics. The Koreas. The stock market. The upcoming election.

I sat up, and my clothes stuck to me. Everything hurt. My shirt still stiff and coarse, pleated into the shape I'd slept it into. My skin was raw. I wanted a shower and a shave.

'We'll need new clothes,' I told her.

She nodded. 'There's a shop up the street. A rental car company, too. The sooner we leave, the better.'

'We're renting a car?'

'Unless you know how to steal one.'

I climbed to my feet and crossed the room to my coffee. It was hot and good. I drank it down. The doughnut I couldn't make myself eat.

'When they catch us, they'll kill us,' she said.

When, she had said. Not *if*.

'So what do we do? We can't just sit here and do nothing.'

'We go to the other hide, like Vickers said.'

'How far is it?'

'Far enough. Two days' drive. We meet up with her and decide what to do.'

'And if she's not there?'

'She'll be there.'

46

We drove west and west, through two states, and into the night. We took turns driving, eating up the miles. The rise and fall of the hills like the waves of some impossible sea. The hypnotic thrum of the engine carried us to dawn.

The plains brought heat and an endless expanse. The doldrums. Horse latitudes.

We ate at a Denny's outside Topeka, and then six hours' sleep at a Super 8 just off the highway.

We hit the badlands at midday. Bright sun shining down. Here the land became alien. As bare and inhospitable as the surface of the moon. The badlands, full of gullies and arid hills. Land that would not level. We drove west for hours more, and then we went south.

'Vickers,' I prompted her.

The sun had gone down, and the world was now defined by what I could see in the headlights. The dotted white line spooled out in front of us and then disappeared behind us again.

'Yeah,' she said.

'Do you believe what she says about Brighton? What he is?'

'You saw them. Make up your own mind.'

She leaned her face against the passenger window, watching the night.

‘And the cascade?’ I asked.

‘The what?’

‘Matryoshka dolls, nested universes. Finite volume but an infinite surface area.’

‘I don’t know physics. Vickers had a different story for me.’

‘What story?’

‘The story of an island,’ she said. ‘The most beautiful place you could imagine, unchanging, until one day rats came to its shores.’

‘Rats?’ I asked.

She nodded. ‘Never mind how they got there. But the point was they got there. These rats were different from the other animals and disrupted the harmony if left unchecked. They had to be controlled, do you understand?’

‘Yeah.’

‘So those in charge of the island tried to control the rats, but the rats were too fast. Traps were attempted, but the rats were too smart. So it was decided that predators would be introduced to prey on the rats. And so it came to pass that snakes were released on the island. Big venomous snakes that could kill the rats with a single bite. What do you think happened?’

‘The snakes didn’t control the rats.’

She nodded. ‘The snakes slithered deep into the heart of the island and did what snakes do, and so now the island had two vermin upon it. Did the keepers of the island stop there?’

‘I guess not.’

‘No, they did not. And a new beast was brought in to

solve the problem. The sly mongoose. Faster than a snake. Smarter than a rat. They shipped them in and set them loose, and what do you think happened?'

'They didn't kill the snakes.'

'Oh, they killed some. The slowest, the weakest. A war was waged. But over time, the mongooses became their own problem, as big as the rats and snakes. And many snakes died, and many mongoose, too, as all around them the rats scurried. And so after that the laws were changed – an unbreakable decree for all time. No more mongooses. No more outsiders. The age of miracles was ended. Nothing new would be added to the island. The curators of the island washed their hands and said, "What will be will be."'

'And Brighton is a snake?'

'The snakes are snakes. I was speaking of an island.'

I drove in silence for a long time. 'What does the snake want?'

'Who can know the wants of a snake.'

'And what of the mongooses?'

'All dead now.'

'And the rats, what do they want?'

'The rats want what rats everywhere want,' she said. She turned her face to the sun. 'Just to survive.'

The heat of the day came on. Mercy offered to drive, but I waved that off. 'Sleep,' I told her. 'I'll be fine.'

At a rest stop, we drank from the water fountain and used the bathroom. We found our place on the map. *You are here.* Low hills hemmed us in on two sides. My eyes in the mirror were tired. *Three hours*, I told myself. In three more hours, I'd let myself rest. I tried my phone, hoping to get the map working, but it was still glitched from the water. The phone turned on, which was promising, but none of the icons worked. I'd heard that bagging the phone in rice did the trick sometimes, but since I had no rice, I tossed the phone onto the dashboard, figuring the sun might dry it out. I thought of Joy.

Mercy slept as I drove.

The land here defied scale. Defied description. The bad lands. The broken lands. Bright red walls rose up in the distance and then fell away. Stone shaped by wind into the flow of a wave. There were no mountains but only strange tables upon which the land resumed. Places where the arid floor of the Earth rose vertically for a hundred feet into the sky, as if God himself couldn't decide at which level the ground should rest.

The road snaked its way through the lowlands between these plateaus – a single traversable ribbon wending its way through the upheaval. Here and there, the road became a bridge, passing over deep crevasses. Other times the road seemed to be in the crevasses themselves as canyon walls rose up around us. It was a landscape in revolt. I wondered what it must have been like here for the first settlers. How many people reached this place and found there was no way forward, the heat of the sun baking down, and no way back.

The heat muddled my thinking. Or maybe it was the need for sleep.

I drove with the accelerator pressed as hard as I dared, but when I looked again, our speed had dropped to fifty. I pressed on, speeding up again, but every time I looked, the speedometer wouldn't stay still. I'd lost control of it somewhere. As I'd lost control of my life.

In the backseat, Mercy made a noise, then lay quiet, sleeping again. So quiet that I looked back, checking her breath. The steady rise and fall, like the land around us.

I turned back to watch the road. The winding gray ribbon.

Minutes later, my chin jerked, and I was suddenly awake – the car straddling the lanes, my speed above ninety. I slowed to seventy and shook my head, trying to clear the cobwebs.

The ribbon unspooled. Miles more. Brown shrubs clinging to the edge of a low canyon wall that finally opened to the expanse. A wide red wild.

As I drove, I gradually became aware that there were two of me. The one who drove, and the one who dreamed, and I saw a hare striding out in the scrublands – a loping run that kept pace with the vehicle. A mystical blackness in the shimmering heat, too faint to see with your eyes, though you could feel it was out there – long legs kicking, maw open, red tongue streaming out from a sly, grinning face, while behind it a coyote chased with snapping jaws, and I was the coyote, and I was the hare, and I was the driver, and the woman in the backseat wasn't anyone, anywhere, not even herself.

The tires squealed as the car followed the curve, and I snapped awake, spinning the wheel, overcorrecting. The sickening pull on my body against the seat belt before finally straightening out, gaining control.

Mercy had come awake but said nothing.

*

She drove while I slept.

Three hours later, she shook me awake. 'We're getting close.'

I opened my eyes to the broken landscape. Low hills. It all looked the same. I wondered how she knew.

'How close?'

'Twenty minutes. Maybe less.'

'How many times have you come here?'

'Once,' she said. 'A year ago.' She slowed and turned off the main road onto a dusty drive that disappeared over a rise. Brown shrubs covered the stony soil. 'I never wanted to come back,' she said.

The car crested another rise. The road went on and on into the distance, brown and dusty, for several miles, following the curve of the upland before seeming to evaporate into the shimmering air. Mercy slowed the vehicle to twenty miles per hour but pressed on.

'Why did you stay with Vickers? You could have walked away, so why didn't you?'

'You mean live a normal life?'

'Yeah. There are worse things.'

I watched her. Her body rocked with the movement of the car over the pitted road. It seemed a track more fitting to four-wheelers than any kind of car.

'What makes you think I could have?'

I looked at her hand resting on the wheel. The missing parts of fingers.

'What happened to your hand?'

She looked at me, following my gaze. 'I don't remember.'

'How can you not remember?'

'There were worse things. Things I lost far worse than

this.' She held her hand up, damaged. 'And *that's* what I remember. I remember them tearing me apart. Toying with me, like a child might pull the wings off a fly. I remember dying – being right at the edge of it.'

The car rocked on its suspension as we crossed another deep hole. I didn't understand. 'You remember things that didn't happen?'

Mercy's eyes were far away, gazing out through the filthy windshield. 'They did happen. It's like there's a fissure, and the world can *pull* you, and I was suddenly on a different track – a track where I'd lived, instead of dying and I was left with this hand that I didn't recognize.' She looked down at her own hand. Her face was grim.

'What do you mean, "pulled you"? Who pulled you?'

'The world. It's like a correction that happens. A fracture.'

I thought of Stuart. *I think sometimes it can get confused.*

'When it happens,' she said, 'you remember the track you come from, mostly. Not the one you're pulled to. Though there's a little bleed-through. Maybe a quick flash of memory, but it's like it happened to somebody else. This' – she held up her hand – 'happened to somebody else.'

'It looks like it happened to you.'

She shook her head. 'A different version of me. What happened to me was much worse.'

We rounded a bend in the rutted track, and the land opened up, dropping slightly, and I could suddenly see for miles.

You hear about people dying in the wilderness, their

car breaking down. I could imagine it easily. Humans are at the mercy of their instruments.

It was a desolate landscape. Dry and inhospitable. More scrub and rock and low, desiccated trees. I squinted through the filthy windshield.

There was something up ahead, maybe half a mile.

Mercy saw it, too. She eased the car to a stop and hit the windshield washer fluid. Precious liquid sprayed across the glass, making streaks in the dust.

The patch of land was maybe thirty yards square, nestled between two low hills. In that spot, the land was greener, with grasses and flowers – and there above it, spread like an umbrella, loomed a huge, gnarled tree, rare in this arid country, and under whose branches crouched a small, dilapidated trailer, shimmering in the summer heat.

We'd seen similar trailers over the last day's drive, on the outskirts of towns, often surrounded by junk and broken-down cars. But this was the middle of nowhere.

'It hasn't changed,' Mercy said.

She shifted the car back into drive, and we continued on, slowly descending the gradual slope. As we approached the settled spot of land, I got a better look at the trailer. Whatever its original color might have been, it had been whitewashed long ago to fight off the sun. Streaked with dust and grime, its chrome trim sandblasted to a cloudy countenance. Even the windows looked fogged – an aging glaucoma, as if the panes had seen too much and wished to see no more. The yard was heaped with cast-offs. A small love seat lay tipped on its side. There were two cars, only one of which looked like it was from this lifetime – a familiar gray sedan. Vickers's car. A small dent in the right front quarter panel. So she'd made it after all. The other car's wheels were sunk into the ground, so that it rested on its belly in the red dirt. The paint was a faded pink that might have once been red. I saw wheelbarrows, and bicycles, and a large metal bucket whose sides were crushed in.

The front door of the trailer was open to the heat. A screen door swayed crookedly in the breeze.

Mercy pulled the car to a stop thirty yards short of the trailer.

I looked at Mercy's face, and I could see the fear. She didn't want to approach.

'What is this place?'

'The last of the hides,' she said. 'This is where Vickers brought Hennig when she nursed him back to health.'

47

We sat. The engine idled.

'We didn't come all this way to stop now,' I said.

She shook her head. 'The car stays here in case things go wrong.'

'And if they do go wrong?'

She was quiet for a moment, considering my words. 'Maybe one of us makes it back to the car.'

I glanced at her. 'I don't think where we park is going to matter.'

She didn't want to drive any closer, but in the end there was no point not to.

'It'll be fine,' I said. Which might have been a lie, of course. I had no way of knowing, one way or the other.

She reached for the window buttons.

It was three o'clock and the worst heat of the day was over, but it was still a killing heat that poured through the opening windows. It might have been 105 degrees. I couldn't imagine the temperature inside that trailer.

She shifted into drive, and the car eased forward. She parked in the shade beneath the tree and after cutting the engine reached under the driver's seat, and pulled out a gun. She tucked it behind her back and smoothed her shirt over the lump.

When we opened our car doors and stepped outside, a hot breeze lifted my sweaty hair from my forehead. The air was oven dry, and the dust of the badlands hung in the wind.

'Come on,' I said.

We made our way up the path to the trailer. A child's metal swing set, decades old, swayed in the breeze. On one side of the swing, the chain was frozen in rust; on the other, it had broken and lay strewn on the ground. The hinge made a rusty squeak as the wind moved the sun-bleached wooden seat.

'Vickers hasn't survived this long by being careless,' Mercy said. 'Or without having contingencies.'

The stairs at the front door looked as old and weather-beaten as the swing. Made of plywood and two-by-fours, bleached gray by the sun. We walked up the crooked stairs to the front door.

Mercy had to close the screen in order to knock. 'Hello?' she called out, knocking on the fogged glass.

There was no response.

'Anybody here?'

She opened the screen door and stepped inside.

The interior of the trailer looked no better than the exterior. The carpet was worn to its threads in a path between the couch and the kitchen. A small TV sat on top of a larger one in the living room. There was a gray, sagging sofa. Coffee table. Cheap glass knick-knacks positioned on a shelf near the front door – ceramic puppies and cats and elephants. I saw a crucifix on the wall. Then another. A statue of Mary stood vigil on a side table by the couch. There were small statues of saints, of various sizes and means of manufacture, located strategically around the room. Some were cheap plastic of the type you saw on car dashboards. Others were larger, hand painted, made of glossy ceramic.

'Hello?' Mercy called out again.

At the far end of the hall, the bedroom door was open. The bed unmade. Bright white sheet waterfalling to the floor. But the trailer was empty. Nobody there.

'Vickers, you here?'

As if in response, a noise drifted in through an open window. An old man's voice, from outside the trailer. I took a few steps deeper into the living room and parted the curtains behind the couch. The backyard was much the same as the front. Part trash heap, part wilderness. Overgrown with weeds and grass. Twenty yards out, the land rose slightly, and a large lean-to had been constructed from an immense white tarp and wooden poles, providing shade for a picnic table. At the table, bent over their work, was an old couple. The man stooped and gray and the woman sitting beside him in a ratty wicker chair.

'People,' I said. 'I don't see Vickers, though.'

Mercy stepped next to me and looked out through the window. She stared for a long time. 'She's here.'

'And who are they?'

'The people who live here. This is their place.'

Beyond the glass, the old man's brow furrowed as he worked with his arms, bent over some task we could not see. The old woman murmured softly, clutching a yellowed newspaper.

'They don't know we're here.'

'They know,' Mercy said. 'Come on.'

I followed her down the rickety stairs and around the side of the trailer. The yard here was more overgrown than I'd realized. Rougher. Tall grass and small green shrubs. As we approached the pair at their picnic table, the old man looked up. He said something in Spanish to the old woman. She glanced at us briefly, green-hazel eyes registering no curiosity, before she went back to her newspaper. I looked down and saw what the old man was working at. He yanked hard, pulling with his knobby hands. The fur pelt came away from the flesh like an overtight sweater. He was skinning a hare. A large butcher knife lay before him.

Along with the knife, there were two other hares on the table. One laid out flat and the other one caged. Wild jackrabbits, by the look of them. Little running machines, with long legs and sleek, narrow bodies.

Of the three animals, one no longer had skin or life, but the other two still breathed, red-brown fur sporadically twitching as the old man worked beside them. The one closest to him flared its nostrils.

The old man took the knife and cut away the skin at the dead hare's front paws. The fur pulled free.

The old couple might have been married, or they might have been kin. The man seemed older and more weatherbeaten. A constellation of age spots across his large nose.

'Is Vickers here?' I asked.

The old man didn't even look up from his work, just waved us farther on with a bloody hand. And that's when I saw the trail.

We followed the path down a gradual slope and found Vickers lying near a small pool that had gathered between the low hills. A natural seep from the uplands. It was cooler down by the water.

'So you made it,' she said, pale green eyes lifting to us as we approached.

She looked terrible. Her once-neat clothes were now ragged and bloody. Her hair hung in matted clumps of dried gore. She clutched something dark and red in her hand, but I couldn't tell what it was.

Mercy dropped to her knees at Vickers's side. 'You're hurt.'

Vickers ignored that. 'You came without Hennig,' she said. 'He's dead then.' It wasn't a question.

Mercy nodded.

Vickers closed her eyes and took the news with the bow of her head. When she finally lifted her face again, she looked at me. 'Now it's down to you two,' she said.

'And you,' Mercy replied.

Vickers shook her head. She tried to smile, but the effect looked ghoulish on her bloody face. 'I didn't make it either,' she said. She sat up, wincing at the pain. She coughed into her bloody sleeve. 'The hounds are fast. Hellish beasts. How did you get away?'

'The tide flats,' I said. 'We got lucky.'

She nodded again and opened her hand, and I saw that the shape she held was a rabbit's foot. The fur streaked in crimson. She caught me looking. 'A present. For good luck, they say.' She smiled. 'But not for the rabbit. Tell me, do you think all good luck must come at a cost?'

'You make your own luck,' I said.

Vickers tried to smile again. 'That's exactly right. You do.' She gestured up the trail where the old man stood at the table. 'He's making some now.' The knife chopped down on the hare's leg.

Vickers extended her hand to me, holding out the foot. It was bloody and raw.

'Go on,' she said. 'Take it. You're either the rabbit, or you hold the foot.'

I took it. It was heavier than it looked.

'Come, help me stand,' she said. 'I've been lying here too long.'

Mercy and I helped Vickers to her feet, and she hobbled to the top of the rise.

'This is a good spot,' she said. She pointed to a shaded place beneath a small, gnarled tree. We lowered her to the ground, and Mercy sat beside her. The grass was long and stiff, but moved with the breeze.

From here, we had a view of the old couple twenty feet away. The man was still skinning his hare. Another thump of the knife, and he shoved the carcass into an empty five-gallon bucket near his foot. He wiped his forehead with the back of his hand, scrawling a line of blood near his hairline.

'How bad are you hurt?' Mercy asked.

'Bad enough,' Vickers said. She opened her business suit, and her blouse was covered in blood. The wound was horrific. I could see the pale white chalk of a rib beneath the torn skin. She coughed into her sleeve again, and when she finished, there was fresh blood on her chin. 'Well past bad enough, actually,' she said.

'We can get you to a hospital.'

She shook her head. 'Too late for that, I think.'

Twenty feet away, the old man placed a second rabbit on the table and stretched it out in front of him. Its fur twitched, and its nostrils flared, but it did not run. Its eyes were big and round and unafraid. He stroked the fur with one hand while the other hand picked up the knife.

'We all see what we want to see,' Vickers said, looking at the old man. 'Does the animal see the butcher's cleaver? Why would it want to see such things? It might run away and tell the story for all the days of its life. Legends might grow. Myths of a vengeful god with a knife.'

'At least let us take you inside.' Mercy said.

'I like it here,' Vickers responded.

The old man brought the knife down hard – stabbing down into the wood, instead of the hare.

The animal's whiskers twitched. It seemed to draw itself up, flexing like a bow, muscles tensing – and then it shot away, launching itself from the table in a single powerful leap. It hit the grass running and leaped over a bush and was gone.

The butcher's blade still shimmied in the bare, sun-bleached wood. The old man looked in the direction that the hare had run.

'You take some, and you give some back,' Vickers said. 'Tomorrow the hunter may catch him, but today he kept his feet and has a story to tell.' She turned back toward us. 'Me, though? My luck has run out.'

I studied her closely. Her face pale and waxy. Her breathing shallow. 'There's medicine at the hospital,' I said. 'They can help you.'

'The only medicine I'll need is one that can wake the dead. Do you have any of that?'

'I'm fresh out of voodoo.'

She smiled. 'Then it looks like we're at the end.' She was quiet for a long while. 'I don't want to die, but we're not given a choice. How much did you see back there at the camp?'

'I saw enough.'

'Good. Then you know what you're fighting.'

'But I don't,' I said. 'Not really.'

'He killed Boaz,' Mercy interjected.

Vickers looked up at me, her face showing surprise. 'And they say the age of wonders is over.' She smiled, then broke into a coughing fit.

Mercy put her hand to the woman's forehead. 'She is burning up,' she said. 'Let's see if we can cool her down.'

I went to the pool at the bottom of the trail and cupped some water in my hand. I carried it back up the slope and held my hands over Vickers's head, dripping the water onto her hair.

She turned her face up to the water and let it clean tracks on her bloody face. 'It's getting late of days,' she said. 'The world's askew.'

'Brighton said I broke the world.'

'Broken, yes.' Her voice trailed. 'Even out here you can sense it – its purpose compromised.'

'What purpose?'

'The purpose of this world is the purpose of every world. To create the next.' She tried to sit up straighter. 'Imagine it. Worlds inside worlds, numbering as the stars. And yet here the gods fight, and here they die. Ask yourself why. Why did they come? Why do they fight?'

'I don't know.'

'Because it's all burning.' Vicker's pale eyes bore into me. 'Burning from the top down.'

'You mean the cascade,' I said.

She nodded. 'The old ones are running. As each world is compressed within the bounds of the world above it, so, too, is time compressed. Dilating from one world to another, an order of magnitude, telescoping milliseconds into millennia. But one day the fires will consume all.'

I sat in the grass. It was a logical corollary to the formula she had shown me earlier. If logic required an endless cascade of worlds, then what happened when the prime world died? As eventually all worlds must. It would all snuff out – the whole cascade. How could you run from such a thing? Where would you go to escape the end?

And the rest of it hit me. I saw the math. 'Time is faster the further in you go.' Space and time interconnected. If you graphed the time dilation against the increasing number of worlds, then over a large enough time scale, you approached the asymptote – world upon world, an arrow shot toward infinity.

'It's a race against the end,' I said. 'That's what the cascade is. That's what civilization is. A race to spawn the next iteration. And then the next, and the next.'

'Yes,' she said.

And the anthropic principle would be at work here, too, I realized, leaving universes optimized for speed. The worlds that reached critical advances quickly would outpace those that didn't, iteration after iteration, time unspooling the further down you went. A moment in one universe becoming an age in the next. Did escape velocity exist? Can you create an eternity inside the cascade? World after world, millions of years, or billions of years all wrapped up inside the last moments of the prime universe?

'What about Brighton?'

'He works to stop the cascade. There are fissures around us you cannot see. Normally, the world corrects itself, choosing only those tracks that best serve the goal.'

'Choosing?'

'Correcting,' she said.

'I don't understand. Correcting how?'

'Imagine space-time as a jewel, with each facet a timeline. As the jewel turns, a new facet catches the light. Our *souls* are that light. And so we shift from facet to facet, depending on where our light is needed.'

I shook my head, but wondered what optimizations were possible. Like Satvik's gate arrays, choosing the best gates for the task. Could a world do that, too? Could an entire universe?

Vickers continued, 'But now the eberaxi is here, and what is broken cannot be mended. The eberaxi warps this world, closing off the time lines. Stopping the corrections.'

'How?'

'I don't know. It is a monkey wrench in the mechanism. With each passing second, we drift farther out of true. Until . . .'

'Until what?'

'A broken world cannot stand.'

I looked at Vickers. 'And that's what Brighton wants?'

'Yes.'

'Why?'

She didn't answer, but I thought of Mercy's words in the car. *Who can know the wants of a snake.*

'Maybe he thinks he can control it,' Vickers said. 'But we are already too far out of line.'

'Out of line in what way?'

'You upset the balance. The universe is built on hidden knowledge. How does society function when some are proven soulless? There are rules. You can know some things but not others. The world must correct if it is to survive.'

'There must be something we can do.'

'It is late of days, but there's still a chance. Only by destroying the eberaxi can things be set right. But even then there will be a cost.'

'What cost?'

Vickers looked at me for a long while before she answered. 'More than you might expect.' She turned away from me then. Her eyes fluttered for a moment before clearing again.

'We won't survive them next time,' I said.

'You made it this far.'

'I told you, I got lucky.'

'It's the best thing to be.' She broke into another coughing fit, and this time I wasn't sure she was going to stop. Her lungs rattled, and her pale face grew flush and pink. When she stopped coughing, she breathed quick and shallow, her eyes glassy.

'When we leave here, they're going to be hunting us.'

'Then be the lucky rabbit,' she whispered.

Her eyes closed, and her face pinched, as if she was going to cough again. Only the cough never came. Her face relaxed, the lines going smooth.

'Vickers,' I said and shook her shoulder.

Her eyes did not open again.

*

I watched as the old man wrapped a blanket around Vickers' body. He and the woman buried her beneath the tree, as if by some previous agreement, and when the earth was patted down, the old man said a few words in a slow, soft Spanish. When it was done, the old man led Mercy by the arm, taking us over the rise. We crossed the grass and stepped to the gravel driveway, moving slowly to the car.

Before I climbed in, the old man spoke in English. 'Don't come back.' His only words to me.

There was no anger in his face. There was nothing. I had an intuition then, as I looked at him. Would he collapse the wave if he saw the detector results?

I climbed in the car and started the engine. In my hand was the rabbit's foot.

I looked down at the furry stump in my hand. Small and dry now. I slid it into the front pocket of my shirt.

From the passenger seat, Mercy spoke. 'Let's get the hell out of here.'

The road was bumpy as we ascended the slow rise. There was some movement out of the corner of my eye, and when I turned to look, I saw a coyote bounding away through the grass.

I drove until we hit the paved road, the badlands all around in the fading light.

'Where are we going?' Mercy said.

I thought of Vickers' words. I thought of my mother.

The pendulum with its long, swaying arm – spooky action at a distance, entangled with the universe. I thought of what Vickers had said. *The universe is an object – a collection of waves. A metaphor for a metaphor that doesn't quite track*. And it *didn't* quite track – not perfectly. The universe wasn't a series of Russian dolls, each one hidden and discrete inside the other. It was more interconnected than that.

A single unbroken whole, information encoded inside itself.

It was a Mandelbrot fractal – an image inside an image.

The world is pattern.

And pattern in pattern.

'I know what we have to do,' I said.

We were three hours down the road when my phone chirped suddenly, some inner component finally dry, rising from the dead.

It was hot against my ear from the dashboard sun.

Three voice messages. All from Joy. She sounded worried. The last one, frantic. 'Call me, *please*.'

'You should toss that,' Mercy said.

And she was right, of course.

But first I made the call. It went to voice mail.

'Joy, I'm okay. I'm out of state and on the road, heading to Indiana. I don't want to involve you in this any more than I already have, so I won't call again. Not until this is done. But I wanted to let you know I was alive. This is almost over, one way or another.'

I hit END. I tossed the phone out the window.

48

It was Sunday afternoon when we pulled into the parking lot. Same empty asphalt, emptier this time than before. No green BMW sat near the entrance.

I turned the engine off, and we made our way up to the building.

The doors were locked. I hit the buzzer. A woman in a tan smock came to the door. White hair. Too thin. The building cleaning crew.

'All the businesses are closed for the weekend,' she said through the glass.

'I work at High-throughput,' I said.

Her brow creased. 'That whole area is closed off now.'

'I'm just clearing out my things.'

'Do you have a pass?'

'I didn't bring it with me. I can give you my name.'

She shook her white hair at me. A stern old grandmother. 'I'm not supposed to let anyone in without a pass.'

Mercy pulled out her gun and pressed it sideways against the glass. 'Here's his pass,' she said. 'Photo ID and everything.'

The woman's mouth dropped open.

'What you wanna bet this glass isn't bulletproof?' Mercy asked.

The woman opened the door.

'We're not going to hurt you,' I said.

'Probably not,' Mercy added, as the cleaning lady backed up, hands raised. 'Keep going,' she said.

'There's no money here.'

'We're not here for money. Do you have keys?'

She held out a black magnetic card.

'Thanks,' I said and took it. 'There's no rope or anything like that around here, is there?'

'I'm just the cleaning crew. There's nothing like that.'

'It's okay,' I said. I pulled the duct tape out of my pack and pulled a strip loose. 'We brought our own.'

Instead of the elevators, we took the stairs up. When we came to the fourth floor, I tried the knob and found it locked. There was a pass reader next to the doorknob.

I swiped the pass, and nothing happened. The door didn't budge. I tried the badge again. Still nothing.

'Let me try.'

Mercy fired the gun, and the doorknob sparked. The sound was deafening in the enclosed space, and the bullet ricocheted terrifyingly up the stairs.

'Let's not do that again,' I said.

The doorknob was the worse for wear – warped to the side with a piece gouged out. Just to the side of the knob, there was a small dent in the metal door where the bullet had struck and bounced away. I tried turning the knob, but it still held in place. 'Fuck,' I said. 'We need a different key.'

'Try that key,' Mercy said, pointing.

I looked. Mounted on the wall one flight down was a stairwell fire ax. That key, it turned out, worked perfectly.

The doorknob snapped loose on the first strike and

bounced down the stairs. Three additional blows brought the locking mechanism to its knees, and we were in.

'After you,' I said, swinging the door wide.

We passed the elevator and walked down the hall into the High-throughput offices. It was much as I remembered. Chaotic. Abandoned. Desks and chairs and empty space. Concrete and carpet. Walking farther in, I saw the yellow police tape. We crossed the room to where one of the windows was broken, its glass shattered into a thousand pieces on the cement floor. Replaced by plywood. Police tape fluttered.

He took his medicine bravely.

I moved farther into the building.

There was a sound. It came from up ahead, down one of the halls. Mercy heard it, too. Our heads swiveled in unison, but there was nothing to see. Just the same empty offices. Nothing moved. The sound didn't come again.

'Stay close,' I said.

Mercy stared at me flatly, eyes half-lidded. She raised her gun. 'You stay close.' We made our way side by side, deeper into the rooms. Mercy with her gun, me with the ax.

Other than the glass and the police tape, nothing else seemed to be disturbed. The rooms looked exactly as I remembered them. A series of offices and work spaces. Eventually, we came to the winding stairwell. 'Down there,' I said.

We descended. The next floor looked like the last. Empty, abandoned, our footfalls echoing in the metal stairwell. And then came the short hall leading to the black door. The final room.

It was already open.

I looked at Mercy. 'This is it.' I could feel my heart beating in my chest.

We stepped inside. The room was empty and dark, but as we crossed the threshold, emergency lights came on, and we could see. The room hadn't changed. Long rows of hardware stood off to the side, draped in shadow. The quartz sphere still sat on its pole at the back of the room.

I let the ax head slide from my shoulder and drop to the floor. The handle was slick in my palm. I gripped it tighter and walked over to the control board.

'Stand back,' I said.

I raised my ax. I thought of Boaz. The way his skull had caved.

The ax came down with a loud crash and carved a gaping hole in the controls. I pulled it from the hole and swung again. The plastic control board seemed to disintegrate, spilling its guts onto the floor at my feet.

Next, I went to the hardware stands. I took a stance like a baseball player, and I swung for the fences – tearing through the thin metal casing to bury the ax head in the machine. I tried to pull it out, but it wouldn't come at first, so I braced my foot against the side of the housing and finally worked it free. I took a step back and swung again, burying the ax deep. I pulled it loose and swung again. Wires and chunks of metal and plastic pulled away, falling to the floor. I moved along the row of hardware, swinging as I went, hitting each part of the machine. It was a long process. I chopped with the ax until each unit housing was hacked open, and my arms were burning, and I was out of air.

Finally, I rested, leaning on the ax handle.

Mercy stood watching. Her eyes tired. It had been a long, hard journey.

'Is it done?'

'One more thing,' I said.

I crossed toward the middle of the room and stood in front of the steel pole. Even in the near dark, the sphere had a sheen. A sixteen-inch diameter sphere of lucent quartz. Had Stuart died for this? The sum of all our work and all my fears.

'The eberaxi,' I said.

Inside the sphere, strange geometries gleamed. The gem. Burned like an afterimage in the quartz.

I shifted my hands on the ax handle, getting a two-handed grip.

'*Ah, ah, ah*' came a voice from behind me.

I turned, and Brighton stepped through the doorway.

49

He came forward, moving into the light. More shapes followed him into the room. Big men. Two, then four, then six. They moved along the walls, flanking us, blocking our exit. They stood in the shadows. I let the ax drop to the floor. Brighton carried Stuart's shotgun in his hand.

'It's been a good chase, Eric.'

Brighton was dressed as I'd last seen him. Dark hunter's jacket. Dark pants. His pale eyes seemed to shine. A half smile on his face. 'But now,' he said, 'the chase is over.'

'How did you find us?' Mercy said, voice so soft that I could barely hear her.

'Now that is a good question,' Brighton said. He crunched across the broken shards of electronics, casually flanking us. Behind him, his men lined the walls. A half dozen bulky shapes in the shadows. 'Step away from the sphere, and I'll give you an answer.'

'You know that's not going to happen.'

Brighton chuckled. 'What world do you live in, that you think this goes your way?' His feet crunched on the shards of quartz as he pivoted. 'But then we are all creatures of our own worlds, aren't we? We fashion them to our likeness, like our gods.' He circled around us. 'Have you ever stopped to ask what kind of world you've fashioned for yourself, Eric? If you hand over the sphere,

I'll let you walk away. And I won't make you watch me kill her.'

'He's lying,' Mercy said. She pulled her gun and pointed it at Brighton.

Brighton's smile only widened.

'Well, mercy me,' he said. 'What have we here?'

'Stay away from us.'

Brighton laughed. 'There is a universal form of communication that I've discovered. Language may be fine for conducting business and infiltrating institutions. Befriending you, when befriending you is expedient. Yet for debate of a more fundamental nature, it is inadequate. I've found that at the core, there will always be misunderstanding. Miscommunication. Until you draw your blade.' He raised the shotgun, but he didn't point it. Its muzzle directed somewhere between them.

His smile widened again, showing gleaming white teeth. 'You show your steel, and then everything changes. No matter what language you speak. I've seen it on the steppes of Asia, the deserts of Africa. I saw it on the icy shores of Greenland, where a thousand years ago the long path east finally met the long path west. No common language is necessary once your blade is out. The rest of human communication falls away as artifice. Only with steel is perfect communication possible.'

He shifted the shotgun in his hands. 'Shall you and I talk, Mercy? Is that what you'd like to do?' He turned toward her, all the good-natured contrivance slowly draining from his face. His eyes were suddenly murderous. 'Shall we *deliberate*?'

They stared at each other.

Her eyes gave her away.

I saw it.

The slightest hint.

Brighton saw it, too. The moment before she moved – the decision, in her eyes.

Brighton's skin seemed to flicker as her finger flexed on the trigger – that same aurora flash, and he surged sideways, rotating his body.

Mercy's gun spat fire in the dim light, just as Brighton struck her arm. I heard the bone snap, and Mercy screamed. The gun went flying.

Brighton smiled. A thing to behold. Runnels of flame seemed to flow along his skin, and I could see him two ways. Brighton, the man. And something else entirely. Something bigger. Skull long and large, a pharaonic deformity. He lifted his own weapon at Mercy, smile widening, arm raised, and he cocked the hammer back –

– and then froze.

Slowly, Brighton swiveled his head toward me. His gun never moved.

I had the sphere, held high over my head.

'Kill her, and I destroy it,' I said.

For a moment he did nothing. 'So you have teeth after all,' he said. He lowered his weapon. Gone was the smile and the runnels of light. He was just a man again. 'But that's not a path you want to go down,' he said. 'Do that, and things will go wrong. For both of us.'

Brighton's voice was soothing and rational. The voice of a negotiator, talking a man down from the ledge. 'Put the sphere on the floor.'

'Smash it!' Mercy snapped.

'Wait,' Brighton said. His eyes moved quickly between Mercy and me. He held up a bare hand. 'There's no need to be rash. We are reasonable people here. The truth is, you don't even know what you're really holding.'

'I do.'

'If you did, you wouldn't have it raised above your head. We've been waiting for this for a long time. Do you know what it's like to have your hard work thwarted? The corrections that shift things the wrong way again and again. What you hold is the end of that. For us and for you.'

'The end of us, you mean.'

He shook his head. 'It was your experiment that broke the world – and it's only that sphere that prevents the correction. Normally, the world moves slowly. But things have progressed now. We're past that. Trust me, you wouldn't like to see the world move quick.'

'Why are you doing this? Why try to destroy civilization? What possible reason could you have?'

'Is that what they told you? That I want to destroy civilization?' He laughed. 'What I want is so much more than that.' For a moment, he flickered – skin crawling with wasp wings. 'I want to stop the cascade.'

'Why? You'll die when it dies.'

'Then I die a martyr. Did you really think this was the only cascade?'

I stared at him, feeling the words sink in.

'There are layers to this that you don't begin to understand,' he said. 'Now put the sphere down.'

'No.'

He raised the shotgun to my face. 'I could just shoot you, instead.'

'Then I drop the sphere.'

'And then what happens? What do you think you're holding?'

I didn't know what to say. What was I holding? The gem. The fabric of space-time. A strange ball of quartz.

'A detector.' Brighton said. 'The greatest detector that's ever been built.'

I looked at him, trying to judge if he lied.

'We knew your friend was on to something, so we funded his projects. What wonders you are. What great things you invent. You never cease to amaze, and here at last, you'd done what we could never do. You still don't see. That sphere takes a perfect picture of space-time. Every proton, every electron, down to the smallest detail. You saw it run, didn't you? The technology to magnify the image might not exist yet, but the image itself now does. The negative. The information is in there if you know how to access it. You managed to detect the state of every quantum particle within range of the sphere. What do you think that does? How does the larger quantum system react to that? It can't.'

'Enough!' I snapped. I raised the sphere higher.

'Wait!' Brighton said. He turned and spoke into the ear of one of his men. The man turned and left the room. 'If you won't see reason,' Brighton said, 'then we have at our disposal another option to help you decide on a less . . . destructive resolution to this.' His blue eyes never left my face while he called over his shoulder, 'Bring her!'

One of his men entered the room, carrying a struggling form.

'You asked how we knew you were here,' Brighton's

said. 'Perhaps you should ask your associate. Imagine our surprise. While we were out looking for you, you were on your way here.'

I knew then that they had me.

The man had one large hand across Joy's mouth; his other arm wrapped her waist, carrying her in front of him like a sack of flour. Her feet dangled a foot off the ground.

'Joy,' I said.

'So here is the exchange,' Brighton said. 'You let us have the sphere, and you can all live.'

'No,' Mercy said. 'He lies.'

'It's your call, Eric, not hers.'

'How can I trust you?' I said.

'You have my word.'

'Not good enough.' My arms were starting to shake. The sphere was heavy; whatever I was going to do, I would have to do it soon, or the choice would be made for me.

'Then all three of you die.'

In the big man's grasp, Joy kicked and struggled. She pulled the hand momentarily from her mouth. 'Eric!' Her voice was high and panicked. The hand clamped down hard over her mouth again.

'You have five seconds,' Brighton said.

I looked at Mercy.

'He's lying,' she said. 'Smash it!'

'You smash it, she dies,' Brighton snapped. 'You can bet your life on that. But there's no reason it has to happen, Eric.' He walked to where Joy struggled in her captor's embrace. He raised his shotgun and pressed the barrel to her temple.

'If I pull this trigger,' he said, 'where will her consciousness go? Do dead eyes still collapse the wave?' Brighton's weapon pushed aside a lock of her hair. 'You like experiments, Eric. Shall we run this one to see what happens? Make your decision.'

'Wait,' I said, trying to buy more time. Trying to think. I couldn't hand over the sphere, but I couldn't let Joy die. I was already responsible for Satvik's death. Stuart's. I couldn't be responsible for another.

'No more time, Eric. You have one second.'

'Wait!' I snapped. I lowered the sphere to my chest.

'No!' Mercy screamed. She lunged toward me, trying to knock the sphere from my hands, and I almost dropped it. I pulled free, clutching the sphere to my chest. Her grasping hand caught on my shirt pocket and tore the fabric.

At that moment, the little rabbit's foot dropped out of my shirt and skidded across the floor.

All eyes followed it.

I looked at Joy.

There is a moment of clarity when you see a way to the solution. As if it was always right there in front of you, and you had only to see it.

The rabbit's foot came to rest on the cement. Joy's eyes had tracked it all the way. Then her eyes lifted and met mine.

She blinked.

'You're not blind,' I said.

'Time's up,' Brighton snapped. He pressed the gun harder into the side of her head.

I looked directly at Joy. Her eyes never moved. She looked directly at me.

'You're not blind,' I repeated.

No one moved for a moment. There was a stillness, like a waiting. The big man holding Joy looked at Brighton, who turned to look at me.

It was Joy who broke the trance. A jerk of her shoulder, and the big man released his hand from around her mouth and set her on the floor.

She stretched her neck, stood up straight. 'Oops,' she said.

Brighton lowered his weapon. He shook his head in disappointment.

My mind raced. My understanding of her shifting. 'But . . . that day at the lab, you – '

'Didn't collapse the wave.' She finished my sentence.

She flickered for a moment – like a brief trick of the light. 'I told you,' she said in a soft voice, 'don't believe your eyes.'

'But . . . why?'

She moved to stand near Brighton. 'We watch all the most promising new research.'

Brighton broke in. 'When you hired on at Hansen, it was a simple thing to plant someone to keep track of your work.'

I couldn't speak. Words failed me.

If I'd had a gun in my hand, I would have shot them both. But I didn't have a gun. I only had the sphere.

Perhaps Brighton saw it in my eye, that moment of decision. The way he'd seen it with Mercy.

'Always the hard way,' he said. He gave a flick of his hand, and two of his men lunged from the shadows. I jerked the sphere high and threw it down with all my strength, but they were too fast. One dove for the sphere, and it crushed his arm instead of hitting the floor – a scream of pain, as the sphere rolled away just as the second man dropped a shoulder into my stomach.

I hit the ground sprawling – the wind knocked out of me.

The sphere rolled across the floor as I wobbled to my feet. Mercy screamed, and then Joy rushed me, grabbing my arm. She flung me. I struck the wall and then slid to the floor. The world grayed out.

Brighton crossed the room toward Mercy, shotgun in hand. Mercy backed away and tripped over the sphere, falling to the floor.

I tried to rise to my feet, but my legs jellied. I slipped and went down hard.

Brighton stood over Mercy.

I wanted to speak, but nothing came.

Brighton crouched, gun in his hand. With his other hand, he reached out to touch the sphere. At the moment his fingers brushed it, it lit up from within. Even without electricity. Even with the hardware smashed and ruptured.

'The sphere remembers,' Brighton said.

Inside the sphere, a scene began to play – a stereographic movie. Shimmering shapes and gunfire and steel. 'That's what your friend didn't understand.'

I realized then that he was speaking to me.

He caressed the smooth surface, and it played the image of Joy throwing me against the wall.

'Once it is created, the sphere remembers. It is a perfect re-creation of everything. Past, present, future. An instrument of immense power.' He turned to look at me. 'It *remembers*. And what it's detected can't be changed, just as your detector results can't be changed. This is why the world cannot correct. It is collapsed in place. Pinned to existence by the fact that these results could someday be read. Would you like to see what happens next?' He smiled. 'No? You'll need no crystal ball for that, now, will you?'

He removed his hand from the sphere, and it went dark again.

He rose and walked over to where I lay.

'Did they tell you the cascade was burning?' he asked. 'Did they tell you eternity was an escape? Well, there's another possibility, Eric. Another inevitable outgrowth of time dilation. The cascade isn't just an escape. It's also a mine.'

He stood over me.

'A mine into time itself. A mine into the future. A mine for ideas. This world is a blur of speed, while those above barely move. It's not your fault. But that doesn't matter. You were going to create the math that was going to make the next great leap possible. You were going to unlock new technologies that others would use to open the next level of the cascade. But that doesn't matter either.'

I tried again to get to my feet, and again, my legs wobbled. I sat.

Brighton bent close, his voice a whisper. 'All that matters now, Eric, is that soon you'll know more than me. You'll know if there is a hell.' He pointed the gun at my head.

There was movement behind him; I saw Mercy struggle to her knees. Brighton saw her, too, his face showing irritation.

Instead of shooting me, he turned and shot her. Her shoulder snapped back, and she spun onto her stomach, sliding across the floor. Brighton crossed the room toward her.

He stood over her and cocked the weapon, chambering another round. 'This time, you'll stay down,' he said.

She was still alive, crawling a red smear across the filthy cement. Instead of backing away, she moved closer. Close to Brighton, as if eager for the bullet. As he raised the gun, she did not flinch away; instead she pivoted her body and lashed out with her leg – connecting with the sphere. It rolled across the floor toward me while all eyes followed.

I dove for it – a last chance. Its smooth surface was hot against my skin. Then I rose to my knees and with the last of my strength lifted the sphere high over my head.

This time, they had no time to react. No time to do anything but stare in horror. Brighton's mouth opening in a frantic scream, 'No!'

He lunged forward, but too late.

I flung the sphere down on the cement as hard as I could.

Time seemed to slow as it smashed onto the floor – a light that wasn't light but its opposite – an unfurling blackness. Every scene from every age, a Mozart concerto in a burst of static – Brighton's eyes squeezing shut as the sphere detonated, blasting shards through our bodies along the cresting shock wave – shredding flesh, the bones of my skull sliding past each other, singing out a soundless tone while the space around me shifted, felt but not seen – like the dark feeling from my childhood – standing too close to a train whistle, as the blackness surged from the middle of the sphere. My old companion, there all along.

The silence was complete.

50

I woke in a white room.

I was on my back, my head spinning.

When I could, I looked around. The bed was fouled. White sheets. White pillows.

The blank white walls were familiar somehow. Like a whiteboard I'd stared at too long. I was in a hospital.

Or I was dead.

I checked my body, running a hand along my torso, but there were no bandages. I wiggled my toes beneath the cover, and the sheet moved.

I slowly slid my legs out and placed my feet on the floor. I stood for a long time, feeling the chill rise up through the soles of my feet. I was off balance.

The place smelled of sickness and disinfectant. If this is death, then Brighton was right – I was in hell. Only hell would have hospitals in the afterlife.

I'm not sure how long I stood there before a nurse walked past the open doorway.

'Nurse!' I called out.

She stopped and looked at me. Dark hair pulled back into a ponytail – an open, expectant face, clipboard in hand. She waited.

I wasn't sure what to ask at first.

She wore blue hospital scrubs and the look of someone who needed to be elsewhere. She was hoping for a question she could answer quickly. I could see it in her face.

'How long have I been here?' I asked.

That changed her expression. Impatience shifted to concern, and she crossed into my room. 'How long?' She repeated my question back to me.

'Yes.'

'Almost a week,' she said. 'You don't remember?'

'But what about my injuries?'

'We took the bandage off your hand yesterday.'

'No,' I said. I looked down at my hand, and I saw the pink skin. The old burn from several lifetimes ago. 'My other injuries.'

Her eyes showed confusion. 'What other injuries?'

I sat in a doctor's office.

He was across the desk from me, my file open in front of him. His face was young. Too young to be a psychiatrist, I would have thought, but his hair was already graying at the front, so maybe he was older than he looked. He stared at me with practiced concern. I imagined it was an expression he'd tried out in the mirror, hoping to get it just right.

'So I understand you're having some memory issues again.'

'Yes.'

'You had a bad reaction to some medication we've been giving you. We're glad you've finally come around. You seem to be responding well to the new meds.'

'How did I get here?'

'You don't remember?'

'No.'

'Memory problems are common with the medications you've been taking, but you seem particularly susceptible. I see in your file that you've had a similar reaction in the past?'

'When?'

'The file says that you reacted badly to medication in Indianapolis.'

'No, I . . . I need to . . .' Nothing came. No end to that sentence. *Need to what?* Instead I asked the question again. 'How did I get here?'

'You were referred to us for a seventy-two-hour hold after being picked up by police wandering the streets. You were incoherent.'

'Police.' I tried to wrap my head around it. That's not what had happened.

'The event has been hard on a lot of people,' he said. 'Some have had more trouble coping than others. Considering your history, it's not surprising that you've had more trouble than most.'

'I don't understand.'

'You're only here until you're stabilized,' the doctor said. 'We've discussed this before, don't you remember?'

'No.'

He frowned slightly and wrote something in my file.

'The retrograde amnesia is a problem with you. I think we need to take you off those meds altogether. How is your mood?'

'Okay,' I said.

'What about your tremors?'

I held my hand out to check. My fingers shook.

'Not too bad,' he said.

I stared at my own hand. If he considered that not too bad, then I wondered how bad it had gotten.

'Are you seeing movement out of the corner of your eye?'

'No.'

'What about circular thoughts? Anxiety?'

'No.'

'Delusional thinking?'

He'd been building up to that one, I could tell. I glanced around the room. His office was nice, I decided. Here there were books and a nice wooden desk. He'd taken the effort. Appearances mattered. There was a window with a nice view of a lawn. Outside, there were trees and blue skies. The sun was shining.

'Just . . .'

'Just what?' he asked.

And I was on the edge of telling him. Spilling the whole thing. Instead, I kept quiet. I kept quiet because outside the window the sun was shining, and I wanted to feel it on my face one more time.

'Nightmares,' I said. 'Just occasional nightmares.'

'About what?'

'There was a woman. Her name was Mercy. She was missing parts of her hand.'

'Her hand?' That seemed to interest him. He picked up his pen again but did not write. 'We've talked about your family,' he said. 'Do you remember?'

'I remember,' I said. Though I wanted to forget.

'That was years ago now. You need to forgive yourself. Tell me more about the dream.'

'I can't remember,' I said, feeling dazed.

I didn't like the way the doctor was looking at me. I

stood. I no longer wanted to talk. I no longer wanted to think about it.

'Am I under arrest?'

'What?' The doctor's eyebrows knitted together. He seemed genuinely confused by the question. 'Why would you be under arrest?'

'So I can leave?'

The look of concern deepened. He wrote another note in my file. 'Soon,' he said. 'Once you're stabilized.'

I leaned forward and rubbed my temples. I thought of my mother seeing doctors like this. So sure of her delusions.

'I need to get out,' I said. 'I can't stay here.'

'I don't think that would be a good idea just yet. Especially considering the events of the last two weeks.'

'What events?'

He stared at me, his gaze evaluating. 'You've watched it on the news every night for the last five days.'

'Watched what?' I thought hard, trying to remember something, anything, from my time in the hospital. Nothing came.

The gaze seemed to harden. 'It's been on every channel.'

'What happened? What was on the news?'

His brow furrowed again. 'We're *definitely* going to change your medication. I've never seen retrograde amnesia quite this bad. This is an abnormal reaction.'

I heard Brighton's voice in my head. *You broke the world.*

'What happened?' I asked. The doctor ignored me while he continued to write in his notebook, I slammed my hand down on the desk. 'What happened?'

51

I drove up to the motel and parked the car in the front. The traffic had been a bit lighter than I remembered. That was the only difference. It felt as if a year had passed, but it had only been weeks. I walked inside.

The clerk eyed me over the top of her glasses. A middle-aged woman, with bluish hair and too much makeup.

'I had a room in this place a few weeks back, and I left some stuff behind.'

'Name and room number?'

I recognized the desk clerk, but she didn't recognize me. She'd probably seen ten thousand faces come and go through these doors. 'Eric Argus. Room 220.'

'We've got a lost and found,' she said. 'What did you lose?'

'Folders. Two manila folders. They were locked in the safety box in the closet. Also a small duffel bag.'

She disappeared for a few minutes. When she came back, she had the folders and bag.

'These them?'

'Yeah.'

She slid a printed sheet across the counter. 'Sign here. You got ID?'

I opened my wallet and showed her my license. She copied down the number.

I signed the printed sheet, and she handed over the

folders. They were nearly weightless. She set the duffel on the counter with a thump.

'I'm surprised they're still here,' I said.

'You're lucky. Anything we find, we keep for thirty days.'

'What happens then?'

She shrugged. 'Employee perk. First come, first serve.'

Behind me, the automatic doors swooshed open as a family came in. A mother, father, boy, and girl. I imagined they were vacationers, here for the ocean.

'Is there anything else you need?' The desk clerk asked.

'Yeah,' I said. 'I want to rent another room.'

I shifted the transmission into park.

The wind was blowing in from the ocean, streaming ghostly lines of sand across the lot.

I opened the paper bag in the seat beside me and popped the seal. I spun the cap off the bottle and smelled the burn.

Good bourbon. Ninety proof.

Music played from my car radio, a soft melody, a woman's voice. I imagined my life different. I imagined that I could stop here. Not take the first drink.

My hands trembled.

It had been three months.

I looked at the folders on the seat beside me, my father's gun resting on top.

Would I drink again?

The folders knew.

The first sip brought tears to my eyes. Then I upended the bottle and drank deep. I tried to have a vision. I thought of Satvik.

Do they know they're different? I had asked him.

One of them, he'd said. *One of them knew.*

When the bottle was half-empty, I looked down at the gun.

I imagined what a .357 round could do to a skull – lay it open wide and deep. Reveal that place where self resides – expose it to the air where it would evaporate like liquid nitrogen, sizzling, steaming, gone. A gun could be many things, including a vehicle to return you to the implicate.

I reached for the first folder.

My hands were steady as I opened it and pulled out the paper. My shakes had faded with the first deep drink – nerves lubricated at last. I was never more myself than after the first drink. By the end of the bottle, I'd be someone else.

I unfolded the paper. I looked at the detector results – and, in so doing, finally collapsed the probability wave of the experiment I'd run all those months ago. As I'd always been meant to do.

When I opened the second folder, the image was there. I stared at what was on the paper, two shaded bands – a now familiar pattern of dark and light.

Though, of course, the results had been there all along.

I grabbed the gun and the bottle and stepped out into the wind.

The smell of the ocean assailed me as I trekked down toward the smooth sand. There were no signs of people here – all wiped away by wind and rain. The sky was dark and brooding.

I walked a crooked path down to the waterline, avoiding some of the biggest rocks. It was midtide, and the waves were low and regular, pushing skirts of gray froth up the beach. The sand was nearly flat here, so the waves lost energy over huge distances. Above me, a white-winged tern pinwheeled in the sky.

There were different names for what had happened. Different acronyms were applied. SUDS, or SUNDS, or other similar variations of an alphabet soup meant to rein it in, make it seem more comprehensible. As if to give it a name was to understand it. In reality, the terms applied were just descriptive. Mass psychogenic illness was another label used. Other people applied a more religious term.

What was known for sure was that people died. All over the world, over the course of the same day. They did not wake. By the millions. Others collapsed in the streets. Others – the youngest and healthiest – drowned themselves. Bus drivers and nurses and teachers and accountants. Bankers in Italy and farmers in India. By the tens of thousands, around the world, they walked into oceans, or lakes, or rivers, and they did not rise.

All across the planet a small but statistically significant percentage of the population took their final breath. Statisticians still argued over the statistical bump – the number of extra deaths that occurred that day.

One other statistical bump existed, I knew, but hadn't yet been noticed. Not yet. None were scientists.

If it's random, why none of us? I'd asked Satvik.

If they're part of the indeterminate system, why become scientists?

And there was another thing I knew.

The researchers who tried to replicate Satvik's work would fail to do so. They wouldn't find the ones who couldn't collapse the wave. The ones who walked among us but weren't us. They would not find what Satvik had found. That evidence was gone. Just another experiment that failed to replicate.

I approached the waterline and followed a wave for a dozen yards as it retreated, draining back into sea, and then I planted my feet and crouched low against the wind, watching the ocean.

Mercy was dead. Though it had taken weeks to find the proof. Web sites dedicated to putting names to the faces of those who died. People without IDs. Jane Does. Another victim of SUDS. The police had found her body, washed up on shore.

I thought of what Vickers had told me. They see nothing because there is nothing inside them from which a vantage can be obtained. Mercy had been one of the fated all along. Fated to what? To fight against Brighton? In some ways, she hadn't existed at all. Not really.

The next wave surged toward me, washing over my feet, shooting past me and up the beach, leaving me standing in a foot of water. The water here had always been cold.

I took a drink from my bottle and pulled the gun from my sweater pocket. The gun was heavy and black. It said RUGER along the side in small, raised letters. I'd been carrying it, in one form or other, since that day it was used, in the same parking spot where my car was now parked.

I thought of my father and the ocean. The wave with your name.

I imagined sailing out past sight of land. There, blue water, where it was all one thing.

The wind picked up; I swayed on my feet. I waited for the next wave, and when it came, I strode out deeper, up to my knees. I looked down at the gun, heavy in my hand.

A view to the implicate.

I threw the gun as far as it would go.

Epilogue

I cross into my office and glance out the window. A new warehouse is being built in the same spot as the old, but an executive decision was made not to call it W building. That name has been retired, like an old pro jersey. So the new building will be labeled *X* on the site maps, and the administration hopes it will be luckier.

I've been back at work for three weeks, getting back in the groove. A one-month chip from AA sits on my desk. A month without drinking. Point Machine and I shoot baskets at lunch some days.

He's returned to his frogs and seems happier now. The events of the past few months have fallen into the background. The fire gave management a new perspective on security; armed guards now serve at the gate. And many a research lab has questioned the wisdom of pursuing a line of inquiry likely to inspire people to burn down your buildings. *A chilling effect* is the term sometimes used when discussing the future of research in quantum consciousness. But the work will go on.

I'd wanted to see what Feynman saw.

I'd seen that and more.

On some days I walk into Point Machine's lab, and I help him with his aquariums. I talk to my sister twice a week on the phone, and one afternoon a thought occurred to me.

If we fashion our own worlds, what would mine look like? It might look like this.

In the hospital, Jeremy had explained how Satvik was found. Dead in a car accident. I'd missed the funeral.

Joy's room is vacant. Her work space empty.

The first day back at the lab, I'd stood in her room and looked for pieces of her personality. I found a book in braille. A music chart.

When I asked Jeremy where she'd gone, he said, 'She didn't leave a two-week notice.'

'Did she give a reason?'

'Nothing. I'd hoped you might know more than me. I know you two were close.'

'Not as close as you'd think.'

The unspoken possibility: She was one of the syndrome. One of those who died. Though her apartment had been searched and turned up nothing. No body had ever surfaced.

Jeremy didn't ask what I was working on right away. He took a few days. Showed remarkable restraint. Or maybe he was half-afraid of what the answer might be. When he finally did ask, cup of coffee in his hand as he stood in the doorway to my office, I said only, 'Quantum mechanics.'

'Meaning what?'

'I'm continuing the research I was doing before I came here.'

He did his best not to let it show. He hid his smile behind the coffee mug. It was the thing he'd hired me for, all those months ago. The thing I'd been afraid to do.

Point Machine showed more surprise when I told him over lunch.

'Why would you do that?'

I thought of the frog in the well. The more you study quantum mechanics, the less you believe.

You are laughing. Why are you laughing?

And that was the key. That's why it was different now.

I believed in the world. But I knew it wasn't the only one.

After lunch, I went up to my office. I stared at the marker board.

I began to write out the formula. The same formula as before. The one I couldn't finish. The one that had driven me away, back to Boston, to this cold place by the water.

From my left hand, the symbols unspooled across the white expanse. Their inescapable logic, assembling a structure like a tower. Higher and higher. There was a beauty in the foundations I laid.

My marker slowed. I was coming to the point where I'd stopped before. Where the known ends and a wilderness begins.

I stared at the board, and this time was different.

A subtle change, and I saw a way forward.

Narrow at first. Like a light under a door.

There was a moment then when I could almost imagine myself in the hospital, in pajamas, scrawling on walls with a black magic marker.

But I pushed the thought away and stared at the board.

And then I knew just what to do. I saw it so clearly, the way it would go, the shining trail that would lead me out from the darkness.

I began to write.

Bibliography

Aczel, Amir. *The Jesuit and the Skull.* 2007.

Bohm, David. *Quantum Theory.* 1951.

Bohr, Niels. *Niel's Bohr's Philosophy of Physics.* 1987.

Bostrom, Nick. 'The Simulation Argument.' *Philisophical Quarterly* 53 (2003).

Feynman, Richard. *The Feynman Lectures on Physics.* YouTube.

Heisenburg, Werner. *Physics and Philosophy: The Revolution of Modern Science.* 2007.

Hughs, R. I. G. *The Structure and Interpretation of Quantum Mechanics.* 1992.

Kirmani, A., Hutchison, T., Davis, J., and Raskar, R. 'Looking Around the Corner Using Transient Imaging.' Computer Vision, 2009, IEEE 12th International Conference.

Meadows, Kenneth. *Shamanic Experience.* 1991.

Ottaviani, Jim, and Myrick, Leland. *Feynman.* 2011.

Peitgen, Heinz-Otto, Jürgens, Hartmut, and Saupe, Dietmar. *Chaos and Fractals: New Frontiers of Science.* 1992.

Plato. Jowett, B., trans. *The Complete Works of Plato.* 2012.

Pribram, Karl H. *Brain and Perception: Holonomy and Structure in Figural Processing.* 1991.

Raskar, Ramesh. 'Ramesh Raskar: Imaging at a Trillion Frames per Second.' TED Talks. 2012.

Talbot, Michael. *The Holographic Universe.* 1991.

Acknowledgments

I'd like to acknowledge all the scientists, mathematicians, cosmologists, and philosophers who have worked hard to push forward the limits of human understanding. If at any point in this story the science is right, the credit is theirs. If at any point in this story the science is wrong, the fault is my own.

I'd also like to thank my family, who put up with me while I second-guessed myself for two years while writing this book.

I'd like to thank my editor, Michael Signorelli, who went above and beyond the call of duty on this, holding up a lamp for me when I was totally lost in the darkness. This book probably never would have been finished without you. You helped me find the real story in the story. I'd like to thank my agent, Seth Fishman, who is more than just an agent, and without whom I wouldn't have had a novel career in the first place. I'd like to thank Stella Tan, Gillian Blake, Steve Rubin, Rachel Selvin, Christopher O'Connell, and the entire Holt team.

I'd like to thank my mother and my father. I count myself very blessed to be your son. Better parents I could never have asked for. I'd also like to thank Richard Feynman.

Lastly, I'd like to thank all my old lab buddies and fellow microscope jockies, you know who you are.